RIGHTEOUS RELEASE

About the Author

Richard Gardner has lived in South East London for many years. Married to a nurse, he has a daughter, a son, and at this moment in time, four grandchildren. Having been awarded a degree in Business Studies he has spent most of his working life in an office. His interests include travel, history, literature and he has a fascination for religion, yet holds no particular beliefs himself.

Richard Gardner

RIGHTEOUS RELEASE

AUSTIN & MACAULEY

A CIP catalogue record for this title is available from the British Library.

ISBN 978 1 84963 079 5

www.austinmacauley.com

First Published (2011)
Austin & Macauley Publishers Ltd.
25 Canada Square
Canary Wharf
London
E14 5LB

Printed & Bound in Great Britain

Dedication

To my wife, Vivien.

Chapter One

"Pass the cakes, David," smiled Hilary Chambers, as ever the perfect hostess.

Two sets of eyes lit up as daughter and mother surveyed the plateful of creamy delicacies thrust in their direction.

"Ooh I shouldn't but I will," giggled Ruth, girlishly claiming a chocolate éclair.

"They look so fresh," beamed Joan Kennedy, launching an even podgier mitt towards a vanilla slice.

With all mouths fully engaged silence momentarily reigned supreme.

For followers of the Eternal Fellowship, cream cakes were a delight to be savoured. In this very strict evangelical sect eating was one of the few pleasures in life tolerated by its spiritual leadership. An inventory of the goods and chattels in the Chambers home would have revealed an absence of just a few of those forbidden fruits, which bring a little cheer and gaiety to the rest of us. There was no TV, radio, computer and a book selection limited to Bibles, dictionaries and the odd gardening manual. Fun activities to be avoided were Christmas and Birthday celebrations, eating in restaurants and trips to the pub.

However, there is something else which distinguishes the Fellowship from other Christians. In the early 1960s, followers were instructed to be separate from the rest of the world and its wickedness. This meant that they were not permitted to be friends with non-believers, enter their homes or even sit down to eat with them. Understandably this new rule met with a great deal of resentment and many left as a result. Only a hardcore remained.

In six week's time David and Ruth were to be married. Joan Kennedy had driven her daughter down from Birmingham that morning to the husband-to-be's home in the Kent town of Brockleby. She was keen to sit down with Hilary, David's mother, to discuss certain details relating to the wedding.

The betrothed couple had not known each other for long.

Premarital sex was strictly forbidden by the Fellowship so most followers are encouraged to have short engagements. In this way the temptation to give into lustful behaviour before the knot is tied is kept to a minimum.

The vast majority of followers are born into Fellowship families. Converts are rare as few outsiders would relish the prospect of entering such a strange world. Therefore young people are expected to marry early and have plenty of children in order to swell the numbers.

David was twenty-three and Ruth had just had her twenty-second birthday. Both were considered to be slightly past their ideal marrying age and pressure had been put on the pair to find a spouse. Five months earlier they had met at a prayer meeting during a visit that David and his family had made to relatives in Birmingham. After that events had moved on very rapidly.

Joan Kennedy was mainly responsible for bringing the two together. Having noticed the good looking young stranger at the Gospel Hall she decided to invite the Chambers' family for a meal at her home the following evening. It might have seemed pushy, but she was determined to see her youngest daughter married off one way or another.

Now of the worldly pleasures permitted to the Eternal Fellowship, perhaps the consumption of alcohol is one of the most surprising. So although David had not been particularly enamoured with Ruth, he had taken a liking to her father's whisky which was being generously distributed. One glass led to another until his mind became so numb he would have been unable to distinguish between a catwalk queen and Whistler's mother. Sitting in a blissfully intoxicated silence he was totally oblivious to the conversation going on around him.

Suddenly he became vaguely aware that his father was addressing him in a hushed whisper.

David tried hard to focus his mind.

"What did you say?"

John Chambers gave a sigh of exasperation.

"I said, do you agree with me?"

"Absolutely," answered David without any idea as to why his opinion was being sort after. Anyway, as he wasn't in any fit state to argue, it seemed a wise course of action just to go along with

13

his father.

John gave his son a fixed stare.

"Are you certain about that?"

"Totally," came the immediate reply.

There followed a great flurry of activity. Telephone calls were made to all parts of the globe and women chatted excitedly between themselves while David watched on with an imbecilic grin.

Soon he and Ruth became the centre of attention as strangers began to arrive at the house. Hands were enthusiastically shook and kisses rained down on the pair as Bob Kennedy busied himself with opening spirit bottles. John Chambers then took it upon himself to read a passage from the Bible and the Lord was thanked by others for his great mercy.

It wasn't until the following morning that David fully appreciated the enormity of his predicament. Quite bizarrely he had agreed to become betrothed to the monster from the Black Lagoon and there seemed to be no escape. Once a commitment to marry has been made, Fellowship followers are expected to take the matter seriously.

"Have you painted the kitchen yet?" asked Ruth who had just finished her éclair and was hopeful of being offered another in the not too distant future.

David shook his head.

"I'll get started on it next week."

Ruth gave him a long hard stare.

"But the last owners moved out over a fortnight ago. What have you been doing all this time?"

David shrugged.

"I've been very busy at work recently."

Ruth looked up at the ceiling as though seeking divine guidance.

"But we are getting married in just over six week's time, and there is so much that needs doing to that house. I live too far away to be able to do anything. It has to be up to you."

"He has been working hard in the last few weeks," chimed in Hilary, feeling the need to support her son.

In an attempt to divert the conversation, David decided it was time to pass the cakes around once more. He was beginning to learn how easy it was to distract the attention of his fiancée with a vanilla slice or a chocolate éclair.

David gave his future wife a sly glance as she scoffed a lemon concoction with a glace cherry perched on top. Like all Fellowship sisters her dark straight hair was uncut and hung freely to the waist, while her drab and sensible skirt fell modestly below the knees. The shoes too were hardly fashionable and looked as though they could withstand the rigours of a long hike.

However, although a little overweight Ruth was not unattractive. Her facial features were small and regular while her clear blue eyes could be very alluring when she smiled. The few inches of leg that were on display on the other hand, looked shapely beneath the light brown tights.

"How do you manage to keep such a big house so spotlessly clean?" enquired Joan Kennedy between mouthfuls of cream bun.

"With great difficulty," laughed Hilary. "Although it is much easier now that the family have grown up."

"Housework can be such hard work," sighed Joan wearily. "Particularly if you suffer from rheumatism like I do."

Hilary offered a sympathetic smile.

"It must be difficult for you."

Joan nodded sadly.

"I just have to pray to the Lord to give me strength."

The Fellowship believe that married women shouldn't go out to earn a living. This is just as well given that followers are expected to have large families and as a consequence, require sizeable properties which require a great deal of housework. What is interesting, is that their homes must be detached as devotees of the faith are not permitted to live in the same building as non-believers. Stranger still, they are even required to have separate driveways and drainage facilities from their next door neighbours.

"It's a lovely day," remarked Hilary brightly as she glanced out of the window. "Why don't you take Ruth for a walk in the garden David?"

"Good idea," said Ruth hauling herself up from the settee with some considerable effort. "There are a number of things we need to discuss."

It was with reluctance that David guided his fiancée through the sliding patio doors of the sitting room and on to the back lawn.

There was no need to remind him of the endless jobs which needed to be done to the new house. All that he required was the time and motivation to get started.

The Chambers' garden was enclosed at the sides by wooden fences. Any visual trace of the non-believing neighbours was further blocked out by several large trees. At the bottom was a privet hedge beyond which was the rolling Kent countryside. Varieties of flowers in bloom added a rich array of colours to the scenery presenting itself to the engaged couple.

Most of the gardening was done by Hilary. Pruning the bushes and weeding the flower beds was a labour of love for the lady of the house. She would often praise God for sending some well needed rain on her tomato plants. Although why the Almighty should see fit to douse scores of children on their way to school, or spoil a day on the beach for holidaymakers just for the sake of one family's salad bowl is a complete mystery.

"How old is your car?" asked Ruth who appeared oblivious to the aesthetic delights that nature had to offer.

"About three years," replied David, casually watching a squirrel darting about on the lawn.

"It's about time you asked your boss for a new one," said Ruth firmly. "We need a reliable car if we are to serve the Lord properly."

David looked at her in astonishment.

"It's extremely reliable. In any case, I have break-down cover should there ever be a problem."

"Listen," said Ruth irritably. "I don't want to arrive at a Fellowship meeting in the knowledge that our car is the oldest one parked outside."

"I should have thought that we have more important things to think about right now," replied David grumpily.

The comment was ignored. Deep in thought, Ruth was trying hard to remember all the jobs needed doing in their new home.

"Now about the garden," she said finally. "You will need to cut the grass before we move in. It is getting very long and…"

David stopped listening as his attention turned to the pursuits of the squirrel. It was now perched on top of the fence clutching an acorn between the front paws. Finally it ran a few steps before disappearing into the garden next door.

16

"Did you hear what I said?" asked Ruth in a raised voice.

David turned to her blankly.

"Sorry I was just…"

"You were daydreaming," said Ruth, changing to her long suffering voice. "I suppose I had better go through it all again."

This time the husband-to-be tried to be more attentive. However, as he stared straight into Ruth's eyes as she addressed him, his thoughts began to stray once more. Suddenly he felt himself being taken over by an uncontrollable urge.

"I want to show you something," he said when his fiancée had finally stopped talking.

"What is it?" replied Ruth without any great enthusiasm.

"Come and see," answered David as he started to head towards the bottom of the garden.

In the corner at the far end was a shed where John Chambers kept his tools. Between this wooden structure and the privet hedge behind it was a ten foot gap, which was the most secluded part of the garden. Away from prying eyes, David in his mid-teens had used this space to experiment with cigarettes.

Walking about twenty paces behind, Ruth finally joined David in his secret hideout. Standing perfectly still he was staring into a blackberry bush with an intense expression on his face.

"If you look closely you can see a robin's nest," he whispered.

Ruth came forward and peered amongst the thorny branches. With her mind suddenly focused on studying wildlife she didn't notice that David was now standing directly behind her. As a consequence, she was unprepared for the two arms that closed around her waist or the passionate kiss on the neck.

"No you mustn't," she exclaimed while trying to pull herself away.

"There is nothing to worry about," answered David as he tightened his grip on her. "Nobody can see us from here."

"God is watching us," replied Ruth anxiously. "We must wait until we are married or he will be cross with us."

More concerned with his own desires than upsetting the Almighty, David refused to stop. Excited at the feel of Ruth's body pressed against his own, he continued to kiss her neck with increasing passion. His heart was pounding so fast it felt as though it would burst at any second.

"Please don't," wailed Ruth who was no longer struggling. "You are hurting me."

Reluctantly removing his arms, David stood giving the ground a sulky glare.

"I was just trying to bring a little romance into our relationship," he muttered.

"But God expects us to be patient and..." began Ruth before suddenly being interrupted.

"David," called out Hilary from the patio door. "Telephone for you."

Without another word to Ruth, David immediately set off for the house. Relieved that he had been spared a lecture on the virtue of patience, he felt indebted to the caller. Therefore there was an exaggerated warmth in his voice when he picked up the receiver and announced his name.

"Good afternoon Mr Chambers, my name is Dean," said a cheery voice. "You recently answered a travel survey I understand."

David vaguely remembered being stopped by somebody with a clipboard but, couldn't remember exactly what had been discussed.

"Yes I think that is correct," he answered hesitantly.

"And you are a homeowner I see," continued Dean.

"Yes I am," replied David proudly.

"Well I am delighted to say that you have won a holiday for two in one of a number of exotic locations," announced Dean happily.

David smiled to himself.

"Sorry Dean but I don't have the time for holidays. My fiancée has given me a list of jobs to do that will occupy my time well into old age."

Dean was taken aback.

"But I have two tickets here just waiting for you to collect."

"Sorry Dean," said David sympathetically. "But I am forbidden by my faith to gamble or be part of a prize draw."

"So what do I do about the holiday?" enquired Dean sounding somewhat less cheerful now.

David stood deep in thought for a moment.

"Tell you what," he said having received a flash of inspiration. "Why don't you go in my place. Get yourself a tan in one of those exotic places."

No sooner had he put down the phone on a surprisingly ungrateful young man, before his father and youngest sister Martha came in through the front door.

John Chambers was an electrician and spent much of his time doing 'the Lord's Work'. He had just driven back from Essex where the Fellowship were building their own church. Of the group of followers who had agreed to apply their skills, his role had been to lay wiring under the floorboards. Martha on the other hand had been selected for the tidy team, which meant clearing up after everyone else.

Helping out on projects like this was not compulsory. However, those who frequently refused an appeal for assistance could be made to feel very guilty

John and Martha greeted the visitors warmly as they sat down for a cup of tea and a cream cake.

"Don't rush," said Hilary checking her watch. "The Bible reading meeting doesn't start for another hour."

"I can't wait to see your church," smiled Ruth, now back from the garden and tucking into her third cake. She seemed to have regained her composure now after the little incident behind the shed.

"It will be your church once you are married and living down here in Kent," replied John.

"A lot of our friends are very excited about meeting you," said Hilary, as she finished pouring out the tea.

"There are lots of people about our age," joined in Martha. "I will introduce you to some of them this evening."

Hilary smiled sympathetically at Joan as she placed a cup of tea into her hands.

"I am sorry that your daughter will be moving so far away from you."

Joan gazed sadly at Ruth.

"Wives must always follow their husbands I suppose."

All heads gave a sagely nod.

"But you must come down at the weekends Mum," said Ruth, licking cream from her stubby fingers.

19

Joan glanced hopefully at her son-in-law to be.

"Well if David doesn't mind."

"Of course he doesn't," answered Ruth without hesitation. "And you must bring the family as well."

David suddenly began to panic as he visualised a horde of Kennedys descending on him week after week. Lots of rotund people scoffing cream cakes and trying to bully him into doing jobs around the house. It was rather like a foretaste of Hell without the fire.

After Hilary had washed up the cups and plates it was time to start getting ready. The women all took turns in front of the hall mirror tying their headscarves. In colours of white and blue, this attire is expected to be worn by Fellowship sisters whenever they leave the house.

The Eternal Fellowship hold church meetings once a day except Sundays when there are four or five. Worship is quite simple with no ritual or liturgy and participation is encouraged from male members. Fellowship Sisters are supposed to remain silent in accordance with the teachings from the first book of Corinthians.

There is an absence of the type of paraphernalia associated with certain other Christian denominations. There are no pews, pulpits, religious icons or stained glass windows. In fact, as far as the latter is concerned, there are no windows at all. The only requirements are a plain square table serving as an altar and rows of wooden stackable chairs.

One feature that Fellowship churches are permitted is air-conditioning. However, with no windows to open, and the size of congregation that many mainstream churches could only dream about, a cooling device of some sort is essential. The six hundred or more worshippers that regularly attended Brockleby Gospel Hall might pass out in the hot weather without it.

It was Friday which meant that the evening's meeting was devoted to Bible reading. As always a Brother stood and read a passage from the sacred book after which other men would rise and provide their comments on what they had just heard. Several hymns were sung but not to the accompaniment of a musical instrument. The Fellowship believe that voices alone were all that was required to praise the Lord.

Women had a very subordinate part to play in proceedings. They were allowed to choose hymns but, their greatest contribution seemed to come from keeping the children amused. Those with younger ones often sat at the back in order that they could take their offspring outside should they become fractious.

The evening meeting was short and sweet. Once it had been brought to a close after the final prayer, followers gathered in groups to exchange a few words before going on their way. A number of people, however, wanted to take the opportunity of introducing themselves to Ruth. It was a rare occurrence to have a new addition to their tightly-knit circle.

Ruth enjoyed being the centre of attention. She had that ability to beguile people with her charm when they first met her. David's older brothers, Joseph and Peter, were soon cast under the spell as they recounted their memories of Birmingham with their sister-in-law to be. The wives too warmed to her when she made complimentary remarks about their children.

Ruth and David were on the point of leaving when Ian Porter stopped them in their tracks. He could best be described as an un-ordained priest who acted as one of the spiritual leaders of the Brockleby Fellowship. He was only in his thirties but had a friendly authority, which was respected by everybody.

"I believe that a good Christian marriage provides a fortress against the Devil and his wickedness," he smiled.

Ruth gave him an enthusiastic nod of approval.

"My father always says that faith is our armour against sin."

"And the Bible is our sword and shield," chimed in Joan Kennedy.

The casual observer might have wondered why they were embroiled in a medieval battle against the forces of evil at the beginning of the twenty-first century. Surely old Satan would have equipped himself with nuclear or biological weapons by now.

"I would like to sit down with you both for a chat before the wedding," said Ian. "Perhaps you could suggest a suitable time."

"My mother and I are coming down again next weekend," said Ruth thoughtfully. "Could I suggest that we meet up on Saturday afternoon?"

"Splendid," beamed the priest. "Would three o'clock suit

everyone?"

There were nods of agreement and Ian promptly scribbled something in his diary. Being a Fellowship priest was a busy life and he needed to keep track of all his appointments.

Soon Ruth waved her final farewell at everyone before setting off in the direction of the car alongside her mother.

"I'm pleased that you are marrying into such a good Christian family," whispered Ian into David's ear just as the young man was about to follow half-heartedly in the footsteps of his betrothed.

Ruth became transformed once she was out of earshot of her newfound friends. All the warmth and conviviality on display moments earlier had mysteriously vanished once she had reached the car.

"I intend to take a good look over the house next Saturday," she said forcibly. "Please would you make a start on the painting and do something about the garden too."

David simply nodded as he had no wish to delay her departure any more than was really necessary.

"And another thing," said Ruth, as she was about to slide into the passenger seat beside her mother, "Get a haircut before I see you next week. You are beginning to look quite scruffy."

David heaved a sigh of relief as he watched the Kennedy car disappear into the distance.

"Don't drive too carefully," he muttered bitterly under his breath.

Chapter Two

David had many fond childhood memories of Broadstairs. Warm magical summer days building sandcastles, searching rock pools for crabs and splashing merrily amongst the waves. Then there was always the ice cream cornet and perhaps a second for extra good behaviour. Today though, more serious thoughts were occupying his mind.

The day after Ruth's visit he had made an urgent telephone call to Simon, his closest friend. He needed to unburden himself of a problem which was threatening to make a complete misery of his life. It was therefore imperative that a meeting was set up without delay.

After some consideration it was decided that Broadstairs should be the venue. They would go and visit Rebecca, Simon's twin sister, who had moved to the coastal town at the time of her marriage two years earlier. She would also lend a listening ear and provide an intelligent woman's opinion.

In fact there had been many discussions between them in the past. As the only Eternal Fellowship children in their class at school they had been faced with the inevitable problems when dealing with their non-believing peers. It had been a case of clinging to each other for support when confronting opposition.

Fellowship children can suffer a hard time at a state school. As human beings they have an innate desire to form good relations with others, yet parents are instructing them to keep their distance from worldly classmates. Therefore like the adults they are not permitted to visit the homes of non-believers or sit down to eat with them in the lunch break. Even accepting a simple Christmas card from the so-called 'Worldlies' is forbidden and has to be promptly returned.

It was about midday when the threesome finally took their place on the beach. Complete with deckchairs, suntan lotion and a picnic basket they discovered a deserted bay enclosed on both sides by white chalky cliffs. Only the cries of seagulls hovering overhead disturbed the peace and tranquillity of a warm late August summer day.

"I'm not getting married," announced David when they were all finally seated.

"Why ever not?" asked Simon, quite taken aback by this sudden revelation.

For a moment David was silent as he tried to gather his thoughts. Then resting back in his deckchair and staring blankly into the distance, he recounted the events which had taken place on that fateful evening in Birmingham. It was the first time that he had revealed to anyone that a ghastly misunderstanding had taken place.

When he had finished, Simon shook his head in disbelief.

"Fancy sobering up next morning and discovering you had become engaged to Dracula's daughter."

Rebecca looked puzzled.

"I don't know why you didn't say something at the time. It's a bit late now to back out."

David gave out a gloomy sigh.

"Things were happening so quickly. At times it felt as though I was being carried along on a tidal wave. Arrangements were being made, all my friends were quickly told about the engagement and finally I allowed myself to be talked into buying a house with that dreadful woman."

"And have you said anything to Ruth yet?" enquired Rebecca, while making a slight adjustment to her headscarf.

"Not as yet," answered David.

At that point Rebecca began unpacking the picnic basket. It had been a long time since breakfast and the sea air was assisting in creating hunger pangs.

"What will you do with the house?" asked Simon, still trying to come to terms with what he had just been told.

David was silent for a moment as he helped himself to a sandwich out of the basket.

"I shall talk it over with Ruth," he said finally. "We will probably decide to put it on the market."

Rebecca produced a thermos flask and began to pour tea into plastic cups.

"Have you mentioned all this to your parents yet?" she asked.

David shook his head.

"You two are the first to know."

"The Fellowship won't be very pleased with you," remarked Simon as he applied suntan lotion to his face. "They expect married couples to stay together and probably engaged ones are required to do the same."

"Unity is very important," joined in Rebecca.

The sun was now getting very strong and David put on some dark glasses to shield his eyes. Then like his friends, although still wrestling with the problem, he sat quietly eating his picnic lunch for a while.

It was Simon who finally broke the silence.

"Why don't you speak with Ian Porter?" he suggested. "As a priest he should be able to advise you on your position."

David shook his head firmly.

"He'll just try to persuade me to change my mind."

Rebecca gave her friend a look of concern.

"I hope the Fellowship don't withdraw from you."

David stared out to sea. He was only too well aware of the control the church had over its followers. The life of anyone withdrawn from, which meant to be excluded, could be thrown into turmoil. Everyone within the sect would be forbidden to associate any further with the unfortunate transgressor. Families might drive them out of a comfortable home and those like himself, employed by a Fellowship company, would most likely lose their job and all the perks attached to it.

The exiled Fellowship follower is like a caged bird who is set free. Having always known the security attached to being part of a large benevolent network of people he is suddenly alone and being forced to confront a strange and terrifying world. For those who have had normal lives it is impossible to imagine what it must feel like.

"I should hate to lose contact with all my friends and family," said David sadly.

"Of course it is possible that you may just be asked to stand up in a meeting and apologise," suggested Simon.

Rebecca began to giggle.

"Like that time when I was seen in a café with that red-haired boy from our class."

"Did you fancy him?" laughed David, struggling hard to remember the boy's name.

Rebecca blushed as she shook her head.

"Actually I was trying to make you jealous but it didn't work."

"I didn't know that," answered David, rather taken aback.

Rebecca gave David a sly look.

"Of course you didn't. You were too infatuated by Alison Johnson with the long blonde hair."

David was shocked at the accusation.

"No I wasn't."

"Yes you were," laughed Rebecca. "It was blatantly obvious."

David's thoughts were suddenly transported back to the classroom. He was sitting across the aisle and two desks behind the most sublime being in the whole universe. His eyes staring dreamily at the long flaxen coloured hair and delicate side features of an angel and following every little move that she made. The sound of her voice was like heavenly music and even the name 'Alison' made him feel weak at the knees.

For weeks David remained desperately in love and spent sleepless nights just thinking about the object of his desire. He would lie in bed and imagine conversations between them or things they were doing together. Of course there was never any chance of a relationship developing. Not only was Alison non-Fellowship, but David was too shy to even speak to her.

"I saw her the other day," remarked Simon, before taking a bite from a pork pie.

"Who are you talking about?" asked Rebecca, waving away a large fly that had settled on her arm.

"Alison Johnson of course," answered Simon. "She works at the central library in Brockleby."

"Is she married yet?" asked Rebecca, offering David another sandwich from a silver foil wrapping.

Simon shook his head.

"Apparently not. She has a small child but the boyfriend and her have split up."

David received this news in silence. He watched as a family of four made their way down a stone path which lead onto the beach. The children were no more than toddlers and were clutching buckets and spades. Behind them strolled the parents hand in hand and looking as though they hadn't a care in the world.

"Did Alison say whether she had heard from any of the crowd from school?" enquired Rebecca, peeling a banana.

"I didn't ask," replied Simon. "We didn't have much time to talk. It was her lunch hour and she was in a hurry to get back to work."

Curiosity was getting the better of David although he was trying hard not to show it. Without knowing why, he suddenly felt a compulsion to see Alison again. He wanted to know whether Aphrodite would still hold some mystery power over him or had she turned into just another member of the human race.

"Which days does she work in the library?" he enquired.

Simon looked thoughtful.

"I think Alison said that she works full-time but I can't be absolutely certain."

Rebecca gave David a sly look.

"Not thinking of borrowing a book are you?"

David smiled as he shook his head. Secretly though he was impressed at how well she had managed to read his thoughts. Visiting the library later in the week was already at the planning stage.

The conversation dried up for a while as the threesome shut their eyes and enjoyed the warmth of the sun. They listened to the screams of the two toddlers who had abandoned their buckets and spades and were splashing around in the sea. The parents watched on from nearby, sitting on a bright red bath towel stretched out over the sand.

"Shall we go home and have a cup of tea?" suggested Rebecca at last.

Everyone began to gather up their possessions before heading off in the direction of Simon's car. Their progress was slow as they stepped through heaps of soft sand while carrying deck-chairs and an assortment of bags at the same time. Two elderly ladies who had recently arrived on the beach smiled at Rebecca as she passed by.

Finally they reached the car and Simon began to fumble for his keys.

"Are you absolutely certain you want to break off your engagement?" asked Rebecca, making a slight adjustment to her headscarf.

"Definitely," answered David firmly.

"Make it soon," said Simon as he began to pack the boot. "There are only six weeks to go before you get married."

"You must have a back-up plan in place," warned Rebecca. "Just in case the Fellowship strip you of your job and home."

"And friends," muttered Simon.

David gave him a concerned look.

"Surely not."

Simon smiled and slapped his lifelong companion warmly on the back.

"Well almost all your friends," he corrected himself.

They drove along the coastal path and passed a brick building with a turret known as *Bleak House*. It was where Charles Dickens had written his masterpiece of the same name. The great Victorian writer must have been inspired by the view as he sat, pen in hand, staring out over the sea. He was fond of Broadstairs and would most probably have approved were he to be miraculously transported to the present day.

The town is largely unspoilt. Quiet and picturesque, it is a magnet to those wishing to avoid the commercialisation so common to many resorts. Although often crowded in summer, it is untainted by theme parks, loud music or noisy bingo callers filling the air with expressions such as 'legs eleven' or 'two fat ladies'.

Further on they looked down upon Viking Bay where most holidaymakers do their bathing. It was August Bank Holiday Monday and many from the great Metropolis and beyond were enjoying a day at the seaside. While the more energetic were swimming or playing beach games, most were spread out on the yellow sand, allowing the sun a rare glimpse of their pale skins.

Rebecca lived in a small detached bungalow. At the back was a long narrow garden and it was here that the threesome choose to sit and drink their tea. The deck-chairs which had earlier been assembled on the beach were now being used as seats on the lawn.

"It's very peaceful here," commented David, who was sat with his eyes closed.

"It's too quiet," replied Rebecca sadly. "The place needs some children to liven it up."

"Any plans to start a family?" asked David, who had suddenly opened his eyes in order to take a sip of tea.

Rebecca sighed.

"There are plans but at present the laws of nature seem to be conspiring against Malcolm and me."

Simon gave his sister a worried look.

"How are things between the two of you these days?"

Rebecca leaned over the arm of her deckchair and irritably pulled a weed up from the lawn.

"Just as bad as ever," she answered with a scowl. "It's impossible living with somebody as pompous as that. He is one of those people who is always right, or so he seems to think."

Simon smiled sadly.

"The problem is that Malcolm is always so certain of everything and you are full of doubts."

"My husband never questions anything," said Rebecca in disgust. "If the Fellowship told him to put his head in the fire he would do it."

"Are you disappointed with marriage?" asked David.

"Totally," answered Rebecca firmly. "The only thing that would make my life more bearable is having children."

"I expect being a father could help Malcolm to become more human," suggested Simon.

Soon the conversation switched to other matters. Deep down, however, David felt depressed that his friend had become trapped in such an unhappy situation. It also occurred to him that in order to avoid ending up in a similar position he was going to have to act very soon.

Later that afternoon Malcolm arrived home. He had just attended a meeting in which the local Fellowship had been discussing the possibility of building their own school in the area. Although nothing had been decided there was a great deal of enthusiasm about the idea.

The sect had built a number of schools for children between the ages of eleven and seventeen, both in the UK and in several other countries. The standard of education was generally regarded very highly, however, they had been criticised by some for not using modern technology such as computers. Although not Fellowship themselves, teachers were selected for their perceived ability in promoting good moral values.

"Where do you think the school is likely to be built?" asked David, as Malcolm was assembling a deckchair which he had just taken from the garden shed.

Malcolm shrugged.

"The location has yet to be decided. We need to find a site which is central to everyone."

"A lot of people are going to be quite busy once the project gets underway," smiled Simon, cheerfully.

"All the effort will be worth it in the end," answered Malcolm, knowingly. "People will be able to have an alternative to condemning their children to state education. It breeds nothing but hooliganism and bad manners with pregnant young girls standing around in the playground."

The others nodded politely even though none of them shared such bigoted views.

"I suppose most of the teachers do their best," said Simon as he helped himself to a biscuit from a plate that Rebecca was passing around.

Malcolm looked scornful.

"The majority of them are either trendy liberals or homosexuals."

"We had a gay teacher who took us for History," said Simon with a broad grin. "You two must remember Mr Chapman."

Both David and Rebecca gave a wry smile.

"We need to keep perverts like that out of our classrooms," snapped Malcolm, angrily.

"Actually Mr Chapman was a very kind man," replied Rebecca, indignantly. "The problem was that most of the class took advantage of his good nature."

"He was just a bloody poof," retorted Malcolm in a raised voice.

Rebecca glared at her husband for a few moments. Then standing up abruptly she retreated towards the bungalow without a word.

"How is the new car?" enquired Simon, deciding it was time to change the subject.

Malcolm's mood suddenly changed.

"Follow me to the garage and you can see for yourself."

Both he and Simon eagerly set off like two small boys heading towards a sweetshop carrying a ten pound note.

The Eternal Fellowship never stint themselves when it comes to buying cars. They generally choose the latest top of the range models possessing every conceivable feature with the notable exception of one. The radio must be removed before a follower will drive it out of the showroom. They don't want to listen to Satan's broadcasting disciples as they promote all their filth and wickedness over the airwaves.

David decided to skip the car worshipping ceremony and instead went in search of Rebecca. While appreciating the convenience of motoring he felt no inclination to go into raptures over large metallic objects. However, he was happy to show tolerance to those that did.

David found Rebecca at work in the kitchen. She had begun to make preparations for the evening meal, which would be eaten once everyone had returned from the Monday prayer meeting. As usual, food cooking in the oven would be left unattended while she was at church.

Fellowship followers need to have a very good reason for missing a religious meeting. Being on holiday is rarely an acceptable excuse as they are expected to go to the nearest venue where the sect are known to worship. Therefore the devotee faces a serious problem if there isn't a gathering of the faithful nearby.

"Need a hand?" asked David cheerfully.

"Not at the moment," replied Rebecca as she began to peel potatoes at the sink. "You can stay and keep me company though."

David pulled out a chair from beneath the kitchen table and sat down.

"I was concerned that you didn't look happy when you came in from the garden," he remarked.

Rebecca didn't reply for several moments.

"Why does Malcolm always have to be so self-righteous?" she said at last.

"Ignorance perhaps," suggested David.

Rebecca stopped peeling and turned to face her former

classmate.

"How can someone be so narrow minded?" she said, looking mystified. "Malcolm always condemns anything he doesn't understand."

"Perhaps he was never encouraged to be receptive to new ideas like we were by our teachers at school," said David with a shrug of the shoulders.

"You are probably right," answered Rebecca, thoughtfully. "At times I get so frustrated with him. He will go on about how the Fellowship are the only ones who preach the truth and yet he knows nothing about Islam, Buddhism, Hinduism or any other Christian denomination for that matter."

"I wish I knew more about other faiths," said David, sadly. "At school our parents never allowed us to attend Religious Instruction lessons. So because we were exempt, twice a week you, Simon and I would sit in an empty classroom in silence and revise other subjects. The only theology we ever learnt was what the Fellowship chose to teach us."

Rebecca smiled to herself as she gazed out of the window. Unknown to any of her friends or family she was a member of the public library and had recently borrowed a hard covered green book. Having taken it from the theology section, it explained the history and beliefs of all the great world religions. Of course the fact that she was reading such material would always have to remain a secret.

"Never mind," she sighed. "I suppose they will never change."

Rebecca was smaller than her brother and possessed a slender waist and shapely legs. Her face had a sweet innocent appeal and was attractive even without the benefit of make-up, which the Fellowship sisterhood are forbidden to wear. With eyes that sparkled when she smiled and a soft gentle voice, it was impossible not to be captivated by her. Dressed in bright fashionable clothes she would have been quite stunning.

"I think at the route of Malcolm's problem is fear," she said suddenly. "He is terrified of being left behind after the Rapture."

Like all Fellowship followers, David needed no introduction to the term. It is the time when God's chosen people are supposed to vanish from the face of the Earth and are whisked off to

Paradise. Those that remain are to suffer all the agonies that are predicted in the Book of Revelations.

"I suppose we are all taught to be afraid," answered David, addressing the back of Rebecca's slim waist.

At that moment they heard the sound of a car engine starting up. Quite obviously the metallic idol worshipping ceremony in the garage was now in full swing.

"There is something else though," said Rebecca, who had finished potato peeling and had now bent down to gather a handful of carrots from the vegetable rack. "Malcolm believes that the reason we have been unsuccessful in having children is because God's punishing me."

David stood up and moving across the room, used his extra height to pass down a dish from the shelf, which Rebecca had been struggling to reach.

"But what exactly have you done wrong?" he asked in amazement.

"Rebecca shrugged.

"It's just that at times I tend to question some of the Fellowship teachings."

David gave out a sigh of exasperation.

"What a load of rubbish. The pair of you just need to go and get some medical advice and try to establish what the problem is."

Rebecca shook her head.

"Malcolm won't hear of it. He says that it is up to the Lord to decide whether we are to have children or not."

David would have liked to have pursued the subject further, but, at that moment Rebecca stopped her meal preparations and hurried into the hall to answer the telephone. It turned out to be one of those protracted female to female conversations and long before the final scrap of gossip had been exchanged the three men were drinking whisky together in the lounge.

The prayer meeting that evening was as predictable as ever. One after the other the men and older boys stood and said a prayer out loud. The women as usual listened with a respectful silence and those that were mothers tried to ensure that their children did the same.

Dutifully David stood up and said his bit. His thoughts, however, kept going back several years to that familiar classroom with its rows of pine desks, pupils in red school blazers and blackboard with words scrawled in chalk all over it. Everything else though faded into the background as his mind's eye focused on Alison Johnson and her flaxen hair. Just the possibility of seeing her again in the next couple of days filled him with excitement. Suddenly Brockleby public library seemed to be the most fascinating place in the universe.

Chapter Three

It was always the same pattern. Nobody was permitted to eat until John Chambers had said a prayer of thanks out loud. Only when this little ritual had finished could the family relax and enjoy their meal.

"I understand the Government has called a General Election," said John while removing the lid off a large tureen and helping himself to roast potatoes.

"When will it be held?" enquired David who took no more than a casual interest in such matters.

There were a few moments of hesitation as John searched his memory.

"Four weeks on Thursday," he answered, finally.

"Who is likely to win?" asked Hilary, passing her husband the gravy boat.

"Everyone is predicting a close result," replied John. "Some say it could end in a hung parliament."

"Martha, David's youngest sister looked puzzled.

"I thought that General Elections took place every four to five years."

"That's usually the case," answered her father, as he lifted up a bottle of white wine and poured a generous quantity of the contents into Hilary's glass.

"It's just that it doesn't seem so long ago when Britain had the last one," said Martha, thoughtfully.

The rest of the family felt that she might be right but nobody could be absolutely certain. If there had have been an election of course, none of those sitting around the table would have gone to the polling station to vote. Fellowship followers are not permitted to do so.

The leadership also forbid watching TV and reading the newspapers. It is mainly for this reason that the Chambers were totally unaware of why the Prime Minister had been forced to call an early election. Unable to keep up with current affairs, the family had little appreciation of the dramatic events which had been taking place.

From the very start, the Labour Government's decision not to support the invasion of Iraq had been highly contentious. Bruce Shaw, the Prime Minister had been demonised by the Conservatives and the right wing press whereas, the left had revered him as a hero. For several months the arguments had raged on and now suddenly the people were being asked to pass their verdict.

Two years earlier in 2001, Labour had been returned to power with a ten seat overall majority. However, this wafer thin advantage had been wiped out at the end of July when a group of back benchers unexpectedly defected to the Tories over Iraq. It had been a savage blow to Bruce Shaw, but he and his cabinet colleagues decided to act quickly. Without waiting to be defeated in 'a vote of no confidence' in the House of Commons, the Prime Minister announced that he was about to dissolve Parliament and hold a general election. This was to spoil the summer holidays of many MPs.

"By the way," said Martha, returning her mind to everyday matters. "Ruth rang up last night."

"What did she want?" enquired David, half-heartedly.

Hilary gave her son a surprised look.

"I expect she called to find out how you were. After all, it is quite usual for engaged couples to be concerned about each other."

"Partly that," said Martha, slightly hesitantly. "I think the real reason she rang though, was to find out how you were progressing with the decorating."

"She is quite right to be worried," joined in John. "You have done nothing to that house since you bought it. Instead of going to the seaside yesterday, you could have used the time to paint that kitchen."

"But I had arranged to go down to Broadstairs with Simon," protested David.

"Surely you should have given Ruth priority," said Hilary, taking a sip of wine.

David decided to make a concession.

"I intend to do some painting tomorrow." He said wearily.

The announcement was met with general approval and soon the conversation moved on to other matters. The fact that only a couple of hours would be devoted to decorating wasn't mentioned. The morning had been set aside for a visit to Brockleby Public Library and nothing was going to stand in the way of that.

That night David slept badly. The following day he awoke feeling tired and washed out, which prompted him to consider postponing the venture until some other time. However, after performing some deep breathing exercises, he began to feel a little more confident.

It was just after ten o'clock when David turned the corner and caught sight of the library. Tucked away in a road off the High Street, it was an old two-storeyed building with two large bay windows and a flight of steps leading up to the entrance. Although slightly austere from the outside, recent decorations had made the interior more welcoming to those that frequented it.

As David approached he suddenly felt his heart pounding fast. Without hesitating he hurried past the entrance steps and stopped outside the nearest shop to take a few breaths. In order to make the very best impression on Alison, he was aware how important it was to stay calm and in control.

While waiting to compose himself he checked his reflection in the window. He had never looked so smart with every little detail of his appearance having been taken care of. Brand new suit, hair well-groomed, shoes shining and a perfectly knotted tie with a shirt that agreeably matched. He could have walked off the pages of a fashion magazine.

However, when the time seemed right to make a move, David found that his feet were rooted to the spot. His courage had suddenly evaporated leaving him confused as to what he should do next. To make matters worse two young female assistants in the shop were staring out at him.

David couldn't believe what was happening. Although no longer in uniform and looking somewhat older he had become the shy and embarrassed schoolboy once again. The adolescent who had worshipped Aphrodite but had done so at a distance for fear of rejection. The one who had loved and lost without ever competing.

Angry with himself for being so feckless he began to trace his steps back towards the High Street. He decided to go for a short walk and then return, hopefully in a more positive frame of mind. However, he hadn't got that far before a young woman with a carrier bag emerged from a shop just ahead of him. Their eyes met for a brief second and instantly David's heart leapt with excitement.

"Excuse me, aren't you Alison?" he heard himself blurt out.

The young woman stopped and stared hard at him. Then her face broke into a smile as she began to recognise the smartly dressed man.

"David Chambers."

David beamed broadly.

"How nice to see you again after all this time."

There was a short pause as both of them searched around in their heads for something appropriate to say.

"I saw your friend Simon Broadbent the other day and he told me you were engaged," said Alison, suddenly recalling the conversation.

David was rather taken aback. It hadn't occurred to him that his impending marriage might have been discussed. His reaction was so instantaneous that he even shocked himself.

"Not anymore," he said with a shake of his head. "We decided to break it off."

"I'm sorry to hear that," said Alison with a sympathetic smile.

Alison had lost that schoolgirl shyness but none of her beauty. The flaxen hair had been cut to shoulder length and the figure was slightly fuller, but the facial features had hardly changed. She had the same clear complexion and shapely lips, while her dark blue eyes still sparkled tantalisingly.

"I hear that you are a mum now," said David, stepping aside to allow an elderly gentleman to pass him on the pavement.

"That's right. I have a three-year-old daughter named Amanda," answered Alison, before quickly glancing at her watch.

"I hope I'm not holding you up," said David, concerned that he might soon be falling out of favour.

"I really should be at work by now," said Alison, anxiously. "It's been really nice seeing you again."

David turned around and spotted a restaurant opposite the

library.

"What time is your lunch break?"

Alison hesitated.

"One o'clock," she answered after a few seconds.

"And do you like Chinese food?" asked David, hopefully.

Alison laughed.

"I love it but that place is expensive."

David shrugged.

"Don't worry. I'm treating you."

Alison gave him an enthusiastic nod as she hurried off down the road.

"See you at one then," she called.

David was jubilant as he headed off towards the parking meter where he had left his car. After checking his watch he noted that there were over two and a half hours to kill before the meal. Ample time to drive home, grab a coffee and reflect on his success.

Hilary Chambers was vacuuming the hall as David opened the front door.

"Joan Kennedy has just been on the phone," she shouted.

David nodded and wandered off to the kitchen to make his coffee. Although feeling ecstatically happy something deep down kept reminding him that there was little prospect of any meaningful relationship with Alison. There were just too many obstacles in the way. Perhaps it was a case of merely enjoying the moment.

Taking his drink into the lounge, David sat on the sofa and shut his eyes. Eager to create a favourable impression he tried to think of things to say in the restaurant, which would avoid any embarrassing silences. In fact he was so deep in thought that he was barely aware of the droning sound of the vacuum cleaner until it was suddenly switched off.

Soon Hilary breezed into the room and flopped down in the armchair facing her son.

"Joan Kennedy and I have been talking furniture," she announced with a smile.

"Why was that?" enquired David, taking a sip of coffee.

"For your new home of course," laughed Hilary. "You can't live in an unfurnished house."

"That's true," answered David, unable to think of an argument against such sound reasoning.

Hilary looked thoughtful.

"Perhaps I will go into the town today and pick up some brochures."

"Good idea," replied David as he loosened his tie. It suddenly felt stiff around the neck and like other Fellowship brothers, it was a garment he wore only for business reasons.

Wetting her fingers Hilary tried to rub a speck of dirt off the arm of her chair. Only when the offending stain had been completely removed did she contribute again to the conversation.

"We will all have to sit down on Saturday and decide what to buy."

David nodded even though deep down he was rejecting the idea. If in the event of him actually finding the courage to break off the engagement, selling the furniture would be yet another headache.

"Why are you wearing your best clothes?" said Hilary, suddenly giving her son a strange look. "I understood you were taking the day off to do some decorating."

"There has been a change of plan," explained David. "I need to call on a client at one o'clock but after that I shall get to work on the house."

"You really need to get stuck in to it," answered Hilary as she stood up and headed briskly towards the door. "Anyway I must be getting on with my chores."

David arrived early at the restaurant. Entering through the swing door he found himself in a long narrow room, which for the moment had no other customers. Bright and cheerful, there was a thick red carpet on the floor, which seemed to match perfectly with the wallpaper. The soft oriental music which greeted him created a soothing background effect.

The tables, which were positioned into three rows were covered in white cloths. Spoilt for choice David selected one by the window with seating for two. Ordering a lager from the smiling waitress he sat studying the menu while mentally preparing himself for Alison's arrival.

As the Eternal Fellowship are strictly forbidden to eat with non-believers, David had never been in a restaurant before. Apart from sandwiches at lunchtime in the canteen at work, most of his meals comprised of home cooked food and partaken in the company of his family and other followers in the sect. Conversation would often centre around everyday matters although religion was always likely to surface in one form or another.

Suddenly he raised his eyes from the wine list to glance out of the window. His pulse began to race as he saw that Alison was about to cross the road. Dressed in a white skirt and jacket with a pale blue blouse, an attire which had been mostly covered by a coat when they had met earlier in the street, she looked exquisite as the sun shone on her hair.

"Just don't mess up," David muttered to himself.

In a few minutes Alison had slipped through the swing door and was advancing towards the chair that had been reserved for her.

"Sorry I'm late," she smiled.

David shook his head.

"Don't apologise," he said politely. "I just happened to arrive early."

Being inexperienced in matters relating to Chinese restaurants David allowed Alison to order first. It turned out to be a good tactical move as he discovered that it wasn't necessary to read out the meal one had chosen. All that was required was to quote the number listed against each selected dish.

Alison looked enquiringly at David.

"Are you still a member of that strange religious group?"

David helped himself to a prawn cracker from the wicker basket which the waitress had brought.

"I'm in the process of breaking away."

Alison smiled as she filled a glass from the large jug of water on the table.

"So that is why you are prepared to sit down and eat with a wicked non-believer."

David laughed a little self-consciously.

"You remember our schooldays then?"

Alison nodded.

"It was incredible. You and the Broadbent twins were dropped off at the school gates just as the bell was ringing and whisked away the minute classes were finished. It was the same every morning, lunchtime and evening. Your parents seemed to take every measure in order to keep the three of you away from the rest of us."

David stared sadly at the table.

"The Fellowship are concerned that their children will be corrupted by worldly influences."

Alison took a sip of water.

"Won't your parents be upset if you leave their church?"

"Much worse than that," answered David with a wry smile. "They will cut me off completely and prevent me from ever entering their house again."

Alison looked stunned.

"But that is a dreadful way of treating your children."

"It's the same with a married couple," explained David. "If one party decides to leave the Fellowship the other one must either go too or separate from their spouse. The followers say that they are obeying the teachings of St Paul in the Bible when he wrote 'Remove the wicked person from amongst you'."

Doesn't sound very Christian to me," replied Alison indignantly. "Would you also lose contact with everyone else in the church?"

"Apart from Simon and Rebecca," answered David, taking another prawn cracker. "I'm sure they would remain friends with me."

At that moment the waitress returned with the starters. Smiling cheerfully she placed a large plate of barbequed spare ribs on the table before turning and rapidly heading back to the kitchen. As the needs of the stomach were attended to it meant that the conversation was temporarily put on hold.

"Would you be interested in coming to a school reunion?" enquired Alison, finally breaking the silence.

"When is it?" asked David.

"Eight thirty on Friday evening," replied Alison, helping herself to the last spare rib. "We have arranged to meet in the Horse and Groom. It's the pub in the High Street opposite the Post Office."

"Sounds good," said David, enthusiastically.

In fact the prospect of a get together with 'the old crowd' was not one that he relished. His strict religious upbringing had made him into an outsider and on occasions, a target for hostility. However, he was willing to tolerate just about anything for the woman who was sitting opposite him.

"We tend to meet up about once every three months," explained Alison, wiping the corners of her mouth with a tissue. "Do you happen to remember Mr Chapman the gay History teacher?"

David nodded.

"I was talking about him the other day with Simon and Rebecca."

"Well he always comes along," laughed Alison. "Everybody is kept up to date with the things he and his partner have been doing."

Their conversation was interrupted by the waitress. Still smiling cheerfully she arrived with a tray and began to clear away the dirty plates. While she was at hand it gave David an opportunity to order two more glasses of wine.

"Who looks after your daughter when you are at work?" asked David once the waitress was gone.

"Amanda goes to playschool until twelve o'clock then my mum takes her for the afternoon," explained Alison.

Suddenly David became aware of two businessmen several tables away. As one was busily studying the wine list the other was gazing intently at Alison with a faint smile. Aphrodite it seemed, had cast her spell over another poor hapless mortal.

David began to experience a strange feeling of pride. It was as though the attention being paid to Alison was rather flattering to him, being the man sitting with her. On the other hand, it also provided a reminder of the competition he was likely to face.

"Does Amanda's father see much of her?" asked David as he tried to ignore the staring eyes.

"Mark comes every Sunday without fail to take her out," answered Alison with a sad smile. "He is devoted to his daughter."

David looked down thoughtfully at the table.

"Why did you and Mark split up?"

Alison shrugged.

"Mark doesn't seem to want a permanent commitment. Every

night he is either out at parties or drinking with friends. The thought of taking out a mortgage and settling down to family life appears to frighten him."

"Is it likely that the two of you will ever get back together again?" asked David as the smiling waitress arrived with the wine and several dishes for the main course.

"Probably not," answered Alison, eagerly inspecting the food. "He may have another woman for all that I know."

During the meal they began to reminisce about their school days. It had been a much happier experience for Alison who talked fondly of teachers and classmates. She had kept in contact with many and therefore had much to update David with.

Finally she glanced at her watch.

"I must be getting back to work in a few minutes. Thank you so much for a lovely meal."

"Thank you for spending your lunch break with me," replied David, saddened by the thought that they were soon to go their separate ways.

He settled the bill at the cash desk and then prepared to leave. Inexperienced in the art of tipping, he squeezed a ten pound note into the hand of the smiling waitress and suddenly her face lit up with delight. Several tables away the staring eyes of the businessman watched sadly as Alison disappeared through the swing door of the restaurant.

David toyed with the idea of inviting Alison out. However, as they were to meet up at the reunion in two days, he decided to postpone it until then. There was a lingering fear in his head that the proposal would be rejected and spoil a perfect day.

David watched as Alison hurried across the road and up the library steps. Turning his thoughts from romance to more mundane matters he decided to drive to Timpson and Duffy to buy paint. He knew there would be no peace until he did something about that wretched kitchen.

The afternoon passed pleasantly enough. David had always found painting to be a monotonous business but today he had happy memories to relieve the boredom. His progress was slow but he was feeling so relaxed it was difficult to get out of first gear. In fact it hardly seemed to matter whether the job ever got done or not.

That evening Hilary had invited the Hendersons for a meal after the Bible reading service. Well into their seventies, they were an odd couple and made an amusing double act. Jim had a rather uneasy manner and was forever quoting from Scriptures, then Vera would follow by repeating the tail end of husband's sentence.

"How are your children?" asked Hilary as soon as John Chambers had thanked the Lord for the food they were about to eat.

"They are all keeping well thank you," smiled Vera. "Ken has just started up his own company and Stephanie is expecting her fifth child any day now."

"What about Eric?" asked John. "I understand that his car was stolen recently."

Vera sighed.

"The police haven't managed to trace it so far."

"There is so much wickedness in the world," lamented John, shaking his head.

Jim who had been sitting with a distant gaze in his eyes suddenly came to life.

"For the wages of sin is death," he chimed in, quoting from Chapter Six of Romans.

"Is death," repeated Vera playing her familiar echoing role.

Martha sniggered before receiving a stern look from her father.

"Was the car new?" enquired David, keen to return to the original subject.

"Eric had only just bought it," replied Vera, gloomily.

"Some people don't seem to have any respect for the property of others," joined in Hilary with a look of sympathy.

After the meal the men adjourned to the lounge for a drop of whisky. The women on the other hand were left to fulfil their usual subservient role in clearing away the dishes. It is a familiar pattern in Fellowship households.

As the two older men talked about nothing of any great significance, David allowed his mind to wander. He wondered what Alison was doing at that precise moment and whether she had given any thought to him since their meal at lunch time. More importantly, was there the remotest possibility that he could defy all the odds and claim Aphrodite for himself.

Suddenly the telephone rang and Martha could be heard scurrying down the hall to answer it.

David," she called out after a while. "Ruth would like to speak with you."

David raised his eyes to the ceiling as he reluctantly lifted himself from his armchair. Then after taking a large gulp of whisky to befuddle his brain he slowly set off to face the ordeal ahead. As he picked up the receiver, however, he paused for a few seconds to take a deep breath.

"How are you?" he enquired, attempting to sound cheerful.

"I'm fine thank you," replied Ruth, pleasantly. "Martha tells me that you were working on the house today."

"I've managed to paint about half the kitchen," replied David slightly wary of the affable tone in the voice of the woman he was betrothed to.

He was right to be suspicious. For what seemed an eternity Ruth provided him with a verbal list of other jobs that were waiting to be attended to. Her voice just droned on like some epic monologue being broadcasted over the radio.

Sitting on the floor with his back to the wall and eyes closed, David decided to do some memory exercises. With the telephone receiver well away from his ear so that Ruth's voice was only faintly audible, he tried to recall all the books of the Bible followed by the Ten Commandments. During his childhood he had used this technique in order to get through some of those long incomprehensible Fellowship meetings.

Having reached 'Thou shalt not kill' in his head, David suddenly became aware that the voice on the end of the line had become a few decibels louder.

"Are you listening to me?" Ruth was asking as David quickly returned the receiver to his ear.

"Every word," replied David with a wry smile.

"You must try to have the house looking nice before we are married," pleaded Ruth in a softer voice.

"I'll do what I can," answered David who had no wish to prolong the conversation by arguing.

"Are you ready for another Scotch?" asked John as soon as his son reappeared in the lounge a few moments later.

David nodded. "Make it a large one."

46

Chapter Four

David was desperate to get away. It was a warm humid evening and after the Friday meeting many of the Fellowship had gathered around in groups outside the Gospel Hall door. It was one of those occasions when nobody wanted to be seen to be the first to go home.

"I am popping down to the house to do a few jobs," muttered David to his father who was standing next to him.

John Chamber gave his son a look of approval.

"I'm glad you are finally starting to take an interest in your new home," he smiled.

"What about your meal?" asked Hilary who was always fussy about regular eating.

David gave a casual shrug.

"Don't bother about me. I'll make something for myself when I get home."

No sooner had David moved a few paces before he was called back by Mrs Harris. A single lady, well known for her ceaseless talking, she was one of those few followers who relied on others for transport.

"Could you give me a lift dear?" she requested with a smile. "I really should be getting home to feed my cat."

David's heart sank. He was already late for the school reunion and having to drop Mrs Harris off was bound to delay him much further. The problem was that because of her endless talking she would never get out of the car when it stopped outside her house.

As he drove off David sat impassively at the wheel. His brain was hard at work trying to decide how to deal with this thorny problem without being downright offensive. Short of making sexual advances, however, no obvious plan of action sprang to ·mind.

In fact it wasn't easy to think straight. Mrs Harris had an annoying habit of sitting in the passenger seat and providing a running commentary on just about anything that caught her attention. Most of her remarks were so inane though, it was surprising that she bothered to waste her breath.

"See those curtains," she said as they drove along. "I have a dress that colour."

"Very nice," replied David without bothering to establish which curtains that she was actually referring to.

Then it was "That hedge over there needs trimming" and "the man in that garden reminds me of my neighbour", and so on and so on.

Finally they pulled up outside Mrs Harris's front gate. Glancing down at the digital car clock David noticed that it was now ten to nine and had mentally resigned himself to a long and dreary wait. So switching off his engine he turned to face his tormentor. However, on this occasion luck was on his side.

"Sorry but I can't stop to talk," said the passenger in rather an agitated voice. "I have probably been drinking too much tea today."

With a broad grin and an immense feeling of relief David watched as Mrs Harris made rapid progress towards her front door. However, not wishing to waste any more time he quickly set off home to freshen up and change into some smart casual clothes.

The Horse and Groom was packed when David arrived. However, amongst a sea of people he was unable to recognise a single face. Fortunately one of the bar staff sensed his unease and came to the rescue.

"There is a private function going on upstairs," he called out. "Go up to the landing and it's the first on your right."

It was now after nine thirty but David decided to delay his entrance just a bit longer. Before making his way to the first floor he decided to buy a pint of beer at the bar. Feeling a little apprehensive about how his old classmates might receive him, he needed a drink to settle his nerves.

There were more people at the reunion than he had expected. Former pupils from different classes were gathered in groups around a room almost double the size of a tennis court. Many had brought partners or friends which had helped to swell the numbers. Although a little older and no longer in those drab red uniforms, people that he had known so well had barely changed.

On the far side of the room several people beckoned to him.

He was about to set off to join them when his path was blocked by a plump man with a shock of dark hair.

"David Chambers," he beamed while throwing out a chubby hand.

"Hello Mr Chapman, how nice to see you again," replied David, instantly recognising his old History teacher.

"Nice to see you looking so well my boy," said Mr Chapman, cheerfully. "What are you doing for a living?"

"I'm a sales rep," answered David as he waved back at somebody he had once sat next to in class.

Mr Chapman looked thoughtful for a few seconds.

"Weren't you from an Eternal Fellowship family?"

David nodded.

"You have a very good memory."

"It's all coming back to me now," said Mr Chapman with his eyes fixed firmly on his former pupil. "You wanted to teach but your parents wouldn't let you stay on at school."

David looked sadly at the floor.

"Like other Fellowship children I had to give up my education before sitting 'A' levels."

Mr Chapman shook his head sadly.

"Are you still a follower?"

"I'm actually on the point of leaving but it's merely a case of making that final leap to freedom," replied David with a smile.

Mr Chapman stroked his chin in the way that had become familiar to his History students over the years.

"How old are you now?"

"Twenty-three," answered David.

Mr Chapman placed his hand on David's shoulder in a kindly avuncular manner.

"Follow your dreams and become a teacher."

"But I don't have any qualifications to begin my training," protested David, as he took a sip from his beer mug.

"It's never too late to get them," smiled Mr Chapman. "Why not study through the Open University and then you can continue working at the same time."

David considered the situation for a few moments.

"Where do I find all the details?"

Mr Chapman produced a scrap of paper from his inside

pocket and began to scribble something down.

"This is my address and telephone number. Just get in touch with me should you need my assistance."

"I might take you up on that," smiled David, carefully tucking the piece of paper into his wallet.

Mr Chapman gave his former pupil a stern look.

"Now I shall be expecting your call."

David grinned.

"It may come a lot earlier than you expect."

"Excellent," replied Mr Chapman with a booming laugh. "Now if you will excuse me, I must go and circulate."

David watched as the History teacher launched himself upon a large ring of people about ten yards away. In the classroom he had been totally inept at keeping control. Now in different circumstances, a few of those people who had treated his authority with such contempt were listening politely to everything that he had to say.

Background music was being played somewhere in the room. David recognised a ballad with a haunting tune, but struggled to remember where he had heard it before. It certainly wouldn't have been in any place owned by the Fellowship. Followers were forbidden to listen to popular songs, believing their lyrics to be undesirable.

On the far side of the room there was a buffet with food spread out over several tables. People were regularly picking up plates at one end and helping themselves to an assortment of sandwiches and other refreshments. Having missed his evening meal, David decided to investigate the situation before everything had been eaten.

Halfway across the floor, however, he stopped in his tracks. Several people who were standing in a particularly large circle waved and called out to him. Against his better judgement, which was to go forward and collect sustenance, he went over to join them. Some of the faces were all too familiar, but the one that stood out was the beautiful Alison.

Meeting some of his classmates again was not as traumatic as he had imagined. People that he had never been on the best of terms with were suddenly shaking him warmly by the hand. They were no longer addressing him by his surname but now he had become David. It was as though the outsider had gained acceptance into the club.

The conversation was polite and friendly. They talked about their jobs before going on to recall funny instances which had taken place at school. Then when these subjects had been exhausted someone happened to mention the General Election.

"I can't see Labour winning in this constituency," remarked Brian Meadows who had always been regarded as one of the brightest pupils in the class. "We've always had a Tory MP here and that is the way it will stay."

"But there have been boundary changes since the last election," replied Alison. "Brockleby has absorbed a large council estate which used to be in the Musselworth constituency and might just swing the vote in Labour's favour."

There was a sudden break in the conversation as a man with a tray of drinks had to disturb a section of the circle to negotiate his way past.

"Labour won't win with Jacqui Dunn as their candidate," stated Wayne Little, a tall thin young man who had once had a fierce fight with David in the playground. "She is only interested in unemployed lesbian asylum seekers."

"There can't be too many of them," joined in a young woman who was standing next to Alison.

"Take my word for it Carol," answered Wayne with a knowing smile. "This town is full of them."

The look on Carol's face suggested that she was far from convinced. Not recognising her as an ex-fellow pupil, David guessed rightly that Alison had brought her along as a partner for the evening. Attractive with fuzzy auburn hair and an attentive expression on her face, she seemed to be quietly observing everyone in the group in turn.

"I think that Jacqui Dunn is a gift to the Tories," said Brian Meadows, loftily. "The people in this town will never elect anyone as left wing as that. Charles Dawkins is bound to retain the seat for the Tories."

"Being a Socialist didn't stop Jacqui from becoming a councillor," said Alison, indignantly. "In fact she increases her majority every time there are local elections."

Shaking heads around the circle suggested that only Carol

held a similar opinion. One person, however, who had little interest in the subject matter stood impassively and kept his eyes fixed on Alison. She was obviously outnumbered and as a Fellowship pupil in a normal state school he knew exactly how it felt like.

"I'm voting for Jacqui Dunn," he piped up boldly. "I actually think that she has a very good chance of winning."

Certain people exchanged a long-suffering look.

"She hasn't a hope," replied Brian Meadows with a superior smile. "Unless of course all the Tory voters decide to take a holiday in the last week of September."

Wayne Little's girlfriend who had looked thoroughly bored during this brief political discussion suddenly perked up.

"We might be going on holiday in the next few weeks."

"Where are you thinking of?" enquired Brian Meadows' girlfriend.

"Down to Cornwall to see my sister," came the enthusiastic reply.

Deciding not to intrude on this cosy conversation, Alison turned her attention to Mr Chapman who had just joined the circle.

"Where is Lenny tonight?" she enquired.

"He has gone to visit his mother on her birthday," replied the teacher with an affectionate smile.

"Isn't he a nurse?" asked Wayne Little with a slight smirk.

Mr Chapman nodded proudly.

"That is correct. He is working very hard on men's medical."

The remark produced sly grins, winks and a snigger, which strangely appeared to bypass the attention of the teacher.

The room was filling up all the time. In the far corner was a bar and David suddenly recognised an old school friend queuing up to be served. On another occasion he would have strolled over for a chat but, at present, there were more important things on his mind. So far he had not had an opportunity to speak with Alison who was now keeping a watchful eye on the time. With a young child at home he supposed, she would not want to be out too late.

Music that had been playing softly in the background suddenly became appreciatively louder. Soon several couples decided to leave their group in search of somewhere to dance and then others followed. Once a space on the floor had been cleared most began to move friskily to a rather bouncy tune.

"Is that one of your CDs being played Mr Chapman?" enquired Wayne Little as he was about to guide his girlfriend towards the dancing area. "Sounds like music from the sixties."

Mr Chapman nodded.

"That is one of my all-time favourites. 'I'm Into Something Good' was a massive hit for Herman's Hermits."

Suddenly David felt a tap on his shoulder. Turning around he came face to face with a stocky young man with a serious look in his eyes. Another of his former classmates, Glen Burgess was one of those people that everyone else makes a special effort to avoid. He only ever talked about himself while appearing to take absolutely no interest in others.

"I'm in advertising now," said Glen in his usual monotonous voice. "Deputy Head of the department, thirty grand a year with a company car."

David tried to look as though he cared. In fact while looking straight at the egocentric bore in front of him he was listening to Mr Chapman's much admired recording. The tune was very catchy but it was the lyrics which were making the bigger impression on him. Something about walking a girl home made him glance quickly across at Alison.

"Would anyone like a drink?" shouted Mr Chapman in order to be heard above the music.

While most people eagerly provided him with their orders, it was Alison's cue to prepare herself for leaving.

"I really must be going," she announced, picking up her bag from the floor. "Are you ready to go Carol?"

Her friend nodded.

"Let me ring for a cab on my mobile."

David had carefully prepared himself for this moment.

"I'd better be off myself," he said, cutting Glen off in mid-sentence. "Can I give you two ladies a lift?"

"We don't want to put you to any trouble," replied Alison, looking slightly concerned.

"No trouble at all," David reassured her.

Mr Chapman who had yet to set off for the bar clasped David by the hand.

"Now don't forget to ring me if you require any advice on teaching."

"I shall be in touch," smiled David, warmly.

It was a while before the threesome were finally on their way. They were delayed by the usual last minute exchanges with promises to 'stay in touch' as well as a profusion of kisses, embraces and handshakes all round.

"Don't forget to pop in the bar downstairs any Friday evening when you happen to be passing," said Glen who was already on the lookout for somebody else to bore. "You are bound to find me there."

"I'll remember," smiled David while making a mental note to stay well clear.

He led the way down the stairs, through the bar and into the pub car park. Although dark now, it was a perfect night for the amateur astronomer with the stars clearly visible in the sky. Through the open windows above, he could still hear the hum of voices from the reunion and the opening bars from another of Mr Chapman's favourite hits from the sixties.

Once the car set off the two women became engrossed in a two-way conversation. For most of the journey Carol in the back seat did most of the talking while Alison in the front, sat listening with her head turned sideways. Sitting in silence like a chauffeur who is aware of his station in life, David was trying to work out his next move.

From what he could gather from the conversation, Alison and Carol were committed Labour Party members. Now with the General Election looming they planned to devote much of their spare time to the campaign. There was enthusiastic talk of canvassing, delivering leaflets, stuffing envelopes and a few other tasks, which the average person might not readily recognise as fun activities.

Soon David was directed to turn off the main road and into a side street.

"It's about two hundred yards on the left," said Carol.

David's pulse began to race. He was praying that Carol would be the first one who would need to be dropped off. Unfortunately God must have had his attention focused elsewhere.

"Along here," announced Alison as the car approached a lamp

post. "I live in that ground floor maisonette."

It was difficult to see a great deal in the dark. However, David was able to make out what looked like a semi-detached house with a concrete staircase just visible at the side. The light from the front window shone out simply over a small square garden surrounded by a low wire fence.

"Who is looking after Amanda tonight?" Carol enquired.

"My mum as usual," laughed Alison with her head still turned to one side. "She must spend more time in my home than I do."

"And is she baby-sitting tomorrow night as well?" asked Carol.

"Of course," laughed Alison.

"So if we come to pick you up about seven thirty would that be too early?" said Carol keeping up the questioning.

"That should be fine," answered Alison.

"Are you going somewhere nice?" enquired David, making an attempt to break into the conversation.

"Not exactly," replied Carol, suddenly remembering that there was a third person present. "We are just going to an election meeting."

David was busy scheming. Feeling largely ignored and with Carol watching on from behind he had abandoned the idea of inviting Alison out just at that moment. Anyway, with the distinct possibility that his invitation could be rejected, he decided that it might be a good time to enter the mysterious world of politics.

"I would love to be involved in something like that," said David, enthusiastically.

"You were saying earlier that you were intending to vote for Jacqui Dunn," said Carol, gazing thoughtfully ahead of her. "Have you ever considered joining the Labour Party?"

Having switched on the light inside the car, David turned around to see Carol.

"Many times," he answered, untruthfully. "I've just never got around to doing it."

"If you are interested I can give you a form to fill out," said Carol with an encouraging smile. "I happen to be the local membership secretary."

"That sounds brilliant," said David.

"OK then," replied Carol, pleased to have found a new

recruit. "Wait outside when you drop me off and I'll go indoors and fetch all the paperwork."

Meanwhile Alison was regarding David with renewed interest.

"Perhaps there is more to you than I thought," she muttered.

Meeting her eyes he smiled modestly.

"There are those of us who feel the need to fight for what we believe in."

Alison gave him a nod of approval.

"If you are free, you are more than welcome to join us tomorrow evening after the meeting," she suggested. "Our premises are at the bottom of Stafford Road."

"Sounds good," answered David who began to feel his heart pounding excitedly. "I can bring my form along with a cheque."

"Right then, I'd better go and relieve my mum," said Alison, making a move to get out of the car. "See you both tomorrow night."

David waited to see her safely indoors before starting up the car. When he was only a few streets away he was directed to stop outside a small terraced house. From the streetlight outside the gate, red posters were visible in every window proclaiming the householder's political allegiance.

"I won't be a few minutes," said Carol before squeezing herself out of the back seat and hurrying up the garden path.

As he waited, David sat idly staring out of the open car window. From the glow of the street lights he could make out rows of terraced blocks similar to the one in which Carol lived. The few he could see clearly were red bricked and had identical doors suggesting that they were council owned. On display outside several gates, were black bins and green recycle boxes that householders had forgotten to bring inside after a recent collection.

Soon Carol returned and held out a sheet of paper through the open window.

"You will find the address and phone number of our premises at the top of the form," she smiled. "Hope to see you tomorrow evening."

"I look forward to becoming a paid up member," laughed David as he started up the engine.

As he made his way home the catchy tune from Mr Chapman's CD kept running through his head. Suddenly recalling some of the words he immediately began to sing out loud. Somehow the lyrics just happened to express his feelings.

"Something tells me I'm into something good," he crooned away to himself while bobbing his head from side to side.

It was now after eleven o'clock and David hadn't eaten since lunchtime. Suddenly the smell of fish and chips wafted through his open window and he felt compelled to stop and try to track down the source of this enticing aroma.

It didn't take long for him to find what he was looking for. Amongst a long parade of shops one was lit up brightly and from the swing door emerged two young men eating from white wrappers. Soon he had parked the car and was hurrying inside to join the queue.

David was still singing as he finally turned into his road. He stopped in mid-tune when he noticed that the sitting room light was still on. Unless there was a special occasion it was rather unusual for anyone in the Chambers' household to be up so late. Expecting a little strife ahead, he mentally prepared himself for a lecture on arriving home at an 'ungodly hour' as his father liked to put it.

Much to David's relief it was his mother who was waiting for him. Hilary was sat in her dressing gown quietly reading the Bible when her son walked in. After a few moments she looked up at the young man who was standing awkwardly in the doorway. Slowly and deliberately she took off her glasses and placed them in their case.

"Did you enjoy yourself tonight?" she asked in a low voice to avoid disturbing the rest of the family who were upstairs in bed.

David shrugged.

"I've been busy painting and doing a few odd jobs."

Hilary gave him a suspicious stare.

"I find it very strange that anyone should dress up to do work on their house."

"But I was wearing my overalls," David protested.

Hilary looked down sadly at the floor.

"Your overalls are hanging up in the shed. I went out there earlier to check."

David began to fidget and rub the back of his head nervously.

"But I've just bought some new ones, which I keep at the new house."

Hilary stood up and crossed the room to put her Bible back in the drawer.

"Don't you find it difficult painting in the dark?"

"But I had a light on in…" David began before deciding to go no further.

Hilary shook her head sadly.

"There wasn't a single light on in your house at nine thirty this evening. I drove right past it on my way over to Mrs Wilkinson's to drop in a recipe."

David was beginning to feel annoyed.

"Look I am twenty-three and it's about time you stopped treating me like a child. Why can't I lead my own life like any normal person?" he snapped, irritably.

With bowed head Hilary squeezed past her son in the doorway to make her way to bed.

"I just don't want to lose any of my children," she sobbed. "You all mean so much to me."

Chapter Five

It was raining heavily as the car pulled up. With his key at the ready, David hurried down the garden path with Simon in hot pursuit. In preparation for the task ahead both carried their overalls in large plastic bags with identical supermarket logos printed on the side.

Unlocking the front door, David led the way to the kitchen. Without carpets their heavy footsteps on the creaking floorboards echoed loudly throughout the house. With the furniture still to be ordered, but for paint tins and an assortment of tools, every room was practically empty.

It was now mid-morning. For the Fellowship, Saturday always begins with a Bible reading service. This, however, is the only religious meeting of the day, meaning that followers are permitted a respite from attending church for a few precious hours.

The two friends soon got down to work. Their plan of action was firstly to finish painting the kitchen and then make a start on the lounge. With Ruth and her mother expected to arrive sometime after one o'clock it was important to get as much done as possible. In any case, that was the opinion held by Hilary and John Chambers rather than their rather laid-back son.

David was pleased to have Simon to keep him company. Having not seen his friend to speak to since the trip down to Broadstairs earlier that week, he had a lot to update him with. More importantly though, he wanted not only to talk about the unusual things he had been doing over the past few days but also seek some advice.

Simon listened in stunned silence. In fact he made absolutely no comment until David had finally provided him with a detailed account of recent events.

"You won't be able to live a double life for very long," he said having eventually managed to collect his thoughts.

"I know," replied David as he stopped to gaze out of the

window. "My mother already suspects something is going on."

Putting down his paintbrush for a moment, Simon turned to face his friend.

"The Fellowship may excuse you for breaking off your engagement to Ruth. However, to then discover that you are dating a non-believer would be stretching their tolerance just a little too far."

David stood thoughtfully looking out over the front garden. A large puddle on the grass was steadily growing by the minute as heavy drops of rain fell in torrents.

"I'm not exactly dating Alison," he replied, keen as ever to get the picture straight. "It's just that as Labour Party members we will probably be seeing a lot of each other in the future."

"And that is another thing," said Simon, prompted by the last remark. "The Fellowship don't get involved in politics. We are taught to concentrate our thoughts on the next world rather than the problems of this one."

Half-heartedly David dipped his paintbrush in the tin and returned reluctantly to his labours.

"Are you suggesting that I should just forget Alison then?" he asked.

Simon nodded.

"In the long run it will probably be for the best."

For a while David considered the advice. However, as he continued to paint his thoughts kept returning to Alison and before long his willpower had crumbled into tiny pieces. His head was capable of putting up a strong argument but in the end the heart was always likely to come out on top.

At last the kitchen was finished. Standing back to admire their handiwork they helped themselves to tea from a flask, which David had brought. Taking a short break provided Simon with an opportunity to announce his news.

"My parents are trying to get me fixed up with a wife," he grinned. "They have just arranged for me to meet up with a girl from Devon next week."

"Did you get any details about her?" smiled David, sipping his tea.

"Only that she is very nice," laughed Simon. "Parents always say that."

"Mine said that about Ruth," said David, acidly.

Simon who had been standing, followed his friend's example and sat on the floor.

"Have you decided yet when you are going to break off your engagement?"

"No," replied David staring blankly at the thermos flask. "But things are beginning to take shape in my mind."

Simon shook his head in disbelief.

"For goodness sake, time is running out fast. Everyone is expecting you to be married in several weeks."

"Give me a few more days," said David, thoughtfully.

After the tea break they started work on the lounge. It was a sizeable room with a high ceiling and was likely to take several sessions before it was finally completed. The first task was to wash down the walls.

As they worked it occurred to David that what they were doing was utterly pointless. There was to be no marriage and before very long the house would be put back on the market again. It could only be hoped that the new buyers appreciated the colour of the paint.

Stopping scrubbing briefly to rest his arm, David glanced out of the window again. The rain had stopped and the sun was shining brightly on the world outside. On the opposite side of the road a boy wheeling a trolley behind him was delivering free papers to ever house. In the distance two middle-aged ladies were holding a conversation over a low privet hedge.

It was early afternoon when the three wise women arrived. Laden with furniture brochures and each with a purposeful look in their eyes, Hilary, Ruth and Joan Kennedy were ready to go on a grand tour of the house. They barely glanced at David who had greeted them at the front door with a wet paintbrush in his hand.

By this time Simon had gone. Now well on his way to Essex, his help had been enlisted in tiling the men's toilet for the new church being built. Such dedication to the cause would doubtless earn him a reward in Heaven.

Before going any further the women stopped to inspect the painting. After a long hard stare and placing themselves in various positions they finally felt ready to give their verdict.

"I think it is a nice shade of blue," commented Hilary without any great enthusiasm in her voice.

Ruth immediately wrinkled up her nose.

"It's too dark for a room this size. You should have gone for something a little paler David."

Joan nodded her head firmly.

"You are absolutely right dear. Personally I would have gone for a light green or perhaps even cream."

David gave the ceiling a look of long suffering.

"But I was told to use my discretion when choosing the paint."

It happened to be the truth. However, preferring to ignore her fiancé's remark, Ruth like her mother turned her head away disdainfully and followed Hilary out of the room. There was plenty to look at and they weren't prepared to waste time arguing with an incompetent male.

The threesome were heading for the kitchen. With what sounded like a herd of elephants who had just spotted a watering hole, they trundled their way on the bare floorboards along the hall. All the while their unceasing talk centred around the subject of furniture.

"I suppose you will have to buy a dark blue three piece suite to match that dreadful paint," commented Joan in a disapproving voice.

"Seems like it," replied Ruth, sulkily.

"On the other hand, you could always get David to decorate the lounge again in a nicer colour," suggested Joan, helpfully.

"That's a good idea," answered Ruth. "I shall speak to him about it."

It was clearly not intended to be a private conversation between mother and daughter. The pair were speaking in such raised voices that their remarks were clearly meant for David's ears as well.

The inspection committee moved slowly from room to room. Each appearing to compete with the others on the amount of suggestions they could squeeze out of their imaginations. Smiling to himself, David was reminded of the three witches from Macbeth.

"We need to buy a cabinet for that alcove," said one.

"I think a shelf should be put up here," said another.

"This room would look nice painted in pink," joined in the third one.

It seemed to go on forever. Ruth who was busily scribbling down notes as she went, must have filled up her pad by the time the threesome had finished. Even as they were standing at the front door preparing to leave ideas were still flowing.

"We are just about to go," called out Hilary, somehow managing to drag her thoughts away from furniture and home decoration. "I have arranged with Martha to have the meal on the table in twenty minutes."

"I'll be there shortly," answered David, who intended to climb out of his overalls the instant the women had gone. He had endured a long session of sliding his paintbrush up and down walls and was thoroughly sick of it.

"Don't forget that Ian Porter is coming to see us this afternoon," shouted Ruth before slamming the front door.

As David drove home he noticed that more and more residents had put up posters in their windows. Unsurprisingly in this affluent part of the constituency, blue was by far the most common colour on view with yellow coming a distant second. However, support for Jacqui Dunn was non-existent amongst those who were prepared to advertise their voting intentions.

In the past David had barely given a thought to such matters. Now with a Labour Party membership form safely hidden behind his wardrobe the situation had taken on a new significance. Because of Alison he now cared which of two mysterious candidates called Dawkins and Dunn actually won the contest to represent Brockleby in Parliament.

Throughout lunch the women spoke of nothing else but furniture. Martha who was also seated around the table added yet another enthusiastic voice to this nonstop conversation. Over soup they discussed kitchens, during the main meal it was three piece suites and the subject as they tucked into fruit and ice creams was whether pine or beech would look better in the big bedroom. Far from finished curtains became the only topic as they washed and dried the dishes. Mercifully, David, however, being advised that his services were surplus to requirements, was allowed to retire to the lounge for a well-earned rest.

Unfortunately this respite was all too brief. Soon the four

fanatics had put away the last dish and were eagerly filing into the lounge to join him. This time they were all equipped with paper and pen to jot down further ideas. Furniture brochures were piled up on the coffee table for reference purposes as and when required.

"So let's start with the kitchen," suggested Joan, staring at everyone in turn with the notable exception of David. "Do we allow the present fixtures and fittings to remain or would it be better to strip the whole lot out and start afresh?"

"Let's get it completely refitted," said Ruth without hesitation.

"It will be expensive," warned Hilary, who had a reputation for being careful with money.

Ruth shrugged.

"We can always go to the bank for a loan," she replied casually.

Like his mother, David had never liked the idea of building up debt. However, in this instance there seemed little point in voicing an objection being that these spending plans would come to nothing. In fact he was feeling rather guilty that all these women were wasting their time and energy.

Further rooms were discussed with even greater expenditure being budgeted for. Just when David thought he was about to go out of his mind, Ian Porter came to the rescue. His arrival prompted the women to put away their pens and paper and adopt a quiet respectful demeanour.

After they had all exchanged the usual pleasantries, Joan presented her master plan to the priest.

"If you would like to be alone with David and Ruth we three women can go down to the couple's new home and do some measuring up."

"An arrangement conceived in Heaven," smiled Ian as Hilary headed for the drawer in which she kept a tape measure.

Soon Ian was alone with the engaged couple. It was like a breath of fresh air for David to listen to something unrelated to the world of furniture, even if it was one of Ian's 'little talks' as the priest was fond of putting it.

As always, when in the company of strangers, Ruth became transformed. Sitting attentively with her head slightly tilted to one side, she sat watching the speaker with a look of admiration. There was almost something angelic about her appearance in that brief period of time.

"You should raise your family to understand the ways of the Fellowship," said Ian, solemnly.

"We will," murmured Ruth, gently nodding her head.

"You must always shield your children from the evils of the world and help them to follow in the path of righteousness," continued the priest.

"We certainly will," replied Ruth with her head now moving up and down like one of those toy dogs, which are hung up in the back of cars.

"Remember David, that all those who reside in your house should observe the teachings of the Bible," said Ian, looking sternly at the young man. "Remember that you are the head of the family."

"That's right," answered Ruth in a small submissive voice.

David managed to resist the temptation to smile. How anyone could so readily change from being such an overbearing person to that of a mild and gentle one had never ceased to amaze him. He wondered how many thespians working in West End plays could have matched such talent.

Ian had finished his 'little talk' by the time the women had returned. With notepads full of dimensions, the subject of furniture would surely have flared up again but for the presence of the priest. However, such matters were put on hold once the distinguished guest had delayed his departure after having accepted the offer of a cream cake.

Ian smiled warmly at Ruth before taking a bite out of his vanilla slice.

"Will you be down again before the wedding?" he enquired.

Ruth nodded eagerly.

"Next Saturday David and I are going shopping for furniture."

This news came as a complete surprise to David. However, it was not a problem that needed to be addressed, being that he fully intended to be a free man in less than a week.

"How is the painting going by the way?" enquired Ian, who had just been handed a cup of tea by Martha.

David grimaced.

"I thought it was going reasonably well but now they tell me that the colour is too dark."

"David will have to go over it all again," explained Hilary, giving her son a sympathetic smile. "I am going out on Monday morning to look for a lighter shade of blue."

This was yet more news to David but, once again, it was of no consequence. His only concern was that the paint might go to waste if nobody were to find a use for it.

Once Ian had gone off to another appointment the notepads came out again. Comparing the dimensions in various brochures with those just taken from the new house, the women were soon deciding whether a wardrobe would fit in this space or if a bookcase would squeeze into a certain alcove. Just when David was considering throwing himself off the roof, Joan Kennedy announced that she and Ruth were about to go. However, before setting off, Ruth issued her final instructions.

"When I come down next Saturday," she began, leaning her head out of the car window, "I expect to see the lounge and kitchen redecorated in light blue paint."

Once the car had disappeared into the distance, David retreated to his bedroom. Moving the wardrobe forward a fraction he retrieved the forms that Carol had given him the previous evening. At that moment he desperately needed to take his mind off furniture and home decorations.

It was almost dark when David turned off into Stafford Road. After driving slowly along it for several moments he spotted a sign outside a large detached Victorian house and on it, printed in bold red letters were the words 'Brockleby Labour Party'. Finding a space on the forecourt to park his car he made his way towards the front entrance.

Once inside, David found himself in a rather crowded bar. It was untidier than might normally have been expected in the average pub with bundles of leaflets, piles of Labour Party newspapers and clipboards scattered around. The walls were covered in posters and notices, while at the far end, a photograph of the Prime Minister smiled down on devotees from behind a long counter where drinks were being served. There were facilities such as a dartboard and pool table, which seemed to be popular attractions for some of the younger members.

David spotted Alison sitting with her back towards him. On the opposite side of the table sat Carol and a man about the same age with a dark pointed beard. The shape had probably been formed by constantly pinching the end of it.

"Good evening," said David as he stopped beside Carol's chair. "You have a nice place here."

The threesome who had been deep in conversation all turned their heads at the same time.

"Glad you like it," smiled Alison. "We were beginning to think you weren't coming."

"This is my husband, Tony," said Carol. "He is our campaign organiser."

Both men nodded to each other.

"Could I buy you a drink?" enquired David, looking down upon three glasses that were almost empty.

With his offer being eagerly accepted he set off for two beers, a vodka and lime and a dry white wine. However, as the one barman on duty appeared to spend more time talking to customers than actually serving them it was a while before David returned. Then after distributing the drinks from the tin tray, which had been provided, he finally took his seat next to Alison.

"I've filled out my membership form," he said, producing a folded up sheet of paper from his inside jacket pocket.

As Carol carefully checked it though, David took out two bank notes from his wallet.

"The exact money I believe."

"Welcome to the Labour Party," beamed Carol when she had finally satisfied herself that everything was in order.

"Thank you," answered the new recruit cheerfully.

Having taken the form from his wife, Tony was studying it carefully.

"Are you able to deliver any leaflets for us?" he enquired.

"Yes of course," replied David, keen to play his part in the campaign.

"I'll see what I can find," said Tony, getting to his feet.

David watched as the party organiser negotiated his way past a large gathering of drinkers before disappearing through a door on the opposite side of the room.

"Make certain you don't take on too much," warned Carol.

"My husband tries to drive people too hard at times."

David promised to heed the advice. He was taken by surprise, however, when two large bundles were presented to him a few minutes later. Tied up in string, they each must have been about four inches thick.

"These leaflets are for your road and several surrounding ones," said Tony. "They need to be delivered by Monday night at the very latest. We have a new one, which is going out across the whole constituency on Tuesday."

Although David smiled willingly, inside he was feeling uncomfortable. It wasn't so much the amount of work involved but rather where he was being asked to do it. His own neighbourhood was the last place he would have chosen to traipse up and down garden paths carrying piles of political literature.

"How did your meeting go?" he asked, taking a sip of beer.

"Very well," answered Tony enthusiastically. "We've just about agreed our election strategy."

"Had you arrived ten minutes earlier we could have introduced you to Jacqui Dunn," said Alison. "She was here for the meeting."

David smiled sadly.

"I would like to have met her."

"Don't worry," laughed Carol. "I'm sure your paths will cross before too long."

"Hopefully as early as Tuesday evening," joined in Tony. "I am getting a team together to deliver our new leaflet on the Gladstone Estate. Please come along if you are free."

"We shall be setting off from here about seven o'clock," added Carol.

David hesitated for a brief moment. It was decision time. Either he could arrange to team up with the group a little later or commit a cardinal sin and miss a Fellowship meeting. There was no way of keeping everyone happy.

"Count me in," smiled David at last.

Tony was delighted to have found another willing worker. Immediately he began to reveal to the new boy how he intended to mastermind a great election victory. However, because of his privileged position in the local party, he was continually being interrupted.

One shaven-headed young man was the main culprit. Having just finished a game of pool with a group of friends he casually strolled over to Tony and tapped him on the shoulder. As he looked down on the election organiser there was a puzzled expression on his face.

"What time did you say we had to be here on Tuesday evening?" he asked.

"Seven o'clock," replied Tony.

There was a short pause as this information sunk in.

"And did you say we were going out canvassing?" asked the pool player.

Tony shook his head.

"As I explained to everyone at the meeting, Ross, we are delivering the new leaflets."

Ross wandered slowly away but was back in less than five minutes.

"If I'm a bit late, how will I know where to find you?"

"Just ring me on my mobile," said Tony. "I'll give you directions as to where we are."

Carol gave her husband a look of sympathy as Ross walked away. However, just when they assumed that the young man had got everything clear in his mind he was back yet again.

"What happens if it is raining hard?"

Patient as ever Tony smiled down wearily at his beer mug.

"Unfortunately we are all going to get bloody wet mate. A tiny drop of water mustn't be allowed to prevent a Labour Government returning to power."

Carol and Alison giggled as Ross strolled back to his friends. Rather than being amused, however, David was a little surprised to learn that these seasoned campaigners were willing to get soaked to the skin for the cause. Politics it seemed was certainly not for the faint hearted.

David continued to listen to Tony's election tactics with interest. It soon became apparent that behind the high ideals that were presented to the outside world, were Machiavellian individuals conniving and scheming away in order to achieve their ends. He became so engrossed that he was unaware that Alison had been keeping a close eye on her watch.

"I think I had better be going," she announced, suddenly.

"We'll be leaving shortly," said Carol. "You can come with us."

"I don't mind dropping Alison off," said David.

Tony laughed.

"But you live on the opposite side of town whereas Alison's place is just around the corner from us."

David tried to think of a counter argument but couldn't. The facts were precisely as Tony had presented them so common sense dictated that Alison should travel with those living close by. It was yet another example of reason sticking her nose in where it wasn't wanted.

Fortunately Lady Luck was smiling down. Ross and one of his friends had approached Tony in order to settle a dispute they were having concerning the whereabouts of Iraq. Helpful as ever the organiser led them off to another room in search of a world map.

Carol gave her friend a long suffering look.

"I suggest you go home with David. Tony is likely to be a while yet."

David followed Alison towards the door. Unfortunately making a quick exit was never an option for any member of the Brockleby Labour Party. It wasn't until they had finally said goodbye to just about everyone left in the bar that they were able to make their way into the night air.

David felt a little nervous as he started up the car. Having longed to be alone with Alison, he was lost for words now that the opportunity had finally arrived. On the other hand, sitting in silence seemed the worst of all options.

"How is Amanda?" he enquired in an attempt to start Alison talking.

He had struck gold. Soon the proud mother was discussing birthday parties, cut knees and the cost of children's clothes. David was utterly confused as to how one subject followed on from another but it really didn't bother him in the least. He was just content to listen to her voice.

"Thanks for the lift," said Alison as they arrived outside her maisonette. "I hope you weren't dragged too far out of your way."

"I enjoyed your company," answered David, regretting that they would soon have to part.

Alison was about to open the car door when she appeared to be struck by a sudden thought. Turning to David she leaned over and kissed him quickly on the cheek.

"See you on Tuesday evening," she whispered.

David was lost for words as he watched Alison hurry up the garden path. It took him a while to recover his senses sufficiently enough to feel confident of driving off. Finally when he did, the lyrics of Herman's Hermits sixties hit began to go through his head once again.

"Something tells me I'm into something good," he sang loudly to the road ahead.

Chapter Six

"I'm just going out for a while," announced David, popping his head around the kitchen door.

Hilary who was swabbing the floor looked up at her son with concern.

"Please keep your eye on the time dear. Don't forget that Scott and Helen's flight is due to arrive at two thirty."

David smiled reassuringly.

"I promise to be waiting at Heathrow to meet them. You really have nothing to worry about."

Hilary's worried expression faded as she returned to her cleaning.

"Thank you dear. It's just that both of them are strangers to this country and I want to make sure that they receive a warm welcome at the airport."

Scott and Helen were a young Australian couple. Only recently married they wanted to take a look at Europe before settling down to start a family. After spending their first two nights with the Chambers, they intended to travel around the UK before crossing the Channel to explore France and beyond.

The Wrights were to be backpackers with a difference. Instead of sleeping in hostels they were to be put up each night by a Fellowship family. This ensured that the couple remained in contact with Godly people who would be responsible for taking them to a service every night.

David closed the front door and headed to his car in the drive. It was ten o'clock on Monday morning, which meant that he was missing the regular weekly sales meeting. Even better still, it was the first of three days extra holiday that his Fellowship boss had allowed him for agreeing to act as chauffeur to the Australian tourists.

David drove around the neighbourhood for a while until he found a suitable place to park. Finally he spotted a small cul-de-sac with three houses on each side of the road. Confident that none of the residents were Fellowship, he brought his car to a standstill next to a high red bricked wall.

Reaching under his seat, David lifted up a white plastic bag. Inside were two items which he hoped would disguise his appearance without making him look too conspicuous. The first was a pair of dark glass, which seemed inappropriate on a day when the sun remained shielded by a thick blanket of grey clouds. The other was a black baseball cap that he had taken from his sister's wardrobe without permission. It was the first time in his life that he had worn such headgear.

Striding around to the back of the car, David unlocked the boot. There where he had left them on Saturday night lay those two monster bundle of leaflets. They must have been intended for a few hundred houses and Tony had wanted them delivered by the end of the day at the very latest.

David referred to his map. On top of each bundle was a list of those roads which were to be targeted with propaganda. Suddenly he became aware that one of the names, a certain Brunton Close, was none other than the very cul-de-sac he was actually stood in. Resolutely he pulled down the peak of his cap and headed boldly towards the nearest house.

To begin with David felt rather self-conscious. He hurried up and down each garden path as though expecting to be hit by a bullet at any minute. It wasn't long, however, before he started to relax and actually enjoy himself.

David soon began to appreciate that there is no uniformity when it comes to letterboxes. Most were waist high but then there are those which barely come above the ankle. They can be horizontal, vertical and then there are the type with springs which are capable of breaking fingers. Not to be forgotten of course is the piece de resistance for all postmen, paper-boys and political activists alike. The type that when the flap is raised, the poor deliverer has to force his material between the stiff bristles of two brushes. The task became increasingly difficult, however, when the item in question happens to be a flimsy piece of paper.

Certain householders had put up warning notices stating that they didn't wish to receive circulars, free papers or junk mail. Like many before him, David on principle simply had to turn a blind eye to such warnings and shoved a leaflet through the door with a little more vigour than normal. Having just marched twenty metres or more up the garden path and with a return journey yet to come, he wasn't prepared to be thwarted in his objective.

At one point David came to a house that he knew to be the home of a Fellowship family. Throwing all caution to the wind he was about to put his hand on the green wooden gate when an upstairs window suddenly flew open. Quite expecting to see a familiar head pop out he was taken by surprise when a bright red duster appeared and began flapping vigorously about on the end of a hand. Keen to avoid detection, even with some slightly odd attire to mask his identity, he turned on his heels and moved rapidly on to the next door neighbours.

Feeling slightly stiff in the legs, David finally returned to his car. It was satisfying to see that the two large bundles that he had set out with had dwindled down to one small pile. The only road still to receive leaflets was his own. This he decided should be remedied later that evening under the cover of darkness.

Slightly wearily, David arrived home to discover that his sister-in-law had dropped by. It was of little surprise to him that she was sat side by side with his mother studying furniture brochures. Both wore that childlike look of wonder on their faces as they flicked through the pages.

"Kate and I were just saying that this would look nice in your sitting room," said Hilary, holding up a glossy picture of a three piece suite.

"Very nice," smiled David, as he craned his head forward towards the brochure in an attempt to appear interested.

"And the colour of the fabric would match the paint which I brought for you this morning," said Hilary, looking pleased with herself.

David tried to look impressed. However, a feeling of nausea was beginning to take route in the pit of his stomach as he contemplated another protracted conversation on furnishing and decorating. It seemed that a change of subject was urgently required.

"Peter has offered to give you a hand with the painting by the way," said Kate.

David immediately saw his opportunity.

"Has he managed to get over that cold yet?" he enquired.

The two women exchanged puzzled looks.

"But that was weeks ago," laughed Kate. "As it happens I'd almost forgotten about it and probably has Peter too."

"Actually you were talking to your brother last night," joined in Hilary. "Did he appear to be unwell?"

"I suppose not," answered David, feeling a little foolish.

Momentarily he contemplated changing the subject yet again but wisely decided against it. However, on the point of announcing that he was about to leave the room in order to answer a call of nature, his five-year-old niece Gemma, who had been playing in the garden, came bouncing in through the patio door.

"Where are you buying your fitted kitchen from Uncle David?" she asked, excitedly.

Before David had a chance to speak, Hilary jumped in first. With her far superior knowledge as to what was going on she was able to report on the latest available information.

"David and Ruth are thinking of buying their fitted kitchen from a local supplier in the High Street," she said.

Unsurprisingly this was news to David. However at this point he slipped out of the room, leaving the little girl to prise more details from her grandmother about the proposed purchase. If at all possible he hoped to preserve at least a few grains of his sadly depleted reserves of sanity.

To escape the obsessive women he set off for Heathrow early. With over half an hour to wait before the Australian tourists were expected to appear in the arrival area he decided to spend the time profitably. Finding a comfortable seat, David sat and read a copy of the Labour Party leaflet he had been delivering that morning.

Jacqui Dunn was featured heavily. On an A4 sheet of paper folded in two, there were three photographs of the parliamentary candidate. She was pictured outside a primary school surrounded by young children, in front of the local general hospital amongst a ring of nurses and sitting down with a roomful of elderly residents in a care home. Each one was headed by a slogan such as 'Jacqui Dunn fights to save local school' and 'Jacqui Dunn cares about health'.

She seemed to be portrayed as a lady knight in shining armour. Probably best described as a cross between a modern day Joan of Arc and Mother Teresa. A medieval heroine ready to take up her sword and do battle against the evil barons who sought to inflict yet more misery on the down-trodden peasants. The baddies of course being her rival candidate Charles Hawkins and his marauding army of Conservative supporters.

David felt moved by what he read. There was something very noble about helping the poor and most vulnerable people in society. After all, wasn't there a powerful altruistic message in the Four Gospels. Unfortunately being new to all things political he had yet to develop a healthy cynicism.

A short while after the flight had arrived David began to keep a lookout for the visitors. Not having seen a photograph of the couple he was relying on a large piece of cardboard to make contact. With the names of Scott and Helen Wright written boldly with a black marker pen he hoped to bring attention to himself by holding it aloft when any likely candidates approached. His job was made easier by the fact that he just needed to spot a young woman with long hair and a headscarf.

People came and went but there was no sign of the Wrights. Finally when David was beginning to think that they had missed the plane, two leaden footed individuals appeared in the distance pushing a trolley. From the amount of luggage the pair were travelling with, it looked as though they might be moving house.

The Wrights were not at all as David had expected. He had a preconceived idea that all Australians were suntanned with athletic physiques due to leading a healthy outdoor life. In fact in this case nothing could have been much further from the truth.

Both had the pallor of people who had spent the winter at the North Pole. However, when it came to size they were at opposite ends of the spectrum. Whereas Scott was large and flabby, Helen had the slender frame of a ballerina.

"Sorry we're late," shouted Scott as he saw his name held up. "Helen and I were searching around for toilets."

"I thought you had missed your flight," laughed David as he led the way towards the terminal exit.

With a struggle and no shortage of ingenuity David managed to squeeze three sizeable suitcases into the boot. The assortment of bags that had also been allowed to make the trip had to fit on the back seat in and around Helen. Had she have been a normal size lady, certain personal effects would probably have remained at the airport.

"This is our first ever trip to Europe," said Scott as they set off along the M25.

"Looking down on Britain from the air we noticed how green and lush the countryside is," said Helen, pushing away a brown bag that was sticking into her ribs.

"It is the result of all the rain we get over here," replied David.

"Do we happen to pass through any quaint little villages once we leave the motorway?" asked Scott, hopefully.

David hesitated for a moment.

"I could show you a particularly attractive one but it means going out of our way a little."

"That would be great," said Helen, excitedly. "I want to take some pictures to show the folks back home."

David was soon to discover that the Wrights were compulsive photographers. Every time they spotted anything remotely unusual the digital cameras would appear. They were like children with a new plaything.

"Hey look!" exclaimed Helen suddenly. "There is a sign over there pointing towards a castle."

David glanced casually out of the window.

"Oh that is Hever."

"Is it very famous?" enquired Scott.

David chuckled.

"I would say so. A love affair began there and ended up creating a religious and political earthquake in this country."

"What happened?" gasped Helen.

David tried to collect this thoughts. He wanted to present the essential facts rather than deliver a history lesson.

"Hever was once home to Anne Boleyn," he began, trying to refer back in his memory to what Mr Chapman had once taught him at school. "Anyway Henry the Eighth, being rather fond of Anne, used to regularly pop down to the castle to visit her."

Not being too familiar with the goings on in Tudor times Helen was starting to look puzzled.

"So the King was having a relationship then. Why was that a problem?"

"Because Henry wanted to marry Anne when he already had a

wife," replied David.

"So what was all the fuss about?" asked Helen, still totally confused. "I don't see why this should have created a political and religious earthquake."

Scott who had been silent during the conversation suddenly decided to make a contribution. Having once read a potted account of British History he began to recall the key events which had led to the Reformation.

"I seem to remember that because England was a Catholic country at the time, Henry needed the Pope's permission to annul his marriage to Catherine of Aragon."

"Spot on," replied David, impressed by the Australian's knowledge. "And when the Pope refused to give his blessing the King decided to break away from Rome."

"After which England became a Protestant country," said Scott, finishing off the story.

"Couldn't we go and see the castle now?" pleaded Helen.

David hesitated briefly. Always keen to visit places of interest he was tempted to turn off the motorway at the next exit and take his new friends sightseeing. However, setting off on such an adventure would most likely annoy his mother who was a stickler for punctuality and keeping arrangements. With an advance warning given that tea and cakes would be served at four thirty, he was expected to deliver the guests to her on time without fail.

"I'm afraid it won't be possible to go today," he replied, sadly. "We would need several hours to go round and see everything."

"Any chance that you could take us there tomorrow?" asked Scott, hopefully.

"If that is where you wish to go then so be it," smiled David. "My services are at your disposal while you are staying in Brockleby."

"Good on you mate," said Scott, switching to a broad Australian accent.

Eventually they left the M25 behind. Soon the constant flow of traffic had given way to quiet winding lanes with hedgerows and overhanging trees on either side. In the distance undulating fields of varying shades of green created a rich tapestry as grazing cattle stared nonchalantly into space as they stood eating.

"Can we stop here to take some photos?" requested Helen, eagerly as they approached a small village.

Having found a place to park the Wrights were quickly taking pictures of everything in sight. Most of the houses were constructed of brick and tile but they managed to discover several that were timber framed and a cottage made from flint. At the heart of the village was an impressive Norman church built in stone and surrounded by Yew trees, which cast lengthy shadows over the gravestones beneath.

The threesome turned a corner and followed a narrow sloping street. Soon they came to a river which must have attracted the first inhabitants of the village to settle there. On the banks beneath the alder and weeping willow trees, young children hung their fishing nets into the flowing river.

As they stopped briefly to take in the scene, Helen suddenly put her hand up to touch her head.

"Just checking that I was wearing my headscarf," she smiled. "Sometimes I go out and forget to put it on."

David turned to her with a look of surprise.

"I thought Fellowship women tied them around their hair without thinking. A bit like putting your shoes on when going for a walk."

"Those that were actually born into the faith probably do," answered Helen, gazing thoughtfully into the distance. "The difference with me is that I am a recent convert."

Having met few people who had left the outside world to join the Eternal Fellowship, David became curious.

"So what made you decide to join our church?"

Helen's mind was elsewhere for a moment. With a smile she watched an excited little boy remove a small fish from his net and place it carefully into a jam jar. His companion who was about the same age looked on in awe.

"There were two reasons which helped me to make up my mind," she replied, finally. "One was that I wanted to find the Lord and the other…"

"You were looking for someone to marry," laughed Scott.

Helen slapped her husband playfully on the arm.

"How did you two come to meet each other?" asked David as he followed the Wrights towards an empty wooden bench overlooking the river.

"We met at work," answered Scott once they were all seated. "Dad and I run a family business and Helen was hired to help with the accounts."

"I didn't want to join the company to begin with," laughed Helen. "Particularly when I was told that women weren't expected to come to work wearing trousers. The problem was that I only had one skirt in my entire wardrobe and it meant going out on a spending spree."

Scott suddenly became serious.

"One day when we weren't too busy, Helen and I sat talking for a while about various things when the subject of religion came up."

"What a surprise," smiled David.

"Anyway," said Helen, taking up the story. "Scott began explaining to me about the love of God and how I could gain Salvation just by following the Bible teachings. It all sounded so tempting that I decided to become a Christian, too."

David suddenly glanced over at the two young fishermen. Having abandoned both nets and jam jars alongside their footwear they were now wading about in the water. Meanwhile on the bank their mothers sat chatting as they kept a watchful eye on the boys.

"Soon Helen was coming along to our Fellowship meetings and became very much part of our church," said Scott with a look of pride.

David looked curiously at Helen.

"Don't you find it difficult adjusting to our lifestyle?"

Helen shrugged.

"I certainly don't miss watching TV or doing any other of those activities which worldly people do. About the only thing that bothers me is not being able to sit down to eat with my family."

"That must be very upsetting for you," replied David, sympathetically.

Helen sat staring into space.

"My parents get very hurt about it. They feel that I am rejecting them."

"Serving the Lord was never meant to be easy," said Scott. "The Devil is always trying to weaken our resolve as we try to follow the path of righteousness."

Producing a tissue from her bag, Helen dabbed the corner of her eye.

"What bothers me most is that I will have to drive a wedge between our children and their grandparents. Never will they be able to experience the pleasure of sitting down to eat a meal together."

Scott gently took his wife's hand.

"Perhaps the answer maybe to help your mum and dad find the Lord as well."

Helen gave him a look of scorn.

"Dad is a staunch Atheist and believes that we all descended from apes. Every time the subject of religion is mentioned he just goes on about how I have allowed myself to become brainwashed."

Scott shook his head sadly.

"I'm afraid the theory of Evolution won't provide him with much comfort in his old age."

During the discussion Scott probably expected some support from his English host. Instead, no longer convinced about the beliefs he had been taught, David sat quietly reflecting on what was being said. He couldn't help but feel sorry for the predicament that Helen faced with her parents.

At that moment drops of fine rain began to fall. The two anxious mothers on the river bank stood up and started to instruct their reluctant offspring to scramble out of the water with immediate effect. An elderly couple out on a leisurely stroll moved hastily towards the nearest tree for shelter.

"Let's make our way before it gets heavy," said David, rising to his feet.

By the time they had reached Brockleby the heavens had opened and it was as if the town had suddenly become struck by a monsoon. Had it been bright and sunny the Wrights would have insisted upon climbing out of the car and taking pictures of the War Memorial, the clock tower and probably the public toilets as well. At present though, they were perfectly content to sit back in their seats and watch the rain lash against the windows.

At one point they passed the library. Huddled inside the entrance were several people who stood anxiously watching for improvements in the weather so that they could go on their way. David conjured up an image of Alison sitting at a desk surrounded by shelves of books. She was busy writing and with her eyes looking down the shoulder length flaxen hair covered her cheeks.

"A lot of people have put up posters in their windows," commented Helen as the car entered the residential part of the town.

"Is our General Election creating much interest in Australia?" asked David.

"Very much so," replied Helen, stooping to pick up a bag which had fallen on the floor. "It is seen as a British referendum on the Iraq war."

"Which it probably is," replied David, thoughtfully. "But why should that matter to the people in your country?"

"Because our Government sent troops to Iraq to support the coalition forces," explained Scott. "It was a controversial decision and there have been massive demonstrations in all our major cities. Therefore the prime minister will feel that if Britain votes against the war, the chances are that Australia will do the same when we hold a general election."

"So do you think it will encourage him to bring your servicemen and women back home?" asked David.

"It's possible," said Scott. "No government wants to get turned out of office."

Although they do not wish to soil their hands through voting, it is not uncommon for the Fellowship to discuss politics. Like the rest of us, what is decided upon in parliaments and council chambers throughout the democratic world has a direct impact on their lives. For them, however, it is a matter of trusting in the Lord that the Ungodly put their crosses in the right boxes.

Hilary as always was the perfect hostess. On their arrival the guests were presented with tea in her best china cups and a plateful of rather exotic cream cakes to feast upon. Furthermore while sitting with an attentive smile she bombarded the Australians with a series of questions.

Did you have a safe journey? Did you manage to sleep on the plane? Where will you be staying when you leave Brockleby? And so forth. The enquiries just seemed to go on and on. David always marvelled at how his mother was able to think of so many and wondered how much she really cared about the answers.

Soon it was time for the family and their guests to set off for the evening meeting. The rain had now stopped and the Wrights were thrilled to be able to take a photo of the church before the service began. Once inside, John Chambers escorted Scott to the front with the other men and older boys, while Helen took her seat next to Hilary towards the back.

It was Monday night which meant that all the males at the front were expected to stand up and pray out loud. David was feeling a tinge of sadness as he waited for his turn to arrive. Great changes were about to take place in his life and most probably this would be the very last meeting he would ever attend. He might never see the inside of this church again and almost every one of the people that were present would soon be treating him as an outcast.

The Wrights were beginning to suffer the effects of jet lag. As soon as they had eaten their evening meal with the Chambers after the meeting, the weary travellers retired to bed. They couldn't even find the energy to read a single chapter of the Bible.

On the other hand, David had one more task to perform for the day. The people in his road had yet to receive those Labour Party leaflets, which were lying in the boot of his car. The matter was beginning to weigh heavily on his conscience.

It was well after midnight as David began to get dressed again. Reasonably confident that everyone in the house was soundly asleep he crept downstairs and quietly slipped out of the front door. To help avoid being recognised by any neighbour who might be suffering from insomnia and just happened to be looking out of the window, he put on his sister's baseball cap once more before setting off. If serving the Lord was difficult he told himself, working for the Labour Party was hardly a piece of cake.

Chapter Seven

The following morning began overcast but dry. Fully refreshed from a good night's sleep the Wrights were eager to squeeze as much sightseeing into the available hours as possible. Therefore shortly after breakfast David and his new friends were back amongst the country lanes heading for Hever Castle.

For the first part of the journey David and Helen talked amongst themselves. Scott was with them in body only as he sat in the front seat studying a large travel guide of London. Finally he shut the book and spent a few moments gazing out of the window.

"How far is Greenwich?" he asked, suddenly.

"Probably less than half an hour's drive from Brockleby," replied David. "Are you interested in going there?"

"Very much," replied the big Australian, enthusiastically. "It sounds a fascinating place."

"What attractions does it have to offer?" enquired Helen who was sitting comfortably in the back seat. Unlike the previous day when she had been penned in by numerous bags her movements were now unrestricted.

"Well to start with there is an old boat in dry dock which you can take a look over," answered Scott who had a passion for all types of transport.

David winced to hear one of Britain's best loved national treasures described in such a fashion.

"The *Cutty Shark* used to carry tea from China," said David who had been taken to see the vessel on a school trip. "On board there is a very impressive collection of figureheads and also visitors have an opportunity to look over the crews living quarters."

"What else is there in Greenwich?" asked Helen

Scott reopened the travel guide to refresh his memory.

"Apparently there is a yacht which sailed around the world, the National Maritime Museum and an amazing park, which overlooks the River Thames. Then there is the Old Royal Observatory where the Meridian, that is the invisible line which divides the Earth's Eastern and Western hemispheres for purposes of time, passes through the building and there are many other fascinating astronomical things to see as well."

"Sounds great," said David. "I've never been to the Observatory so it would be a new experience for me, too."

He was beginning to feel very much at home with the Wrights. The couple seemed to take a keen interest in everything while at the same time appreciating the funnier side of life. Scott would roar with laughter while his oversized body would shake as though an earthquake was erupting inside. Always ready to support her husband, Helen would join in with a more subdued titter.

Finally they arrived at their first destination. However, the moment the Wrights set eyes on Hever Castle they were lost for words. Only in photographs had they seen a building quite as ancient as this one.

There was something almost magical about the fortified manor house. The symmetric gaps at the top of the grey walls through which men with crossbows would have showered arrows down upon any attackers below. The ornate drawbridge which would have been lowered only for welcome guests and of course there was the surrounding moat with fish swimming in the water.

"We have nothing like this at home," gasped Helen.

"Truly magnificent," agreed Scott. "And to think that it was built as far back as the thirteenth century."

Having been thoroughly impressed with the exterior the Wrights were keen to have a look inside. Therefore for the next half an hour the threesome were transported back to a bygone age as they wandered in and out of a banqueting hall, a vast kitchen, a chapel and any number of bedrooms. It was fascinating but there was just too much information to absorb in one go.

Having been in existence since 1270, Hever Castle had passed through many hands. Therefore although its Tudor character had been well preserved, later owners have undertaken extensive restoration. In particular, the wealthy American, William Wardorf, who purchased the property in 1903. It was he in fact who created a thirty-five acre lake and many well-laid out gardens with exotic flowers and plants.

As usual the Australians took photographs of just about anything which caught their eye. It was only when Scott felt the need to rest his weary legs that they stopped to sit down on a wooden bench. At this point David who had been watching on from a short distance away came over to join them.

"Your mum was telling us that you are getting married in four weeks," said Helen with a broad smile.

"Is that all?" replied David with little enthusiasm in his voice.

"Aren't you looking forward to your big day then?" asked Helen with a quizzical look.

It was a few moments before she received a reply. The bench the threesome had chosen to sit down on overlooked the Splashing Water Maze, a major attraction for young children. Briefly it managed to capture David's attention.

It was a circular pond with a difference. Above the water were stone slabs, which could be used as stepping stones to reach a folly at the centre. This in itself was fairly simple but the difficult part was to arrive at the middle without getting wet. At regular intervals jets of water would spurt up between the slabs and douse any youngster attempting to negotiate their way across.

"I'm not getting married," said David, finally.

The Wrights both looked at him in amazement.

"But your mum told us that you and your wife-to-be had bought a house and were preparing to buy furniture for it," said Helen.

"And she also said that under pressure you had finally started to decorate it," added Scott with a smile.

David shook his head firmly.

"I'm afraid that the property will be back on the market before too long. Any painting being done is purely for the benefit of the new owner."

The Wrights were bemused by this revelation and there was a short silence as the information was given time to sink in.

"If your mum isn't aware that you have no intention of getting married, is there anyone else in the family who knows?" enquired Scott at last.

"Not at the moment," answered David.

"And what about the women who you are engaged to?" asked

Helen. "Does she have any idea?"

David smiled sadly.

"Not at present. It is kindest if I let events just take their course."

Scott looked blank.

"Surely somebody is going to have to mention it to her."

David glanced at his watch.

"Let's head off for Greenwich," he said, slowly getting to his feet. "We can sit in the park and eat the picnic lunch my mother has prepared."

The Wrights sensed that David was struggling with a major crisis in his life. However, frustrated that the conversation had been ended so abruptly they were determined to raise the subject again at the earliest opportunity. Helen in particular was dying to find out what on earth was going on.

Soon the threesome were climbing up a steep slope as they made their way to the car park. At the top they turned around to take one last look at the enchanting castle with its glorious surroundings. Earlier there had been only a handful of visitors but, the arrival of several coachloads of day trippers had helped swell the numbers.

Suddenly David was transported back in time to 1530. He imagined that down below Henry and Anne Boleyn were enjoying a romantic encounter. Strolling hand in hand and dressed in their finery the couple were talking and laughing as though they hadn't a care in the world.

David was thinking of Anne as he drove off. How this young woman had been brought to the throne by her husband the King, only to be executed with his consent after only three years. Even if the accusations of adultery were true the penalty seemed harsh in the extreme. Probably her courtship with Henry in those early days had been the happiest period of her short life.

At that moment his train of thought was broken by the oversized passenger sitting next to him in the front seat.

"Now returning to this matter of your engagement," said Scott with an accusing look in his eye that evaded the attention of the driver. "If you don't intend to marry this poor woman, hadn't somebody better let her know before the wedding day?"

"Oh she will be told," replied David, reassuringly.

"So can we assume that you are getting someone else to do your dirty work?" enquired Helen.

"I suppose you are right," answered David. "I had never thought of it like that."

"Aren't you being rather cowardly?" suggested Scott.

David felt rather wounded by the remark. What he proposed to do would take courage and probably a great deal of sacrifice as well. It occurred to him that it was time to confide in the Wrights.

"Over the next two days I expect the Fellowship to withdraw from me," David began, unsure as to how this news would be received. "I shall just announce that I intend to stop going to Fellowship meetings and everything should fall conveniently into place after that."

The Wrights were stunned. For Scott in particular, who had never had reason to question his religious beliefs, it was impossible to comprehend how anyone would be prepared to sacrifice so much. If losing contact with family and friends was bad, then surely giving up the chance of Salvation was far worse.

"Have you prayed for guidance?" asked Helen. "I'm sure God will show you the way."

"Many times," replied David, sadly. "But I don't seem to be getting an answer."

"If it were me," said Scott, thoughtfully, "I would sit down with this lady and tell her in a kindly way that I didn't feel we were suited to each other."

It was a reasonable suggestion. However, it is difficult to arrive at the perfect solution to a problem when one only has half the facts. Therefore the Wrights were in for a further shock when David began to tell them about Alison and his involvement with the Labour Party.

The Wrights listened in silence. When everything had at last been revealed Helen asked the question that had been on her lips for the last five minutes.

"Do you think this lady would be prepared to join the Fellowship?"

"Highly unlikely," smiled David, recalling his conversation with Alison in the Chinese restaurant.

"You need to be on your guard," warned Scott. "Sometimes Satan uses people to tempt good Christians away from the paths of righteousness."

"I'll bear that in mind," answered David, a little testily.

The Wrights were quick to pick up the signal. Concerned that David had been offended by the suggestion that Alison was being used as an instrument of the Devil, the couple decided it was time to change the subject. Before parting company with him the next day though, they were determined to make a further attempt to save his soul.

It was early afternoon when they arrived at Greenwich. Making straight for the Royal Park, they found a bench high on the hill which provided an excellent view of the Thames and Isle of Dogs on the other side of the river. In the distance they could make out the skyscrapers of Canary Wharf, the City of London and the Millennium Dome.

For a while the threesome sat in silence eating their picnic lunch and taking in the view. On the lower level of the park they could see a children's playground and a boating lake. However with the summer holidays now over only parents with small toddlers seemed to be in evidence.

"You were saying earlier about not attending any more Fellowship meetings," said Helen, suddenly. "Does that mean that you are not coming along tonight?"

David nodded.

"I have promised to deliver leaflets for the Labour Party. With the General Election coming up there is a lot of work to be done just now."

"Couldn't you just come along tonight?" pleaded Helen. "I should hate for there to be any unpleasantness while we are staying at your house."

David hesitated. Already counting down the hours before seeing Alison again, there was no way that he was prepared to cancel the evening's arrangements. On the other hand he was determined to spare the Wrights any unnecessary embarrassment.

Fellowship members need a valid excuse to avoid attending religious meetings. Absence without a good reason in the Chambers family always resulted in confrontation, followed by a sustained period of frostiness towards the guilty party. It didn't seem to matter to John and Hilary whether guests were staying with them or not. If the Lord had been badly treated, they had a moral duty to be angry with their children.

"Don't worry," said David, trying to sound more confident than he was actually feeling. "Everything will be fine."

The Wrights that afternoon were enthralled with the attractions that Greenwich had to offer. Continually taking photographs, accompanied by their English host the Australians explored the *Cutty Shark*, browsed in the National Maritime Museum before finally arriving at the Observatory. Perched on top of the hill in the Royal Park, it is a complex containing a treasure trove of scientific wonders.

Once inside the threesome were peering through telescopes, touching meteorites, marvelling at John Harrison's maritime chronometers for measuring longitude and in a theatre, gazing up at a film of the moon's landscape projected onto the domed-shaped ceiling. No less interesting was a line of telephones of contrasting shapes and designs. The four on display were examples of different generations of this instrument of communication with an early black cumbersome model at one end and a more contemporary lightweight version at the other. However, apart from being able to appreciate the evolving styles, the visitor was invited to pick up each receiver and listen to how the Speaking Clock would have sounded in different eras.

Later when driving home, David had an idea. It was a possible solution to how he could avoid having to attend the evening church meeting without upsetting his parents. The only problem was that he was going to need some help.

When he put his plan to the Wrights they were rather shocked. To begin with neither of them wanted to be involved as it meant deceiving their Fellowship hosts, but at last they reluctantly agreed to assist. Helen in particular was anxious that harmony should reign supreme for the remainder of her stay.

As it happened Helen put in a performance worthy of an Oscar. The scene was set with the Australians sitting down for afternoon refreshments and some polite conversation with the Chambers family. Hilary as usual was peppering her guests with questions such as: Did you like Hever Castle? Was it expensive to get in? Were there many visitors? And so on.

"Oh no," gasped Helen, suddenly. "Don't say I have left my camera behind at the Observatory?"

Both David and Scott turned to her with horrified expressions. It was as if she had announced that the Earth had just been invaded by little green men.

"Was it expensive?" asked Hilary when it became apparent that Helen's frantic search through the contents of her bag had been fruitless.

"It was," answered Scott, gloomily. "I bought it for Helen as a birthday present."

"Somebody should ring the Observatory and find out whether it has been found," suggested John Chambers, helpfully.

"I'll do it," said David before anyone else had an opportunity to volunteer." I've got the number on this leaflet that I picked up."

Marching out into the hall he lifted up the telephone receiver and dialled three digits only. After a brief interval he found himself being addressed by a lady with a clear and precise voice.

"At the third stroke it will be eighteen hours, seven minutes and twenty-five seconds." Then there were three short pips.

David hesitated momentarily, then spoke.

"Good evening, is that the Royal Observatory?"

Unsurprisingly the Speaking Clock avoided the question and continued to announce the time.

"My friends and I were visitors this afternoon and we think we may have left a camera behind," explained David. "Has it been handed in by any chance?"

David was quiet for about ten seconds.

"You have," he cried out excitedly. "Can I come and collect it tonight?"

After yet another pause his voice became rather less enthusiastic.

"So you say I need to be there by seven o'clock," he groaned. "And what about tomorrow morning?"

Everyone who had been listening in the lounge looked at one another anxiously. Then after hearing David put down the receiver with a weary sigh they waited for him to confirm what was already obvious.

"Isn't it possible to go tomorrow then?" enquired Hilary when her son returned from the hall.

"The lost property office doesn't open until twelve o'clock," replied David, giving her a resigned look. "The problem is that

Scott and Helen need to be at Brockleby Station by then."

"What a shame you can't go tonight," said Helen with her head in her hands. "I shall be lost without my camera."

All eyes turned towards John Chambers. According to Fellowship teachings, as the senior male in the family, it was his responsibility to try to keep members of his household on the straight and narrow. Granting permission to avoid meetings was therefore down to him.

It took a while for John to make up his mind. Quotations from separate books of the Bible were pulling him in different directions. It was a matter of deciding whether to be guided by Jeremiah in the Old Testament or Luke from the New. Finally he came to a decision.

"You had better set off for Greenwich before it gets too late," he said, grudgingly.

David resisted the temptation to give the Wrights a smile. He was just relieved that the plan had succeeded and he was now free to do as he pleased without causing the Australians any embarrassment. He just hoped the rest of the evening went so well.

A number of activists were already assembled when David arrived at the Brockleby Labour Party headquarters. Tony was looking flustered as he darted about from one group to another, handing out bundles of leaflets and stopping occasionally to answer questions. Looking more composed, Carol was wandering around with a map in order to assist any deliverer who required directions. There was, however, no sign of Alison.

It was just after seven and some of the party members were restless to get started. There was nothing to stop them of course but, as comrades in a common cause, they preferred the idea of setting off en masse. On the other hand they weren't prepared to wait around indefinitely for latecomers to arrive.

"What time are we leaving, Tony?" shouted a tall thin man with shoulder length hair.

The election organiser checked his watch.

"You might as well all get going," he answered. "I'll wait here for another ten minutes to see if anyone else shows up."

David watched dejectedly as people become to file past him on their way to the front door. The magical evening that he had been looking forward to so much was doomed to failure for him if Alison failed to arrive. All of a sudden he felt very little appetite for tramping the streets delivering folded up sheets of paper.

Once the crowd had disappeared Tony seemed to notice David for the first time. Looking less harassed now he strolled over to the new recruit with a friendly smile.

"I've put you down to deliver with Alison," he said stroking his beard. "Unfortunately she has been delayed so would you mind picking her up at home?"

"No trouble at all," replied David, cheerily.

"I'll come with you," said Carol holding up an enormous bundle of leaflets tied up with string. "It is going to take at least three of us to deliver this lot tonight."

Alison was waiting on the pavement as David pulled up outside her maisonette. Having scrambled into the back seat she began to explain in great detail how a series of domestic disasters had contributed to her delay. It seemed that a broken hairdryer, burnt sausages and a lost bag had all been partly responsible.

David listened with sympathy. Had anyone else in the entire world given such an in-depth account of a rather mundane sequence of events, it is quite possible he would have fallen asleep at the wheel. Such is the power of devotion.

"Stop along here," shouted Carol suddenly as the car turned into a housing estate.

For the next five minutes everyone sat and studied a map that the organiser's wife had brought. With the roads which were to be leafleted, it was a matter of agreeing between themselves the most efficient route to take. There then followed a heated discussion before finally a collective decision was reached.

David soon discovered that leafleting in groups was preferable to doing it alone. The prospect of delivering to a never-ending line of houses didn't seem so daunting when there were others to share the burden. It was also pleasing to have somebody else there to exchange a bit of banter with to keep the spirits up.

To start with David felt that the whole operation was altogether easier than it had been the previous morning. As a rule the houses in this less affluent part of the town had much shorter gardens to walk up and down. However, his opinion changed somewhat when he came to a tower block of flats. Passing through the glass door he was confronted by a handwritten sign reading 'Lift out of use'. Therefore he was left with no alternative but to climb ten flights of steps in a building stinking of urine.

The two women had no shortage of advice for the political rookie.

"Make sure you push the leaflet right through the letterbox," warned Carol. "It has not been unknown for the Tories to destroy any that are left sticking out."

"I see," said David who was appalled by such devious behaviour.

"Don't be put off if you see a Tory or Lib Dem notice in the window," advised Alison. "Put a leaflet through the door just the same. There could be somebody in the house who could be persuaded to vote for us."

In little over an hour they were finished. The large bundle of leaflets they had begun with had dwindled down to just a handful. Feeling a little weary but, nevertheless satisfied with their evening's work, they trudged back to the car.

"Are you two going back to the bar for a drink?" enquired Carol.

Alison shook her head.

"I had better get home and do some ironing," she smiled, sadly. "Otherwise Amanda won't have anything to wear in the morning."

"I can't stay either," said David.

"That's a pity," replied Carol. "Are you both helping tomorrow night?"

"Just as long as I can get my mum to baby-sit again," smiled Alison.

"She won't refuse," laughed Carol. "Your mum enjoys looking after Amanda."

"There's always a first time," muttered Alison more to herself than anyone else.

Carol turned to David.

"Will you be joining us?"

"Count me in," answered the new political recruit.

David was beginning to feel excited as he dropped Carol off at Labour Party headquarters. It was wonderful to be walking the streets with Alison delivering leaflets but he was craving for something much more than a casual friendship. He didn't want to remain just another fellow political activist of hers.

On the journey home Alison did most of the talking. David merely listened and made the appropriate responses when required. Politics was beginning to fascinate him but there were other matters on his mind just then.

"Are you coming with us on the march in London on Saturday?" enquired Alison as the car pulled up outside her maisonette.

"First time I've heard about it," replied David. "Why are you marching?"

"It's a protest against the American invasion of Iraq," answered Alison. "The organisers are hoping that at least a million demonstrators will take part."

David gave a low whistle.

"OK, I'm up for it. Are there many of our crowd coming?"

Alison looked thoughtful.

"Just a few of the very keenest I expect."

David had not turned on the light in his car. Therefore he could just make out Alison's soft facial features from the streetlight some twenty metres away. The pale delicate skin, the straight regular shaped nose, the high cheekbones and of course the hair that nestled gently about her shoulders.

It was time to be bold. Turning in his seat, David leaned over and kissed Alison gently on the corner of the mouth. His heart pounded fast, partly with excitement but also fearful that his advances would be rejected.

Inexperienced in these situations he was taken completely by surprise. Instead of pulling away as he had dreaded, Alison threw her arms around his neck and kissed him passionately on the lips. So firm was her hold on him that for a while David was unable to move.

Silently they sat for some time clutching each other tightly. Then through David's partly open mouth Alison slid her tongue inside to meet his. Both enjoyed the sensual experience as they tasted each other's warm saliva.

"Must go now," whispered Alison as she gently began to extricate herself. "See you tomorrow night."

David was in a complete daze. He arrived home without

being able to recall any part of his journey. It was rather like being in a drunken stupor without having touched a drop of alcohol.

It was quite early and everybody was still up. When David strolled into the lounge the Chambers and the Wrights were sat thumbing through pages of some rather ancient looking family photograph albums. Without fail, Hilary would produce these dilapidated volumes for the dubious entertainment of visitors who happened to be staying any length of time.

All eyes looked up expectantly at David as he was about to sit down.

"Have you got the camera?" enquired Martha, eagerly.

David gave his younger sister a vacant stare.

"It's over there in the drawer if you want to take a picture."

Hilary gave her son a look of exasperation.

"She is talking about Helen's camera. The one you were supposed to have collected from Greenwich this evening."

After a few seconds the fog began to clear.

"Oh I've left it in the car," said David with a nervous laugh.

His remark was met with long-drawn out sighs of relief.

"Make certain that you give it to Helen before she leaves in the morning," warned Hilary.

"No worries there," chimed in Helen. "I intend to take lots of photos of Brockleby before I go."

Slowly the Wrights and the Chambers returned their attention once more to the albums. In a moment, however, Martha looked up and clicked her fingers as she suddenly remembered the telephone message she had promised to pass on.

"Could you ring Ruth by the way. She wants to know how you are getting on with the painting."

"I might leave it until tomorrow," replied David, casually checking his watch. "It's getting a bit late to make telephone calls."

Hilary looked up in surprise.

"But it's only just gone nine thirty. I shouldn't think Ruth would be in bed yet."

Nods around the room suggested that others were of the same opinion.

David groaned inwardly. However, as he made his way to the

96

telephone in the hall he was suddenly struck by an idea. With a little bit of acting he told himself, it should be possible to avoid the unpalatable deed.

Having dialled the three numbers so easy to memorise he stood and waited for a few minutes. Then when the time felt right he spoke in a loud and clear voice.

"Good evening Ruth how are you?" he began before stopping for a short pause.

The female on the other end of the line totally ignored the question. The truth was that she really was quite a tedious person with only one mission in life. Telling the time to anyone who cared to listen.

"At the third stroke it will be twenty-one hours and thirty-five minutes and thirteen seconds," she announced.

After a long conversation with the Speaking Clock, which he insisted on calling 'Ruth', David put the phone back in its cradle and returned to the lounge.

"Ruth sends her love to everybody," he said, cheerfully.

"That's nice," replied a chorus of voices, without anyone actually raising their eyes from the photograph albums.

Chapter Eight

It was the day of the Wrights departure. At breakfast everyone tucked into bacon and eggs. Hilary was putting a string of questions to her Australian guests sitting on the opposite side of the table. Having made enquiries about Helen's family she suddenly changed the subject.

"What time does your train arrive in Cambridge this afternoon?" she asked.

The Wrights looked blank.

"I'm not really sure," answered Scott with a shrug of his shoulders.

Alarm bells immediately began to ring inside Hilary's head. She was one of those very organised people who rarely left any little detail of their life to chance. Forward planning she believed, was the safety net which protected her life from descending into a world of uncertainty and chaos.

"Where do you catch your train?" she enquired, already considering whether to take control of the situation.

The Wrights looked at each other for assistance in answering the question. They were an easy going couple who left everything until the last moment, including checking their travel arrangements. As a consequence, no allowance was ever made for setbacks such as traffic jams or delays on public transport.

"Is it Victoria?" asked Scott.

Helen looked doubtful.

"That doesn't sound right. After breakfast I'll go upstairs and get my bag. I may have written it down in my notebook."

"It can't be Victoria?" piped up John Chambers who was something of an expert on such matters. "Trains out of that station head south. For Cambridge you are more likely to need King's Cross."

"Or Liverpool Street?" suggested Martha.

"That's the name I was trying to remember," cried Scott, slapping the edge of the table and almost overturning a jug of milk with the impact.

For the remainder of the meal Hilary brought a cessation to her barrage of questions. Getting the Wrights to their next destination at a reasonable hour was just one of the problems which was troubling her. Another concerned her son David who had hardly touched his food and was sat with a rather stupid grin on his face.

As usual, Hilary single-handedly cleared the table and washed-up. Standing at the sink she heard first John then Martha slam the front door as in turn they set off on their journey to work. Also clearly audible from the lounge was Scott's booming voice and hearty laughter almost seeming to shake the foundations of the house.

Once the last plate had been stacked away Hilary went to join David and her guests. Having discovered that the Wrights immediate travel plans were in disarray, she suddenly became a woman with a mission. Somebody sensible needed to take charge of the situation otherwise, well goodness knows where these woolly minded Australians would end up spending the night she told herself.

"Right, now we've established that your train leaves from Liverpool Station," she began, taking a seat on the settee. "Do you have any idea of the departure time?"

Scott shook his head blankly.

"We'll just jump on the first one going out."

Hilary's concerns were now growing by the minute. She was already visualising the Wrights boarding the wrong train and finding themselves in the Scottish Highlands at three o'clock in the morning.

"Have you any idea how long the journey will take?" she asked.

Scott shrugged.

"About twenty minutes. It doesn't look very far on the map."

Totally exasperated, Hilary scurried out of the room to gather up some details. First she rang British Rail enquiries and then turned her attention to finding a London Underground map. With her usual efficiency she had soon amassed and jotted down on a scrap of paper all the required information.

"At Victoria you need to get on the Circle Line to Liverpool

Street," she explained, repeating all the facts that were already written down and had been given to the Wrights. "Make absolutely certain that you get an Eastbound train. Going Westbound will get you there eventually but it means more stops."

The Wrights managed to look both grateful and baffled at the same time.

"From Liverpool Street there is a train at thirteen twenty-eight, which arrives in Cambridge at fourteen forty," continued Hilary, still repeating what was already on paper. "Should you happen to miss that, the following one is a thirteen fifty-eight."

Even while speaking though, she felt that further assistance was required. Many would have called it intuition, but Hilary recognised that it was the voice of the Lord that was speaking to her. Therefore as soon as the Wrights had disappeared upstairs to pack, she took the opportunity to have a quiet word with her son.

"I think you had better go with them," she said, anxiously. "At least see that they catch the right train at Liverpool Street."

David made no protest. Unlike his mother he felt confident that the Wrights would muddle through and find their ultimate destination in the end. However he had no objection to spending a little more time in their company.

On his mother's advice David set off for the station earlier than the Wrights had planned. Scott and Helen had spent much of the morning taking photographs of Brockleby to show the folks back home. A significant amount of time had also been required to fill up the car with the Wrights huge quantity of personal effects.

Hilary still felt uneasy as she waved goodbye to her guests. David had been acting so strange recently it wouldn't have surprised her if he didn't get lost with the Australians. She really would have to speak to him when the opportunity arose.

"So this is your big day then?" said Helen, wedged in again between numerous bags of different shapes and colours.

Held up at traffic lights, David was able to turn his head around and give her a broad grin.

"This is the one."

"It isn't too late to change your mind," Scott reminded him.

David shook his head firmly.

"I can't now. Not after last night."

There was a brief pause as the Wrights reflected on this remark.

"Did things go well?" asked Helen as she pushed away a large shapeless green bag that was digging into her ribs.

"Perfect," answered David as the traffic lights suddenly changed to green.

"Are you in love?" ventured Helen, a little coyly.

David hesitated briefly. Just hearing the question put in that way sent a warm glow radiating throughout his whole body. At that moment he wanted to share his secret.

"Yes I suppose I am," he smiled.

"In that case the Fellowship have lost you for good," replied Helen. "Nothing can compete with love."

"Poor Ruth," muttered Scott, more to himself than anyone else.

It was the last word said on the matter for the time being. However, the subject of David's forthcoming withdrawal from the Fellowship surfaced again soon after the threesome had boarded the London Victoria train. With a carriage entirely to themselves, they felt able to speak freely.

"If you are forced out of your home, where will you live?" enquired Helen, looking more confortable now that the assortment of bags were filling the luggage racks rather than sticking into her ribs.

"Probably a hotel room until I can find something more permanent," answered David, thoughtfully.

"What if your parents throw you out tonight?" enquired Scott with a worried frown. "They will be livid with you for skipping a Fellowship meeting."

David shrugged.

"As a temporary measure I'll go and sleep down at my new house."

"I hope you have a bed," said Helen, giving him an anxious look. "According to your mum, there isn't a stick of furniture in the place at present."

"And make certain you have something to eat for the morning," warned Scott who always placed food at the very top of his priority list. "You can't function on an empty stomach."

"And don't forget to take a change of socks and underwear," added Helen.

Soon David was compiling a list. In fact it had never seriously occurred to him that he might instantly be evicted from the house. On the other hand there seemed no harm in taking precautions. The minute he returned home he was determined to sneak out a number of items and put them in the boot of his car.

As soon as the threesome arrived at Victoria they followed the signs to the tube. However, choosing to cross London by Underground rather than taking a cab was a decision they were soon to regret. Loaded up with cases and bags they were having difficulties even before stepping on to the platform. Firstly there was the problem of Scott squeezing his massive bulk through the ticket barrier. Then they had to battle to gain a foothold on the escalator against some fierce competition from other members of the travelling public.

Unfortunately their troubles didn't end once they had boarded the train. A shortage of luggage space meant that the threesome had to stand guard around the towering pile of personal effects to prevent fellow travellers from tripping over them. Then to add insult to injury, Scott and a black suitcase were almost cut in half by the sliding door as the oversized Australian attempted to get off.

Wearily they arrived on the concourse of Liverpool Street's main line station. Looking up at the giant departure board they noted that the Cambridge train would be leaving in less than ten minutes. Just enough time to say a brief goodbye.

"Thanks for taking us around and being such a good guide," smiled Scott, fondly, while extending a chubby hand.

"And for helping us to find this station," added Helen. "I'm sure we would have got lost without your assistance."

David felt a lump in his throat as he shook hands. It had been not more than forty-eight hours since he had first spotted the Wrights at Heathrow Airport but somehow it seemed much longer. In just a short space of time a strong bond had developed between them.

"I hope you enjoy the rest of your trip," said David, cheerily.

"Thanks mate," replied Scott. "And I really hope that things turn out well for you. Both Helen and I will pray for you."

It was the last words they exchanged. David stood watching sadly as his Australian friends slowly made their way along the platform and out of his life. The large bulky figure of Scott pushing a mountain load of baggage in a trolley with Helen, looking tiny in comparison, following in her husband's tracks.

Hilary was out when David arrived home. With the house to himself it meant that filling the car with emergency items in the event of sudden eviction, became that much simpler. He could go about this task without the likelihood of detection.

Clothes and washing accessories were easy for David to lay his hands on. He faced more of a problem, however, climbing down from the loft with a fold-up bed. Finally though he was able to slam the boot shut, happy in the knowledge that the contents within would at least cater for his basic needs.

There were still several hours to go before David was due to set off for the evening's leafleting session. To begin with he took a chair out into the garden and tried reading a chapter of the Bible but, in his present state of mind, it was impossible to concentrate for more than thirty seconds. Finally he went upstairs and just lay flat on his bed and stared vacantly up at the ceiling. His thoughts just seemed to bounce backwards and forwards between Alison and the inevitable family confrontation that lay ahead.

At six thirty David emerged from his room. Taking a deep breath he slowly descended the stairs towards the rest of the household who were gathered in the hall. Hilary and Martha were standing side by side in front of the mirror adjusting their headscarves, while John Chambers was hovering by the coat stand anxiously checking his watch.

Suddenly Hilary glanced up at her son.

"Are you ready dear?" she called.

David paused for a moment in his tracks. He felt like a mischievous boy about to release a hive of bees into a nudist colony.

"I'm not coming tonight," he answered, attempting to sound casual.

There was a prolonged silence as everybody gaped at the speaker in astonishment.

"Where are you going?" demanded John at last.

David gave a dismissive shrug.

103

"I've promised to go out and deliver leaflets for the Labour Party."

There was a further silence as this latest announcement was given time to sink in.

"You are abandoning the Lord just to go and do that," gasped John when he had finally got his thoughts together.

"What has got into you recently?" joined in Hilary who was recalling other incidences during the past week or so where her son had acted strangely.

"The Devil is attempting to capture his soul," answered John, bitterly. "Satan looks for any signs of weakness in one of God's children and then he pounces."

David glanced at his watch.

"We will have to continue this discussion later. I have to be on my way."

Hilary gave her son a look of desperation.

"What do I say to Ruth if she rings?"

"Just take a message," smiled David as he squeezed past his father in order to get to the front door.

David could feel three sets of eyes follow him as he strolled down the path. Even though he knew there would be bitter arguments waiting ahead it was a relief that the opening salvos had been fired.

"You must resist Satan and his empty pleasures," called out John as his son shut the garden gate behind him.

David climbed into his car without looking back. To avoid being blocked in on the drive, which might have been problematical under the present circumstances, he had chosen to park out on the road. Unsurprisingly he had no desire to hang around a moment more than was really necessary.

Unlike the previous evening Alison had arrived early at Labour headquarters. When David walked into the bar she was stood at the far corner of the room speaking to an elderly couple. The expression on the three faces suggested that the subject under discussion was of a serious nature.

Spotting David, Alison waved to him to join them.

"Meet Bert and Sandra Vine," she smiled. "Bert is the chairman of this association and Sandra is the treasurer."

"Always good to see a new face," beamed Bert, grasping

David's outstretched hand. "Particularly a young one like yours. Most of our membership these days are getting on in years."

"The younger generation don't seem interested in politics," remarked Sandra, sadly.

"It isn't trendy," replied Alison with a wry smile. "Everybody now just wants to get their hands on the latest gadget that comes on the market."

"Anyway," smiled Bert, who always liked to be upbeat about everything. "Which ward have they stuck you in?"

David stared blankly at Alison for assistance. The only wards he was familiar with were those in hospitals.

"It hasn't been discussed yet," answered Alison. "I expect it will be the Upper Oakham ward which is where he lives."

Suddenly the conversation was brought to a halt as Tony at the other end of the bar shouted for silence.

"We are about to go," he announced. "Come and see me if you haven't got your leaflets yet."

Once again David formed a team with Alison and Carol. Armed as usual with a massive bundle of leaflets they parked at the top of a street not too dissimilar from several that the threesome had delivered to on the previous evening. Lines of grey terraced houses, small rectangular front lawns in varying degrees of neatness and often bordered on three sides by waist high brick walls.

It was the third day in a row that David had been out leafleting. As he walked up and down one path after another it occurred to him that politics could drag a person into a world of hard work and drudgery. Were it not for the presence of Alison he wondered whether he would be such a willing participant.

When they had finished, all three went back to headquarters for a drink. Wearily they trudged into the bar where many of the other deliverers had already returned and were sat relaxed in small groups. As ever political literature, paper and clipboards were scattered about in every nook and cranny.

David bought drinks and followed the women in search of a table. After standing in the middle of the floor and gazing around the room for a few moments, Carol finally caught sight of Tony sitting by himself in a corner reading the *Guardian*. After cautiously stepping in between bundles of leaflets left lying on the floor, she led her two companions over to join him.

Once they were all settled down Alison gave David a thoughtful look.

"About the march on Saturday. I can't remember whether you said you were coming or not. We seemed to get a little diverted last night."

David smiled as he recalled their period of intimacy in the car. It was hardly surprising that all other matters faded into insignificance in comparison.

"I'm coming," answered David, enthusiastically. "Where do I meet you all?"

"Quarter past ten at Brockleby Station," replied Carol, taking a sip of her red wine.

David smiled to himself. It occurred to him that Ruth was supposed to be coming down from Birmingham on Saturday so that they could shop for furniture together. If only she knew what her betrothed were planning for the day instead.

"Just a small group of us will be travelling up by train," explained Tony. "Many other members from here will be making their own arrangements."

"Are you bringing Amanda?" asked Carol, turning to her friend.

Alison nodded.

"Her future will be at stake as well. Money should be spent on education not wars."

David noticed that much of the attention in the bar had become focused on a middle-aged woman who had just arrived. Dark haired and attractive, she was dressed in a white lightweight jacket with a red rose in the lapel and carrying a clipboard under her arm. Several people nearby strolled up to kiss her on the cheek while others further away called out or waved.

"That lady is Jacqui Dunn," whispered Alison in David's ear. "She is the party's parliamentary candidate for Brockleby."

"She always manages to look so fresh," commented Carol with admiration. "Ever since the election was called she has been out night after night canvassing."

"Labour are not going to win this election without a lot of hard work," joined in Tony. "We intend to knock on every door in the constituency with the candidate herself doing a high proportion of it."

Jacqui had begun to wander around the bar. Beaming broadly and with the clipboard gone and now replaced with a half pint of bitter, she made regular stops to speak with supporters.

At last she came to a halt behind Carol's chair.

"Nice to see you all," she beamed, showing a perfect set of white teeth. "I hear you've all been out this evening delivering leaflets."

"That's right," grinned Carol. "I would much rather do that than knock on doors though."

Alison and Tony both nodded in agreement.

"Having canvassed dozens of voters now, how do you think it's going?" asked Carol.

Jacqui suddenly looked serious.

"I would say we are running neck and neck with the Tories. It wouldn't surprise me in the slightest if it doesn't go down to a recount on election night."

"I couldn't stand the tension of that," shuddered Alison.

Jacquie switched on her broad smile again as she turned to David.

"And did this lot get you out delivering tonight as well?"

Before David had a chance to answer Carol spoke up first.

"Yes and he has been working very hard."

David stood up politely to shake hands. Deciding on a less formal introduction, however, Jacqui slipped around the table and kissed him on the cheek. Then moving back a step she smiled warmly at the new recruit.

"Thank you for your help. It is so important that we get our message over to the voters."

"I understand that you have been very busy yourself," replied David, taking an instant liking to this attractive lady with a magnetic charm.

"We have to stop the Tories winning this election," she said with determination in her voice. "If Britain joins forces with America there will be even more carnage in Iraq. We will read in our newspapers of more children losing their sight or having limbs blown off."

"I don't want that to happen in my name," said Tony, angrily.

"Or mine either," added Carol and Alison almost

immediately.

David felt deeply moved as he sat down. He could tell from the emotion in Jacqui's voice that her words weren't just empty rhetoric but had come directly from the heart. Beneath the smiles and kisses lay a passionate conviction that had the power to inspire others.

Suddenly everybody switched their attention to the TV in the far corner of the room. The volume had been raised so that those that were interested could listen to a party political broadcast by the Conservative Party. On the screen was the familiar face of the Right Honourable Jonathan Canning, leader of the Opposition.

"If this nation hadn't stood up to Adolf Hitler in 1939, the British people wouldn't enjoy the freedom they have today," he began solemnly.

Tony looked incensed.

"How can he possibly make a comparison between the mighty German army of the thirties and the feeble forces of modern day Iraq. It took six years to defeat Hitler whereas Saddam's lot were toppled in a couple of weeks."

Jacqui touched Tony's arm.

"Calm down. The British people are smart enough to see through the Tory Party and its propaganda."

"I only hope you're right," answered Tony, glaring at the screen.

Soon the message of the Right Honourable Jonathan Canning was being drowned out by boos and hisses. David from his distant position just sat and watched the changing expressions and moving lips of the Tory leader. Then suddenly his image was replaced by a dog food commercial as somebody decided it was time to change channels.

Alison suddenly glanced up at the wall clock above the bar.

"I really must be on my way in a minute."

"Actually it's getting late for me as well," said David, finishing off his drink. "I will give you a lift home."

Carol gave the departing couple a mischievous look as they stood to their feet. The temptation to suggest that they should behave themselves on the way home was very strong. In the end though she decided to spare their blushes.

As ever saying goodbye became a prolonged affair. To begin

with Jacqui had more than a few parting words to say to Alison, and then there were several people who walked up and introduced themselves to David. Eventually after many hands had been shaken and kisses exchanged the couple were finally free to stroll out into the night air.

"What are you doing on Sunday?" asked David as he fastened his seatbelt.

Alison laughed.

"Washing, ironing, scrubbing floors and probably going out in the evening canvassing for the Labour Party."

"Take a couple of hours off," suggested David, switching on the car engine. "There is a lovely restaurant just outside Sevenoaks. Perhaps I could take you and Amanda out for a drive and we could stop off there for lunch."

Alison turned to him with a mischievous smile.

"Sorry to disappoint you but Amanda goes out with her dad on Sunday. I'm free though if you are still interested."

"Very interested," laughed David, both overjoyed and relieved that his invitation hadn't been rejected.

For part of the journey home Alison sat almost in silence. Turning her head sideways she gazed thoughtfully out of the window, barely responsive to David's almost desperate attempts to strike up a conversation. Finally as the car turned into a side road she suddenly seemed to come to life.

"Let's stop here," she said, softly.

David obediently pulled up by the kerb and switched off the engine. It struck him as a rather odd request as they were still some distance from Alison's home. His main concern was that he may have said something to upset her and she had decided to walk the rest of the way.

For a few seconds David thought that his worst fears were coming true. Without a trace of a smile Alison began to unfasten her seat belt and then gradually rose up. In the next moment she turned her body round, bent over David and began forcing her lips on his. Then they embraced tightly and each slipped their tongue inside the other's mouth.

As they sat caressing, David felt the urge to allow his hand to explore. Looking downwards in the half-darkness he was just able to make out two bulges gently heaving beneath Alison's white T-shirt. As much as he wanted to touch, however, the fear of causing offence restrained him.

Suddenly Alison straightened up.

"It's getting late," she whispered. "I really must be getting home."

Without speaking David started the car once more and continued the journey. In contrast to the previous evening he didn't feel dreamy and woolly headed but unusually strong and self-assured. It was rather as though he had been taken up to Paradise and been empowered by the experience.

"What time shall I pick you up on Saturday morning?" he asked as they came within sight of Alison's maisonette.

"Make it about nine thirty," she answered, leaning over to kiss David quickly on the cheek.

David watched Alison walk up the garden path before setting off. Driving home he savoured those magical moments of intimacy that they had shared together. Reliving every second and recapturing the memory of those soft lips, the sweet breath and the feel of her body against his. It was only as he parked behind his father's car in the drive that he rapidly came down to earth.

His parents were sat reading their Bibles as David entered the lounge. It was something that John and Hilary Chambers did together most evenings before finally retiring to bed. Often the pair of them would read the same passage and then share their thoughts on it once they had finished.

John looked up and glared hard at his son.

"Ian Porter wants to see you urgently."

David settled down in an armchair and looked his father directly in the eye.

"What exactly is the problem?"

"Like the rest of us, he is concerned that you should choose to deliver those leaflets rather than to worship in the house of the Lord," replied John, sternly.

"When does Ian want to meet me?" asked David, staring down at the carpet.

"He will ring you at work tomorrow," answered Hilary closing the Bible, which was resting on her lap.

David nodded but said nothing. He would have his say tomorrow but, for tonight, there seemed little point in antagonising his parents too much. Although the car boot was full of items which would help come to his rescue in the event of being evicted, it was something he preferred to avoid if at all possible.

"We are off to bed now," said John, raising himself from the settee. "Your mother and I will pray for you."

David sat and watched sadly as his parents filed out of the room. Although he was excited by the prospect of making a fresh start to his life, he was also aware that the cost of departing from his old one would be high. Later as he turned off the light and scrambled into bed it occurred to him that this would probably be the very last night he would sleep within those four walls. A room that had provided him with a haven of rest for as long as he could remember.

Chapter Nine

David woke up long before the alarm clock had been set to go off. Lying tucked up in bed he tried to focus his mind on the rather mundane subject of earning a living. With so much going on in it had completely slipped his mind that he was meant to give an important sales presentation later that morning. After a significant downturn in business in recent months, pressure was now on his shoulders to secure the order.

The atmosphere had a definite frosty feel to it at breakfast time. John Chambers was sat quietly reading his Bible between mouthfuls of cornflakes, while Hilary breezed backwards and forwards to the kitchen performing her usual waitress role in stony silence. Even Martha who was generally so talkative around the house seemed unusually subdued. It was therefore with some relief when David was finally able to shut the front door behind him and step out jauntily into the morning air.

'Fine Choice Furniture' was a small family company. It was owned by the two Boswell Brothers who had gradually built the business up over a period of twenty years. Success had come through a simple formula of buying cheaply from manufacturers in Easter Europe and the Far East and selling on to customers in the UK at a tidy profit.

The owners and management were all Fellowship. In accordance with their beliefs, computers, fax machines and mobile phones were strictly forbidden. As all office tasks were performed manually it meant that administrators with neat handwriting were highly regarded.

Over half of the workforce were not adherents of the faith. It was not permissible for these worldly decadents to listen to the radio, blaspheme or use obscene language on the premises. They also had their own canteen so that sinners and the righteous did not have to sit down together to eat.

David sat staring from his office window on the first floor. Warehouse staff were loading up one of the company's seven and a half ton vehicles with chairs and settees ready to despatch. The supervisor and the driver stood side by side and looked on from a short distance.

There was a relaxed atmosphere at Fine Choice Furniture. The owners were good employers and felt a loyalty to their staff that is fast disappearing in many organisations these days. Few people were ever spoken harshly to and sackings were almost unknown. To be dismissed a person would have to do something unthinkable, such as a member of the Fellowship deciding to break away from the faith.

Suddenly Maurice Hopkins poked his head into David's office.

"Are you fully prepared for your presentation this morning?"

David tried to appear more confident than he was actually feeling.

"I can't wait to get started."

Maurice looked reassured. As a sales manager he was an excellent motivator but lacked the necessary energy levels to contribute a great deal of work himself. In truth he owed his position in the company to marrying Samuel Boswell's daughter rather than his ability to perform as a salesman.

"If anyone can win this order for us you can," beamed Maurice.

"I don't intend to let Robsons take the business from under our noses," replied David, resolutely.

The name of the company's main competitors made Maurice wince.

"The quality of our products is far superior to anything that Robsons have to offer. All you need to do is to demonstrate that to the client."

David nodded even though he was unconvinced that such a gulf in quality actually existed. He often wondered in fact whether certain items of furniture could have been produced by the same manufacturer.

"By the way, I'm taking Des with me to help carry the samples."

"Take who you wish," grinned Maurice. "Just bring me back the business."

In less than an hour David was ready to set off. All the

113

brochures he was likely to need were tucked away in his briefcase, while the samples had been carefully loaded inside the company van. Then resting back in the passenger seat he signalled to Des to start driving.

Des was an amiable man in his mid-forties. He had an unhurried approach to life and spent much of his working life strolling around the office looking for someone to chat to. It was for this very reason that most of the tasks he was set had to be completed by a colleague.

"Didn't see you at the meeting last night," said Des after they had been driving for a few minutes. "Not well then?"

David gave a casual shrug.

"I decided to go and deliver some leaflets with friends."

Des gave a little gasp.

"So has Ian Porter spoken to you about it yet?"

"Not so far," replied David, sounding rather indifferent. "I understand he wants to meet up with me urgently though."

"I'm not surprised," replied Des. "Anyway who are these friends of yours?"

At that moment they pulled up at a set of traffic lights. Des hurriedly dipped his hand into the glove compartment and pulled out a liquorice allsort. He was one of those people who always had an endless supply of sweets and little snacks within easy reach.

"Just a few people that I know from the Labour Party," replied David with a yawn.

It took a few moments for Des to digest this startling information. It was against the beliefs of the Fellowship for any follower to have 'worldlies' for friends. They were supposed to remain separate from the rest of the humanity.

"I hope that Ian isn't too cross with you," said Des, anxiously. "He can be quite severe at times."

"Anyway, how is your wife?" enquired David, eager to change the subject. "I understand she is expecting a baby very soon."

Des nodded his head gloomily.

"We've already got four children all under the age of fourteen. I just don't know how we are going to cope with another one at our time of life."

"You should have considered using contraceptives," replied David.

Des looked shocked.

"I can't believe you said that. As Christians you and I have always been taught that contraception is an abomination in the eyes of God."

David looked thoughtful as he helped himself to one of Des's sweets from the glove compartment.

"I am beginning to question that," he replied. "The world is already over populated and the numbers are growing steadily. The time will come when there won't be natural resources left to sustain everybody."

"We must all put our trust in the Lord," answered Des.

David felt he had said too much and decided to allow his companion to have the last word. Putting forward an intelligent argument against a person with blind faith was unlikely to achieve a great deal. Therefore, with a few probing questions he managed to direct the conversation towards the less contentious subject of Des's kitchen garden.

They were travelling along a country lane when Des spotted a large board ahead. It had been erected to advise passers-by that Conningvale House, the venue for the presentation, was a mere two hundred yards further on. Then after turning a bend in the lane, a red bricked building with scaffolding at one end came into view.

They arrived twenty minutes early allowing David adequate time to get organised. Lifting his briefcase off the back seat he began rummaging inside for the brochures that he intended to hand out. Then having just assembled a few on his lap he received a gentle dig in the ribs.

"Look who has just appeared," remarked Des in disgust. "It's Ryan Pritchard from Robsons."

David looked up to see his rival salesman emerging from the entrance of the red bricked building. Ryan and his assistant were cautiously negotiating their way through the swing doors carrying a blue armchair between them. They were being keenly watched by a member of staff concerned about possible damage to the property.

"Look at that bit of old junk," muttered Des with a snigger.

"I'm sure I saw that chair recently at a jumble sale," replied David with just a hint of a smile. "They were trying to flog it off for a fiver."

For a little while Des and David watched on in amusement. With a disgruntled expression on Ryan's face he and his assistant carried a succession of furniture pieces through the car park and on to a white van. When the vehicle had been finally loaded up the salesman slammed the back door shut with some considerable force.

"Shall we get out and say hello?" suggested Des with a big grin.

"Might as well," answered David, fastening his briefcase. "We need to be making a move in any case. It is almost time for our appointment."

Ryan tried to brighten up when he spotted David and Des coming towards him.

"You two might as well turn round and go home," he jeered. "I've got the business in the bag."

"We wondered why you were looking so happy Ryan," replied David, turning to Des to give him a wink.

"Your furniture is a load of old crap," shouted Ryan as he and his assistant climbed into their van.

"Crap it maybe, but, it's still superior to the rubbish that you try to flog," retorted David, before Ryan managed to slam the door.

David and Des smiled to each other as they headed towards the red bricked building.

Conningvale House had been built for people with behavioural difficulties. The local council were investing a great deal in providing a suitable environment for their charges. Furniture that could withstand extremely violent treatment was a top priority.

David and Des entered through the swing doors and strolled over to the reception counter. A middle-aged woman in a white coat sat at a desk totally engrossed in a telephone conversation. As the pair stood waiting to announce their arrival David had a quick look around him.

The reception area was quite large. Everything seemed bare without furniture and the floor was covered mostly in white sheets. With another ten weeks still to go before the official opening day there was evidence all around of the work that was in progress. Ladders were propped up against the walls, toolboxes lay open on floors and the monotonous beat of hammers seemed to be coming from all directions.

Finally the receptionist put down the telephone.

"Can I help you?" she enquired in a rather superior voice.

David gave her his details with a broad smile. He had learnt from first-hand experience that it was wise to make a favourable impression on everyone within the organisation when selling. One never knows who might be called in to offer an opinion on a particular piece of furniture.

David's attempt at charming the receptionist appeared to have failed. Giving him a weary look she picked up the telephone once more and repeated the details that the visitor had just given her.

In a few minutes a door opened and a grey haired woman in glasses appeared.

"Please come this way Mr Chambers," she called out.

David and Des were ushered into a long narrow room with a number of cardboard boxes stacked up against one of the walls. At the far end was a man in a suit sat behind a wooden desk covered in papers. Standing up to shake hands he introduced himself as Harvey Jennings, a health and safety executive from the council. He was extremely tall and had the look of a person who had a very bad smell under their nose.

The woman who had appeared at the door was Shirley Bromage, soon to be the care manager for the home once it was in operation. In contrast to Harvey she was small and plump but, facially, she had a similar contemptuous look to his.

David cursed his luck. He had the distinct feeling that these two people who had been given the task of selecting furniture for the home had taken an instant disliking to him. If his instincts were correct he would need to be at his very best to clinch the order that was so desperately needed.

Once the introductions had been completed David followed Des to the van to collect the samples.

For a full hour the frosty twosome poked, prodded and jumped upon the furniture that was put in front of them. They flung questions at David and always appeared less than satisfied with his answers. Eventually the uncomfortable ordeal came to a close as the final chair being scrutinised received a hefty kick.

"We can't be too careful you know," said Harvey Jennings still with the look of a man with an offensive odour beneath his nasal passages. "A loosely fitted leg or arm could be pulled off and used as a lethal weapon."

Shirley Bromage nodded as she gave David's furniture a rather disdainful glance.

"Also we need to know that there aren't any tight gaps down the side of a chair which could be used to stash away a knife or razor."

David was only too well aware of the hazards that such a home could face due to poorly constructed furniture. As the group talked on for a while, he tried to convince the frosty pair how safe and reliable the products of Fine Choice really were until gradually he began to feel that they were beginning to thaw.

Finally when there was nothing left to discuss the council executive shook David and Des warmly by the hand.

"We must now sit down and try and reach a decision," he smiled, glancing briefly at Shirley. "The company which receives our order will hear from us by ten o'clock tomorrow at the very latest."

David checked his watch as he and Des left the building. Like any salesman who has ever tried to clinch a major order he knew that he was about to experience an agonising wait. The outcome was outside his control.

"Feeling confident?" enquired Des as they drove back down the country lane.

David shrugged.

"It's difficult to know what to think. I had the feeling for a while that they weren't very impressed with my presentation."

Des laughed out loudly.

"Ryan Pritchard didn't look too happy when we saw him. I've seldom seen somebody looking so disgruntled in all my life."

David was still thinking back over the meeting as he sat down at his desk. It was difficult to focus his mind on anything else as he stared blankly at several handwritten messages that had been left for him. At last one in bold capitals caught his attention and read: 'PLEASE RING IAN PORTER URGENTLY'.

A faint smile flickered across David's face as he reached for the telephone. It seemed absurd that with all the serious problems affecting the world, missing a single routine meeting should be of such monumental importance. He felt that God should be directing his attention elsewhere.

"Can you arrange to be at my house this afternoon at four?" enquired Ian, anxiously when he recognised the caller's voice.

David stopped for a moment to consider the request.

"I am very busy right now. Can't it wait for a few days?"

"I'm afraid not," answered Ian. "It's extremely important that we meet up right away."

"See you at four then," said David, wearily.

After putting down the phone he strolled out into the open office. Several of the juniors were in the middle of a cold calling session in an attempt to boost flagging sales. Each had the same script in front of them so that every potential client would have the same monotonous spiel rattled off to them.

Slowly David made his way down to the canteen for a coffee. Opening the door he was not surprised to find Des and Austin Matthews the post boy standing by the vending machine talking 'cars'. Austin had just passed his test and was keen to get a 'set of wheels' as he called it. He had managed to track down the one man in the company with the time on his hands to advise him on what to buy.

When his drink was ready David stood back and half listened to the discussion. Cars were hardly his favourite topic of conversation but at least it was a diversion from his problems. There was also something very comforting about wasting time with colleagues when there was a pile of work waiting to be done. To get the maximum amount of satisfaction though, it was important to be like Des and just switch off that conscience, which continues to nag away inside the head.

Eventually the group dispersed and David returned to his office. He had no sooner sat down before Maurice Hopkins popped his head around the door.

"How did the presentation go?" he enquired with a nervous expression.

David shrugged.

"You never really know in these situations. Quite often it is

119

down to how good or bad the competition is."

"So do you think you are in with a chance?" asked Maurice.

"Of course," replied David.

Maurice's features began to relax. Managing a smile he took a seat opposite his senior salesman and for a while the two of them discussed the presentation in detail. Talking wasn't going to affect the outcome of course, but at least it could provide some comfort to two anxious people.

David had other things on his mind, however, when he pulled up outside Ian Porter's house later in the day. For much of his life he had been in awe of the priest and the time had now come to confront him. In order to make that leap to freedom though, he needed to be strong.

The Porters lived in a large house even by Fellowship standards. Alongside the front lawn, which was roughly the size of a tennis court, was the drive which at times resembled a forecourt for brand new top of the range cars. Today though there were only three vehicles and David was rather taken aback as he recognised that the Mercedes nearest to the road belonged to his father.

Ian Porter looked impassive as he opened the door. Without a word he turned to lead the way through to the living room where his other visitor was sat on the settee drinking tea. John Chambers had been requested to arrive an hour earlier in order to give an account of his son's recent conduct.

Once everyone was seated Ian lay back in his armchair and fixed his eyes on David.

"Everyone is very upset that you chose to turn your back on God last night," he began, sternly.

"I am very sorry to hear that," replied David, staring straight back at Ian.

Ian and John quickly exchanged glances.

"Your father and I feel it would be entirely appropriate for you to stand up at the meeting tonight and make an apology," continued Ian.

David gave a wry smile.

"That might be a little difficult. You see, as it's a nice evening I've been thinking of delivering some more leaflets on the council estate."

John turned to the priest in astonishment.

"My son has become a different person recently. He used to be so God fearing."

"I'm afraid it's the Devil who is talking to him," replied Ian sadly.

John looked anxiously at his son.

"You must fight Satan and his wickedness," he pleaded.

David somehow managed to resist the urge to laugh.

"You just don't understand Dad," he replied, sadly, shaking his head. "This has nothing to do with dark forces. It is about me wanting to think for myself rather than just slavishly doing what I am told all the time."

John thumped his fist on the arm of the settee.

"I expect anyone who is living under my roof to walk in the ways of the Lord," he snapped, angrily.

David glared back at his father defiantly.

"You needn't worry," he replied, trying to keep his temper under control. "When we have finished our conversation here I am going home to pack my things."

John and Ian looked at each other in surprise.

"And where are you planning to go?" enquired John.

"This afternoon I booked a hotel room for a few nights," answered David. "It will give me time to find somewhere permanent to live."

At that moment Ian's elderly mother hobbled in with a tray of tea. Everyone sat in silence as the old lady, who had long white hair trailing down to the waist, made her way falteringly in the general direction of the dining table. Passing David's armchair she stopped briefly to greet him with a smile.

"Just put it on the floor Mum and we can go and help ourselves," said Ian with just the slightest hint of impatience.

Once the old lady had finally departed the Fellowship priest turned his attention once more to his wayward guest.

"Have you given any thought to Ruth?"

It was the question that David had dreaded most.

"I have decided that Ruth is too good for me," he answered, fidgeting nervously in his armchair. "I'm certain that she would be far happier married to somebody else."

John looked horrified.

"But you have to get married," he gasped. "Everything has been arranged. Your poor mother will be absolutely devastated if the whole thing is called off."

"Ruth and her family aren't going to be happy either," chipped in Ian.

David suddenly felt bolder.

"I am not going to get married for the sake of other people. This is my life and it is up to me to decide who I am going to share it with."

John Chambers put his head in his hands.

"Please leave," he said in a low voice. "You are a great disappointment to both me and your mother."

Ian stood up and showed David out. Standing at the front door he placed his hand on the young man's shoulder and looked directly into his eyes. For a moment the priest was motionless as he tried to choose his parting words.

"I shall pray for you each day," he said at last. "Remember that those who walk with Satan are damned for eternity. There will be wailing and gnashing of teeth as all those tormented souls burn in Hell."

"I'll bear that in mind," replied David, offhandedly as he turned to walk down the garden path.

David's face glowed with anger as he drove away. As a child those images of Hell that the Fellowship were always so keen on describing had given him many terrifying nightmares. Now he began to see how he had been controlled by fear.

David arrived home and hurried up the stairs. With so many possessions that he had collected over the years he knew it would take several car journeys in order to remove everything. Those items, which would not be required over the next few days could be temporarily stored at his new house. Everything else would be taken in a suitcase to the hotel.

It was a sad moment when David looked around his bedroom for the last time. Having slept within those four walls for most of his life it seemed unbelievable that he would never return. Unless he was to repent, his parents wouldn't allow him to enter the house again. As far as they were concerned he had rejected the ways of the Lord and was now the 'wicked one' who had to be cast out.

Hilary Chambers could be heard preparing the evening meal in the kitchen. The door was shut and David guessed that it would remain that way until he was safely off the premises. Once the acrimonious meeting had ended his mother would have received a telephone call giving her a full account of the proceedings. She would also have been instructed to avoid making contact with her decadent son at all costs.

David could feel the tears well up in his eyes as he stood in the hall.

"Goodbye Mum," he called out loudly.

Suddenly the clatter of pans came to an abrupt halt. David stood motionless for a while waiting for the slightest murmur, but there was total silence. Reluctantly he closed the front door for the last time and made his way slowly towards the car.

Chapter Ten

David had picked out the Brockleby Park Hotel at random from the telephone book. The advertisement that had taken up about a quarter of the page, informed him that it was a large Victorian house with six spacious rooms for guests, each with an adjoining bathroom. Having then established from the jovial proprietor that the rates for bed and breakfast were reasonable, and that evening meals and packed lunches were an option, he decided to book himself in for three nights.

He had never stayed in a hotel before. When the Fellowship travel they always go to visit other sect followers who will put them up. This allows the 'righteous' to have a holiday while remaining separate from those dreaded 'worldlies'.

Surprisingly David had been given a double room at no extra cost. The walls were tastefully decorated in light blue embossed paper which coincidentally, happened to be the colour of the silk curtains, the tufted woollen carpet and the lampshade in the corner. The pine bedroom furniture looked almost new, while the bed with a thick foam mattress and goose feather and down filled duvet resting neatly on top appeared soft and inviting.

Laying his suitcase on the floor he began to unpack. Clean socks, underwear and shirts were jumbled up with all the other essentials he needed over the next few days. When finally everything had been put away in drawers and cupboards he turned his attention to the TV.

Having never had access to a set in his entire life he was soon hooked. Laying on the bed with the remote control he switched from channel to channel with his eyes transfixed on the screen. One minute he would be watching a cartoon for toddlers and the next, a serious documentary. He was like a child with a new toy.

Eventually he switched off the set and went down to the restaurant for his evening meal. A number of people were already eating as he was guided by the waitress to a small table by the wall. Looking around it appeared that he was the only guest who was alone.

The atmosphere was quiet and relaxing. A piano recording of some of Chopin's most soothing nocturnes were playing gently in the background. At the far side of the room, tropical fish in a large tank swam gracefully around displaying their exotic colours. Covering one wall was a mural in which an artist had made an excellent attempt at replicating Leonardo's 'Last Supper'.

It felt strange sitting down to eat by himself. At home the evening meal was regarded as an important social event in the day when the family and, any friends who had dropped in, could gather around the dining table and talk. There would always be plenty of laughter as everybody partook of Hilary's excellent cooking. Tonight though, only the waitress spoke to him while taking his order for dinner.

Having eaten, David returned to his room. After organising a hot drink for himself from the tea making facilities left on the sideboard by the hotel, he lay down on the bed again. Lazily he reached over to the bedside table for the remote control and then made himself comfortable.

He was busy channel hopping again when something suddenly caught his attention. It was the start of the news and as the music slowly petered out there were images of people standing around a smouldering van. Some were shouting angrily, others were weeping but most just seemed to be in a state of shock.

The picture faded and was replaced by the solemn face of a newsreader.

"Today there was a massive bomb attack in the centre of Baghdad killing at least thirty people and injuring dozens more," he announced. "It is understood that Al-Qaeda have claimed responsibility."

There were further pictures on the screen of the injured being carried away after the explosion. Nearly all were adults but the most disturbing image was that of a small child screaming in pain.

"Tell the Americas to go home," shouted an Iraqi woman dressed in western clothes. "People may have lived in fear under Saddam Hussein, but at least we could walk the streets without the threat of being blown to pieces."

David felt quite shocked at what he had seen. Suddenly he

began to realise what a powerful tool television was in helping the viewer to appreciate the devastation that such atrocities were having on the lives of other people. Reading about such things just didn't have the same impact.

David began to feel annoyed with the Fellowship. He had been brought up to believe that TV was a mechanism that Satan employed to spread his wickedness. It now became apparent to him that the whole argument could be turned entirely on its head. By making the viewer aware of the terrible things that were happening in faraway countries could inspire him or her to protest and demand change.

It began to become clear to him that the beliefs he had been brought up with were both simple and very selfish. By setting themselves apart from others, in a sense the Fellowship became detached from all the suffering in the world. For them, thinking about poverty, famine and wars was only a distraction from obtaining the one thing that really mattered. Achieving everlasting life in Heaven for themselves.

David slept badly that night. He dreamt that he was burning in Hell alongside the newscaster that he had seen on TV, while Ian Porter and his father were watching from above with smug looks on their faces. At one stage he woke up in a cold sweat and had to search around for a pillow which had fallen on the floor.

The following morning David had little difficulty in adjusting to the new routine. Having a bathroom to himself was a luxury and meant that nobody would be hammering on the door urging him to hurry up with his ablutions. It was also a pleasure to stroll down to the restaurant and order what he liked for breakfast.

Arriving at work David felt rather tired after his restless night. As normal he headed straight for the canteen for a drink and hopefully exchange a few friendly words with anyone who happened to be lingering there. It was no surprise to see Des standing by the vending machine with a plastic cup in one hand and a bag of crisps in the other.

"Have you heard anything from Conningvale House yet?" enquired Des.

David shook his head.

"Nothing so far," he replied, glancing at his watch. "Remember though that they promised to let us know by ten o'clock if we had got the business. There is still over an hour to go."

Des finished his crisps and tossed the empty packet into the rubbish bin.

"Are you beginning to get nervous?"

David withdrew his plastic cup from the vending machine before turning to his colleague.

"I'm beginning to quake in my boots. We need this order desperately."

Des produced a chocolate bar from his trouser pocket and started to peel off the wrapper. He really was like a mobile tuck shop.

"It is all in the hands of the Lord. There is little we can do about it now."

David nodded.

"Perhaps you are right."

He had momentarily considered arguing about God's likely involvement but quickly dismissed the idea. The decision on which company would be supplying furniture to Conningvale House clearly seemed to rest with the frosty couple they had met the day before. In fact, if the Almighty had any decency at all, he should be concentrating all his efforts on sorting out the bloody conflict in Iraq.

A few minutes later David set off for his office leaving Des to find someone else to chat to. Having finished work early on the previous day meant that an important message might have been taken in his absence. Sadly his hopes were dashed when he discovered that his desktop was just as he had left it.

Picking up the telephone, David rang the senior secretary to verify the situation.

"I'm not aware that there were any calls for you yesterday," replied Angela Barton. "If you hold on a minute, I'll check with the other secretaries."

David sat doodling on a scrap of paper as he waited. Suddenly he glanced out of the window and spotted Samuel Boswell climbing out of his car. Dressed in a well-cut suit he looked like any other senior executive but for the absence of a tie. It was the one conventional garment that Fellowship men were not supposed to wear.

Soon Angela was back on the telephone.

"No messages I'm afraid."

David thanked her and hung up. Glancing briefly at his watch yet again, he consoled himself that there was still almost another hour to go before all hope should be abandoned.

Deciding to shut his mind off from work for a while, he opened his briefcase and took out the local paper he had picked up at the newsagent. Quickly he turned towards the back in search of the 'rooms to let' column. Having finally located it he cast his eyes down the list of advertisements before spotting one under the heading 'Brockleby bedsit'. After reading the details through a second time he decided to ring for an appointment to view it.

"Hello," said a rather gruff voice at the other end of the phone.

"Sorry to bother you," answered David, attempting to sound a little more friendly. "Has the bedsit been taken yet?"

"No," replied the short but not so sweet reply.

"Would it be possible for me to call around this evening for a look please?" enquired David politely.

"What time?" asked the gruff voice.

"Would eight thirty be convenient?"

"Sounds OK."

David quickly grabbed a pen.

"Could you give me the address please?"

The gruff voice suffered a noisy coughing attack before eventually replying. "Number 32a, the High Street. Look for the fish and chip shop a few doors up from the Post Office. It's the flat above."

After putting down the telephone David wondered whether to keep the appointment or not. Living on a busy street with the smell of fried food wafting up through the floorboards was hardly idyllic. Added to that though was a landlord who sounded more sinister than Bill Sykes, the cut-throat villain from *Oliver Twist*.

David continued to study the advertisements and put rings around those rooms which looked remotely promising. Eventually he was interrupted by one of the junior secretaries who had pushed open the door and was presenting him with his mail. Reluctantly he slid the newspaper back into his briefcase and tried to focus his mind on work.

The time seemed to be moving rapidly. Suddenly David who had been busy drafting out a letter to a client happened to glance up at the wall clock and was quite shocked to see it was showing ten fifteen. Sensing failure he flung his pen down on the desk in frustration.

He was about to wander down to the canteen for a coffee when Maurice Hopkins popped his head around the door.

"Any news?" he asked, anxiously.

David shook his head despondently.

"They must have chosen to go to Robsons."

Maurice gazed thoughtfully out of the window.

"Let's give the client a call," he suggested. "There is absolutely nothing to lose and after all, we need to know one way or the other."

Maurice plugged a lead into David's telephone and picked up the earpiece at the other end.

"If Fine Choice have failed to win the order I want to know why we have lost out to the competition," he explained.

With a feeling of apprehension David lifted up the telephone and began to dial. Out of the corner of his eye he saw Maurice adjusting his earpiece with the right hand and nervously tapping the desk with the fingers on the left.

"Conningvale House," answered a voice managing to sound both bored and superior. "How can I help you?"

David immediately recognised the person on the other end to be the middle-aged receptionist in the white coat.

"Good morning," he replied, cheerfully. "This is David Chambers of Fine Choice Furniture. May I speak with Mr Jennings or Mrs Bromage please?"

There was an agonising pause during which David and Maurice exchanged worried glances.

Finally a man with a precise, no nonsense voice answered.

"This is Harvey Jennnings here."

David felt his heart thumping as he introduced himself.

"That's right," said Harvey, sounding a little more relaxed. "You were one of those chaps who came to give a presentation yesterday."

David gave a little nervous laugh.

"Yes I was. Is it possible to tell me whether you have

129

managed to reach a decision regarding the furniture?"

Harvey hesitated for a moment.

"To be perfectly honest I couldn't make up my mind between the two companies," he replied finally. "In the end I took the easy way out and allowed Mrs Bromage to have the last say."

David glanced quickly at Maurice. The sales manager was sat with his eyes tightly shut and appeared to be mouthing a prayer.

"And has Mrs Bromage been able to decide?" asked David who was now beginning to find the tension unbearable.

"Wait a minute," replied Harvey sounding quite affable now. "I will hand you over to her. She has just walked into the room."

The two salesmen could hear whispering at the other end of the line and then a female voice suddenly broke the silence.

"This is Shirley Bromage speaking. I must apologise for not getting back to you."

David saw from the corner of his eye that Maurice was still praying.

"Please don't apologise," replied David. "I was just thinking that if you had made up your mind to buy from Fine Choice Furniture I could arrange to come over next week and discuss all your requirements in detail."

There was a brief pause and then Shirley let out a little chuckle.

"Actually the other representative was on the telephone a few minutes ago asking exactly the same question."

David felt the hairs standing up on the back of his head.

"I am sorry if we are causing you any inconvenience," he answered.

"Not at all," answered Shirley. "As if happens, I got a great deal of satisfaction from telling Mr Pritchard that we were buying from you. I didn't like the man one little bit. You were much more professional."

Although feeling like dancing around the office, David managed to remain calm.

"That is very kind of you to say so Mrs Bromage," he replied, courteously. "I shall make certain that we provide you with an excellent service."

"Mr Jennings and I were hoping you could come over on Monday morning so that we could go through a number of things."

"Sounds fine," replied David without even bothering to check his diary. Anything booked would have to be rescheduled he told himself.

Maurice had heard all he needed to hear. Dropping his earpiece on the desk he disappeared into the main office to broadcast the good news, leaving David to tie up a few loose ends with Shirley. Before too long, word had spread to Samuel and Oscar Boswell.

David felt elated once he had finished the call. Like all salesmen he suffered so many disappointments in the course of his work that the successes were sweet and had to be savoured. With a broad smile he hurried off to enjoy the moment with Maurice and all the rest of the sales team.

The weather was hot and sunny so David decided to eat his hotel packed lunch in the park. He managed to find a bench beneath the trees, which looked out across the lake with its still blue water and a small wooded island in the centre. At the edges mothers and children threw bread at the large variety of ducks gliding gracefully over the surface.

Some distance from the nearest road everything was so quiet and peaceful. David sat studying the advertisements in the local paper once more while helping himself to the sandwiches and other food items that the hotel catering staff had provided. Apart from bedsits he was also considering the possibility of flat or house sharing. It certainly seemed to be a more appealing option than living alone.

After a while he closed his paper and sat back. Apart from finding somewhere to live, there was still the problem of what to do with the house. It had been bought in joint names so Ruth would obviously need to have a say in the matter. Like it or not he was going to have to get in touch with her.

Finally he stood up and started to slowly make his way back to work. Still deep in thought he suddenly became aware of a child shouting from the direction of the lake in a shrill voice. Looking up he saw his five-year-old niece Gemma waving excitedly at him. She and her mother Kate were standing on the bank feeding the ducks with bread from white paper bags.

David smiled and waved back.

"Have you a bit for me to throw in?" he joked.

David was startled by his sister-in-law's reaction. Looking quite anxious she bent down and whispered something in Gemma's ear before steering her away. The little girl clutched her paper bag tightly as she tried to keep up with her mother.

Sadly David watched as they headed towards the children's playground. Kate with a blue headscarf covering the crown and long fair hair bouncing up and down on her back while Gemma, no longer linking hands, walked briskly behind. Deep down he knew he was being ostracised for daring to offend the Fellowship.

The sect was of the opinion that every word in the Bible had to be taken quite literally. Therefore when Saint Paul had written in his second epistle to the Corinthians that 'be ye not unequally yoked together with unbelievers', it became an edict to be obeyed. To their simple minds the word of God could hardly be clearer.

In the middle of the afternoon David was summoned to Samuel Boswell's office. Imagining that the purpose of the invitation was to congratulate him on winning the important order, he was surprised to see the boss looking so sombre. He had the appearance of a man about to announce bad news and that in fact turned out to be the case.

Samuel Boswell was a man in his late fifties. He was the senior partner in the company and made all the most important decisions, while his mild mannered younger brother, Oscar, seemed happy to play second fiddle. Together though, they had built up a very successful business.

"First of all," began Samuel, hesitantly, "I must offer my thanks to you for making a very important sale for Fine Choice Furniture."

David smiled but deep down he was feeling decidedly uneasy.

"However, I've been speaking with Ian Porter," continued Samuel, gazing sadly at his fingernails. "He tells me that you are planning to follow in the way of the world."

David shrugged.

"I just want to be free to lead my own life."

Samuel looked grave.

"Ian wants me to dismiss you and I am inclined to agree with him. This company has been built on strong Christian values. I'm therefore concerned that if you are allowed to stay here it may have an unsettling effect on everyone else."

David was stunned. It was difficult to collect his thoughts as he sat staring blankly at a calendar on the wall just behind Samuel's desk. This was the only job he had ever known and it had never occurred to him to look for another.

"So are you telling me to go straight away?" asked David, finally.

Samuel looked thoughtful.

"Not at this minute. I would like you to pray very hard over the next week. Ask God to give you guidance and help you through this very difficult time. Then we will meet up next Friday at the same time to see how you feel."

David felt the position needed to be clarified.

"Does it mean instant dismissal if I am of the same mind?"

Samuel nodded.

"Of course you will get your normal redundancy entitlement plus enhancements."

David felt there were numerous other questions that needed to be asked but his mind had just gone numb.

"It seems a very bad time to get rid of me," he said, bitterly. "There are going to be a lot of loose ends to be tied up with this Conningvale House order."

Samuel smiled reassuringly.

"I am sure Maurice will be able to cope."

Like others in the company David had reservations about the ability of Samuel Boswell's son-in-law but it seemed pointless to express them. Maurice was little more than a figurehead in the sales office and was carried by the efforts of everyone else. It was a classical example of the nepotism which exists within any Eternal Fellowship organisation.

David was in no mood to watch TV. Returning to his hotel room that evening he dropped on the bed and stared up at the ceiling. Having now made that leap for freedom he was not prepared to contemplate remaining in his present job and facing all the consequences that he had been trying to escape. It was time to look for alternative employment.

His ultimate goal was to teach. For the immediate future though, it was necessary to find work which didn't require long-term training and qualifications. Perhaps aim for another position in a sales office or to explore other alternatives.

Once again he turned to his local paper but this time it was to scan the 'employment opportunities' section. However, he soon began to realise that the type of job that he was looking for always required knowledge of various computer systems. Unfortunately, due to the Fellowship's rejection of such technology he had absolutely no previous experience in that area.

He decided to call Simon in the morning. It might help to crystallise things in his own mind if he was able to sit down with someone else and discuss a few ideas. His friend might also come up with an invaluable suggestion.

After dinner David set off for his appointment to view the bedsit. His hopes of finding something suitable were not high but he decided to have a look all the same. As the High Street was only a short distance away he chose to go on foot and enjoy the warm early September evening.

The fish and chip shop was going through a slack period as David stopped outside. With more assistants than customers one older man in a white trilby hat was stood at the window looking out. He was short and plump with a large reddish face.

Having spotted David he strolled casually over to the open door.

"Are you Mr Chambers?" he enquired in that gruff voice that David recognised from their earlier telephone conversation.

David smiled.

"If you wouldn't mind showing me the room."

The man produced a large set of keys.

"The name is Don Sharp by the way," he said. "Just follow me."

Don walked a few steps along the pavement and stopped outside a black door beside the fish and chip shop. Trying several keys he finally found the one capable of turning the lock and was soon leading the way along a dark narrow passage and then up a flight of stairs. There was a very noticeable musty smell in the air.

Don came to a halt at the top of the landing and turned to David with a big wide grin.

"I let out two rooms," he announced, proudly. "A professional gentleman has the one at the back but yours in the front is better. From the window you have a good view over the High Street."

David had already lost interest even before he was shown the bedsit. Actually standing inside the small square room and peering around did absolutely nothing to rekindle the slight enthusiasm he had started with. Everything was just so gloomy and depressing.

It was certainly no place to entertain Alison or anyone else for that matter. To start with, the smell of fish and chips from the shop below penetrated into the room even more than he had expected. On top of that were the faded carpets and curtains, the dingy wallpaper, battered furniture and a stained duvet, which barely covered the off-white sheets underneath.

"No cooking facilities then?" remarked David.

Don gave a little laugh.

"I'm sure a young bloke like you doesn't want to be bothered with that type of thing. The High Street is full of good restaurants and just downstairs you have got fish and chips."

David wondered about the expense of eating all his meals in restaurants and takeaways but said nothing.

Don pointed to a gap between the wardrobe and chest of drawers.

"See this silver metal box attached to the wall here?"

David moved a couple of steps to take a look.

"I see it."

"This is the electric meter," explained Don. "Now if you ever run out of coins, just come downstairs to the shop."

David smiled his appreciation.

"That would be very helpful."

Don suddenly turned to the door.

"Now let me show you the bathroom."

David followed the landlord several paces up the landing and through another door at the end. After what he had just witnessed, his expectations of being over-impressed with anything in that place were not high. He was now desperate to get away as soon as possible.

David soon discovered he had been right to fear the worst. The bath and toilet were covered in dark stains while the sink was full of washing that had been left to soak. The walls looked no better with cracked tiles everywhere and others which had come away completely.

"If you want to take the room I will need a week's rent in advance," said Don.

David nodded as he edged his way back to the landing.

"I need to go away and have a think about it."

A look of disappointment appeared on Don's face.

"You need to make up your mind quickly," he warned. "A lot of people have rung up making enquiries. In fact I have a gentleman who is coming to have a look in the morning."

David shook his head.

"I don't want to reach a decision straight away."

"There are no restrictions here," said Don with a gleam in his eyes. "My lodgers are free to do as they please. The young man who had that room before used to hold parties in it."

David smiled as he turned to make his way back down the narrow staircase.

"I'll be in touch," he called.

"Have you still got my number?" Don called back.

"Yes I do," replied David as he hurriedly turned the lock of the front door and finally smelt fresh air again.

Walking back to the hotel he began to feel quite light-headed. The evening had hardly been a resounding success but, at least he had something to smile about. In his mind's eye he was trying to visualise a crowd of young pleasure seekers having a wild party in those cramped and miserable premises. Even a funeral parlour might have provided a more suitable venue for such purposes he laughed to himself.

Chapter Eleven

News spreads quickly in Fellowship circles. Less than three hours after David's acrimonious meeting with his father and Ian Porter an announcement was being made to the Brockleby congregation that the young man had left their ranks to serve the Devil. However, even before the locals were informed, a telephone call had been made to a certain Birmingham number.

Ruth was stunned when everything had been explained to her. Not exactly besotted with David, she regarded her forthcoming marriage to him as a Christian duty. It was to be a union to create a brood of children that would grow up to serve the Lord. Although never expecting to fall wildly in love, she hoped eventually to develop an agreeable understanding with her future husband.

"I'm sorry to have to break this sad news to you," said Ian Porter, gently.

Ruth could feel the tears well up in her eyes. All those wonderful life changes that she had looked forward to making were now not going to happen. She would not be resigning from her monotonous job or moving into that new house in Kent. Dreams too of motherhood would also be dashed for the foreseeable future.

"Where is David now?" she sobbed.

"He has moved into a nearby hotel but at the moment I couldn't tell you which one," answered Ian.

"Could you find out for me," pleaded Ruth. "I am driving down to Brockleby on Saturday morning and it is important that I speak with him."

Ian paused for a moment to consider the situation. Having only recently spoken with David he didn't think it likely that the young man would have come to his senses just yet. The Devil it seemed had a powerful hold over him for the present at least.

"I shouldn't come down at the weekend if I were you," he advised. "Let's allow David a little time to reflect on things."

"You may be right," replied Ruth, tearfully. "Before very long he is bound to become disillusioned with the world and its empty pleasures."

"Exactly," said Ian, attempting to sound upbeat.

Throughout the call Ruth had managed to remain relatively calm. However, once she had returned to the lounge to join her mother all attempts at remaining dignified were instantly abandoned. She wanted sympathy and plenty of it.

"The wedding is off," she wailed, flinging herself on the settee.

Joan Kennedy looked sternly at the chocolate éclair that she was in the process of eating. Having been listening to her daughter speaking on the telephone she had managed to get the gist of what was going on. She was anxious though to be filled in with the exact details. It took a while but between sobs Ruth finally managed to provide her with the full story.

"Fancy forsaking the Lord just to go and join the Labour Party," she said with a loud snort.

"Not to mention abandoning me at the same time," cried Ruth before blowing her nose into a small white handkerchief.

Joan turned to the mantelpiece and gave David's photograph a ferocious glare.

"I thought he was a good Christian and then he does this to you. I suppose we should be thankful to the Lord that all this has happened before the two of you went ahead and got married."

"Of course I still may marry him," perked up Ruth as she dabbed the tears from her eyes. "Sometime soon I intend to go down to Brockleby to speak with him."

"Just forget him," answered Joan with a shake of her head. "I always said that he was never the right man for you. There was something shifty about his eyes."

It was typical for her to be wise after the event. Up until the past five minutes she had always given the impression that she had regarded her son-in-law to be the best thing since cream cakes. Having said that of course, she had often warned her daughter that David would be one of those husbands who might benefit from the occasional kick up the arse.

"But if the wedding is off what am I going to tell everybody?" asked Ruth, staring down gloomily at the carpet. "What about all the presents that people have probably gone out and bought for us?"

"Don't worry about that right now dear," smiled Joan. "Look, have another of these chocolate éclairs. They are from that nice little cake shop in the High Street."

Ruth's reddened eyes suddenly opened wide.

"They are rather scrumptious," she grinned. "Perhaps I will have just one more."

***

It was on the following day that the news of David's exploits reached Rebecca down in Broadstairs. From the kitchen window she had been watching groups of children making their way to school when the telephone rang. Not being a frequent caller she was surprised to hear her brother's voice on the other end of the line.

"Guess what has happened?" began Simon, somewhat dramatically.

"What is it?" asked Rebecca breathlessly.

"The Fellowship have withdrawn from David Chambers," announced Simon.

Rebecca smiled to herself as she listened to the details. Having seen David only the previous week she was aware that he didn't want to marry Ruth and seemed generally restless with life. However, it still came as a surprise to learn that her old classmate had found the courage to rebel against the Fellowship.

"I wonder what made him decide to join the Labour Party?" she said, thoughtfully. "He never struck me as being politically minded."

"Because Alison Johnson is a member," laughed Simon. "Apparently he goes out delivering leaflets with her."

Rebecca gasped.

"Are they having a relationship?"

Simon paused briefly to consider the question.

"When I spoke to David earlier this week he seemed hopeful that things were moving in that direction," he said, finally.

"I hope that she isn't stringing him along," replied Rebecca with more than a hint of concern in her voice.

"Only time will tell I guess," answered Simon.

At that moment Rebecca glanced up at the calendar which was hung up on the wall beside the telephone table. It was the type that could be used to pencil in future engagements and anything else that the user needed to be reminded of.

"Why have you bothered to ring me?" she laughed. "I shall be seeing you this evening. Mum has invited Malcolm and me up for a meal."

"I wasn't aware of that," replied Simon, cheerfully. "But then nobody bothers to tell me anything."

Shortly after putting down the phone Rebecca began to vacuum the sitting room carpet. Friday mornings were always set aside for coffee with some of the younger Fellowship sisters. Each would take it in turn to act as hostess and today her bungalow was to be the venue.

Although Rebecca looked forward to these weekly gatherings she often felt the odd one out. As the only woman in the group who was not a proud mother she sometimes found it difficult to fully contribute to conversations which centred around children. Of course she pretended not to mind and smiled sweetly while listening to the mundane occurrences surrounding the lives of little Johnny and baby Susie.

This morning Rosemary was the first arrival. Stopping to remove her headscarf at the front door she was surrounded by three noisy children all pre-school age. Beneath her white silk blouse there were visible signs of a fourth, which was expected to be born in the very near future.

Suddenly she turned and beamed at Rebecca.

"Last night I dreamt that you'd just had a baby."

"That's nice," replied Rebecca, who could think of nothing better to say on the spur of the moment.

"Perhaps it is one of those prophesies that you read about in the Bible," said Rosemary, excitedly, as she ushered her three children along the hall.

"Let's hope so," smiled Rebecca who was more inclined to put the dream down to poor late night eating habits rather than any supernatural explanation.

Soon the sitting room was full of young women with hair to their waist and small children crawling on the floor. With so many people talking at the same time it was rather like being in a chicken run with clucking mother hens keeping a watchful eye over their chirping offspring. One voice, however, was attracting more attention than all those in competition.

"Last Sunday I had thirty people staying for lunch," announced Miriam Foster, proudly.

"Gracious!" exclaimed Rosemary who was always easy to impress. "That must have been hard work."

"It could have been an absolute disaster," answered Miriam shuddering as she looked back on the event. "When I was about to serve the meal I discovered that there weren't enough plates to go around."

Rosemary threw her hand to her mouth in horror.

"How awful," she gasped.

"Of course I had some plastic plates but they are not the same as china ones," continued Miriam with a shake of the head.

"No substitute at all," agreed Lucy Young who was listening intently. "Whatever did you do?"

"I had no choice but to send my sister home to fetch me some of hers," answered Miriam.

There were sighs of relief all round.

"Lucky that your sister lives close by," said Lucy.

Most of the other women nodded in agreement.

Now that Miriam had finished her little narrative Rebecca called for attention. With pen and paper at the ready and smiling sweetly she announced that she was about to take orders for coffee, tea and soft drinks. It was always a task that required a bucket load of patience.

"I'll see what everyone else is having," replied Rosemary who was the first to be asked.

"Could I have tea with no sugar?" requested Lucy. "I'm trying to lose weight so it means having to cut back on sweet things."

"I'm on a diet too," chimed in Rosemary to murmurs of approval from most of the other women.

Determined not to be distracted Rebecca ploughed on with the job in hand.

"What about you Miriam?"

"I'll have a black coffee with one sugar," replied Miriam,

before bending forward to address her small son. "What do you want Ben?"

"Apple juice," answered the boy without hesitation.

Rebecca gave mother and son a long apologetic look.

"Sorry I don't have any. There is orange, lemon, blackcurrant or milk."

Ben looked scornful and then threw a colouring pencil at the settee in disgust.

"I want apple juice," he screamed.

All eyes suddenly fixed on him. Embarrassed by the outburst Miriam picked up her son and tried to comfort him. Sensing his mother's anxiety, however, Ben was not prepared to be pacified without some form of bribery. He therefore began to wail at the top of his voice.

Witnessing Ben's distress seemed to upset Rosemary's youngest daughter. Without warning she lay face down on the floor with her feet kicking the carpet and began to howl loudly. It was almost as though the two children were in competition as to which one could make the most noise.

"Could I change my mind and have coffee instead of tea," requested Lucy who always had trouble making up her mind.

Rebecca finally wrote down the last order for drinks. Politely refusing all offers of assistance she slipped into the kitchen with the list. Feeling a headache coming on she preferred to be alone for the moment.

Rebecca was thinking of David as she waited for the kettle to boil. While admiring his courage for breaking free of the Fellowship she was also concerned that things could go sour for him. Deep down she knew it was that fear of failing to cope with the outside world that actually kept her trapped in an unhappy existence.

It was something of a relief to wave goodbye to the last of her departing guests. Then having restored her bungalow to its former state of tidiness she hurried along the hall to the spare bedroom. Kneeling on the floor she poked her hand into the narrow gap between the heavy double wardrobe and the wall. It was a tight squeeze but, after a few moments, she managed to withdraw a green hard covered book.

It was a secret that Rebecca dared not share with anyone.

Soon after her marriage she decided to join the local library in Broadstairs. Unable to enjoy a great deal of intellectual stimulus from those around her, she was determined to expand her knowledge. In particular, she wanted to read the works of notable people that had always been demonised by her parents.

Of course it wasn't long before new ideas started Rebecca thinking for herself. If Darwin was right and man had indeed evolved from apes, where did God fit into the picture she wondered. Perhaps as Marx had suggested, religion with its threat of eternal damnation for wrongdoers, was merely a tool devised by the ruling classes to keep the lower ranks from rising up. It was also feasible that in their ignorance, the writers of the Bible could have invented the concept of a divine force just to explain the phenomena, which modern science had now found answers to.

Books had now become an essential part of Rebecca's life. However, it was only safe to bring them out in the day when Malcolm wasn't around. The lord and master would have doubtless accused his wife of heresy had he discovered the type of material she was reading. Even to venture into a library was a mortal sin in his eyes.

The green covered book she was reading at present was of a particular interest to her. The author had provided a detailed account of the history and beliefs of each of the world's major religions. Apart from a very negative portrayal of Catholicism that she had been taught by the Fellowship, Rebecca had practically no knowledge of other faiths.

Taking the book into the sitting room she decided to allow herself an hour's reading time. Usually her mind began to wander after that and in any case she wasn't prepared to neglect the housework. She didn't want to give Malcolm the opportunity to criticise her on that front.

The master of the house was in a bad mood when he arrived home. However, he became even more irritable when Rebecca reminded him that his mother-in-law had invited them up for a meal that evening. The problem was that the auditors were arriving the following week and Malcolm wanted to run through the books beforehand.

"You should have given me more notice," he snapped.

"I mentioned it to you last night just before we went to bed," protested Rebecca.

"No you didn't," replied Malcolm, angrily. "If you had have done I would have rung your mother up straight away and cancelled."

Rebecca gave the ceiling a long suffering look.

"We will have to go now," she, said wearily. "It has all been arranged. Anyway there isn't much to eat in the house if we stay here."

"But I've got work to do this evening," shouted Malcolm.

"Then you can phone up for a takeaway," replied Rebecca. "I'll go tonight without you."

Malcolm glared hard at his wife.

"I want a proper meal not some fried muck."

"Then cook it yourself," answered Rebecca storming out of the room and slamming the door behind her.

Malcolm stood smouldering for a while. Were Rebecca to have a better understanding of the teachings of the Bible she would know that wives are expected to fulfil a subservient role in marriage he thought bitterly to himself. The duty of a husband on the other hand as every good Christian knew was that of provider and decision maker.

Grudgingly he decided to accompany Rebecca. The prospect of spending the evening alone and having to make do with junk food was not appealing. He was, however, determined to take every opportunity to make his wife feel guilty about dragging him away from his work.

The atmosphere was tense in the car. Conversation had never flowed easily between them but tonight they merely snapped at one another like two dogs fighting over territorial rights. Hostilities didn't even come to a halt when they eventually sat down to eat.

"I'm thankful that you didn't marry him," said Mrs Broadbent as she passed the tureen of roast potatoes to her daughter.

Rebecca looked bewildered.

"Who are you talking about?"

"Why David Chambers of course," answered Mrs Broadbent. "To think that he has just rejected the Lord and gone off into the world to serve the Devil."

Mr Broadbent nodded.

"Had Rebecca married him she would have been left on her own."

"What makes you think that I wouldn't have gone with him?" answered Rebecca, indignantly. "You've always said that a wife should support her husband."

"Because we have brought you up to be a Christian," answered Mr Broadbent, rather taken aback by his daughter's last remark. "You have been taught that those who follow Satan will suffer eternal damnation."

Suddenly attention switched from religion to alcohol as Simon lifted up a bottle of red wine. For a few moments there was total silence as those glasses that were advanced in his direction were served an ample measure of red liquid. Then the conversation returned to where it had broken off.

"I think that both Rebecca and David Chambers have forgotten much of what they were taught," said Malcolm with a self-satisfied smile.

Rebecca gave her husband a disdainful glare.

"Perhaps David and I have learnt to think for ourselves. Somebody of your limited intelligence wouldn't be capable of that."

Mrs Broadbent stared at her daughter in astonishment.

"Do you have doubts about what the Fellowship believe?"

Rebecca took a sip of wine. Having spoken out in a moment of anger she was already considering retracting her last comments. She had no wish to receive an unwelcome visit from one or more of the local priests. As long as she remained dependent on the Fellowship for so much, these people could control her life in any way they thought fit. Therefore rebellion was pointless unless a follower intended to break away as David had done.

Sensing the predicament that his sister was in, Simon decided to come to the rescue.

"I think that Rebecca just enjoys an argument," he laughed. "Deep down she is as true to her beliefs as anyone around this table."

Malcolm and the two senior Broadbents looked far from convinced. However, Simon's intervention helped to take the heat out of the situation and soon the conversation moved on to more

145

general matters. Not surprisingly though, the subject of Rebecca's faith resurfaced after dinner.

The sexes had temporarily gone their separate ways. The three gentleman had retired to the lounge to relax over a drop or two of whisky leaving the two ladies to wash and dry up in the kitchen. The usual arrangement in Fellowship households.

"It's such a shame that you and Malcolm don't seem to be able to get along together," commented Mrs Broadbent as she scrubbed away at the inside of a large pan with a wire brush.

"But Malcolm is so pompous," protested Rebecca. "He always thinks he is far superior to everyone else."

Mrs Broadbent stopped scrubbing and turned around to face her daughter. Usually a mild mannered woman, it was clear from her expression that at the present moment she was not best pleased. The warning signs were that somebody close by was about to receive a piece of her mind.

"You are extremely fortunate to have such a good husband," she said, indignantly. "Malcolm is a perfect Christian and works hard to provide you with a lovely home and a comfortable lifestyle. You should be very grateful to him."

Rebecca looked thoughtfully at the tea towel in her hand. It was true that materially she was well blessed but that hardly compensated for those more precious things that were missing from her life. There was little point in having an expensive home when all the hours she spent in it were miserable.

"I want children," she suddenly blurted out, "and if that isn't possible then I want a job to keep me occupied. My life seems to be so pointless. It's just one long round of entertaining guests and keeping the bungalow clean and tidy."

Mrs Broadbent's angry expression began to fade.

"You must trust the Lord," she said, gently. "He knows what is best for each and every one of us."

As Rebecca had grown older she had become increasingly frustrated by responses such as this. Even assuming there was an all-powerful divine being, did he really have a grand plan worked out for each and every one? It seemed just as likely that he expected people to be proactive and make choices for themselves. Still there seemed little to be gained from arguing such profound theological matters with her mother.

"Perhaps you're right," she said with a sigh.

"Of course I am," smiled Mrs Broadbent. "I always say a special prayer that you and Malcolm will find harmony in your marriage."

"Thank you," answered Rebecca, picking up another dinner plate to dry.

The men were talking cars when the women eventually joined them in the lounge. This was hardly surprising as they seemed to discuss little else when the three of them met up. They were forever comparing the features of one model with that of another.

While pretending to sit back and listen Rebecca switched herself off. She had absolutely no idea why anyone would go into raptures about a motor vehicle any more than a washing machine or a vacuum cleaner. As far as she was concerned, cars served a very useful purpose and that was about the end of the matter.

Of those present Rebecca was the only one not partaking of alcohol. There was an understanding that when they went out for the evening, Malcolm was permitted to drink as much as he pleased. Her role was to remain sober and do the driving on the way home.

At eleven o'clock Rebecca got to her feet.

"It's getting late," she said with a yawn. "I think we had better be on our way."

"OK," answered Malcolm as he struggled to get out of his armchair.

As usual he was drunk. Being that alcohol is the one vice Fellowship followers are permitted, Malcolm had a tendency to overindulge himself. He would then wake up the following morning with a hangover and be extremely irritable over breakfast.

"Would you just pop this in the box for me?" requested Mrs Broadbent as her guests were about to depart.

Malcolm who was the closest took the long white envelope from her. Leaving Rebecca on the doorstep to say her final goodbye to the family he set off on his errand. Even in his drunken stupor he was vaguely aware that the red post box was on the opposite side of the road. Tragically he was dead before the deed was done.

The driver didn't see him until it was too late. Malcolm was buffeted hard in the leg before being thrown to the ground. The impact may have killed him before the front wheels crushed his ribs.

Hearing the sharp thud Rebecca hurried over to investigate. Much to her horror, there beneath the bright glare of the streetlights lay Malcolm's battered and blood stained body. Shaking with fear and revulsion she quickly turned her head away.

For the next few hours she felt like the central character in a surreal play. Like ghouls, neighbours slipped silently out of their front doors to get a glimpse of the prostrate figure lying in the road, while others peeped discreetly behind net curtains. Mr and Mrs Broadbent stood close by and attempted to comfort their traumatised daughter but she was barely aware of their presence.

An ambulance responded quickly to Simon's call. Hurrying quickly to Malcolm's side the paramedic held the limp wrist for a few minutes before sadly shaking his head. It was quite clear to him that his only responsibility now was in removing the body to a mortuary.

Two police officers walked amongst the neighbours looking for witnesses. They were keen to seek out somebody who had seen the accident and could help them catch the offending driver who had fled the scene. Everyone they spoke to though just looked back blankly and shook their heads.

Simon guided his sister back inside the house. The police would return in the next few days to question her but tonight she would be left to grieve in peace. The job of providing details of the deceased therefore fell to Mr Broadbent.

"Of course your daughter could receive counselling," said the senior officer once he had got sufficient facts about Malcolm.

"That really won't be necessary," smiled Mr Broadbent. "You see she is fortunate enough to have the Lord in her life."

Rebecca sat in the lounge sobbing. Even though she had grown to hate Malcolm it was terrible to see him come to such a gruesome end. It filled her with guilt now to think of the many times she had wished him dead. She also tried hard to shut out that gleeful voice inside her head which kept repeating the same words over and over again.

'At last I am free. At last I am free.'

Chapter Twelve

The warm weather continued on into Saturday. With a gentle breeze in the air the conditions were exactly as the organisers of the peace march had been praying for. Huge numbers of demonstrators were needed to pour out on the streets of central London, to have any chance at all of making the White House sit up and take notice.

After breakfast David went in search of the hotel proprietor. With only one night remaining of the three originally booked he wanted to reserve his room for an extra week. He was beginning to appreciate how important it was, to search at leisure for a permanent place to live.

Having secured himself further time at the Brockleby Park Hotel, David went up to his room to make a telephone call. There was ample time to have a long chat with Simon before setting off to collect Alison. After dialling the number he sat on the edge of the bed sipping tea.

It was the familiar voice of Simon's mother who eventually answered. She sounded far from her happy self, however, when the caller introduced himself.

"I'm sorry but Simon doesn't wish to speak with you right now," she said, sharply.

David was taken aback.

"I promise to make it brief Mrs Broadbent."

"I'm sorry," came the abrupt reply. "At present he only wishes to talk with those who accept the word of the Lord."

Had David been aware that the Broadbents had just suffered a tragic death in the family he would have been more sympathetic. As it was, however, he was simply furious when climbing into his car shortly afterwards. It seemed to him to be yet another example of Fellowship parents feeling that they had a perfect right to interfere in the lives of their children. Surely at the age of twenty-three Simon was more than capable of speaking for himself so why had he not been called to the telephone.

149

By the time David had pulled up outside Alison's maisonette he had cooled down. Walking up the garden path he blissfully recalled their intimate moments in the car a few nights before. The pure feeling of ecstasy that had given him a glimpse of a world he never knew existed.

Alison looked harassed as she opened the door. Her hair was dishevelled and in one hand she was holding a face flannel. Beckoning her visitor to come into the hall she immediately hurried off to be with a screaming child in another room.

"Don't argue," she shouted. "We are going up to London on the train."

"I want to go and stay with grandma," shrieked back the unseen child.

The confrontation raged on for a few more minutes, then finally everything went quiet. Eventually a door swung open and Alison appeared followed by a little girl with blonde flowing hair, who looked like a miniature version of her mother. Peace it appeared had been restored for the time being.

Alison handed David a child's folded up buggy, which he duly loaded into the boot. Then stone faced and resentful the little girl climbed into the rear of the car with her mother and slumped back in the seat.

"This is Amanda by the way," said Alison when they were both settled.

"Pleased to meet you," replied David, cheerfully.

Amanda seemed unimpressed as she turned her head and glared bitterly out of the window.

"I want to stay with grandma," she muttered, sulkily.

Before starting the car David rummaged around in the glove compartment.

"Would you like a sweet, Amanda?"

Alison intervened before the child had time to answer.

"Not at the moment thank you. She has just brushed her teeth."

Amidst the howls of protest the car set off for the station. They were running late now because of Amanda's tantrum and it was important to catch up on lost time. The arrangement was that all members of the Brockleby Labour group were to travel up on the train together.

"Could Amanda have the radio on please?" requested Alison after a few minutes.

David began to feel slightly uncomfortable.

"Unfortunately it has been removed."

"Was it taken by thieves?" asked Alison who was using the journey to brush her hair.

David laughed.

"Actually my company had the set taken out when the car was bought."

Alison stopped brushing briefly and let out a gasp of surprise.

"What is the point of doing that?"

"The Fellowship disapprove of radios," explained David. "They believe them to be the tools of the Devil."

Alison shook her head in disbelief.

"What a load of rubbish."

They were the last to arrive at the station. The little group of supporters were already beginning to board the train as the three latecomers hurried along the platform. David was carrying the buggy while Alison and Amanda ran hand-in-hand.

Tony, Carol's husband, who was leading the way, found an empty compartment in the last carriage. With four seats on one side of the gangway and six on the other it suited their requirements perfectly. Everyone was in high spirits as they took their places and waited for the train to set off. The slogans on their T-shirts and the several banners which they had brought, left fellow travellers in little doubt as to their eventual destination.

David found himself sitting opposite Jacquie Dunn. Even in a white T-shirt and jeans she looked as elegant as ever with her slim waist and dark hair. It was as always though, the vivaciousness in her eyes which captivated the most.

"By the way," began Tony, stroking his beard. "The Prime Minister is expected to be at the club on Wednesday evening at about five o'clock. Are you all able to make it?"

David looked across at Jacqui.

"Where is the club?" he asked in a low voice.

"That is how we often refer to the Brockleby Labour Party headquarters," she smiled.

"A free meal will be thrown in as well," added Tony. "We shall sit down to eat about six before the Prime Minister goes off to give an election address at the Methodist Church in Maple Road."

David needed less than a few seconds to decide. It would mean finishing work early but, he could feel very little loyalty to a company that would almost certainly be sacking him at the end of the week.

"Put my name down," he smiled, enthusiastically.

The train suddenly started to pull away. Alison who was sitting on the other side of the aisle from David slowly got to her feet. Taking Amanda by the hand she began to shepherd her daughter towards the front of the carriage in search of a toilet.

"If you get elected to Parliament, what happens about your seat on the Council, Jacqui?" asked Carol. "Presumably you won't be able to do both jobs."

Jacqui shrugged.

"I shall have to stand down as a councillor. After that it will be a matter of finding a suitable candidate to fight the seat for Labour."

"I wonder who might be interested?" asked an older man who was answering to the name of George.

"I understand that Sid Davidson might be keen," replied Tony.

There were groans all round.

"He is far too right wing," protested Carol. "Upset him once and he is liable to defect to the Tories."

Most people nodded in agreement. He was one of those individuals who had voted Labour all his life yet seemed to be opposed to every principle the party stood for. He despised the poor, distrusted the trade unions and often argued for the privatisation of parts of the public sector.

"I see he isn't joining us on the march today," smiled a young man in glasses who was sitting next to Jacqui.

"It's hardly surprising Kenny," said George, bitterly. "He believes we should be supporting the Americans in Iraq."

Jacqui turned to Tony.

"We simply can't afford to allow Sid to become the party candidate. Somebody must be found who will stand against him."

Tony shrugged his shoulders.

"A lot of people are put off standing in council by-elections.

There is always a lot of coverage in the local papers and candidates fear being put under the microscope."

The arrival of the ticket inspector put a temporary halt to the conversation. A few anxious moments followed in which George stood up and began to empty his pockets out. Finally his face relaxed when he managed to produce the necessary evidence proving him innocent of fare dodging.

David looked thoughtful.

"Isn't there somebody here who could stand?"

Jacqui smiled.

"Tony, George and Kenny are already on the Council. In fact the four of us spend half our lives sitting on committee meetings."

"What about you putting your name forward David?" suggested Tony.

"It would certainly be a way of impressing a certain lady," grinned Carol, nodding her head towards Alison's vacant seat.

Seeing David's shy smile, Tony realised that his wife might be on to something.

"I bet Alison would love to see her picture in the paper," he laughed. "Dressed up to the nines as the new councillor's partner."

David began to visualise the picture in his mind's eye. He being the local hero surrounded by admiring party workers and standing next to the most beautiful woman in the world. The chance of such glory might never come again in his life.

"What exactly are the duties of a local councillor?" he asked, trying to contain any outward signs of excess interest.

"There is a good booklet about it at the club," replied Tony. "I'll find you a copy."

It was just before midday when the group arrived at the Embankment. Hordes of people were already gathered waiting to follow a route which would eventually take them to Hyde Park. It would not be a long journey but one that would be watched by many in high places.

There were men and women of all ages. Some like Alison had brought their children as a reminder to all that the planet didn't belong to one generation alone. For many it was the first demonstration they had ever experienced while others were seasoned campaigners.

The atmosphere was friendly and good humoured. Protestors and the large gathering of police stood patiently in the sunshine waiting for the march to begin. The peacefulness was only disturbed by chanting from a small group of young people calling for an end to the war.

Finally the organisers gave the signal. Raising their banners, those at the front began to lead a million or more people past some of the world's most famous landmarks. Brothers and sisters who were united in their desire for peace.

Strangely, not everyone appeared to be protesting against the war in Iraq. David noticed that slogans on certain banners and T-shirts expressed opposition to issues such as laboratory testing on animals and the proliferation of nuclear weapons. It was as though certain individuals had accidentally tagged on to the wrong march.

The demonstrators proceeded into Whitehall and past the high security gate at the entrance to Downing Street. For once the current occupant at No. 10 was a hero of the protestors rather than a villain. He was the man who had dared to stand up and oppose the Americans.

Alison who had been busy chatting to Carol suddenly called to David who was a few paces in front.

"I hear you may be putting yourself forward for the Council."

"I am just thinking about it at the moment," he replied, stopping to allow the two women to catch him up.

Alison, who had the buggy to push made a brief stop. Being an attentive mother she pulled the canopy forwards a little over Amanda's head to protect her from the midday sun. The little girl looked up serenely as she cuddled her teddy bear.

"We are going to need a good candidate," said Alison while smiling at her daughter. "Winning the seat is not going to be easy. The Lib Dems have been working very hard in the Bassington Ward."

"It's a matter of campaigning on those local issues, which people are most concerned about," joined in Carol.

Satisfied that her daughter's head was well shielded from the sun, Alison was ready to continue marching.

"Unfortunately national politics can influence the outcome of the election," she said, ruefully. "Many a good local candidate can be beaten because the party at Westminster is unpopular.

"David has a much bigger problem that than," grinned Carol. "He needs someone to be his partner at the count."

"I'm sure there won't be a shortage of volunteers," laughed Alison.

Carol turned to give David a sly look.

"Looks as though you will be able to take your pick then. Is there anyone that takes your fancy?"

"Possibly," replied David, shyly, before turning his head away.

Tony arrived at that moment saving David from further embarrassment.

"Are you free to deliver some leaflets tonight?"

David readily agreed. The prospect of being in the company of his new found friends seemed preferable to sitting in his hotel room. It would also give him the opportunity to spend yet more time with Alison.

"Tomorrow night I am hoping to get a team to go out canvassing," continued Tony, pulling at his beard. "Can I count you in for that, too?"

David stopped to consider for a moment. Knocking on strangers' doors seemed a lot more daunting that dropping leaflets through letterboxes. However, he was happy to do what was necessary for the cause.

"I'll give it a go," he smiled.

Carol looked concerned.

"I don't think we should go bothering people on a Sunday night. It might just put them off voting for us."

"It's a good time as any to get our message across," replied Tony, dismissively. "I can't see anyone objecting on religious grounds in this day and age."

David could think of a number of people who were likely to get upset. However, as the Fellowship never used their vote anyway, it hardly mattered whether they were offended or not.

Soon the marchers were passing Trafalgar Square on the south side. Many of those not familiar with London stopped to admire one of the Capitol's great tourist attractions. Admiral Lord Nelson, diminutive when alive, was now 165 feet tall perched up on his famous column. At the base sat Edwin Lanseer's four impassive lions, much admired by very young visitors.

Soon the hordes of demonstrators were streaming along the Haymarket before turning into Piccadilly. Curious to see what was happening, many West End shoppers stopped to watch the never ending procession of people making their way steadily along. Respectable types in the main, chanting and carrying banners proclaiming their anger at the latest outbreak of American imperialism in the world.

"There's the Ritz," shouted Carol, pointing to her left.

Alison smiled.

"Anyone for tea?"

Tony who was walking hand-in-hand with Carol gave David a friendly nudge in the ribs.

"If Alison agrees to be your partner at the count I think you should offer to take her there as a reward."

"I'll start saving my pennies," grinned the would-be councillor.

Alison who was pushing Amanda's buggy with a single hand squeezed David's arm with her free one.

After the Ritz they passed Green Park. Those marchers who turned to their left would have spotted scores of sunbathers spread across the landscape, all stretched out on the grass enjoying the warm weather. A few were fully dressed but most were exposing large quantities of flesh.

Finally the Brockleby group arrived at Hyde Park Corner. Those protestors who had already filed through the gates were massing around a large stage. Looking less relaxed were two of the organisers who were busy checking the sound equipment for the speeches, which were soon to follow.

Amanda, who had seemed quite contented during the march suddenly became restless. Having spotted a small boy with a brightly coloured ice lolly, she decided to make demands for something similar a little too forcefully. Realising that Alison's attempts at consoling her daughter were failing, David chose to come to the rescue. Noticing an ice cream van close by he hurried off to join a rather lengthy queue.

The speeches had already started by the time David was finally served. A famous actress was the first to take the microphone followed by a senior army officer who had fought in the first Gulf War. When they had finished addressing the crowd each one left the stage to rapturous applause.

David returned holding three cornets with a large topping of ice cream and a chocolate stick in each. Realising the importance of making a favourable impression on Amanda he was relieved to see the little girl's eyes light up as she eagerly threw out her hand. Then sitting down next to Alison he tried to concentrate on what was being said on stage.

Speakers came and went until it was the turn of Robin Davies, the Liberal Democrat leader. As someone regularly demonised by the right wing press it was no surprise that he was a hero with the crowd. Just the announcement of his name was greeted by thunderous applause.

"Why this great dash to war?" he began, giving his vast audience a look of bewilderment. "Why weren't the weapons inspectors allowed to finish the job they had been entrusted to do? The White House need to wake up and realise that every time they kill an Iraqi fighter, America doesn't have one less problem it has got itself ten more. Friends and family of that dead man are soon lining up in some back room in Baghdad signing up to the Al-Qaeda."

Robin continued to give a powerful performance. Finally he left the stage to mighty cheers and clapping, which grew even louder as one great orator was replaced by another. The Prime Minister stood perfectly still as he waited for the sound to die away.

"We must never give in to terrorists," he began before pausing a moment. "And this country must never join a coalition which aims to unleash untold misery on innocent people."

The crowd erupted with delight and from then on they were in the palm of his hand. Seldom glancing down at his notes he charmed them with his smile and easy manner, before bringing them to their feet with a passionate attack on the War and the American President who launched it. He seemed the complete showman and this was a sublime performance.

"We must learn from the lessons of the past," he warned preparing to end his speech on the highest possible note. "Let us put an end to the bloodshed and wars that scarred the last century. We must build a brighter future and let peace and prosperity be our goal."

David felt deeply moved. He tried desperately to keep the tears from welling up in his eyes amidst the deafening sound of cheers and clapping. Until that very moment he had doubted the existence of charisma, but now he was a believer. If there was one person who could win an election for his party and keep Britain out of that unjust war it was surely this man.

On the way home the Brockleby group were fired up. Having been reminded by Bruce Shaw, the Prime Minister, that polling day was less than three weeks away they were all determined to increase their efforts to gain a Labour victory. They talked enthusiastically about producing more leaflets, canvassing every home in the constituency and trying to think up further issues that could win extra votes.

Goodbyes were not prolonged as the group dispersed at Brockleby station. Everyone agreed to meet up again at the club in several hours and they were intent on getting home to freshen up. It seemed a good idea to put the feet up for a while, before tramping the streets delivering leaflets.

Having missed her afternoon sleep, Amanda was starting to get fractious as children do. Alison was too preoccupied with soothing her daughter to pay any attention to the driver. It was very frustrating but David knew that he needed to be understanding in situations like this.

Once he had dropped his passengers off, David returned to the hotel. On entering his room he was about to head for the tea making facilities when he spotted a note lying on the bedside table. As he moved closer he read the message that was written in bold capitals:

PLEASE RING IAN PORTER URGENTLY

Lifting up the telephone, David was rather puzzled. He was sure he had not given his temporary address to any of the Fellowship and wondered how Ian had managed to trace him.

"Thank you for ringing back," said Ian on recognising the caller's voice. "I was just wondering whether you had come to your senses yet?"

"I never parted with them," answered David, frostily.

"That remains to be seen," replied Ian. "Anyway the purpose of my call was to speak with you about Ruth."

"What about her?" asked David, suspiciously.

Ian hesitated for a moment as he tried to choose his words carefully.

"Ruth is very distressed at the moment. She had been expecting to get married in a month's time, move into her new home and eventually start a family. Now suddenly she discovers that none of that is going to happen."

"I'm sorry that Ruth is upset but I am not entirely to blame," protested David, irritably. "Presumably you wouldn't want her to marry a worldlie like me?"

"Absolutely not," agreed Ian. "However, Ruth rang me up this morning and pleaded with me to try and set up a meeting between the three of us."

David was puzzled by the reply.

"Why should you be involved?" he asked, acidly. "Surely this matter concerns only Ruth and myself."

"For some reason Ruth has expressed a wish for me to be present and therefore I feel I am obliged to do as she has requested," explained Ian.

David paused briefly to consider the situation.

"OK then, so when and where do we meet?"

"Ruth is driving down from Birmingham on Tuesday and is having lunch at my house," replied Ian. "I suggest that you call round about two o'clock after we have eaten."

"Sounds fine," answered David without enthusiasm.

He was beginning to feel quite guilty as he laid down the phone. With so many things happening in his life over the past few days he had given little thought to Ruth and any anguish she might have been suffering. It had crossed his mind, however, that there was a pressing need to meet up and talk at some stage. Most importantly of course, a joint decision would have to be taken concerning the house they had bought together.

It was after nine when David and the others finally sat down in the bar with their drinks. The same group that had gone on the march gathered around two square tables, which they had joined together. Having delivered leaflets over a wide area of the Bassington Ward they were more than satisfied with the evening's work. It was time to relax and chill out.

"Sid Davidson isn't doing much to help in the election," whispered Carol, nodding her head disapprovingly towards a man with a very large stomach, who was sitting on a stool at the bar.

"He never does much work for the party," commented Tony in a low voice. "It's another reason why I don't want to see him elected to the Council."

"Careful what you say," muttered George. "He is heading this way."

Sid came to a halt at the end of the joined tables. He was a man in his fifties and would have been entirely bald but for a few wispy tufts of grey hair at the sides. Standing with a pint in front of his enormous pot belly, he smiled cheerfully at everyone.

"Been waving your banners about in Hyde Park today?"

Most of the group greeted him with a frosty stare.

"We were protesting against an unjust war," answered Tony, sourly.

Sid shook his head sadly.

"The Americans have stopped buying British because Bruce Shaw is refusing to send troops to Iraq."

"Sometimes in this life you have to stand up for your beliefs and do what is right," replied Jacqui.

"Mark my words," said Sid wagging a short stumpy finger. "Failing to back the Americans is going to cost Labour the election. The press are now calling Bruce Shaw a traitor for not helping our friends."

"I believe the British people will support our Prime Minister," smiled Tony. "Many of them are sick and tired of being the fifty-first state of America."

"You may be right. On the other hand, voters will feel angry if the Government's foreign policy ends up costing them their jobs," replied Sid, before finishing his pint and moving unsteadily in the direction of the gents' toilet.

"We've just got to stop him getting on the Council," remarked Kenny as Sid disappeared through the swing door.

"It isn't just his right wing views," added Tony. "I can imagine him turning up at committee meetings in a drunken stupor."

Suddenly heads began turning to David.

"We need you to come to the rescue," said Carol.

David looked thoughtful.

"If Sid and I were both to put our names forward, who decides which one of us is to be the Labour Party candidate?"

"It is down to the branch members," replied Tony, smoothing down his beard. "They are invited to a selection meeting in which Sid and you would each be given a set amount of time in which to speak and impress them. Once that process has finished votes are cast and whoever wins the ballot becomes the candidate."

David was beginning to feel apprehensive.

"How many people arc likely to be in the audience?"

"Possibly a hundred or so," said Jacqui. "Not too many."

David shuddered.

"Sounds an awful lot to me. The trouble is that I know practically nothing about local politics."

Tony produced a small booklet with a red paper cover and passed it across the table to David.

"This is the book that I promised you earlier," he said. "Read it through when you have a few moments. It explains everything you need to know about being a local councillor."

"That takes care of that side of things," replied David. "My big worry is that I have no solutions to the problems facing education, housing or anything else for that matter. They will just laugh at me in a selection meeting."

"Don't worry," said George, reassuringly. "We will give you tips on what to say."

Kenny laughed.

"Anyone who hangs around us for long enough will have politics pouring out of their ears. You will know far more than Sid Davidson ever knew."

"Of course, if Jacqui doesn't get to Parliament there won't be a vacancy on the Council," said George with a note of caution.

"She is going to win," shouted Kenny with a look of defiance.

First one, then all glasses were raised in the air, followed by loud cheers.

David felt on edge as he was driving Alison home. There was always a nagging fear in the back of his mind that he was going to say the wrong thing. It made him wonder whether he would ever feel totally relaxed in her company.

"There is one thing that I have been meaning to ask you," said Alison, suddenly. "Where are you living now?"

"The Brockleby Park Hotel," replied David, casually. "It's just a temporary measure until I can find somewhere permanent."

"Sounds very posh," laughed Alison.

"It should be at the prices they charge," answered David, acidly.

It was now well after ten and quite dark. There was not a soul in sight as they arrived at a stretch of road with high brick walls on either side. Both were formed in the front perimeters of businesses empty of their work forces over the weekend.

"Let's stop here for a while," suggested Alison.

David pulled up alongside the kerb. As soon as the car came to a halt, Alison unfastened her seat belt and then sat perfectly still for a moment. Staring straight ahead she seemed to be deep in thought.

"Do they serve midday meals in your hotel?" she murmured, finally.

"Of course," replied David.

Alison rested her head on David's arm.

"Can we have lunch there tomorrow instead of driving into the country?"

"If you like," replied David, turning and gently kissing her golden hair. "You will be very impressed with the restaurant."

"That's good," said Alison, dreamily. "Then can I come and see your room?"

"Of course," whispered David.

"And do you have a shower with hot water and a big comfortable bed?" giggled Alison.

"All of that and tea making facilities."

"Perfect," smiled Alison.

David's heart beat fast as he lowered his head to kiss her on the lips. As they embraced he could feel Alison's shoulder length hair on his neck and began to feel aroused by her soft body. He could smell her gentle feminine fragrance as he pushed his tongue through her slightly parted lips.

David was taken by surprise at Alison's strength. At one point she stretched her arms around him and squeezed so tightly he could barely breathe. Finally she drew herself away.

"I'd better be getting home. My mother will wonder what has happened to me."

"What time should I pick you up tomorrow?" asked David as he started the car.

"After eleven," replied Alison as she adjusted her hair. "Mark usually comes to collect Amanda about ten thirty."

For the rest of the journey they remained in silence. It had been a long and eventful day and the exhaustion was gradually creeping up on them. For David, it had ended perfectly.

Chapter Thirteen

After breakfast David turned his attention once more to finding permanent accommodation. Taking the local paper he had bought a few days earlier, he focused purely on those advertisements aimed at people wishing to share a house or flat. Any that looked hopeful he marked with a pen.

Having identified six possibilities he started to make telephone calls. By the time the job was completed he had managed to secure two appointments for the following evening. Both were to view flats in Brockleby and would mean sharing with several young people.

Satisfied with his work he lay on the bed and stared blankly up at the ceiling. He reflected on how Sundays would be much more leisurely now, free from the jurisdiction of the Fellowship. The day would no longer be taken up with travelling manically backwards and forwards to church to attend five separate meetings. It also meant the end of rising at the crack of dawn for the 'Breaking of the Bread' service.

David's room was in the process of being cleaned when he returned to the hotel with Alison later that morning. Retreating back down the stairs they made their way to the lounge and found two sumptuous armchairs to sit back in. For the moment at least, there were no other guests about.

"Tell me about the girl you were engaged to," said Alison when they were both settled.

David looked thoughtful. It was not a subject that he felt entirely comfortable about discussing. Deep down he was feeling guilty about Ruth and it concerned him that Alison would regard her as the innocent victim.

"Ruth was always so certain of everything," he said, finally. "She had allowed herself to be brainwashed by the Fellowship and seemed to believe implicitly in just about everything they had ever taught her."

Alison smiled sympathetically.

"And you were full of doubts."

"How can you not question?" said David looking mystified. "Take one example. It says in the Bible about loving our neighbour and yet I was taught by my parents never to sit down to eat with non-Fellowship. Isn't that a contradiction?"

Alison picked up her bag from the floor and placed it on a coffee table close by.

"Probably poor Ruth wasn't smart enough to think for herself. You must have been in love when you proposed to her."

David looked doubtful.

"It's not always like that with arranged marriages. Sometimes people agree to spend their lives together out of a duty to their parents."

As they were speaking a middle-aged couple entered the lounge and slowly made their way towards a settee by the window. The man was in shorts and had a strong muscular appearance, while the woman who was much smaller looked rather frail. Both were holding rolled up newspapers which they unfurled once the pair of them had sat down. David first remembered seeing the couple that morning at breakfast.

"So which one of you decided to break it off?" enquired Alison continuing her cross examination.

"The engagement inevitably came to an end once I had made the decision to leave the Fellowship," explained David. "The sect would have withdrawn from Ruth had she decided to go ahead and marry me."

"Weren't you sad?" asked Alison.

David considered his answer carefully before speaking.

"In a way but it was probably for the best," he said, finally.

Alison rested her head against the back of the armchair and gazed at David through partly closed eyes.

"How does Ruth feel about the situation?" she asked.

"She is quite upset," replied David, rubbing his hand along the arm of the chair. "Actually we are meeting on Tuesday to sit down and discuss a number of outstanding issues, such as the house that we bought together."

Alison smiled.

"I expect she will burst into tears and you will end up going back to her."

David shook his head firmly.

"It's all over between us. Anyway, I've fallen in love with somebody else now."

"Who?" enquired Alison, lowering her voice slightly as though a great secret was about to be revealed.

Before David had a chance to answer the proprietor came and stood by his chair.

"Just to let you know that the restaurant is now open for lunch Mr Chambers," he beamed.

"Thank you," answered David as he watched the genial hotel owner stroll up to the couple by the window to make the same announcement.

"Come on tell me," prompted Alison, eagerly.

David reached out and took her hand but said nothing. Having never been at ease in expressing his innermost thoughts he suddenly felt that his courage was deserting him. Therefore he decided to wait for one of their more intimate moments to open up his heart to her.

"I will tell you later," he said, getting to his feet. "Anyway let's go and get something to eat."

They were the first to arrive in the restaurant. David walked over to his usual table for two, happy in the knowledge that the chair opposite would be occupied for once. Smiling warmly, the waitress wandered across and presented them with menus.

"I love the mural," said Alison, studying the reproduction of Leonardo's *Last Supper* on the wall facing her.

"The proprietor was telling me that he commissioned a local artist to do the work," replied David, looking up momentarily from his menu.

Alison turned to smile at the waitress who had just placed a jug of water on the table.

"Could I have a glass of white wine please?" she asked.

"Make that a bottle," said David with a smile.

Once the waitress had gone Alison gave him a sly smile.

"You're not trying to get me drunk are you?"

David looked surprised.

"Why would I want to do that?"

Alison giggled.

"So you can lure me up to your room and take advantage of

my innocence."

David was uncertain how to respond. It was not the type of comment that would ever be made in Fellowship circles. Followers never discussed sex in a light-hearted manner, although married couples were encouraged to be active in between the sheets in order to procreate.

"We could go for a drive in the country this afternoon if you would prefer," suggested David.

Alison smiled as she shook her head.

"I want to see how comfortable that mattress is of yours first."

Conversation flowed easily between them during lunch. They both ate hearty meals, washed down by a bottle of white wine and a liqueur before finally leaving the restaurant and heading for the stairs. Linking hands they passed the proprietor in the hall who gave them a knowing look.

David turned the shiny Yale key in the lock and pushed open the door. In a couple of hours the room had become presentable once more now that the chambermaid had finished with it. She had changed the sheets, vacuumed the carpet and put a number of items back in their rightful place.

"Pure luxury," sighed Alison as she lay on top of the bed and bounced gently up and down.

David looked down on her fondly.

"You really are like Aphrodite."

Alison gave him a quizzical look.

"Why do you say that?"

"She was the Greek goddess of love, beauty and fertility," replied David as he laid down by her side. "When we were at school it was the name that I gave you in my daydreams."

Alison snuggled up to him.

"Did you fancy me?"

David tilted his head and kissed the top of her hair.

"It went far deeper than that. I would think about you all day and then dream about you at night."

Alison stared at him aghast.

"Were you in love with me?"

"I was crazy about you," smiled David.

Alison giggled.

"Actually, I quite liked you but not at seriously at that."

David stared up at the ceiling.

"It seems unbelievable that we are together like this. Probably at any moment I am going to wake up and find it has just been another of those dreams."

Alison laid her arm across David's chest.

"Anyway, who is this woman you have fallen in love with now? Downstairs you promised to tell me later."

David caressed her arm.

"It's still Aphrodite," he whispered. "I only want the very best."

Suddenly tears began to well up in Alison's eyes.

"You are putting a great weight of responsibility on my shoulders."

David looked surprised.

"Why do you say that?"

"Because I'm so frightened of hurting you," she answered with a sob.

"I didn't mean to upset you," answered David, who was inwardly cursing himself for having said the wrong thing.

Suddenly Alison sat up.

"Can I use your shower?"

David shrugged.

"Feel free."

David continued to lie on the bed as Alison disappeared into the en suite bathroom. After a few minutes he heard the shower curtain being drawn across the railing above and the hiss of water spraying out from the hose. Surprised that these sounds were so clearly audible he turned his head to see that the door had been left wide open.

"Oh David!" called out Alison in that distinctive way, common in games of Hide and Seek. "Come and join me."

David's pulse began to race. It was impossible to think clearly as he stood to his feet and headed towards the bathroom. As he advanced further he could hear Alison quietly humming to herself.

Outside the shower cubicle clothes were scattered on the floor. David stood still for a moment and watched the movements of the shadowy silhouette behind the curtain. Then slowly he started to undress.

However, panic set in when he came to pull down his boxer shorts. Much to his embarrassment he had an enormous erection standing in a ten o'clock position. For a moment he couldn't decide whether to make a hasty retreat or to stand his ground.

All of a sudden the shower curtains opened about a foot and Alison's face appeared in the gap. Studying David from the head downwards, her eyes came to rest on a part of his anatomy just below the naval.

"My word," she giggled. "We won't be able to stand too close together in here."

Clearly the shower was never designed for a woman and a man beside her with an untimely erection, to indulge in excessive movement. Instead they made do by standing as close as circumstances would allow and let the warm water cascade over them. Passionately they kissed as each explored the other's body with their hands.

"Let's go to bed and make love," whispered Alison, finally.

First one and then the other stepped out on to the bathroom floor and grabbed large white towels supplied by the hotel. As they dried themselves off, David's eyes were drawn towards Alison's naked form. It was not the skinny shape of a supermodel but rather more curvy, voluptuous and infinitely more desirable.

David felt weak at the knees as he surveyed her soft creamy white body from head to toe. He watched with fascination as her perfectly rounded breasts swung gently from side to side while she rubbed her back with the bath towel. His eyes rested momentarily on the pink thimble shaped nipples, which struck out so boldly and unashamedly. Further down he admired her narrow slender hips, the long shapely legs and the small bush of her pubic hair, which seemed just a shade darker than the flaxen hair which flowed from her head.

David now had a secret that he had no intention of sharing with Alison. She had been the very first woman that he had ever seen naked in the flesh. Of course he had looked at photos in books and pornographic magazines that had been thrown away in public places. Nothing though could possibly compare to the real thing.

Single Fellowship men have little opportunity to see nude women. Sex before marriage is strictly forbidden and the same is true of popping out on a Friday night to watch strippers parade their wares on stage. Their best hope probably rests on spying through bedroom keyholes on unsuspecting family members getting undressed.

"Do you like my body?" asked Alison when she had finished drying herself and had hung up the towel. "Mark used to say that I was overweight."

"I think you're gorgeous," smiled David, dreamily, as he slowly cast his eye over her once more. "Even better than Aphrodite herself."

Alison reached out her hand to David.

"Come on."

Blissfully they returned to the bed and lay down in their original positions. Alison kissed David forcefully on the lips and taking his hand placed it on the lower part of her pubic hair. Then she slowly rubbed his finger over a small slightly moist area.

"Just keep doing that," she whispered.

David duly obliged and he watched longingly as she shut her eyes contentedly and experienced the sensation down below. Obeying an uncontrollable urge he leaned over and kissed the beautiful pink nipples that were now projecting upwards. Then gently rolled his tongue over each of them.

"That's nice," sighed Alison as she stroked the back of his head. "Now get on top of me."

It was the moment of truth. Having never had intercourse or been given any tuition on the art of making love, he would have to rely on Alison's guidance. He inwardly cursed himself for his lack of experience.

Quickly David got the general idea. Thrusting himself gently upwards he looked lovingly down at Alison while trying hard not to ejaculate too early. Unable to hang on any longer he remained still on his love partner and felt the pleasurable sensation of an orgasm.

For a while they lay side by side staring up at the ceiling. Eventually Alison turned her head and kissed David on the cheek.

"Thank you darling, that was perfect," she murmured.

David was thrilled and taking her hand he began to caress her fingers.

"Hopefully as perfect as you," he smiled.

Alison patted his arm playfully with her other hand and then her expression became a little more serious.

"You know I was lying there a few moments ago and thinking about our schooldays."

"Most of my memories depress me," replied David, mournfully.

Alison smiled and squeezed his hand affectionately.

"You know the prettiest girl in our class was Rebecca, Simon's sister," she continued. "Nearly all the boys fancied her."

David gave her a surprised look.

"I never realised that."

"Poor Rebecca," said Alison, sadly. "It seems so ironic that the boy she fancied didn't reciprocate because he was crazy about me."

David sighed.

"I had no idea about that until about two weeks ago. Rebecca just happened to mention it when Simon and I went down to visit her in Broadstairs."

"Typical man," replied Alison with scorn. "You must have been the only person in the class not to realise."

David gave her a quizzical look.

"Let's complete the picture then. Who did you actually fancy?"

Alison gave him a sly smile.

"I had a crush on Mr King, the gym teacher. He always looked great in shorts."

David was disappointed.

"I always hoped you were secretly in love with me."

Alison smiled sympathetically.

"I always thought you were quite cute. The problem was that you always blushed and seemed uncomfortable whenever we spoke."

David suddenly found himself taking an interest in Alison's naked body once more. A certain very sensitive organ began to stir as his eyes fixed on those beautiful rounded breasts. His heart beat faster as he leaned over to kiss her passionately on the lips.

"I want to make love again," he whispered.

"So do I," giggled Alison as she placed her arms around David's neck. "Then after we have taken afternoon tea in the lounge downstairs you had better drive me home."

"I prefer your first suggestion to the second," replied David as he tenderly kissed her neck. "I hate it when we have to separate."

Alison began to run her hand up and down David's thigh.

"We won't be away from each other for very long," she laughed. "You and I are out canvassing tonight remember?"

It was just after four when they finally parted. Before getting out of the car Alison kissed David quickly on the cheek and was about to open the door when she had a sudden thought.

"Thank you for a lovely afternoon by the way."

David merely smiled by way of reply but had something more serious to say.

"Look I said that I was in love with you," he began, hesitantly. "Do you feel the same about me?"

Alison was silent for a moment as she contemplated the question.

"Please don't rush me," she answered, finally. "Let's just take things as they go."

It wasn't what David wanted to hear but it was far from being a rejection. When he actually came to consider the situation while driving back to the hotel, it seemed unreasonable to have expected her to fall in love with him so early in their relationship. It was really a matter of remaining patient for the time being.

David recognised most of the faces when he arrived with Alison at the club. It was early evening and only the keenest activists ever volunteered to go out canvassing. Some of the other less committed party members, however, might look in a bit later for a drink at the bar.

"Where are we going tonight?" enquired Alison when she spotted Kenny and George sitting at a nearby table.

"Upper Oakham," replied Kenny with a scowl. "Where all the snobs live."

Alison groaned.

"I hate it around there."

David smiled but said nothing. He was only too familiar with the area having lived in it all his life, and had only recently bought a property in one of the more exclusive roads.

George turned to him and shook his head.

"For the first time canvasser it is a baptism of fire. You won't come across many Labour Party supporters."

"And many are pig ignorant," added Jacqui Dunn who had just strolled across the room to join them. "It seems that the richest people are always the rudest. Give me the council house tenants every time."

George and Kenny nodded.

Tony who had been busy sorting out a pile of papers on a separate table, suddenly stood up and began to make his presence felt. Having invited the assembled party workers to select a partner he then proceeded to distribute a sheet of paper to everyone. Printed on one side were the names and addresses of eligible voters in any given street in the constituency. With sheets for both even and odd numbers, the pair that had requested to be together could concentrate on canvassing different sides of the same street.

David was familiar with the road that he and Alison had been allocated. Before moving into the hotel he had driven down it daily on the way to work. The large detached houses were probably home to some of the wealthiest people in Brockleby judging by the number of gleaming top of the range cars parked in every drive.

David came to a stop at the top of the road and switched off the engine. Then siting back in his seat he took a deep breath in order to calm himself before facing the ordeal ahead. It was something he often did in preparation for sales presentations.

"Are you worried?" asked Alison, showing concern.

David turned and gave her a sly smile.

"I'd rather be back in the hotel making love to you."

Alison leaned over and kissed him.

"We must do it again soon."

David reached over to the back seat and grabbed the two clipboards they had been given.

"Come on," he said, resolutely. "Let's get it over with and then we can go back to the club for a drink."

David felt a little less confident once Alison had crossed the road to do her side. With no previous canvassing experience and with little more than a vague awareness of the policies which the Labour Party were fighting the election on, he felt he had been thrown in at the deep end. He dreaded that his ignorance would be discovered by unforeseen questions that were likely to be thrown at him.

The first house that he came to was a large mock Tudor property. Stopping for a moment he peered through the vertical bars of the tall cast iron gates and noted the inevitable gleaming cars in the drive. There were three and each one looked as though it had just arrived from the showroom.

A few moments later David was stood on the doorstep pressing the bell. When there was no immediate reply he was tempted to walk away but then he heard a scuffling sound from within. Slowly the door opened and all of a sudden he was face to face with a middle-aged man in shorts.

"Good evening," smiled David, cheerfully. "I am calling on behalf of the Labour Party."

The man stood and glared at him.

"Bugger off," he said sternly and slammed the door.

It was hardly the start that David had hoped for. However, turning to his canvass sheet he had little difficulty deciding which box to tick in describing the resident's voting intentions. Clearly 'wouldn't say' seemed to sum it up pretty well.

Walking back along the drive he smiled to himself. It occurred to him that if everyone slammed the door in his face he would be finished in no time. On the negative side though, such an outcome was hardly likely to further Jacqui's electoral prospects.

David received a friendlier welcome at the next house. After introducing himself the elderly lady shook his hand warmly and invited him into the hall.

"Actually I'm a Liberal Democrat, but, I can't decide what to do in this election," she said, thoughtfully. "Do I vote tactically or support the principles which I believe in?"

As a person who was used to moral dilemmas, David was sympathetic.

"What do you consider to be the most important issue in this election Mrs Cook?" enquired David, memorising the name from his canvass sheet.

Mrs Cook's genial smile gave way to a look of anger.

"The Iraq War," she replied without hesitation. "The situation will only get worse if British troops are sent out there to support the Americans."

David nodded.

"I went on the anti-war march yesterday with some of my friends."

"Me too," replied Mrs Cook, eagerly, with the twinkle returning to her eyes.

Soon they were chatting like lifelong friends. Time passed quickly and eventually it was Mrs Cook who was responsible for bringing the conversation to a close.

"Hadn't you better go and speak with some of my neighbours now?" she smiled.

"It was almost with sadness that David began to walk towards the door.

"Can we count on your support then?" he enquired, turning around on the doorstep to face his new friend.

Mrs Cook beamed at him.

"You've finally managed to convince me," she said as they shook hands once more. "The Liberal Democrats haven't much hope of winning Brockleby so I am going to vote for Jacqui Dunn."

David was less successful at the next house. An attractive middle-aged woman who was more than happy to talk made it perfectly clear where her political allegiance lay.

"I shall be voting Tory because they have promised to lower taxes," she said.

David gave her a suspicious look.

"How can they afford to do that and take Britain to war at the same time?"

The Tory voter had a ready reply.

"By cutting benefits to all these scroungers."

David considered arguing that this was likely to increase crime rates but thought better of it. Instead he set off in search of someone with a more open mind.

By the time Alison had finished, David had called on less than half the houses on his side of the road. Making a joint decision to call it a day, they linked hands and made their way back to the car. The prospect of a drink in the bar seemed too enticing to put off any longer.

The mood back at the club was one of despondency. Sitting

around the two tables that had been put together again, Labour's keenest activists in Brockleby stared forlornly at their canvass sheets. It had not been a successful night for any of them.

"Let's try another area tomorrow," suggested Kenny. "Upper Oakham is too depressing."

There were nods of agreement all around.

"Actually," began Tony with a sly smile. "We are getting help this week from some supporters who are coming up from the coast. I shall send them to Upper Oakham and we can concentrate on friendlier territory."

"Sounds like a good idea," laughed Jacqui. "Is everyone free tomorrow evening?"

David shook his head.

"You will have to count me out. Unfortunately I am flat hunting."

George immediately pricked up his ears.

"What sort of thing are you looking for?"

David stared down into his pint of beer.

"I'd like to move into a house or flat and share with a few people."

George and Kenny exchanged glances.

"When my mother died she left me her house," explained George once he felt he had Kenny's support. "But instead of selling it I decided to live there and charge a reasonable rent to any friend who was looking for a roof over their head."

"Do you happen to have a vacancy at the moment?" asked David, eagerly.

"You are in luck," replied Kenny. "At present only George and I are living there so we could easily fit another person in."

George smiled as he rubbed his hands together.

"Feel free to come and take a look."

If was an offer that David readily accepted. He was beginning to feel very much at home in this little group and the thought of moving in with two of them seemed the answer to a prayer. Not that he had been doing much praying in the past week, however. It was almost as though religion had become an irrelevance in his life.

Having been given the address, David arranged to call in on George and Kenny on his way home from work on the following evening. Then if everything seemed satisfactory there would be no need to keep the appointments to view the two flats, which he had arranged over the telephone. It would leave the rest of the evening free to go out canvassing again.

While driving Alison home, David stopped the car in the very same spot as he had the night before. Once again it was quiet and there was not a person to be seen in any direction.

With some urgency both he and Alison unfastened their seat belts before falling into each other's arms. As they kissed their tongues touched and David could taste Alison's saliva. Then he slid his hand beneath her T-shirt and moved it gently upwards, exploring the soft warm flesh with all its contours. Suddenly the tips of his fingers came into contact with the underside of the right breast.

"You have reached a point where my T-shirt becomes a little tighter," Alison giggled as she lifted the garment just above her nipples. Then sinking back in the passenger seat and half closing her eyes, she enjoyed the sweet sensation as David tenderly kissed her breasts.

Eventually Alison leaned forward and checked her wristwatch.

"You had better take me home soon," she whispered. "I have to be up early in the morning."

Later that evening David lay on top of his hotel bed and pondered on a question that had been going around in his head. If the Fellowship were right he would have to endure the agony of eternal damnation for rejecting their teachings. On the other hand, did he really want to end up in Paradise without the woman he loved.

Finally he dreamt that he and Alison were lying in a bed making love. Suddenly he became aware that towering flames had surrounded them and high above Ian Porter was looking down wearing a smug smile. Dressed in a white gown, the priest had managed to sprout wings and was gently floating skywards.

"Good bye David," he called out. "Don't say I didn't warn you."

Chapter Fourteen

On Monday morning David arrived at work dressed in his best suit. Having won the order for his company to furnish Conningvale House he now had to return to discuss matters in greater detail. Seated at his desk he began gathering together all the paperwork required for the meeting. Conscious that this was likely to be his last week as an employee of Fine Choice Furniture made him no less determined to give of his very best.

Reading through his notes reminded him that Shirley Bromage had requested to see a particular dining chair she had noticed in the brochure. Having finished his work on the clerical side he left his office to go and find a sample from the warehouse. Luckily it was a stock item so it was just a matter of helping himself.

Carrying the chair back he happened to pass the loading bay. As usual the warehouse staff were busy conveying furniture on to one of the company's seven and a half ton vehicles in readiness for the days deliveries to customers. Close by Donald Perkins, the despatch manager was in discussion with the driver as they stood studying a piece of paper together.

"Jesus!" exclaimed a young man who was helping to carry a wardrobe. It was his first day and the item of furniture was far heavier than he had expected.

Donald looked horrified. Like most of the Fellowship devotees he could tolerate a reasonable amount of swearing but blasphemy was a different matter. Angrily he hurried over to the young man to have a word.

"This is a Christian company and you must not take the name of our Lord in vain on these premises."

The young man who was still struggling with the wardrobe seemed to be taken by surprise. However, concerned for his job security he muttered an apology just before disappearing inside the vehicle with his cumbersome load.

David walked away disgusted. With so much suffering in the

world he wondered why the utterance of a solitary word mattered so much. It was just typical of the small minded mentality of the Fellowship.

Having placed the sample chair that he intended to show to Mrs Bromage, inside the company's transit van, David returned to his office. He had barely sat down though before Maurice Hopkins poked his head around the door.

"Could I have a word please?" requested the sales manager before bringing the rest of his body into the room.

"You will have to make it brief," answered David, shortly. "I am setting off for Conningvale House in about ten minutes."

Maurice looked down sheepishly at his feet. Breaking bad news to the staff was a part of his job, which made him feel distinctly uncomfortable. At heart he was a kindly soul and hated upsetting anyone.

"Samuel Boswell would like Des and I to visit the customer instead of you," he said, pulling nervously at the lobe of his ear.

"That is crazy," replied David in astonishment. "I've done a great deal of preparation for this meeting. What is Samuel's reasoning for this decision?"

Maurice turned his head sadly towards the window. For a moment there was silence as he tried to think of the kindest way to phrase his explanation.

"Samuel feels that if you aren't going to be with us for much longer, then it is better that I take over the order as soon as possible," he replied at last.

David stared at him suspiciously.

"In that case if I am going to hand over to you, wouldn't it make a great deal more sense for the pair of us to go together?"

Maurice shrugged.

"Yes but it isn't down to me," he answered, sadly. "Anyway you must excuse me. Once I have managed to round up Des, the pair of us had better be on our way."

David was beginning to feel like an outcast and the situation was to get worse. Having no sooner stepped into the canteen at lunchtime to eat his sandwiches he sensed something was not quite right. Several colleagues watched him keenly as he crossed the floor and sat down on a table with two of the sales administrators.

"We do not eat with non-believers," announced Donald Perkins who was standing by the microwave waiting for something to heat. "I suggest you go and use the warehouse canteen."

David decided not to budge. He was feeling in a confrontational mood and the only way they were going to get him to move was to use force. However, knowing the Fellowship, he could be fairly sure that the chances of being physically ejected were highly improbable.

"You appear not to have heard me," continued Donald realising that he was being ignored. "We would all like you to leave."

David had never liked Donald Perkins. He was one of those self-righteous, Bible quoting individuals that most normal people give a wide berth to. His bullying behaviour in the warehouse that morning was typical of the man.

Slowly David stood up and tucked his chair under the table. Then putting on his most menacing glare he strolled over to Donald and stopped only when they were inches apart. Everybody else in the room was now transfixed as the two men stood eyeball to eyeball.

"I'm warning you," said Donald, anxiously. "You will end up in court if you hit me. I have a number of witnesses in here."

David who was a good six inches taller continued to glare down menacingly at Donald.

"I can think of nothing more nauseating that having to spend eternity with a creep like you," he said, finally before turning around and then going back to his seat.

After that Donald became subdued. However, concerned at the prospect of having to eat with a 'worldlie', the two sales administrators got up sheepishly and moved to another table. One murmured an apology before leaving David to eat by himself.

The afternoon dragged on. The earlier events of the day had made David feel even more desperate to find alternative employment. It was just a matter of where to start looking but the name 'Robsons' kept coming into his head. Could Fine Choice's main competitor actually come to his rescue he wondered.

Having hesitated for a while he finally picked up the telephone. After stating his reason for calling he was transferred to the sales manager, a person who introduced himself in a cheery well-spoken voice.

"You are through to Roger Green. How can I help you?"

"Do you have any vacancies for salesmen?" enquired David, attempting to sound more confident than he actually felt.

"I'm sorry old chap but we aren't looking to recruit at this precise moment in time," replied Roger. "However if you would like to send me your CV I will happily keep it on file."

This wasn't the sort of response that David had been hoping for so he decided to play his trump card.

"I do have experience in selling furniture to your type of markets," he said, eagerly. "For the past five years I have been a salesman for Fine Choice."

There was a brief silence on the other end of the line as Roger took into account this information.

"What exactly is your position in the company?" he asked with a little more enthusiasm in his voice.

"I am the sales rep for the whole of the south-east," answered David, proudly. "Since taking over the area turnover has more than trebled."

"Splendid," replied Roger drawing out the word in a hearty voice. "So why exactly to you want to leave?"

David had naturally anticipated this question and had jotted down his answer on a scrap of paper.

"I am keen to join a more progressive company. One which has the ambitions to match my own," he read out grandly.

"Super," exclaimed Roger. "If you have your diary handy perhaps we could arrange to meet up."

David punched the air as soon as he put down the telephone. An interview with Roger Green had been booked for Thursday morning and a gut feeling was sending him positive signals. Already he was getting excited about the possibility of a fresh challenge.

After work he kept his appointment to drop in on Kenny and George. They lived in a quiet road of semi-detached houses all built in the same style. The cars that were parked in the drives, however, suggested that the residents enjoyed a more modest lifestyle to those in Upper Oakham.

George gave David a guided tour of his home. Most of the

rooms were quite large but much of the space was taken up with boxes of printed material. It was rather like being back at Labour party headquarters.

"As councillors, Kenny and I have so much information to read," explained George, apologetically. "Every week a van arrives with several cartons of literature."

"Do you ever get round to reading it all?" asked David in amazement.

George gave a guilty smile.

"Not a chance. What with work and all those committee meetings that we have to attend. There just aren't enough hours in the day."

When David had seen the whole house he and George joined Kenny in the sitting room for a cup of tea. It was difficult to stay off the subject of politics for too long but, business had be to given priority on this occasion. The weekly rent, housework duties and rules that had to be obeyed were all matters which needed to be discussed.

"Are you interested then?" asked George, finally.

David smiled broadly.

"Seems perfect."

The deal now done he arranged to move in on Saturday morning. David would have preferred to have made it sooner but the hotel room had been booked up until Friday night. The only consolation was that he would be free from cleaning and catering for himself for a few more days.

Canvassing went well that evening. The voters in the area were much more sympathetic towards Labour than those from Upper Oakham and nearly everybody returned to the club in an upbeat mood. Once again the group were daring to talk about possible victory.

Only David was feeling a little downcast. He was missing Alison who had been prevented from coming out after her mother had gone down with a heavy cold and there had been nobody else willing to baby-sit. For once there would be no beautiful period of intimacy on the way home.

The following morning passed without incident. At lunchtime David decided to eat his sandwiches in his office rather than risk another confrontation in the canteen. Although it seemed rather like conceding defeat to Donald Perkins he realised that there were far more important things to worry about.

His afternoon at work was short. Soon after lunch he tidied up his desk before setting off for his appointment with Ian Porter and Ruth. Although not a meeting that he had been relishing, he knew there could be no running away from it.

Ian greeted him at the front door with little more than a half smile. Then having followed the Fellowship priest into his sitting room, David came face to face with the woman he had once been expected to marry. It had been little over a week since they had last seen each other but somehow it seemed much longer.

"Are you beginning to regret your recent actions?" asked Ian once they were both seated.

"Not in the least," answered David, scornfully. "In fact I am relieved to be free of your closeted little world."

Ian gave him a steely look.

"I take that to mean that you don't wish to repent and return to the Lord."

David nodded.

"Nothing has changed since we last met."

"What about me?" joined in Ruth. "Doesn't it matter to you that our engagement has come to an end?"

David felt uneasy as he turned to look at Ruth. There were distinct traces of redness around her eyes, which suggested recent tears had been shed. In addition to that her facial expressions for once didn't seem to exude excessive self-confidence.

"Blame the Fellowship," answered David. "It is they that forbid their followers from marrying non-believers."

Ian was about to speak when the door, which was slightly ajar, suddenly flew open. Standing in the hall holding a silver tray and smiling cheerfully was Ian's elderly mother. For several minutes the conversation was adjourned as Mrs Porter senior hobbled across the room before carefully laying three cups and a plate of cakes on the table.

"Don't worry Mum," said Ian a little brusquely. "Don't pour out the tea. Because David has forsaken the Lord, Ruth and I won't be able to eat and drink with him."

When the old lady had finally left the room Ian turned accusingly on David.

"I believe that it isn't us Fellowship followers who are responsible for the break-up of your engagement but rather a certain blonde-haired lady."

A surprised looked appeared on David's face.

"What are you talking about?"

"Somebody saw you on Sunday evening in Upper Oakham holding hands with this young lady."

David gave the priest a look of defiance.

"Is there a law against it then?"

"You bastard!" cried Ruth, before running out of the room sobbing.

Ian and David sat silently as they listened to the thud of her feet as she ran up the stairs to the bathroom.

"Sometimes these things just happen," muttered David.

"They do when you don't have God in your life," replied Ian curtly. "And are you happy to be damned for eternity for the sake of this woman?"

"I'd rather rot in Hell with her than spend an eternity in Paradise with a crowd of bigots," retorted David, bitterly.

Ian was taken aback by this outburst. Briefly he considered continuing the argument and even throwing in a few biblical quotations for good measure, but quickly dismissed the idea. Clearly the young man was beyond redemption.

"We may have found a buyer for your house by the way," he said deciding to change the subject. "Jeremy Wright is getting married in a few weeks and would like to make an offer."

"Even without seeing it?" asked David in surprise.

"Your dad showed him and his future wife around yesterday and it seems that they were both impressed."

"Sounds good," replied David. "We can at least avoid estate agents fees."

"Ruth is pleased," said Ian, unsmiling. "The house is just one more sad reminder of your engagement and she is keen to be rid of it as quickly as possible."

Ian went to a drawer to fetch a pen and paper.

"I'll jot down Jeremy's number so that you can get in touch."

David got to his feet and waited for the priest to finish writing. It was with a little sadness that he cast his eyes around the room for the very last time. In one corner was the piano made in mahogany with half a dozen photographs of family members lined along the top.

Near to where he was standing stood the brightly polished table. In the centre was the silver tray with a plate of cream cakes that had remained untouched besides which, was the teapot and the three teacups which had not been used. Closer to the edge was a small pile of religious tracts and then the black leather Bible that Ian was forever thumbing through.

Finally the priest handed over the slip of paper before leading his visitor into the hall.

"Is the Brockleby Park Hotel comfortable?" he asked, casually.

"Very," replied David, giving Ian a curious look. "I was amazed to find a message from you when I returned to my room at the weekend. How on earth did you know where I was staying?"

Ian grinned as he opened the door.

"One of the Fellowship just happened to be passing as you were about to drive out of the entrance on Friday morning."

"Typical," muttered David as he strolled down the garden path. "That lot never miss anything."

Returning to his hotel room David headed straight for the shower. Relieved that the dreaded meeting was now behind him he began to sing out loud as the warm water flowed over his body. It was hardly surprising therefore, that he failed to hear a timid little tap on the door.

However, he couldn't fail to hear the harder more persistent raps which followed. Quickly climbing out of the shower he rubbed himself down before slipping on a white hotel bath robe. Then grabbing a comb from the dressing table he tried to tidy his damp dishevelled hair.

Having checked that his private parts were fully covered he opened the front door. Half expecting to see the chambermaid with her brush and cleaning trolley, he was taken aback to see Ruth standing on the landing. Even more surprising was the sweet smile on her face.

"Can I come in," she said, meekly.

David nodded as he stood aside.

Walking slowly up to the window Ruth drew back the curtain

very slightly and stared thoughtfully out.

"Sorry I swore at you earlier," she said, finally.

"You had every right," replied David taking a seat on the edge of the bed. "It must be terrible telling all those people that the wedding has been cancelled."

"People are being very kind and understanding," answered Ruth who seemed to rub a tear from the corner of her eye. "Anyway let's change the subject. Tell me the name of the lady with the blonde hair."

David was beginning to feel uncomfortable.

"Alison."

Ruth nodded.

"Tell me a few things about her."

"What can I say?" answered David with a shrug. "She works in a library, has a little girl called Amanda and supports the Labour Party."

Ruth turned away from the window and sat down in an armchair facing David.

"Is she an unmarried mother?"

"Yes she is," answered David, proudly. "And a very good one, too."

Ruth took a look around the room before her eyes came to rest on the television set.

"Is she a Christian?"

"I really don't know. Anyway it doesn't bother me whether she is or not."

"That's because the Devil has got hold of you," answered Ruth, sadly.

Irritated at this line of questioning and the criticism of his new lifestyle, David couldn't stop himself from going on the offensive.

"Why do you always have to be so morally superior?" he said, accusingly. "Has it ever occurred to you that the Fellowship have got it all wrong?"

Ruth gave her ex-fiancé a long suffering look.

"Anyone who follows the teachings of the Bible has to be right. After all, it's the word of the Lord."

David immediately seized on this remark.

"But we are told in the Gospels to sell our goods and give to

186

the poor. It seems to me that the Fellowship's main concern in life is to see who has the flashiest car parked outside the church."

Ruth became indignant.

"Our cars are used to do the Lord's work. They are needed to get everybody to worship each day."

The argument failed to impress David.

"It just amazes me. The Fellowship despise the world and yet they crave for all the finest material possessions it can produce. Top of the range cars, large detached houses and the very best furniture money can buy."

Ruth was taken aback by the passion in David's voice. However, it was something else that prompted her to cut short the visit and head off back to Birmingham. The bathrobe that her host was wearing looked perilously close to falling open at any minute.

"I must be on my way now," she said, making certain not to look down. "I shall always mention you in my prayers. Remember that it is never too late to repent."

David suddenly felt sad to think that he would never see her again.

"I'm sorry that things didn't work out for us."

"It was probably for the best," she said with a smile. "Better to part now than after we were married."

David bent down and kissed her on the cheek.

"Take care."

"And you," replied Ruth.

"Are your parents planning to introduce you to any young men in the near future?"

Fearful that the bathrobe would fall open at any second Ruth edged her way towards the door.

"I expect so," she laughed. "They must be desperate to get rid of me."

David stood at the window watching as Ruth got in her car and drove away. Although relieved that a line had finally been drawn under their relationship he knew that a part of him would always feel guilty. It was something he would just have to live with.

That evening he went out with the canvassing team again. It turned out to be another very good session and everyone returned to the club later sensing that the tide was beginning to turn in their favour. Earlier in the day a bomb had exploded in the centre of Baghdad killing many innocent victims. Having seen the carnage on the television news many voters were ready to express their anger on the doorstep.

"What are your feelings Jacqui?" asked Carol, looking thoughtfully at the local party candidate. "Are we going to win?"

Jacqui gave her a blank look.

"It's so hard to say. A lot of people are still trying to make up their minds."

"It's a matter of getting our supporters to come out and vote," said Tony with a look of determination. "I don't care whether we have to physically drag them down to the polling station."

David was only partly listening. For the second evening in a row Alison had been unable to find a babysitter to stand in for her mother who was still unwell. Suddenly he was beginning to miss her desperately.

Carol who had been studying him for a while finally stood up and walked past the back of his chair.

"Can I show you something?" she whispered in his ear.

Slightly puzzled David got to his feet and joined her in front of the main notice board just inside the entrance.

"Why are you sitting there looking like a schoolboy who has lost his pocket money?" Carol muttered, while appearing to read a leaflet which had been pinned up.

David was taken aback.

"I'm fine."

"No you're not," answered Carol with a half smile. "Why don't you buy a box of chocolates at the bar and then go round to see Alison?"

David felt uncomfortable.

"Do you think she would mind?"

Carol gave him a sly sideways look.

"Of course not. She is probably wondering where the bloody hell you have got to."

Deciding to take the advice David was soon standing outside Alison's front door. It had occurred to him in the car that she may have decided to go to bed early, so it was a relief to see that the front room light was on. Then after a few nervous moments of indecision he finally rang the ball.

Suddenly through the frosted glass in the door he saw a moving figure.

"Who is it?" called out Alison.

"It's only David."

For a moment he watched as Alison from within fiddled with a chain. Then at last the door swung open and they came face to face.

"I hope I haven't called too late," said David, slightly awkwardly.

"No it's all right," smiled Alison. "Come on in."

She turned to lead the way down the hall and into a slightly cluttered up sitting room.

"Excuse the mess but I haven't had time to tidy up. Amanda has only just gone to bed."

"Don't worry," replied David, sympathetically. "I've come to see you not the inside of your house."

Alison immediately began to fold up the ironing board in the middle of the room. Lined up along the back of the settee were an assortment of clothes that looked recently pressed and on the floor, a plastic orange basket full of jumbled up garments awaiting the same treatment. Then there were toys of various descriptions scattered about in every corner.

"How is the canvassing going?" enquired Alison as she began to clear away.

"We've had two very successful evenings," replied David sitting down in an armchair suddenly free of books, which had been piled up on the seat. "Also a number of people have been arriving from outside Brockleby to give us a hand."

"I'm surprised that you didn't want to stay on at the club tonight," said Alison as she began to pick up toys from the floor and place them into a large cardboard box.

"I thought I would call on you instead," replied David.

Alison smiled as the clearing up operation continued.

"I'm flattered."

"How is your mum by the way?" enquired David. "Is her cold any better?"

Alison turned to him looking guilty.

"Very well thank you. Actually I only said she was unwell in order to get out of canvassing."

"You naughty thing," grinned David. "I shall have to tell on you."

"They just can't expect me to go out every night," explained Alison. "The ironing and cleaning won't do itself."

At that moment she bent down to pick up something by David's foot. The neck of her red jumper she was wearing hung down to reveal a sizeable portion of her breasts. Quite clearly she was taking a break from wearing a bra.

"I agree that Tony and Jacqui can be quite demanding," replied David as he felt a sudden stirring in his boxer shorts.

When everything was finally shipshape Alison flaked out on the settee.

"Come and sit here," she said, patting the cushion beside her.

David was quick to accept the invitation and soon they were in each other's arms. To begin with the kisses were quite gentle but passions were raised a notch as Alison became more responsive.

"Let's go to bed," she whispered as David's hand beneath her red jumper began to fondle her left breast.

Chapter Fifteen

Malcolm had now been dead for four days. Despite appeals the Kent Constabulary had so far been unsuccessful in finding a witness who could assist them in tracing the hit and run driver. They were beginning to pin their hopes on the free newspapers which would be delivered to local residents over the next few days. The front page coverage promised by one editor might help jog the odd memory or two.

After the accident Rebecca had stayed on with her parents. The prospect of returning home to a lonely bungalow was not something to be relished, but of course she would have to face up to it sooner or later. All of a sudden there seemed to be so many pressing matters that required attention. Certainly sitting down with Malcolm's business partner and funeral arrangements featured high on the list.

From now on though, Rebecca was determined to take control of her life. It was as if the ideas she had absorbed from all those secret reading sessions had given her a new self-belief. No longer would she be prepared to acquiesce so readily to every pronouncement made to her by the Fellowship priests.

"Keeping an independent mind won't be easy," warned Simon, thoughtfully as he took a sip of tea.

There was an expression of defiance in Rebecca's face as she relaxed in her deck chair.

"According to the Declaration of Independence, the pursuit of happiness is a right of all men," she replied, bitterly. "So why should I be excluded?"

"Because in 1776 Thomas Jefferson forgot to get his famous words printed in the latest edition of the Bible," grinned Simon.

The Broadbent twins were waiting to set off to the Tuesday evening Fellowship meeting. Sitting at the bottom of the garden they were well out of earshot of their parents who were up in the front bedroom getting changed. Rebecca was taking a rare opportunity to unburden herself on the person she trusted most of all in the world.

"If it isn't possible to have children then I want a challenging career," she said, with eyes closed and her face tilted in the direction of the sinking sun.

"Now that you are a widow the Fellowship will expect you to return to work in any case," replied Simon, waving away a fly which had settled on the rim of his teacup. "But if you are employed in one of their companies, it is unlikely to be in a very high-powered position. Usually women tend to be given the more menial jobs."

Rebecca opened her eyes and gazed dejectedly towards the house.

"And no doubt it would upset them if I were to be employed by 'worldlies'."

"Most definitely," said Simon, with a smile. "You could become corrupted by all forms of undesirable behaviour. The next thing we know is that you have been down the High Street buying a TV or using naughty words like 'bum' and 'shit'."

Rebecca laughed at her brother's crude sense of humour.

"I might even go as far as to say 'boobs' and 'willies'," she giggled.

"You see," said Simon, "where would it all end?"

Momentarily Rebecca fell silent as she spotted the next door neighbour's ginger tomcat in the garden. With arched back and in a position suggesting that he was about to pounce, the animal's gaze was fixed firmly on the apple tree. The object of his attention was a small sparrow perched on a branch only several feet above the ground. The poor creature seeming quite oblivious to the mortal danger it was in.

In an instant Rebecca stood up and clapped her hands loudly. The sudden disturbance had the desired effect of sending both predator and prey in opposite directions. A flurry of leaves floated downwards as the bird flapped its way to safety. Then with a faint smile of self-satisfaction the wildlife protector resumed her seat.

"Of course is it quite reasonable to suppose that you may marry again," suggested Simon, taking a sip of tea.

Rebecca looked dubious.

"Once bitten twice shy," she replied. "The problem is that with arranged marriages, couples don't get the opportunity to get to know one another before making a commitment. We should be permitted to go on dates and have a period of courtship like 'worldlies' do."

Simon gave an emphatic nod. Only the previous week his parents had traipsed him down to Devon to introduce him to a 'nice young lady' as they had termed it. Without question she had a certain charm but still he returned home feeling uneasy. Could he actually agree to marry a woman after one meeting or even several. Much to his father's annoyance he had still to make a decision.

"Of course without a husband you won't be able to have children," he warned.

Rebecca shrugged.

"Even when I had a man I couldn't conceive."

"Surely now that Malcolm is no longer alive to object you could always go and get medically checked," suggested Simon. "Then if you have a problem it may be possible to resolve it."

Rebecca gave her brother an appreciative smile. Whenever life was dark and depressing Simon could always be relied upon to show her the light at the end of the tunnel.

"It seems funny to have fertility investigations when I'm not married," she mused.

"I can't think why," replied Simon, scornfully. "Out there in the real world even single people are allowed children."

At that precise moment the senior Broadbents appeared at the back door. As usual father was getting into a state about the possibility of being late for church. Mother on the other hand was trying to perform her familiar role as the calming influence. It was a double act that the two of them had played for many years.

"Let's go then," called Mr Broadbent in an anxious voice. "We don't want the meeting to begin without us."

Rebecca gave her brother a mischievous wink.

"That would never do."

***

Charles Dawkins QC had forsaken the legal profession to enter the more precarious world of politics. After Labour's landslide victory in the 1997 General Election, Charles was one of a small band of new MPs appearing on the Conservative benches. Sadly for the party many distinguished members had been swept out of office.

With a majority of over 8000, Brockleby was considered to be a reasonably safe seat for the party. Therefore when in 1995 the sitting MP made the decision not to stand at the next general election there was a mad scramble to be the future Tory candidate. Amongst the many contenders was a little known barrister by the name of Charles Dawkins.

By necessity, choosing the right person was a tortuous process. To begin with the names of all the applicants had to be checked out with Central Office to ensure that each one was on the list of approved Conservative Party Candidates. The task then for Henry Fordham, the local party chairman, was to decide which members would be best suited to join him on the selection board. The remit of the group being to produce a shortlist of the finest people.

As soon as the closing date for written applications had passed, Henry's team set to work. Of course it wasn't simply a matter of reading what the contenders had to say about themselves. It was also important to make contact with those sources which were acquainted with their past lives.

Finally the job was done. Henry and his panel had managed to eliminate every applicant in the field with the exception of four. All that remained was to advise each one when and where they were required to present themselves before the Brockleby Conservative Association.

The clear favourite was Adrian Thomas. He had the great advantage of being a local man, the leader of the Borough Council and most importantly of all, a long time member of the Brockleby Tories. Not only was he known personally to many who were eligible to vote, but a few were very close friends.

However, those who had predicted that Adrian was all set for a comfortable win were in for a shock. As it happened the local man was the first one called upon to take centre stage and the large audience who had packed the hall waited expectantly. Much to their disappointment, however, he appeared to be overwhelmed by the big occasion. Not only was his speech flat and uninspiring but he was also thrown off balance by many of the questions put to him at the end.

The performances of the next two contenders were equally lacklustre. Many members were beginning to wish they had not bothered to brave the cold night air but instead, spent the evening in front of the TV. One or two were considering heading for the exit even before the last of the quartet got to his feet. However, everyone remained seated and decided to see it through to the finish.

At last it was the turn of Charles Dawkins to try and make an impression. Immaculately dressed in a black pin-striped suit from Saville Row, he was tall with good looks and clearly undaunted by the sea of faces staring up at him. Then with his charming smile and silky smooth voice he entertained the audience with a virtuoso performance.

He had written his speech several weeks earlier. Then having memorised every single word it was merely just a matter of concentrating on the actual delivery of what was in his head. In particular, ensuring that the humorous little quips were timed to perfection.

Charles knew how to please the large gathering. If elected he promised to support cuts in just about every tax the Government levied, to argue for stricter immigration controls and to speak out every time Brussels attempted to impose yet further bureaucracy on Britain. Each point he made was greeted by a warm ripple of applause.

However, the accomplished advocate had decided to leave the best until the end. Using his skills of persuasion learnt in the courtroom he was about to promote an issue which was guaranteed to win him popularity. It was the reintroduction of the death penalty.

"It is my belief that just the threat of Capital Punishment would greatly reduce the number of murders committed in this country," he began slowly. "If there was the slightest risk of being condemned to the gallows, what hardened criminal would not be deterred from performing an act of extreme violence. Who in their right mind would not tremble in fear at the prospect of facing those few final terrifying seconds of life, blinded by a hood, arms and legs bound securely and noose gripping tightly around the neck. All that remains between this life and the next is the trapdoor that is just about to collapse beneath their feet."

Charles paused and cast his eyes around the room. Much to his satisfaction the audience were riveted to their seats in absolute silence. Nobody as much as twitched.

"Advances in DNA testing now mean that the innocent are highly unlikely to be executed for the crimes of others," he continued. "This must eliminate the most powerful argument against the Death Penalty. Now only the guilty will die."

Charles had to give way to the loudest round of applause heard all evening. The pause gave him an opportunity to prepare to end his speech on a high note.

"Opponents of Capital Punishment argue that it is wrong for the state to take human life," he continued at last. The smile in his face had now given way to a look of anger. "I say who cares. In my view it is better that ten thousand violent criminals swing on the end of a rope that one vulnerable person is battered to death. But who they ask is to be the executioner?"

Charles's eyes searched around the hall as he gradually raised his right arm.

"Are there any more volunteers out there?"

Many hands swiftly shot up in the air. The women it appeared seemed more eager to fill the role of hangman than their husbands.

There was an eruption of hand clapping when Charles resumed his seat. While the members queued up to register their vote by dropping a folded up slip of paper into a large open box, Adrian was feeling tense. Having fully expected to be selected as the Conservative Parliamentary Candidate he was now beginning to have doubts. Even though many people had pledged their support to him, there was no reason to believe that they would be true to their word in a secret ballot.

There was an interlude of twenty minutes as the votes were counted. When at last Henry Fordham stood up to announce the result there was a hushed silence. Looking grim faced the chairman began to call out the names of the contenders in alphabetical order.

"Philip Barker," he called out. "Seventeen votes."

There followed a rather half-hearted round of applause.

"Charles Dawkins," cried out Henry with a little more

enthusiasm in his voice. "Seventy-nine votes."

This time loud cheers rang out around the hall. The chairman was forced to wait for a few moments to allow the noise to die down.

"Caroline Jenkins," he called a little more quietly. "Thirty-one votes."

The audience this time reacted with merely a generous round of applause.

"And finally Adrian Thomas," said the announcer staring hard at the sheet of paper in front of him.

The entire audience were now sat with hearts in their mouths. However, if the tension was bad enough for them it was sheer agony for the two men whose political futures now lay in the balance. In only a split second all would be revealed.

"Seventy-five votes," called out Henry in an almost apologetic voice.

There was thunderous applause as the adversaries stood up to shake hands.

Adrian's warm smile as he congratulated the victor managed to disguise his great disappointment. Deep down he realised that the chance of achieving his life-long ambition of becoming an MP had probably been swept away for ever. If he couldn't win the support of his local association then he was hardly likely to be selected as a parliamentary candidate elsewhere.

Not surprisingly Charles Dawkins was jubilant over his success. Of course, possessing immense self-control he conducted himself with great dignity when the result became apparent and during his acceptance speech to the audience. He despised any outward display of triumphal behaviour so common amongst sporting heroes.

In the years that followed Charles began to attract the attention of the party leadership. Having won the Brockleby seat in 1997 he went on to increase his majority in the following election of 2001. By this time, however, he was a shadow junior Home Office minister and many predicted that he could rise to the very top.

Meanwhile Adrian continued in his role as the Borough Council leader. He never seemed to bear any resentment towards Charles and in fact, during the current election campaign the two

197

of them were almost inseparable. Often they would be seen drinking alone together in the Conservative club bar.

It was one Friday night as they sat sipping scotch and soda that Charles broke the news to his friend.

"I have been earmarked to become the next Home Secretary," he smiled, proudly. "Of course it all depends on me holding my seat and the Tories being in a position to form the next Government."

Adrian raised his eyebrows in surprise.

"When were you told?" he said, aghast.

"Yesterday afternoon," answered Charles, staring down into his whisky glass. "I was summoned by Jonathan Canning, the big white chief himself."

"Congratulations old chap," said Adrian, patting his friend warmly on the elbow. "Even more reason why we need to get you elected in three weeks' time."

Charles looked a little dubious.

"It is going to be very tight this time. What with boundary changes we now have another large council estate in the constituency, which will help Labour enormously."

Adrian smiled confidently.

"According to our canvass returns it is level pegging at the moment. That is always good news for us."

Charles gave him a quizzical look.

"I would say that the position is extremely worrying."

"Not at all," smiled Adrian, downing the last drop of his drink. "A lot of Labour supporters are too apathetic to go out and cast their vote. On election night they will be curled up on the settee glued to their TV sets."

Charles looked far from convinced by this analysis.

"I understand that Jacqui Dunn is a very popular lady. People might be prepared to make a special effort to get down to the polling station for her."

"Highly unlikely," grinned Adrian. "Having worked with Jacqui for many years, I believe she is one of the best councillors in the chamber, but that alone won't help to get her elected. The problem is that most people have no idea how hard she works."

Following Adrian's example Charles finished off his whisky and soda in one gulp before going up to the bar for a refill.

Stressed out after several weeks of hectic campaigning the two men were soon buying rounds of drinks with considerable regularity. Without being aware of it they were starting to become quite drunk.

At ten thirty Charles began to drag himself reluctantly to his feet.

"Better be on my way. The wife will wonder where I am."

"Sure you're fit to drive old chap?" enquired Adrian, giving his friend a look of concern. "You could always order a cab and leave the car parked here overnight."

"I'll be fine," replied Charles as he made his way unsteadily towards the door. "I only have to drive through a quiet residential area. There is rarely anyone else around at this time of the evening."

Charles was used to driving while over the limit. This time though he was experiencing severe difficulties in keeping his mind focused on the road ahead. It was as if part of his brain had shut down for the night and the bit still functioning was shrouded in mist.

In a while he became aware of ring tones. In fact is was the third time in rapid succession that a rather tinny version of Mozart's Fortieth Symphony had suddenly broken the silence in his car. Instinctively Charles began to fumble around in his jacket pocket before producing a mobile phone.

"Charles Dawkins speaking," he said with an unmistakeable slur in his voice.

"It's Madeleine here," replied the caller, cheerfully. "When are you coming around to my flat for a bite to eat and a few carnal pleasures?"

"It may have to wait for a few days," answered Charles, sadly. "With all this campaigning it is impossible to find any free time at the moment."

"I can't wait for this election to be over," said Madeleine, dreamily. "Then you can divorce your wife and we can be together all the time."

"Of course," chuckled Charles, merrily. "And then you will be the new Mrs Dawkins."

Madeleine gave a short excited gasp.

"Fancy being the Home Secretary's wife. I shall be on

television and there will be pictures of me in all the newspapers."

Charles smiled as he turned the corner into a quiet side road.

"We'll be like movie stars. The media will love the fact that a high ranking cabinet minister is to marry a beautiful model. Every gossip writer…"

At that point his flight of fancy was brought to an abrupt halt. Without warning a tall figure emerged from between two parked cars and stepped out just in front of him. Even had he been cold sober there was no way he could have avoided a serious accident.

In that split second Charles felt his blood run cold. From the glow of the headlights he could just make out the profile of a young man before the sudden sharp impact sent the helpless pedestrian hurling backwards. Then in a flash there was a jolt as the front tyre ran over a large obstacle lying on the ground. It felt soft and seemed to flatten out under the weight of the car.

Charles panicked. Without even stopping to think he put his foot down hard on the accelerator and fled the scene as quickly as possible. Even in his drunken condition he was still able to appreciate the serious charges that he faced if caught by the police. Once they had established that amount of alcohol in his bloodstream he would almost certainly be spending the next few Christmases in prison.

Soon Charles arrived home and parked in his drive. Instead of immediately going indoors though he sat for a time trying to recover from the shock of what had just happened. No longer the cool, calm and collected professional so familiar to all those who knew him, he was now close to tears and trembling with fear.

At last he slowly climbed out of the car. Almost reluctantly he walked around to the front of it to make an assessment of the damage the vehicle had suffered. It was too dark to make a thorough examination but, quite clearly, extensive repairs would have to be undertaken. The bonnet in particular appeared to be badly buckled.

He was beginning to feel composed enough to face his wife. Although he had a pressing desire to unburden himself, a voice inside was warning him to act as though nothing had happened. In several weeks when he approached the thorny subject of divorce, Sally would have a lethal weapon with which to take revenge on him.

"Is that you?" shouted the lady of the house as soon as she heard the front door beginning to creak open.

"Who do you think it is?" replied Charles, gruffly.

Sally appeared in the hall wearing a blue silk dressing gown and looking a little surprised at being spoken to in this way.

"It could be anyone," she replied indignantly.

"And how many people have got a front door key to this house?" Charles sneered.

Sally was stuck for a suitable retort. Therefore feeling slightly bruised by her husband's sarcasm she began to climb the stairs.

"I'm off to bed. Let's hope you are in a better mood in the morning."

"You won't find me here," answered Charles. "I've just had a scrape in the car so I shall be taking it along to the garage first thing tomorrow."

"Is it serious?" asked Sally.

Charles shook his head.

"Just a few small dents in the front. Unfortunately I happened to run over a fox on my way home."

"What will you do for transport while the repairs are being done?" asked Sally, clearly feeling that this matter was of greater importance than the welfare of the fox.

"I shall get a car from that hire company near the park," answered Charles as he headed for the kitchen to make some black coffee.

For much of the following day Charles felt as though he was living through a nightmare. The only time that the black clouds seemed to roll away was when his thoughts turned to Madeleine. Finally he decided to drop in on her that evening and share his guilty secret. In all the world, she was the one person he felt able to trust.

The glamorous model listened to the account of the accident in stunned silence. The peroxide hair and heavy make-up were no longer able to disguise the fact that she was approaching middle-age. At thirty-four it was harder to get work out of advertisers and fashion magazines than in her earlier years in the beauty business. Having decided it was time to find a rich man to arrest her declining living standards, she had fortuitously stumbled across Charles Dawkins at a party. He was it seemed an answer to a prayer.

"Poor you," she murmured on at least three occasions while listening attentively to her lover's outpouring of grief.

"I don't even know whether he is dead or alive," moaned Charles.

Madeleine looked thoughtful.

"Where did you say it happened?"

"Westwood Avenue," answered Charles as he buried his head in his hands.

"A friend of mine lives there," replied Madeleine. "I'll give her a ring and find out what she knows."

Charles looked up in alarm.

"Don't sound too interested," he pleaded. "She might become suspicious."

"Don't worry," smiled Madeleine, already dialling the number on her mobile. "Midway through the conversation I shall casually bring up the subject of careless driving and hopefully, she will be prompted to talk about your accident."

Once Madeleine had got through there was a brief pause before she gave a firm shake of the head.

"My friend has switched off her phone. I will try again later."

In fact it wasn't until the following evening that Charles finally received the news that he had been anxiously waiting for. Having spent the entire day tied up with the election campaign, there simply wasn't enough time to deal with personal matters. It had been with heart in mouth that he had finally rung his mistress's home number.

"Didn't you get my message?" asked Madeleine. "I left it on your mobile."

"Sorry but I seem to have mislaid my phone," answered Charles. "The last time I remember having it was at the time of the accident. I shall ring the garage in the morning to see whether they can find it lying on the floor."

Madeleine hesitated for a moment as she tried to build herself up for what she was about to say.

"I'm afraid a young man is dead," she said, finally. "Apparently the impact killed him instantly."

Charles felt as though the room had started to revolve around him. Surrounded in his study by shelves of reference books he was alone in the house apart from a caged hamster in the lounge. The rest of the family were in church.

"Do you know whether he had any children?" asked Charles, immediately thinking of his own.

"I'm afraid my friend wasn't able to give me any details like that," answered Madeleine, apologetically. "Apparently the family don't mix very much with the neighbours. It seems that they are followers of some strange religious sect."

For further information Charles had to wait until later in the week. Under the front page headlines 'Police hunt for road death driver' the *Brockleby Times* had provided a detailed account of matters relating to the accident. The weekly newspaper had also printed a head and shoulders photograph of a serious looking young man with neatly combed hair. According to the caption underneath it, the name of the victim was Malcolm Baverstock.

Charles felt riddled with guilt as he studied the face. The unsmiling eyes seemed to stare back accusingly at him from the page. It was almost as if the deceased were about to come to life at any moment and take his revenge.

Charles read the story through for a second time. It was an agonising experience but he was partly consoled to discover that the victim had no children. Unfortunately though, the accident had created a young widow somewhere down in Broadstairs.

For a while he sat deep in thought. Would it at all be possible to compensate this lady while remaining completely anonymous he wondered. Perhaps an expensive gift or a substantial sum of money might just help to lighten her grief. At last, however, Charles dismissed the idea and threw the newspaper in the nearest waste paper bin. If the bereaved wife were suddenly to receive a present from a mysterious donor it would undoubtedly raise suspicions. It wasn't worth risking a promising career just to ease his conscience he told himself.

Chapter Sixteen

David continued to feel largely ignored in the office. His colleagues tended to be both courteous yet distant whenever they came into contact with him. Even Des seemed reluctant to stop and talk when they met at the coffee machine.

After work on Wednesday evening David drove straight to the club. A number of people, including Alison were already drinking in the bar while awaiting the arrival of the Prime Minister. Of the keenest activists only Jacqui Dunn was missing.

It wasn't long, however, before the Parliamentary Candidate made an appearance. She was part of a small entourage accompanying the party leader through the main entrance. Looking serious and dressed in a smart pale blue top with matching skirt, she looked like a woman who was destined to go places.

The sight of the Prime Minister induced a loud cheer. Soon Jacqui was escorting the illustrious guest around to introduce him to everyone. Being on a tight schedule, the head of Her Majesty's Government had to limit himself to a quick handshake and a few words to each person. With so much practice it was something he had become quite adept at.

At last it was David's turn to meet the great man.

"This is David Chambers, a recent addition to the party," announced Jacqui. "He has been working very hard for us."

The Prime Minister beamed warmly at the young man as they shook hands.

"I am greatly indebted to you for your efforts. When Jacqui is elected it will be a major boost to the Government and the country as a whole. Thank you so much."

David was overawed and could feel his cheeks burning.

"I enjoy being part of the campaign," he heard himself saying.

Like most people David was left with a favourable impression of Bruce Shaw. An attractive man physically, he had an easy manner and was not at all like the imposing figure that had appeared on stage in Hyde Park at the weekend. In the present atmosphere he seemed more like the man next door rather than the leader of a great democracy.

After the Prime Minister had shaken the last hand it was time to eat. Carol who had been keeping an eye on the catering, suddenly emerged from the kitchen and began to usher everyone into the main meeting room next to the bar. Inside four rows of tables, arranged into the shape of a large letter 'M' with a flat top, had been set in preparation for the meal.

On the top table all the places had been reserved. Tony had selected the keenest activists, councillors and senior members of the Association to sit close to the Prime Minister. Apart from wanting to reward the commitment of the most loyal members, he was keen to keep known troublemakers such as Sid Davidson at a safe distance from the honoured guest.

The cooking facilities were quite limited at the club. However, as the weather was still warm, prawn cocktail followed by ham salad was reasonably well received. Certainly David and Alison seated at the end of the top table had no complaints.

Looking around David spotted a number of unfamiliar faces. Some were quite elderly and Alison pointed out several who had been distinguished councillors in years gone by. Although they were never seen drinking in the bar, it seemed that they were a certain group who frequently attended functions such as this one.

"It's the first time I have ever been introduced to anyone famous," commented David as he tucked into his salad.

"It's a funny feeling to meet a public figure," replied Alison, thoughtfully. "Because their faces are so familiar they can often seem like old acquaintances."

"Mind you," grinned Carol who was seated next to Alison. "You sometimes learn more about their private lives than you do about intimate friends."

"Just as well," answered Alison, giving David a wink. "I would probably be disgusted if I knew what she gets up to."

The two women began giggling like schoolgirls.

"I bet that David could tell a tale or two about you," replied Carol, when she had finally managed to regain control of herself.

"I'm sworn to secrecy," answered David with a wry smile.

Although hardly an hilarious riposte it was funny enough to

trigger off another giggling fit in both women.

At the end of the meal Jacqui stood up to speak. She began by praising everyone for their efforts towards the campaign before going on to thank the Prime Minister for coming. It was short and sweet but it received enthusiastic applause.

Then it was the turn of the man sitting next to her to say a few words. Climbing to his feet Bruce Shaw waited for a few minutes to allow the cheers to die down. Then finally, with a broad smile he began to speak.

"Two weeks tomorrow this nation has a very important decision to make. Whether to elect a Government committed to spending billions on sending troops to Iraq or one that would rather use that money on health and education."

It was typical Bruce Shaw rhetoric and received rapturous applause. Of those that were assembled in the room only Sid Davidson remained impassive as he sat sipping his beer. Feeling nothing but contempt for the Labour leader, however, he was boiling over with anger inside.

"This constituency has always been in Tory hands," said Bruce as he was about to conclude his speech. "Because of the boundary changes it has now become a marginal seat and I firmly believe we can win it. Please help as much as possible so that we can get Jacqui Dunn elected to serve the people of this country."

"Labour won't win this election Shaw," shouted Sid amongst the cheers. "You are being seen as a soft touch for terrorists."

The hearts of the faithful sank. The occasion had been going so well and suddenly the Association's biggest loud mouth was threatening to spoil it. However, Bruce Shaw seemed unfazed by the outburst.

"Terrorism will never be defeated by invading countries such as Iraq," he answered, addressing Sid directly. "We need to understand what it is that drives a young person to strap explosives to their bodies, with the intention of killing themselves along with many others."

Sid who had been drinking all afternoon wasn't going to be beaten. As a man who enjoyed being the centre of attention he seized the opportunity to stand in the spotlight.

"You are a coward Shaw," he snarled, angrily. "You should be standing shoulder to shoulder with America instead of running

206

away."

Having faced that same accusation on many occasions Bruce Shaw had a readymade reply prepared.

"In recent times Britain has become too subservient to America. I have been the first Prime Minister in living memory to have gone to Washington and said 'No Mr President'. Believe me, to do that on the world's stage takes guts."

Amid the cheers that followed there were hoots of derision. Having taken a gulp of beer, Sid somehow miscalculated the exact position of the table and dropped the glass in his lap. Such accidents rarely occur to those in a sober state.

Sid stood up and began dabbing at his soaking trousers with a paper serviette. Then with all eyes in the room following his progress, he began walking crab-like towards the door. Before leaving, however, he was determined to have the last word. Red faced with anger he swung around to face the Prime Minister.

"The Tories are going to hammer you in this election," he shouted.

There were jeers mixed with a sense of relief after Sid had departed. The Prime Minister's two bodyguards standing discreetly at the back, had both been ready to pounce had the situation demanded such a course of action. For those who knew the loud mouthed party member better though, the incident was more about the embarrassment he was causing rather than a breach of security.

"That happens to be one of the people who might replace me on the Council if I have to resign my seat," whispered Jacqui to Bruce Shaw.

"Good gracious," exclaimed Bruce in a much louder voice. "I hope that the others in the frame are more promising."

Fingers on the top table started pointing at the young man sitting at the end.

"We are hoping that David will stand," replied Tony who had a seat on the other side of the star guest.

The great man craned his head both forwards and sideways to give the potential candidate an encouraging smile.

"You certainly get my endorsement David, for what it is worth," he called down to him.

The young man felt his cheeks burn as he returned the smile.

He was still savouring those precious words of encouragement long after Bruce Shaw had said his last goodbyes, before setting off to give his election address at the Methodist church. Having agreed to go out canvassing, it was a meeting that David would sadly have to miss.

David was feeling a little apprehensive as he pulled up alongside the premises of J Robson Ltd the following morning. Having never been interviewed for a job in his life he had no idea as to the questions that might be thrown at him. At Fine Choice Furniture such formalities had been by-passed as the partners had known him and his family for many years.

Robsons was located on the Brockleby Trading Estate. Rather bigger than his present company, the red bricked office block had four floors, double that of Fine Choice. The warehouse at the rear and the yard where the delivery vehicles would be parked at night were also more spacious.

It wasn't just the size that set the two companies apart. Having embraced modern technology the office staff at Robsons were each provided with a computer terminal rather than having to make endless journeys to the filing cabinets for information. Fax machines were also on hand to provide an instant means of communication and not seen as a tool of the Devil as they were at Fine Choice.

David was met in reception by a young secretary in a tight skirt. Having been greeted with a warm smile he was escorted up two flights of stairs, through a swing door and into the Sales Department. It was contained within one very large room filled with a dozen or more people, barely recognisable to him as a working environment.

Here desks were not cluttered up with paper and files. Men and women were staring straight ahead at a screen rather than looking downwards as they would when writing with a pen. Apart from using the fingers to tap on the keyboard very little physical effort seemed to be required.

The young secretary suddenly stopped outside a large office. As she gave a sharp rap on the door, through the glass David noticed two men facing one another across a desk. The older man was unfamiliar to him but the other one he recognised as Ryan Pritchard.

"Mr Chambers to see you Roger," said the young secretary as she partly opened the door.

With a wide smile the older man stood up and extended his open hand towards David.

"Delighted to meet you," he said, cheerily. "I'm Roger Green."

After shaking hands with the Sales Manager David turned to exchange a friendly nod with Ryan. They both appreciated that any rivalry that had existed between them in the past would have to be put to one side for the present.

"Congratulations on winning the Conningvale House contract," said Ryan, magnanimously. "I thought that Robsons had got that one in the bag."

"It was just luck," replied David, modestly.

"Nonsense!" joined in Roger, heartily. "It was quite an achievement."

At that point Ryan gave his manager an enquiring look.

"Do you want me to stay?"

Roger nodded.

"If David joins this company you will be working very closely with him. Therefore I need to be certain that everyone is happy with the situation."

David was already forming a favourable impression of Roger Green. He sensed that beneath that over the top charm lay a strong personality which commanded respect. Unlike Maurice Hopkins, his opposite number at Fine Choice Furniture, this was almost certainly a man who had earned his position on merit rather than because he happened to marry the senior partner's daughter.

The interview began with Roger discussing the company. Firstly he provided a potted history before going on to outline an overall view of the way Robsons actually operated. Then he turned the spotlight on to the job applicant.

"How much notice do you need to give your employer?" he asked, having finally exhausted questions relating to work experience.

"None," replied David. "I am free to start next Monday if required."

Roger was clearly taken aback.

"But senior sales people can't leave just like that. Surely there must be a clause in your contract requiring you to give a period of notice?"

With some difficulty David was forced to explain why his company were prepared to release him so readily. As he spoke he could see the expression of amazement which crept over the faces of his two listeners. Ryan at times shook his head in disbelief while his manager just looked dumbstruck.

"I can't believe it," said Roger when David had finished. "A salesman wins a major order for his company and ends up receiving an ultimatum. Accept our narrow-minded beliefs or we sack you."

"At Robsons we judge people only by the quality of their work," joined in Ryan. "One guy here is in a naturist club and spends his weekends parading around in his birthday suit. However, we take the view that he is free to do as he likes in his spare time."

"Just as long as he doesn't arrive at the office in that state," grinned Roger.

David was beginning to feel at ease in the present company. However, he was also becoming increasingly anxious to know whether or not a job offer was going to be made to him. Earlier some concern had been expressed as to his total lack of computer skills and he was worried as to how much this would count against him. Eyebrows were also raised at his failure to produce a CV.

Just when he had given up all hope of being recruited Roger's expression suddenly turned serious.

"Normally I never hire anyone after just one interview," he said, thoughtfully. "However, because time is against us, I shall make an exception in your case. Would you like to start on Monday?"

David could hardly believe his ears.

"Fine by me," he replied, trying to keep his composure.

Picking up a pen Roger jotted something down before pushing the sheet of paper in front of David.

"That will be your starting salary," smiled Roger. "Your current income plus an extra ten per cent."

"Sounds perfect," answered David, staring down at the figure.

Ryan turned to Roger with a puzzled look.

"Which area are you giving him?"

"None to begin with," replied Roger with an artful grin. "Our friend will start by introducing new customers to the company."

"But you can't ask him to cold call," protested Ryan. "We have juniors to do that."

Roger shook his head as he looked straight at his latest appointment.

"Do you have a list of contacts for all your customers?"

"Of course," replied David. "In my office I keep a card index system with names and telephone numbers of buyers within each organisation."

At that precise moment the telephone rang. Looking a little irritated at the interruption Roger almost wrenched the receiver from its cradle.

"All right," he said after a brief pause. "Show him into the conference room, Sophie. I shall be along there in about five minutes."

Once the call was finished Roger immediately put forward his master plan.

"Bring your cards in at lunchtime and I will get one of the secretaries to photocopy them. If you then pick up the box after work, nobody at Fine Choice will be any the wiser."

"Sounds good," joined in Ryan. "Next week you can ring all of your contacts and introduce them to Robsons. Just say that you are working for a better company and offer to send them one of our brochures."

The idea of being part of a conspiracy appealed to David. Beneath the surface a growing resentment festered because of the way his present company was treating him. He would take his revenge on the Boswell brothers for depriving him of his job.

David gritted his teeth as he glared down angrily at the desk.

"I'm going to put those bastards out of business," he snarled.

His fellow conspirators gave him a look of approval.

"What a splendid idea," replied Roger with a glint in his eyes.

"I like your style," added Ryan. "You are going to fit in well at Robsons."

As soon as David got into work he headed straight for the drinks machine. Like Des who was standing idly by and tucking into a bag of crisps, he had no desire to do anything useful. It was impossible to motivate himself when the only concern he had left for his company lay in plotting its downfall.

"How is Maurice coping with the Conningvale House order?" he enquired.

Des glanced around anxiously before replying. It was as if he had been asked to reveal state secrets by a Soviet agent during the Cold War years.

"Slight problem yesterday," he answered in a hushed voice. "Maurice had an appointment with Shirley Bromage and forgot to show up."

David shook his head in disbelief.

"What did Shirley have to say about that?"

"She wasn't happy," answered Des as he dropped his empty crisp packet into the rubbish bin. "Apparently she had driven up from Portsmouth especially for the meeting."

"So when has Maurice arranged to see her again?" asked David.

"He hasn't contacted her yet," smiled Des, taking a sip of coffee. "Maurice had gone home when Shirley rang here and one of the secretaries took the message."

"He has probably rung her this morning to reschedule," suggested David.

Des shook his head as he produced a chocolate bar in a blue wrapper from his trouser pocket.

"Maurice has gone on holiday and won't be back until Monday. He has taken the family up to Scotland to visit some friends. He has probably forgotten all about the Conningvale House order."

David was hardly surprised at the news. It was typical of Maurice's whole attitude to clients and work in general. Had a non-Fellowship employee in the warehouse acted with such negligence, they would probably be facing the sack.

Finishing his coffee, David strolled upstairs to his office leaving Des to go in search of someone else to gossip to. Sitting down at his desk a few minutes later, he noted the number of Conningvale House which was pinned to the wall in front of him, then lifted the telephone receiver. His pulse began to race as he listened to the rings.

Quite expecting the sullen receptionist to answer his call, he was surprised to hear Shirley Bromage's voice.

"Hello Mrs Bromage. It's David Chambers of Fine Choice Furniture speaking. I'm ringing to offer my apologies for the very poor service you are receiving from my company."

After a brief pause Shirley launched into a tirade. Clearly frustrated by the events of the past few days she began to list out her complaints in the sequence that they had occurred. Although Maurice was clearly the arch villain, some of her anger was directed at David himself.

"Why didn't you tell me you were leaving?"

Having anticipated the question David had a reply already prepared.

"I didn't know myself until last Friday," he said, sadly. "It seems that the company are close to bankruptcy and they are making me redundant in order to save costs."

Shirley was silent for a moment as she tried to work out the implications of this latest information.

"Does this mean that I may not be getting my furniture?" she said at last.

"It's quite possible," answered David. "At the moment Fine Choice are having difficulty in paying suppliers and some are threatening to halt delivery to us."

"Now you have got me panicking," replied Shirley who was clearly stressed. "I must have my furniture in place by the time this home opens."

So far David was pleased with his performance. His exaggerated portrayal of the company's poor financial state was so persuasive he was beginning to be taken in himself. Therefore having successfully raised the alarm bells, it was time to come to the rescue.

"Of course there are other firms which can supply your needs," said David as he drew a matchstick man on a piece of paper.

"Do you know of any?" asked Shirley, anxiously.

"There is always Robsons," suggested David. "As it happens, I am joining the company on Monday. You may recall that you had a presentation from one of their reps on the day you saw me."

"Very well then," said Shirley, wearily. "When can I see somebody?"

213

"Give me five minutes while I speak to the sales manager."

Roger Green was delighted when he heard the news.

"Splendid," he replied, heartily. "Let me ring the good lady myself and make the appointment."

"Will you be sending Ryan again?" enquired David.

Roger gave a thoughtful sigh.

"I don't think that would be wise. From what I can gather he didn't get on too well with Mrs Bromage on the last occasion. Perhaps it is time to send in the 'A' team."

David was puzzled.

"Who are they?"

"Why, you and I of course dear boy."

"Sounds OK to me," answered David, cheerfully.

Roger gave a little chuckle.

"A winning combination I feel sure."

As planned David made another two visits to Robsons during the day. By the time he arrived on the second occasion every card containing his customer's details had been photocopied. He could now return the whole box to his office the next day and nobody at Fine Choice Furniture would be any the wiser.

The Labour Party activists were given a respite from canvassing that evening. Instead they were asked to go out and deliver a new leaflet that Tony had just produced. It contained a hard hitting message which he believed would damage the Tories.

The bold heading read 'vote for schools and hospitals not war'. It then went on to quote figures produced by an independent source estimating the cost of sending British troops to Iraq. To add effect, the annual cost was printed with ten large digits spread across the page.

The following day was David's last at Fine Choice. Having first restored the customer cards to their usual position on the windowsill he began to clear out his drawers. By nature an untidy person, he felt uneasy about leaving the unenviable task to somebody else.

Midway through the morning he received a surprise call from Simon.

"I gather you rang at the weekend," he began.

"That's right," laughed David. "But your mother seemed anxious to protect you from dark forces like me."

"I'm sorry but when you called she was still trying to recover from a terrible shock," explained Simon. "You see only hours earlier Malcolm had been killed in a tragic accident."

David was aghast. For several minutes he listened in silence as he was furnished with the details. It seemed unbelievable that anyone as sensible as Malcolm would simply walk out in front of a moving car.

"And how is Rebecca taking it?" he asked when his friend had finished speaking.

"Remarkably well," answered Simon. "Yesterday she went home to Broadstairs to sort out some of her affairs. I believe she wants to carve out a completely new life for herself now that Malcolm is gone."

"Good for her," said David, feeling a sense of admiration that she was standing up so well to adversity.

"Look I fancy a day at the seaside," said Simon. "We could go down to visit her in a couple of weeks. Both she and I are eager to know how you are coping with your new life."

"Sounds good," replied David, thumbing through his diary. "How about two weeks tomorrow?"

"Saturdays are always good for me," replied Simon. "Where shall I pick you up?"

"You had better take my new address," said David. "As from tomorrow I shall be sharing a house with two friends."

Simon's call was the biggest event of the morning. With so little work to do now, time passed very slowly and David found himself continually checking his watch. Finally at three o'clock he received his expected call from Samuel Boswell.

The senior partner looked a little downcast as David walked into his office. To many of his employees he appeared brusque and authoritarian but underneath lay a kindly soul. He hated hurting the feelings of others but there were times when God's will had to be obeyed.

"Are you ready to repent young man?" he asked as David took his seat on the opposite of the desk.

The rebel shook his head firmly.

"I want to be free to lead my own life."

"I thought you would say that," answered Samuel with a weary sigh. "You will soon tire of sinful pleasures I expect."

"We will have to wait and see," replied David who was in no mood for a lecture. "Now can we get down to discussing my redundancy pay out?"

Taking the hint Samuel handed him a letter with a cheque fastened at the top by a paperclip.

"The payment includes both your statutory entitlements together with certain enhancements. I have provided you with a detailed analysis of how that figure is made up."

David briefly read the contents of the letter before tucking it away in his inside pocket.

"You have been very generous," he replied with a grudging smile. "I certainly didn't expect to be allowed to keep my company car."

A look of concern suddenly spread across Samuel's face.

"Do you have another job to go to?"

"Not yet," replied David, casually. "I shall have a good look around next week."

He could think of no good reason for telling the truth. As in poker it made no sense to reveal one's hand in advance of the game. The shrewd operator always keeps his cards close to his chest.

"I wish you luck," answered Samuel. "Life is tough out there."

"There is nothing like a challenge," replied David, who could think of nothing else better to say.

Samuel was silent for a moment as he tried to collect his thoughts.

"Had Maurice been in today I would have asked you to run through some of your customers with him," he said at last. "You could have pointed out any that might be looking to buy from us in the near future and any other useful tips about them."

David nodded.

"Perhaps I could write some notes for him."

"I would appreciate that very much," said Samuel, enthusiastically.

Following Samuel's example, David stood up and the two men shook hands.

Having known each other for many years both felt more than a tinge of sadness. However, in Fellowship parlance it was time for the Righteous and the Ungodly to travel their separate paths.

"Have you found anyone to replace me yet?" asked David, casually.

"I have decided to appoint Des," replied Samuel. "I believe he possesses all the qualities to be a great success. A brilliant mind, good people skills and a tremendous enthusiasm."

David almost collapsed in amazement. The only talent he could credit Des with was his ability to take an incoherent passage of the Bible and give some bizarre meaning to it.

"But he doesn't have any selling experience," David protested.

"Des will have an excellent manager to guide him," answered Samuel, fondly. "Maurice knows everything there is to know about selling."

David smiled to himself as he conjured up a picture of Des and Maurice at a sales presentation. One day very soon Samuel would come to regret his decision to put so much faith in the feckless couple. For the moment though it was better that he kept his delusions.

Back in his office David carefully compiled a list of customers to be contacted. Instead of being the best prospects, however, each one was amongst the very worst. Selected mainly for their rudeness they could all be relied upon not to buy from Fine Choice Furniture, now or ever.

David had a few regrets as he left the building for the very last time. He would miss some of his colleagues who had just shook his hand and the little office that had been his workplace for the past five years. Soon of course it would all be just a distant memory but, for the moment, it was sad.

Later that evening David lay on his hotel bed and stared up at the ceiling. He had been out delivering leaflets again with the other activists and had enjoyed an intimate period with Alison in the car afterwards. However, at the present moment his thoughts were on other things.

In his mind's eye he was looking down on three men. The trio of Samuel Boswell, Maurice Hopkins and Des were sitting around a table looking grief stricken. Fine Choice Furniture had just been declared bankrupt and it was all because of an ill-advised decision to dismiss a brilliant young salesman. Finally the picture faded and David fell asleep.

Chapter Seventeen

David glanced around his hotel room for the last time. Although the stay had been short, inside those four walls had provided the scene for two memorable events. He would never forget his final encounter with Ruth and those feelings of relief mixed with a certain amount of guilt. More importantly though, it was where he had lost his virginity on that blissful Sunday afternoon.

In a little over an hour he was unpacking in his new bedroom. Not only had David made several journeys collecting up his possessions from the hotel but, also from the house he owned jointly with Ruth where he had stored bits and pieces. George who had helped him carry some of these belongings up the stairs now stood in the doorway watching on in case further assistance was required.

"Kenny and I will have to leave you by yourself for a while," he said, apologetically. "We have to go and do our Saturday morning surgery."

"What exactly is that?" enquired David, giving his new landlord a quizzical look.

George gazed down at the floor as he tried to think of a suitable explanation.

"Well we sit in an office down at the Village Hall and people pop in to see us if they have a problem which involves the Council," he said, finally.

"Such as?" enquired David, stopping to take a short break from hanging his clothes up in the wardrobe.

"A wide range of issues," answered George. "It can be anything from rubbish collection to helping people to find a council house."

"Is that what being a councillor is all about?" enquired David.

"That and attending countless committee meetings," laughed George.

"And being a school governor," added Kenny, who had suddenly appeared on the landing polishing the lens of his glasses with a small cloth.

"I'm glad to see you are ready at long last," said George, glancing over his shoulder. "What time are we setting off?"

"Right now," replied Kenny.

George was just about to follow his friend down the stairs when he suddenly turned back to David.

"There is a meeting at the club at one," he announced. "Tony wants to talk to everyone about election day."

"I'll see you there then," answered David, enthusiastically.

"Feel free to help yourself to tea," called George, just before he slammed the front door behind him.

Once David had finished unpacking he sat on the edge of his bed and glanced around. His new sleeping quarters seemed very small after the size of his hotel room and considerably shabbier. The rug on the floor was old and frayed while the curtains looked as though a good cleaning was overdue. The blue faded wallpaper, too had a dingy appearance, which didn't assist the overall effect. However, he felt more than compensated by having such good friends around him.

He was making his way downstairs to have a nose around when the telephone rang. In a split second of indecision he wondered whether to answer it or not before finally lifting the receiver.

"How can I help?" he enquired, after providing the caller with the number.

"They haven't been around to fix my windows yet," replied the voice of an elderly woman.

David was taken aback. It seemed odd that anyone should start a telephone conversation without first revealing their identity. However, concerned that this mysterious person could be somebody closely connected to his new housemates, he decided to be courteous.

"How did they break?" he enquired, politely.

"Bloody kids playing football in the street," answered the caller grumpily. "They seemed to be using my house as a goal."

"That's awful," replied David, who still had no idea who he might be speaking to. "When exactly did this happen?"

The caller appeared to ponder briefly over the question.

"It must have been about nine days ago," she said at last.

"That's a long time," said David, sympathetically, still mystified as to why he was being given this information.

"Too long," agreed the caller. "How soon can you get someone to fix it?"

Having concluded that the poor woman was feeble minded David resisted the temptation to resort to sarcasm. Feeling reasonably certain that she must have been connected in some way to George and Kenny though, he felt obliged to offer her some assistance. In any case the solution to her problem was fairly simple.

"If you would kindly give me your name," he said, grabbing a pen and notepad lying on the telephone table.

"Mrs Dorothy Winter," answered the caller.

David scribbled the name down before taking details of the address.

"I shall try to get somebody to repair it for you today."

David was true to his word. Once he had put down the phone he began thumbing through the pages of the local directory. Finally he came to a bold heading marked 'Glaziers'.

"It will cost more if you need someone to come out today," said a chirpy voice.

"I'm sure Mrs Winter won't mind the extra cost," replied David, confidently.

Happy with his good deed David set off for the kitchen to make a cup of tea. It seemed crazy to him that the poor old soul had to live with a broken window for over a week. Surely a friend could have advised her what to do to get it fixed.

Soon the matter faded into insignificance. There was no way of course that David could have foreseen how, what had seemed such a trivial incident would come back to haunt him. At present he was still a rookie in political terms.

David felt certain he would soon settle into his new surroundings. It was, however, in stark contrast to the home which he had known for so many years. The one in which his mother was forever scurrying about, cleaning this and that or putting some item into its rightful place.

George's house had a relaxed ambience to it. A burglar who had just broken in would quickly make the assumption that the occupiers were not of a fastidious disposition. Washing-up was piled high in the sink, clothes were strewn around in unusual places and the rubbish bin in the kitchen was overflowing with an assortment of unpleasant objects.

Then there were those boxes. Large brown cardboard containers full with reports on committee meetings and various other matters relating to council business, which were delivered weekly. When moving around David needed to keep his eyes fixed to the ground to avoid a nasty accident.

Scattered about also were Labour Party leaflets. Stacked in piles, some were recent but others had faded with age. Sitting down with his cup of tea David spent a while scanning through several of the older ones which caught his eye. One of the most discoloured ones had a picture of a much younger George, standing triumphantly alongside some friends after being elected as a councillor for the very first time.

Tony had reserved a room next to the bar for his election day talk. A number of tables had been arranged in a full circle, with chairs in place for about thirty or more people. All the keenest activists were in attendance plus some unfamiliar faces.

"Let me begin by giving you all some good news," beamed Tony. "Having analysed our canvassing sheets I am pleased to say that Labour are on course to take Brockleby. It appears that we are three per cent ahead of the Tories."

Most people in the room smiled broadly and a few clapped.

"How much of the constituency have we canvassed so far?" enquired George.

"Roughly about three quarters," replied Tony.

"How many voters are still undecided?" asked Kenny suspiciously. "That is always an important factor at this stage in an election campaign."

Tony quickly consulted the figures he had compiled the night before.

"About twenty-two per cent," he answered at last.

"It's too close to call," said Jacqui with a shake of the head. "We still need to give every last drop of sweat if we are going to win."

There were murmurs of agreement from certain members.

"These figures are never reliable," joined in a young man who was sat next to Kenny. "You only have to read what the polling organisations are telling us nationally. Yesterday the *Telegraph* put Labour ahead by four per cent whereas in the *Guardian* I see that the Tories are winning by about the same."

"And each one allows itself three per cent margin of error," smiled George.

"There is only one thing that we can be sure of," said Jacqui. "Both nationally and locally the result is going to be very tight."

David who had been listening intently suddenly became distracted. Beneath the table Alison who was sitting next to him, placed her hand lightly on his leg and began to manoeuvre it in the direction of his crutch. The expression on her face, however, was one of angelic innocence.

"Now on to election day," said Tony, stroking his beard. "I want tellers at every single polling station throughout the day. We need to be absolutely certain that all our supporters have been out to vote."

The hand beneath the table had finally reached its targeted destination. For a moment there was a pause in operations before the fingers began gently massaging a sensitive part of David's anatomy. Then leaning sideways, Alison put her mouth to his ear.

"Are you free to come around for a meal tonight?" she whispered.

David turned and nodded.

"What time?"

"About eight," she answered. "Amanda will be in bed by then and I shall have had time to tidy up."

"Sounds good," smiled David. "I shall bring a bottle of wine."

Suddenly they became aware that Tony was no longer speaking and all eyes in the room were gazing in their direction.

"If you would kindly give me your full attention," pleaded the election organiser. "It is very important that everyone listens to what I have to say."

The two offenders looked slightly embarrassed. Alison swiftly removed her wandering hand and both of them made an effort to focus on the great words of wisdom that were being imparted. Much of it of course, they had already heard during their evenings in the bar.

"From our canvass sheets I have created lists of all those people who have pledged their support to us," said Tony, finally.

"Over the weekend we need to see that each one of them puts a poster up in their window. I am handing out rolls to all of you."

"How is that going to help the campaign?" asked David, suspiciously.

"It is a way of advertising," answered Tony. "If people see that their neighbours are intending to vote Labour it may encourage them to do the same."

"It is the herd mentality," smiled Kenny.

At last the meeting came to a close and everyone filed out of the room. A group of people led by Tony and Jacqui headed for the bar while others went their separate ways. Alison needed to go home in order to take Amanda to a birthday party, while George and Kenny had arranged their weekly trip to the supermarket.

"I'd better come with you," said David. "This shopping business is a bit of a mystery to me."

"It's pretty easy once you get into the swing of it," Kenny assured him. "The key to it is to draw up a list of the things that you need before setting off."

As it turned out, the experience turned out to be a lot less irksome than David had imagined. Following his two flatmates along one aisle after another he was able to fill his wire trolley with anything that took his fancy. It occurred to him that he was no longer reliant on somebody else to decide what he was going to eat. From now on he would be in control.

At last the three of them arrived at the checkout. Cautiously David stood at the back so that he could keep a watchful eye on how the process actually worked. Surprisingly it was all reasonably straight forward and soon he was free to set off pushing his trolley of goodies.

It was four o'clock when the threesome eventually staggered through the front door laden with plastic bags. In his room David had been provided with a fridge freezer and a cupboard to store his food separately. When finally he had put all his shopping away he joined his housemates in the sitting room.

George and Kenny were sat on the edge of their seats watching TV. Both keen football fans the pair of them were waiting anxiously for news of goals that were likely to have an impact on the teams they each supported. Not fully appreciating the importance that many people attached to the world's favourite game, David thought their behaviour to be quite bizarre.

"Yes!" shouted Kenny as the presenter announced that Manchester United had just scored a third goal at Old Trafford.

George, however, found little consolation in his friend's joy. In contrast he was staring gloomily at the screen hoping desperately that somehow Charlton could force an equaliser in the dying minutes of the match. Sadly for him there were no further goals and his beloved team were condemned to another defeat.

"You should support a decent side," crowed Kenny, triumphantly.

George gave him a contemptuous look.

"Bloody Manchester United. You've never been north of Watford."

"Yes I have," protested the younger man. "I've travelled all around Northern England and Scotland, too."

"Well you've never set foot inside Old Trafford," scowled George.

"Granted," answered Kenny, chirpily. "But I intend to pay a visit before long."

The repartee ended at that point. In an attempt to forget his recent disappointment, George snatched up a local paper and began to flick through the pages.

The rivalry between them didn't end with football. They also had differences of opinion when it came to politics as David was soon to discover. George was a traditional Labour supporter with routes in the trade unions whereas Kenny was much further to the left.

It was after nine when David and Alison sat down to their meal. Eating by candlelight they tucked into a rice and chicken dish, which the hostess had stumbled across in an old recipe book. The white wine on the table having been supplied courtesy of the guest.

"You've known Kenny and George much longer than I have," commented David, thoughtfully. "Do they have any women in their lives?"

Alison shook her head.

"Both of them just seem to live for politics. George was actually married once but it didn't last. His wife got tired of him going out to meetings night after night."

"What about Kenny?" asked David.

For a moment Alison gazed into her wine glass.

"He doesn't appear to show much interest in the opposite sex," she said, finally. "I believe that deep down he despises women. In particular, the materialistic type that are forever following the latest fashion."

"Sounds as though he would get on well with the Fellowship," laughed David. "They don't approve of trendy clothes either."

"Don't ever say that to him," warned Alison. "He believes in the Marxist doctrine that religion is the opium of the masses. The rich preach it to the poor to help them accept their poverty."

"He may have a point," said David, reflectively. "Put up with hardship in this life and God will reward you in the next."

"Exactly," smiled Alison.

David looked thoughtful as he poured a little more wine in Alison's glass.

"Funny when you come to think about it. Our little group meet up practically every night at the club yet I know hardly anything about their private lives."

"Most of the time we just talk politics," replied Alison, helping herself to more rice from a bowl in the centre of the table. "I suppose that is what happens when like-minded people become fanatical about something."

At that moment they were interrupted by a small cry from the next room. With a resigned smile Alison got to her feet and wearily set off for the door.

"Coming," she called before muttering an apology to her guest.

Later that evening David again approached the topic of private lives. Having just made love in bed and now lying dreamily in Alison's arms a picture of Jacqui Dunn suddenly came into his head.

"Does Jacqui have a partner?" he enquired.

"She lives with a chap," answered Alison, staring up at the ceiling through half-closed eyes. "Alistair is a cabbie."

"Does he ever get involved in politics?" asked David, as he lowered his head slightly to kiss the silky white shoulder that peeped out from beneath the sheets.

"He did until a few months ago," replied Alison, turning her face towards David. "There was even talk of him standing as a candidate in the local elections next time. However, Alistair stopped supporting Labour after Bruce Shaw refused to send troops to Iraq."

"But becoming an MP is so important to Jacqui," said David, indignantly. "For her sake he should put his principles behind him and be out there every night with us campaigning to get her elected."

Alison lay quietly reflecting for a few moments.

"You may be right," she, said finally. "On the other hand people must be allowed to remain true to their convictions."

The discussion might have continued for much longer but both of them were too tired. After his sexual exertions David slept so soundly that he didn't hear Amanda cry out in the night. When he finally awoke the sun was beaming a shaft of light through a crack in the curtains and Alison was standing by the bed offering him a cup of tea.

The opportunity for further romance had disappeared though. Amanda had woken up in high spirits and was demanding to be played with, read to and fed all within a short space of time. Feeling a little neglected and unable to compete for attention, the guest decided that an early exit might be advisable.

After breakfast David returned to his new house. He had been advised in advance that Sunday morning was always set aside for domestic chores. Each person was assigned a number of tasks after which the house would become a hive of activity for an hour or so.

About eleven the housemates stopped for a break. Once they had settled down in their armchairs Kenny switched on the radio to listen to the hourly news bulletin. Like George his appetite for election information had become insatiable. They had both scrutinised three Sunday newspapers for the political coverage and were still hungry for more.

The BBC headlines concerned a television interview that had been conducted earlier that morning. Colin Sudbury, one of the Labour MPs who had defected to the Tories was now seeking to damage the Prime Minister even further. In a bitter attack he accused his former party leader of putting the security of the nation at risk.

"Before too long Saddam's weapons of mass destruction will be found," he warned. "Then we will all be congratulating the American President on taking such decisive action."

"How can you be so sure?" asked the interviewer. "After all, it has been six months since the US troops took control in Baghdad and they have still to uncover anything."

"It won't be long before they find what they are looking for," replied Colin. "Reliable sources, once close to Saddam's regime, assure us that there are a vast stockpile of chemical weapons hidden somewhere."

Red with anger Kenny switched off the radio.

"Bloody traitor," he snarled. "That bastard got elected to Parliament with the help of Labour Party funds and the efforts of its workers, then he stabs us all in the back."

"Also by defecting to our opponents he has cheated his constituents," joined in George. "If they had wanted a Tory MP they would have elected one."

For a few moments David reflected on the situation. In a strange way he felt both bitterness and yet a certain amount of admiration for Colin Sudbury, for having the courage to stand up for his convictions.

"I read recently that if Labour lose this election Bruce Shaw will probably be told to step down as party leader," remarked David, thoughtfully, as he sipped his tea.

"That is often the case in politics," replied George. "As the man who is in overall charge he will probably take the blame if we are defeated."

"Does that mean that somebody new might reverse some of our policies?" enquired David, sounding more than a little concerned.

"Most probably," answered George. "If the party takes the view that the position we have taken on certain issues have cost us votes."

"What about Iraq?" asked David, suspiciously. "Surely we can't abandon our principles and support military action?"

George shrugged.

"To gain power it is necessary to take account of what the people are telling you."

"But that is terrible," protested David. "We should be trying to stop the suffering of those poor souls in Iraq rather than helping to make the situation worse."

"What is the use of having principles without power," answered George with equal passion. "I want to see a Labour Government elected, which will provide a good health service, better schools and give help to the poor and elderly."

David was beginning to feel his blood boil. He was becoming a passionate opponent of the War and it was unthinkable that his party might be prepared to abandon the cause.

"Surely we should try to influence public opinion, not follow it?" he argued, with his voice growing steadily louder. "Anyway, think about all those protestors on the Peace March. Who will continue to represent their views?"

Suddenly George's face began to soften. As a young man he too had despised political expediency but, in later years, he had learnt to accept the need for compromise. Without it there seemed little prospect of bringing about change.

"Don't worry," he smiled, reassuringly. "Britain won't be sending her troops out to the Middle East. Labour are going to win this election in eleven days' time."

The afternoon had been set aside for political activities. After a bite to eat the three housemates made their way to the club to join forces with the other activists. David took his own car in order to pick Alison up on the way.

Tony as usual was at the centre of operations. Each person was handed a sheet of paper listing the names and addresses of all constituents who were intending to vote Labour. As had been discussed at the meeting the previous day, each of them was to be revisited and encouraged to put up a poster in their window.

Alongside the usual helpers there were a number of strangers. Because Brockleby was a key marginal more and more party workers from neighbouring constituencies were lending a helping hand. Tony and Jacqui had both worked hard in convincing other associations that the seat really could be won.

David and Alison were part of a group that was sent to Upper Oakham. In a staunchly Tory area, Tony was keen to see at least an occasional red poster on display. To Labour eyes like his, it was too demoralising to see just blue ones on view.

Having knocked on a few doors David realised what a difficult task he had been given. On the council estates where support for Jacqui Dunn was strong, Labour voters had no reservations in putting up posters. In the more affluent areas, however, people were more reticent.

Soon he arrived at a house that he had canvassed the previous Sunday. It was home to Mrs Cook, the elderly lady who had been on the anti-war march. One of the very few people that he had spoken to on the doorstep during the past seven days, who had managed to stick out in his mind.

Meeting for the second time, they greeted each other like long lost friends. Although there was a very large gap between their ages, they both felt a strange affinity.

"Would you be prepared to put up a poster in your window?" David asked, hopefully, after they had exchanged a few pleasantries.

Mrs Cook hesitated for a few seconds.

"Give me two," she beamed, enthusiastically. "I will put one in the sitting room and another in the front bedroom. That should upset some of my neighbours."

David was delighted.

"Thank you very much. Unfortunately though, you appear to be our only supporter in the road."

A cheeky smile flashed across the elderly lady's face.

"Wait there for a moment. I may have another one for you," she replied, before hurrying down the hall.

Soon David could hear Mrs Cook speaking in a raised voice.

"I have a good looking young man at the door who would like to have a word with you Beryl. He is from the Labour Party."

"Show him in Joyce," answered another equally loud female voice.

Mrs Cook suddenly reappeared at the end of the hall and beckoned to her visitor.

"Please come this way," she called out.

David followed her into a spacious sitting room. It was tastefully decorated, but the most striking feature were two large cabinets full of dolls dressed in national costumes from many different countries. Also very prominent were many large figurines of very elegant ladies and gentlemen in the clothing

229

common in Europe during the sixteenth and seventeenth centuries.

Beryl was roughly the same age as Mrs Cook but considerably larger and rounder. In fact her size was so immense that it would have been difficult to have wedged another person on the three-seated settee she was spread out on. As standing seemed to be a strenuous business, David politely indicated to her to remain seated as they were about to shake hands.

"For the first time in my life I am going to vote Labour," she announced. "It is about time we had a new MP in Brockleby. Several times I have written to Charles Dawkins with my problems but he never bothers to reply."

"If you ask me, he is more concerned with impressing his party leader than the people who elected him," added Mr Cook, indignantly. "Our Mr Dawkins only has his sights set on becoming the next Home Secretary."

David nodded as he unfurled another poster from the roll he was carrying.

"One or two?" he enquired with a smile.

"Make it two," answered Beryl, as she held out her hands.

"By the way," said Mrs Cook. "Will you be sending a car to take us down to the polling station? The Lib Dems generally give us a lift, but we can hardly ask them to do it this time if we are voting Labour."

"I shall come and collect you myself," beamed David, as he scribbled a note in his diary. "What time would suit you both?"

"About eleven if possible," answered Beryl, after a moment's hesitation.

"Consider it done," said David, as he shook the two ladies warmly by the hand. "I shall look forward to seeing you both again on Thursday week."

David greeted Alison with a broad grin when they met in the road a few moments later. He was able to give her the news that among a sea of blue posters the neighbourhood would get four splashes of red. Hardly earth shattering but at least it was a start.

Just then a car swung around the corner. Being some distance away the two activists casually stepped on to the pavement where they continued their conversation. However, it wasn't until the vehicle was actually passing them by that David took any notice of the occupants.

Staring forlornly at him were two women. Both in white headscarves, his mother sat in the front passenger seat and youngest sister Martha behind her, were doubtless making one of their five Sunday trips to the Gospel Hall. On the far side and partly obscured by Hilary Chambers was his father sitting at the wheel.

David was stung by a pang of sadness. In less than two weeks the family he had once been so closely bonded to were now a little more than strangers. It was as though he had become so distant that they no longer felt any inclination to as much as smile or give him a friendly wave.

"Wasn't that your family?" asked Alison, as she watched the car moving away. "I'm sure I recognised your mother from when she used to meet you at the school gates."

David nodded.

"They just sat there and ignored me," he replied, resentfully.

Alison turned and patted him gently on the arm. Having had very supportive parents it was very difficult for her to comprehend how David was feeling. Even harder than that was trying to imagine how she could ever disown her own daughter later in life.

"Come on," she smiled, grabbing David's hand. "Let's go and knock on some more doors."

Chapter Eighteen

It was over a week since the fatal accident. Charles Dawkins was still being haunted by the memory of that terrified face seconds before the young man had been crushed beneath the wheels of his car. At night in his dreams he would relive the whole scene again before waking up in a cold sweat. If the truth be told though, he was more concerned for himself and his career than any remorse for the victim.

He was well aware that his whole future depended on whether there had been witnesses. As a barrister Charles knew better than most, that he was likely to be charged with manslaughter if found guilty of causing the fatality. No doubt there would be members of the local Conservative Association who would be happy to testify that he had been drinking heavily on the evening in question. Furthermore, to make matters worse he had fled the scene of the accident.

Fortunately the election campaign had managed to occupy his mind in the daytime. With so much at stake and the result likely to be close he was giving every last ounce of energy to the cause. Like Jacqui Dunn, the only other serious contender in the contest, he spent much of his time knocking on doors.

Canvassing was not something that Charles enjoyed. However, he had decided from the start of the campaign, who to target and what the message to them should be. The plan was to concentrate on those areas where Labour's support was strongest and focus mainly on the issue of crime.

At many houses Charles was greeted with a hostile reception. However, as a possible future Home Secretary in a new Conservative administration, many constituents were eager to listen to what he had to say. As in most deprived areas many residents had been burgled or had suffered from having their cars broken into. Therefore very high on their wish list from the new Government was that strong measures should be taken to remedy the situation.

With the General Election now less than two weeks away Charles was more than satisfied with the way things were going. It was Saturday afternoon and as usual the Conservative candidate was trudging up and down garden paths with his clipboard in hand. The smile as ever was broad and cheerful.

By chance he came to a house where an unpleasant argument was in progress. The resident, an elderly lady, was being confronted by a man, in overalls who appeared to be on the point of leaving. Both were speaking in raised voices.

"You will be hearing from my solicitor about this," shouted the man angrily. "I'm not a bloody charity."

"But how many times have I got to tell you," screeched the woman. "The Council are meant to come and fix my window for free."

The man in overalls looked up at the sky in exasperation.

"Then why didn't you contact the Town Hall rather than ring a private firm?"

"But I didn't ring you," snapped the woman. "It must have been my local councillor. I asked him over the telephone this morning to get someone around here to fix my broken window."

Charles Dawkins pricked up his ears. He had stopped halfway down the garden path in order to get the drift as to what was at the root of the disagreement. It was the words 'local councillor' which really started his pulse racing.

"Good afternoon," said Charles, with a genial smile. "Look I couldn't help overhearing your conversation and I wondered whether I could be of any assistance?"

The man in overalls looked the newcomer up and down suspiciously.

"And who are you exactly?"

Still smiling Charles thrust out his open palm.

"Charles Dawkins, MP for Brockleby."

"Andy Jackson," replied the man, slightly taken aback.

As they shook hands Andy seemed to be growing a little less hostile. Then with some input from the elderly lady he began recounting the facts which had led up to the present dispute. There wasn't really a lot to tell yet the glazier managed to drag out the story much more than was probably necessary.

Charles looked grave as he switched his attention to the

elderly lady. Having taken a quick glance at his canvass sheet he already knew the name of the resident without having to ask.

"It's nice to meet you Mrs Winter," he said, as they shook hands. "Would you happen to know the name of this councillor that you spoke to this morning?"

Mrs Winter looked down thoughtfully at her carpet slippers.

"I can't think of his name just at this moment," she answered with a shake of the head. "However, I do know that he is quite a young chap."

"Would it be Kenny Simpson?" prompted Charles.

"That's it," said Mrs Winter. "He hasn't been on the Council very long."

Of course she was mistaken. However, having rung Kenny's number she could have been forgiven for expecting the councillor to answer rather than a complete stranger. Particularly as the young man she spoke to had been so willing to help.

Charles's mind was working rapidly. For whatever reason the councillor had acted incorrectly and the Conservative MP intended to exploit the situation to the full. With the election result on a knife edge this was a golden opportunity to strike a decisive blow.

"Could I impose on you Mrs Winter?" asked Charles, politely. "Would you mind if we all came inside and discussed this problem over a nice cup of tea? It is my intention to resolve this matter to everyone's mutual satisfaction."

Andy glanced down anxiously at his watch.

"Just as long as it won't take too long. I have to be at another job very shortly."

Charles stood back and allowed Andy to be the first to follow Mrs Winter into the house. Then quickly withdrawing his mobile phone from his jacket pocket he made a call.

"I need somebody to meet me urgently with a camera," he instructed in a whisper. "Now take down this address."

Soon Mrs Winter and her two guests were sat back sipping tea in a small but tidy living room. Overhead two green budgerigars in a cage chirped away noisily as they hopped from perch to perch. Far less energetically a sleeping black cat lay curled up on an armchair completely oblivious to the humans who had just arrived.

"Now first things first," began Charles looking straight at Andy. "How much does Mrs Winter owe you?"

"Sixty-five pounds plus VAT," replied Andy, without hesitation. "It costs more than usual being an emergency weekend call-out."

"I can't afford that sort of money," protested Mrs Winter. "I have to try and get by on the Old Age Pension."

Charles gave her a sympathetic smile.

"Of course I understand it is a lot of money for you to find. That is precisely why I am going to settle up with Mr Jackson myself."

The faces of Mrs Winter and Andy lit up almost simultaneously. For the next few minutes both of them sat watching the Brockleby MP as he wrote out a cheque.

"That is very kind of you sir," muttered Mrs Winter, with a radiant smile.

"It is a pleasure," answered Charles as he handed the cheque to Andy. "We Conservatives care passionately for the less well-off in our society. It is outrageous that your Labour councillor should enlist a private firm to fix your window and then leave you to pay the bill. It is something that I need you both to help me put a stop to straight away."

"What can we do?" asked Andy in surprise.

Before Charles had a chance to answer the doorbell rang. Very soon Mrs Winter was leading a third guest into her living room. This one, however, was carrying a very expensive camera.

"I would like pictures of you both in a leaflet that my party is about to print," explained Charles. "Hopefully I can embarrass young Kenny Simpson so much he will think twice before he treats vulnerable council tenants like this again."

Of course both Mrs Winter and Andy felt obliged to agree. Immediately Charles began to issue the photographer with his instructions. All he required was a shot of himself taken alongside an appreciative Mrs Winter, and one of Andy Jackson peering out through the open side window of his white van holding up a cheque.

"That's prefect," beamed Charles when the pictures had been taken. "Now finally I want each of you to tell me in just a few words, how you feel about the way Councillor Simpson has treated you."

"Bloody disgusting I call it," replied Mrs Winter.

Charles smiled to himself as he put pen to paper. It was hardly the greatest quote in the world but it was blunt and to the point. No doubt the tenants on the estate would have little difficulty in appreciating its meaning he mused.

"And what to you make of Councillor Simpson's conduct Mr Jackson?" asked Charles, turning to the glazier. "After all as a small businessman there was a great risk that you wouldn't get paid for your hard work."

"He needs a good kick up the arse and if ever I get my hands on him, that is precisely what he is going to get," answered Andy.

Later that evening Charles dropped in at the Conservative Club. Having already written his article for the leaflet he was eager to share his story with a few of the members. No doubt they would concur with the view that it was yet another classical example of Labour hypocrisy in their dealings with the poor.

Adrian Thomas shook his head in disbelief.

"There must be some sort of misunderstanding. I have worked alongside young Kenny for about two years on the Council and for him to do a thing like that would simply go against the grain. He is always standing up for the less well-off."

"Well now I've found out the truth about him," smiled Charles like the cat who had just licked up the cream. "And it is my intention to let all those Labour devotees know about one of Jacqui Dunn's closest cronies."

Adrian sat staring down thoughtfully at his whisky glass. As the Leader of the Council he had come to respect Kenny for his hard work and sincerity. With most of the modern generation turning their back on the political process he had been pleased to see the young councillor's dedication. It didn't matter that the two men represented different parties when they were working side by side on various committees.

"I don't feel entirely happy about this situation," said Adrian, slowly shaking his head. "We should be sure of our facts before we blacken Kenny's name."

Charles waved his hand dismissively.

"I have gathered all the evidence I require," he replied, disdainfully. "I have absolutely no doubt that my two sources of information are totally reliable."

"So when do you want this new leaflet delivered?" enquired Adrian now resigned to the fact that he had little chance of saving the young man's reputation.

"Next weekend," replied Charles, without hesitation. "Most people will be at home and should have time to read any literature that arrives through their letterboxes. Also, with only a few days left before the election, Labour will have little opportunity to respond."

For a moment Adrian fell silent. The plan seemed to make perfect sense but he was able to detect one major flaw. Quite obviously it appeared to be something which had completely escaped the attention of his drinking companion.

"There is a snag," he began. "How are we going to find enough party workers prepared to distribute leaflets over the whole constituency in only two days?"

Charles looked unfazed as this problem was pointed out to him. As was typical of the man, he had already thought the entire plan through before discussing it with others. What he had in mind this time had a certain Machiavellian flavour about it.

"I just want to target council tenants," he explained simply. "Few homeowners are likely to be very sympathetic to the thought of Mrs Winter having to pay for her broken window. After all, they are expected to find the money themselves for their repair bills."

With a grin Adrian finished off the last drop of whisky in his glass.

"Will you be joining me for another?"

Charles shook his head firmly.

"Better not seeing that I'm driving."

Adrian raised his eyebrows in mock surprise.

"That's never stopped you in the past."

Charles made no comment as he got to his feet. As the memory of the fatal accident was still very painful he was determined never to risk repeating it again. Outwardly he was composed and self-assured as ever, but the two women in his life had noticed a change in him over the past week.

Sally, his wife, merely put his irritability down to stress as a result of his hard work in the election campaign. Madeleine on the other hand, the one person who shared his guilty secret, noticed that he appeared to be less attentive towards her. It was for this very reason that she had invited him around for a meal on Sunday evening.

In preparation for the occasion Madeleine had gone out to buy several cookery books. The time had come to get some practice in for the years ahead. It was just beginning to dawn on her that the role of the Home Secretary's wife would require a considerable amount of entertaining. Therefore she needed to be as good in the kitchen as she was in the bedroom.

During dinner Madeleine did most of the talking. For much of the time Charles just sat eating with a distant look in his eyes. It quickly became apparent to the anxious hostess that her guest had something on his mind.

"Are you still worried about the accident?" she asked with a sympathetic smile.

Charles nodded.

"It haunts me whenever I'm not thinking of politics. Each time a stranger approaches I'm afraid that he or she is about to arrest me. Whenever the telephone rings now my heart almost stops, fearing that the police are on my trail."

"I'm sure everything will be all right," answered Madeleine, taking a sip of red wine. "Even if there were witnesses it would be very difficult to identify the driver in the dark."

Charles appeared less than impressed by this argument.

"They might not be able to spot me but they might recognise my car."

Madeleine looked thoughtful.

"If that was the case I would have expected you to have heard something by now. Surely had there been witnesses they would have come forward."

Charles shrugged.

"For all I know they could be speaking to the police at this very moment."

Madeleine was beginning to feel she could be fighting a losing battle. Any positive argument she might be able to conjure up was likely to be countered by another negative one. Therefore in an attempt to bring Charles out of his present state of mind she decided to provide him with a few carnal pleasures.

By the time they had eaten Madeleine had devised her plan of action. Leaving all the dirty crockery on the table she silently took Charles by the hand and guided him down the hall of her small apartment. Then once inside her dimly lit bedroom she began slowly undressing.

The previous day she had been on a shopping spree. Not only had Madeleine been investing in cookery books but she had also ventured into a store which specialised in sexy underwear. Managing to conceal any embarrassment she had calmly strolled around examining a selection of lacy and somewhat skimpy garments. Finally she had slipped back on to the High Street, hoping not to be noticed by passers-by, carrying a small black carrier bag.

Tragically all her efforts were unappreciated. Charles hardly seemed to pay any attention as she stood before him naked but for a blue see-through negligee. Instead he just slumped down on the edge of the bed and buried his hands in his hands.

"Do you realise that everything I have ever worked for could be lost?" he groaned. "Why did that bloody idiot have to go and walk in front of my car?"

Madeleine felt deflated. At that precise moment she couldn't decide whether to offer her sympathy or throw a heavy object at him. It seemed unbelievable that somebody who commanded so much respect in the outside world could act so pathetically.

"It's a pity he is not able to apologise to you," replied Madeleine, sarcastically.

"It's all right for you," answered Charles, sulkily. "You are not threatened by a possible prison sentence."

By now Madeleine was already getting dressed again. It felt rather ridiculous standing almost naked in the middle of the room while trying to take part in a serious conversation. Smiling to herself she wondered whether to donate the negligee to the next church jumble sale. It could be useful in reinvigorating the vicar's sex life.

"Did you manage to find your mobile phone by the way?" she asked in a desperate attempt to change the subject.

"No I don't know where it can be," replied Charles, sounding like a man who was just about to be executed. "I've hunted high and low. I searched the car when it came back from the garage and none of the mechanics had come across a phone either."

Madeleine looked puzzled.

"Have you searched the house and garden and gone through all your pockets?"

Charles nodded.

"It just seems to have vanished into thin air. I've actually bought a new one now so I had better jot down the number for you."

The missing mobile was becoming quite a concern for Madeleine. She hadn't dared mention it to Charles, but having been cut off during her telephone call to him at the time of the accident she had attempted to ring him again. When there was no reply she had left a rather panicky message. In fact she had made a succession of calls that evening and the following morning, none of which had been answered.

Her mind was finally put at rest when she had heard from Charles the next day. However, now she was worried that the mobile had fallen into the wrong hands and her messages could be used to incriminate the MP in some way.

In fact Charles had been vaguely aware of the intermittent ring tones. However, as his mind was in a total state of confusion the sound of Mozart's fortieth Symphony had been little more than background music in a supermarket to him. What had happened to the mobile phone once he had got out of the car on that fateful evening though, would have to remain a mystery for just a little bit longer.

***

Mark had woken up with that 'morning after feeling'. Memories of the previous evening were dim but, a throbbing headache was sufficient evidence to suggest that he had consumed a significant quantity of alcohol. He did, however, have a vague recollection of staggering home from a nightclub long after midnight.

In most people's eyes Mark seemed to lead a rather aimless existence. Were he able to remember the numerous jobs he had started since leaving school, sitting down to write a CV would have been a lengthy process. His poor work record was almost entirely due to a combination of two factors. His over consumption of beer and an inability to get up before ten o'clock in the morning.

"At twenty-four it is time you were taking life seriously," warned Mrs Wright.

Once Mark would have dismissed such a comment. However, over the past few weeks he had gradually come around to the same opinion. Perhaps at last it was time to grow up and act responsibly.

"It's a question of knowing just where to start Mum," replied Mark, blankly.

It was now late afternoon. Mother and son were both sat by an open window in the lounge watching Amanda play by herself on the lawn. The small girl's face was shielded from view by her long blonde hair as she gathered up daisies to make a chain. All the while she could be heard singing contentedly to herself.

"You could start by marrying Alison I suppose," suggested Mrs Wright. "Then you would be able to see more of your daughter."

Mark gave a long sigh.

"I'm afraid I've messed Alison around too much in the past. Anyway I understand she is going out with someone else now."

"You have one very big advantage over him," replied Mrs Wright, with a sly smile. "You happen to be Amanda's father."

Mark gave his mother a dubious look.

"Why should that make a great deal of difference?"

"Because you dote on that little girl," answered Mrs Wright, nodding in the direction of Amanda. "Alison is well aware that her daughter would never get the same love and attention from a step-father."

At that precise moment Amanda looked up and exchanged a wave with the two adults.

"I think I would need a great deal more going for me than that, to persuade Alison to marry me," replied Mark, with a smile.

"Perhaps you should consider joining the Labour Party," suggested Mrs Wright. "That would certainly impress Alison."

Mark screwed up his face.

"That seems too high a price to pay for a reconciliation," he laughed.

"It could be worth it in the end," answered Mrs Wright, slowly rising up from her chair to go to the kitchen.

Sundays seemed to follow a similar pattern for Mark. He would pick Amanda up before lunch and then take her out for something to eat. If the weather was fine they would go to the park and feed the ducks, then it was back to grandma's for tea. Finally the two of them would catch the bus to mummy's house after which daddy and 'the Little Fairy Princess' would be separated for another week.

Mark was deep in thought as he and Amanda approached Alison's maisonette. He knew it would be absurd to simply propose to his ex-partner on the doorstep right out of the blue. However it was just possible that she might accept an invitation to join him for a meal in a restaurant. After that things could progress from there.

Still holding Amanda's hand Mark rang the doorbell. Having prepared a speech of sorts, he was fretful of fluffing his lines when coming face to face with Alison. On the other hand he was also wary of appearing too slick.

For a few moments nothing could be heard inside the maisonette. Then there was the distinct sound of shuffling feet before the door suddenly swung open. Much to Mark's surprise though, he found himself looking at an older person than the one he had been expecting to see.

"Is Alison in Mrs Johnson?" he enquired, feeling a little uneasy.

Mark had always been under the impression that his ex-partner's mother had never really approved of him. Although her smile was friendly enough, there was always a slight note of disapproval in her voice whenever they spoke. It was rather as though she wanted to strangle him but was trying hard to conceal the fact.

"I'm afraid she is having a bath at the moment. Can I take a message?" replied Mrs Johnson, sounding like the managing director's secretary in a large corporation.

Mark hesitated for a split second.

"No it's really not important," he smiled, as he bent down to kiss his daughter goodbye.

Feeling a little deflated Mark wandered back to the bus stop.

242

He had once owned a car but circumstances had forced him to sell it in order to make ends meet. His dole money was insufficient to permit him such luxuries.

It was time Mark decided, to join the rat race. He would discard his aimless existence and become a respectable member of society. Instead of living off the state he would get a good job and acquire all those material things that defines one as middle class. If she was agreeable, he would marry Alison and they would buy an expensive house in Upper Oakham with a large garden for Amanda to play in.

No sooner had Mark reached the bus stop before he received a call on his mobile phone. Having a gut feeling as to who might be ringing he wondered whether to ignore it. If he were to turn over a new leaf this would be an excellent starting point. On the other hand the prospect of having a quiet night at home was unappealing.

"A group of us are off to a party tonight. Shall we pick you up at eight o'clock?" asked the caller.

Mark smiled broadly.

"Plenty of women and booze I hope?"

"Goes without saying," laughed the caller.

"See you at eight then," answered Mark, suddenly feeling quite light-hearted.

He always enjoyed a good party. Of course he still needed to get his life together but perhaps there was no reason to be in an almighty hurry. It was always wise to think things through before making any rash decision he told himself.

Chapter Nineteen

David's first day at Robsons went well. After being introduced to everyone the rest of the morning was spent sorting through the photocopied leads from his former company. No longer with an office of his own he felt strange working alongside colleagues. On the other hand it helped him to start forming close ties that much quicker.

The atmosphere was friendly and relaxed. Banter was plentiful while sexual innuendo was frequent and took place without causing any apparent embarrassment. There was also a constant use of swear words and blasphemy, which for some people, seemed to form part of their normal vocabulary.

Wesley Chapple was the first friend that David made. The grandson of Jamaican immigrants who had arrived in Britain in the nineteen fifties, he was one of those people who was forever smiling. Because of his good-natured friendliness it was difficult not to feel instantly drawn to him.

As soon as David had settled in at his new desk, Wesley, who sat close by, struck up a conversation.

"Which football team do you support?"

David thought for a split second. As the Fellowship reject worldly pastimes his knowledge of sport was limited, to say the least. However, he was eager to disguise the fact if at all possible.

"I support Manchester United and Charlton," he replied, deciding to select the sides that were favoured by his two flatmates.

"I'm a Crystal Palace season ticket holder," announced Wesley, proudly.

David tried to look suitably impressed. However, he was anxious to change the subject in order to avoid exposing his ignorance of the game.

"Have you worked here long?" he enquired, while sharpening a pencil.

"It will be three years in January," answered Wesley, with his smile appearing to grow wider by the minute.

"Would you say this is a good company to work for?" asked David.

Wesley shrugged.

"It's a job I suppose," he replied casually. "The thing I enjoy here most is the social life. People in this department tend to spend a lot of their lunchtimes and evenings down at the pub."

David was about to press for more information when Wesley was interrupted by the telephone. Returning to the sheets of customers he suddenly came to one which sent his pulse racing. Back in May he had written in bold capitals 'Client requires a call towards the end of September. Intends to order furniture for a care home that opens in December'. Firmly of the belief that there was no time like the present, he began eagerly to ring the number.

"Do you know, I was just about to call you," replied Arthur Bell, the purchasing manager that David had known for several years. "It's about time that we started to set the wheels in motion."

"I'm not calling from Fine Choice," warned David. "Unfortunately the company are on the brink of bankruptcy and had to release me last Friday."

Arthur seemed genuinely alarmed at the news.

"Sounds as though we had better look around for another furniture supplier then. Do you happen to have any ideas?"

Of course like a knight in shining armour, David was able to come to the rescue. Then having made an appointment for the following week he went in search of a brochure to send to the purchasing manager ahead of the meeting. Once the large A4 sized envelope had been handed in at the post room, he returned to his desk to make an entry in his diary.

Roger Green was naturally delighted with the prospect of another large order. That afternoon as they set off for Conningvale House he began to lay out his plans for the new salesman. He could already foresee an exciting future in the company in which David would be playing a key role.

"At Robsons we work hard and play hard," he said, cheerily. "When we win a major order I take the Sales Department down the pub and buy everyone drinks."

"Sounds good," answered David, enthusiastically. "That

would never happen at Fine Choice. In fact the Fellowship won't socialise with those members of staff who don't belong to their church."

Roger sighed.

"Team unity is very important. Encouraging colleagues to become friends outside the office helps cement good relations in the workplace."

"Makes good sense to me," replied David.

At that moment Roger, who was driving, slowed the car down as they approached a roundabout. Having never visited Conningvale House before he was reliant on his passenger to direct him.

"Take the second exit," David instructed.

"Do Fine Choice ever entertain their clients?" enquired Roger as he turned into a quiet country lane.

David laughed.

"They might send them complimentary hampers at Christmas but that is about it. As the salesmen are all Fellowship it means that wining and dining clients it out of the question."

Roger shook his head in disbelief.

"I take a lot of my most important clients out to expensive restaurants. It's amazing how much people enjoy a good meal when someone else is paying for it."

"And does that help you bring in many big orders?" asked David.

Roger turned his eyes off the road for a brief moment and gave his passenger a cheeky grin.

"It provides me with a lot more than just business. There are a lot of very nice lady buyers in this industry."

Appreciating that his new boss enjoyed being 'Jack the Lad' David decided to play along.

"Sounds like a lot of fun."

"I'll see to it that you get some of the action," promised Roger. "A good looking chap like you should score well with some of these women."

When the two salesmen arrived at Conningvale House they were met by Shirley Bromage, who was waiting in reception for them. David detected the same frosty expression that he recalled from their first encounter. It was the disdainful look that one might give when stepping into a cave full of bats guano.

"Thank goodness you are more reliable than the gentleman who was supposed to meet me last week," she began, testily. "He made me waste the best part of the day, which I could ill afford."

David could have informed her that Maurice Hopkins had been preparing to gallivant around in the Scottish Highlands but thought better of it. Instead he quietly followed Shirley into the narrow room where he had given her his original presentation. As before the cardboard boxes were stacked up against the wall.

"There's just me here today to impress," said Shirley, taking a seat behind the wooden desk.

Picking up the brochure that Ryan had left on his visit, she began thumbing through the glossy pages. There was still that disconsolate look on her face of the disapproving headmistress. Sensing the frostiness in the atmosphere, Roger decided to try introducing a little warmth.

"This should make an absolutely delightful home," he said turning to David. "I love the building and it is so peaceful out here in the middle of the countryside."

The first trace of a smile appeared on Shirley's face. The frost was beginning to melt and soon she and Roger were laughing and joking like lifelong friends.

"Well I am certainly going to buy my furniture from your company Roger," she said, finally with a coy smile. "But I would like to take a closer look at some of the chairs that you have here in your brochure."

Roger looked thoughtful.

"Look, why don't I take you out for lunch one day this week. Then afterwards we can go back to Robsons where I can show you our whole selection of furniture."

Shirley's face lit up.

"As it happens I am free tomorrow during the middle of the day."

"Excellent," beamed Roger. "David and I will pick you up here at about twelve. I know a charming little restaurant close by which serves exquisite food."

The following day Roger treated his client like royalty. Having booked in advance, he had ordered champagne in an ice bucket to welcome them on the table when they arrived. Then with a broad smile he encouraged Shirley to select from the most expensive dishes on the menu.

After the meal they sat leisurely sipping brandy for a while. Roger lent a sympathetic ear as Shirley poured out all the problems she was facing in trying to get the home ready by the deadline set by the Council. Getting her furniture in place before the opening day was just one of her major problems.

"Don't worry," smiled Roger, reassuringly. "I will ensure that Conningvale House is fully furnished by whatever date you care to give me."

"Thank goodness I've found a company I can rely on," said Shirley, gratefully.

Her remark prompted David to ask the question, which had been gnawing away at him over the last two days.

"Did anyone from Fine Choice ever get back to you?"

"Not a word," replied Shirley in disgust. "If Mr Hopkins does have the cheek to ring me up, I shall give him a piece of my mind."

"Please do," joined in Roger. "I think he has treated you appallingly."

"Thank you Roger," said Shirley, favouring the sales manager with a warm smile.

"You seem to be making quite an impression on Mrs Bromage," said David when the client had slipped out to the ladies washroom after the meal.

Roger gave him a sly look.

"We both know the business is in the bag. It is now my intention to get her to spend as much as possible with us."

"And boost our commission," added David, with a grin.

"Exactly," answered Roger as he finished off his glass of brandy in one gulp.

At four o'clock the two salesmen returned to their department. They had just waved Shirley Bromage off in a taxi and now Roger Green was left holding a lucrative order that the client had just signed. His face looked a picture of absolute contentment.

Returning to his office Roger sent an email to all the sales staff. It was one that he knew would be well received.

'Company has just secured a large order. Pack up early and

join me for drinks at the Queens Head.'

The invitation took David completely by surprise. Although welcoming it as an opportunity to get acquainted with his new colleagues, he would have preferred an advanced warning. Having arranged to go out canvassing later that evening he was beginning to foresee problems ahead. Finally he made up his mind to 'down a swift half' and then go home.

The plan, however, was doomed to failure for the hero of the hour. Word having spread round that David was responsible for securing the large order, many were eager to express their gratitude. It was quite apparent that he was in great demand.

Being a new recruit, David was having difficulty in sorting out who was who. The previous day Roger had escorted him around the office in order to introduce him to everyone but most of the names had just failed to stick. For no particular reason though, some people had managed to make a deeper impression on him than others.

The staff at Robsons were gathered around several tables that had been placed end to end. David was sat facing Roger and Ryan Pritchard who were explaining to him about a motivational prize that was presented each month to the most successful salesman. By nature a very competitive person, it was an idea that appealed to him.

"Last month I won two tickets to see Spurs up at White Hart Lane," beamed Ryan.

"This guy wins nearly every month," laughed Roger. "It's about time somebody provided him with some rivalry."

Wesley Chapple who had sat quietly sipping his pint of beer suddenly perked up.

"I'm sure that David will give him a run for his money."

David gave Ryan a sly smile.

"I'll see what I can do."

Roger eagerly rubbed his hands together.

"Let the battle commence gentlemen."

There might have followed some friendly banter between the two competing salesmen. However, at that precise moment they were interrupted by the barman who had come to collect up the empty glasses. After that the conversation progressed on to another topic.

Time was passing quickly. When David strolled up to the bar to fetch his third free drink he had already abandoned any thought of canvassing. The party activists he concluded, would have to manage without him for one evening.

By nine thirty most of Robsons' sales staff had gone home. Roger and Ryan had been two of the earliest to leave and David had spent the last hour listening to Wesley discussing football with a couple of male colleagues. With little understanding of the game though, his attention was being drawn elsewhere.

Sitting at the other end of the table were three secretaries. The two older women were in deep conversation whilst the younger one was watching David through half-closed eyes and a faint smile hovering around her lips. She was slim and pretty with light brown hair.

Suddenly the young secretary stood up. She whispered something to her companions before walking a semi-circle around the back of a few colleagues who still remained at the table. Then finally she stopped beside David.

"May I come and join you?" she asked with a glint in her eye.

"Please do," replied David, taken rather by surprise.

The secretary then slowly lowered herself into the vacant chair on David's right.

"I'm Samantha in case you've forgotten."

"I'm afraid I did," answered David a little sheepishly. "It will take me ages to get used to everyone's name."

"Anyway, congratulations on winning the big order," she smiled. "You've given us all a good night out in the pub."

"Glad that I've made myself so popular," grinned David. "Have you worked for Robsons long?"

"Only a few months," answered Samantha, taking a sip from her wine glass. "They don't exactly pay me a fortune but the social life is good."

Already David was beginning to feel attracted to the young secretary. So captivated was he by her dark blue eyes and soft feminine voice, that all other thoughts had completely gone out of his head. The amount of alcohol that was circulating around in his bloodstream was making it very difficult to resist temptation.

"Do you live locally?" he enquired, casually.

"I share a flat in Station Road with two girlfriends," answered

Samantha. "How about you?"

David looked pleasantly surprised.

"Parkwood Drive, just around the corner from you. Last weekend I moved into a house with two other guys."

Just then David happened to look up. He became aware that Wesley Chapple and the two other football enthusiasts were watching him with some amusement. The oldest of the trio, a rather stocky man with a drooping moustache very fashionable in the seventies, gave the embarrassed new boy a cheeky wink.

"You're not married then?" asked Samantha, who seemed completely oblivious of the spectators.

David shook his head.

"I was engaged but we recently decided to break it off."

Samantha gave him a sympathetic smile.

"Are there any other women in your life?"

"Not at the moment," replied David, glancing down at his beer mug. "Perhaps someone will come along one of these days."

Of course it wasn't true. In fact until the past few minutes he would never have dreamt of denying the existence of his relationship with Alison. It was rather as though dark forces had taken over his whole being and were trying to lead him astray. However, he decided to deal with his feelings of guilt in the morning.

"I'm actually divorced," said Samantha. "My husband and I were only together for nine months."

David was taken aback. He had been brought up to believe that marriage should only be terminated when one spouse died. However, not for the first time, he quickly reminded himself that he no longer lived in the world of the Fellowship.

"What a shame that it didn't work out for you," replied David as he was about to take another sip of beer.

"Actually, it's fun being single again," smiled Samantha saucily. "I'm free to do just what I like now."

They continued to talk for a long time. In fact the pair of them were so engrossed in conversation that they were unaware that the rest of Robsons' staff had drifted away. Finally Samantha glanced at her watch.

"Look at the time," she gasped. "I had better be going."

"Can I give you a lift?" enquired David, hopefully.

"Where have you parked your car?" asked Samantha, putting on a rather smart red jacket.

"In the yard not far from the loading bay," replied David, finishing off the beer in his glass.

Samantha looked concerned.

"The security guard locks the gates at nine before going off for a sleep in the warehouse. I'm afraid you won't be able to get to your car before the morning. Somebody should have warned you."

David felt exasperated.

"How am I expected to get home then?"

Opening her shoulder bag, Samantha took out a mobile phone.

"We can share a cab. Let me ring the number of a firm I regularly use."

Very soon they were sitting side by side on the back seat of a Ford Focus. David was facing that age old male problem of what to do next, when suddenly Samantha rested her head on his shoulder. Immediately the sensuous fragrance of her hair began to fill him with desire.

Turning in his seat David gently kissed her on the forehead. Then caring little for what the driver might be thinking he started to caress Samantha's thigh. Much to his delight, she responded by placing her arms around his neck and they sat locked in a tender embrace.

All too soon their period of romantic bliss came to an end. Having turned the corner into Station Road the driver broke the silence by seeking further directions.

"Just stop about fifty yards on your left," said Samantha.

"When will I see you again?" whispered David.

"About nine o'clock in the morning," giggled Samantha. "See you by the photocopying machine."

"I was hoping that we could arrange to meet one evening after work," he said, hopefully.

Samantha kissed him quickly on the cheek before scrambling out of the car.

"I'm sure that we can arrange something," she smiled. "Let's talk about it tomorrow."

George and Kenny were sat sipping coffee when David

arrived home. They greeted him with surprised looks as he popped his head around the living room door.

"We thought you'd gone off to join the Tories," said Kenny, giving George a wink.

David stared down at his feet a little sheepishly.

"Sorry guys but all the sales staff were invited out for drinks and I couldn't really refuse."

"Not to worry," smiled George. "We were just concerned that you were OK."

"I should have phoned but I just didn't think."

No sooner had he uttered these words before he was struck by a feeling of déjà vu. Only two weeks earlier he had stood before his parents in their sitting room and been made to feel guilty for arriving home late. It suddenly flashed across his mind that perhaps he had broken out of one prison only to enter another.

The smile began to disappear from Kenny's face.

"If it wasn't so late I would suggest that you give Alison a ring. She was very worried that you might have had an accident."

David started to feel guilty for the first time that evening.

"I'll give her a ring at the library in the morning," he muttered, before turning to make his way towards the stairs.

***

Maurice Hopkins arrived back to work on Monday as planned. Unfortunately he had picked up a rather nasty cold during his Scottish holiday and was feeling out of sorts. The last thing he wanted was to be greeted by the pile of queries that were waiting for him on his desk.

The Conningvale House order had barely crossed his mind while he had been away. However, now he was back in the office he was determined to ring up and apologise. It was only a matter of finding a spare minute to make the call.

Of course poor Maurice had no idea that the business was about to be taken from under his nose. It did strike him as odd, however, that amongst the numerous messages which had been left for him during his absence, not one had been from Mrs Bromage. It occurred to him that perhaps the order wasn't so urgent after all.

Several times throughout the day Maurice tried ringing the home but, on each occasion, the line was engaged. Finally, as he was about to go home that evening the idea came to him of delegating to his new right-hand man. Being so dependable Des seemed to be an ideal choice.

Maurice managed to catch the man in question as he was in the process of clearing up his desk for the day.

In answer to the request Des looked rather worried.

"I'll see what I can do," he replied, hesitantly. "At the moment though I am being rushed off my feet. There just aren't enough hours in the day to complete everything."

In fact there was some truth in what he was saying. Des had been so busy telling everyone how much he had to do it hadn't been possible to get on with much work. It was really the story of his life.

The following morning was particularly hectic for him. Mostly standing by the coffee machine Des could be heard listing out all the tasks he was expected to carry out during the day to any colleague who happened to be around. It therefore wasn't until after lunch that he found time to make the all important call.

"She isn't here," announced the surly receptionist brusquely. "Mrs Bromage has gone out to lunch and I am expecting her back later this afternoon."

Des left a message and hung up. Sitting back in his chair he gazed around his new office. For five years the domain of David Chambers, it was small and square with a good view over the loading bay. The present occupier, however, decided that a facelift was long overdue. In fact he was determined to give it top priority.

The choice of colour was essential he told himself. Disregarding a number of urgent messages which had been left on his desk, he tried to decide whether the walls would look better painted in cream or light blue. It was certainly a dilemma, so throughout the afternoon he called in a number of colleagues to offer an opinion.

Finally Angela Barton, the senior secretary seemed to come up with the perfect solution.

"You could have two walls painted in cream and the other two in light blue."

Des gave her an appreciative smile. What this woman lacked in looks she definitely made up for in imagination he thought.

"And what colour would you suggest for the wall facing the window?" he asked the Oracle.

Unfortunately, before the advice could be imparted to him he received his long awaited call.

"Thank you for ringing back Mrs Bromage," said Des when he recognised the voice. "Maurice Hopkins and I would like to make an appointment with you to discuss your order. When would it be convenient?"

"You and your sales manager can go and fly a kite," said Shirley, angrily. "All my furniture requirements are going to be supplied by Robsons. I signed an agreement with them about three quarters of an hour ago."

Des was stunned.

"But I understood you were going to buy from us."

"Actually I am amazed that you have the cheek to ring me," replied Shirley, icily. "A week ago I drove all the way up from Portsmouth to meet Mr Hopkins and finalise everything but he didn't arrive."

"Unfortunately there were unforeseen problems," answered Des, who could think of nothing better to say on the spur of the moment.

"And I suppose he was stranded up at the North Pole with no access to a phone," said Shirley in a raised voice.

"I am sorry that you have been unhappy with the service we have provided," replied Des, deciding that making excuses would be fruitless.

"It's too late now to apologise," snapped Shirley, before slamming down the receiver.

Des felt annoyed that he had taken a scolding for someone else's negligence. He therefore sort solace in a large jam doughnut that he had been saving in his top drawer. Feeling it was time for a complete break he leaned back in his chair and put his feet up on the desk.

Angela Barton had disappeared during the telephone conversation. However, Des, having benefited from her advisory service on interior design, had himself come up with an idea. Instead of light blue on two opposite walls he wondered whether a delicate shade of pink would go better with cream.

Suddenly Maurice popped his head around the door.

"Any news yet?"

"We've lost another sale I'm afraid," replied Des, dragging his mind away from various colour schemes for the office. "It appears that Mrs Bromage is buying her furniture from Robsons."

Maurice was horrified.

"Buy why?" he muttered in dismay.

Des shrugged.

"It seems she didn't like the way we treated her."

Maurice needed a few moments to reflect on the situation. With a haunted expression on his face he gazed down on one of the company's lorries as it pulled into the yard. He had the look of a man who expected the vehicle to explode.

"I bet it was David Chambers who upset her," said Maurice with his eyes still fixed firmly on the lorry. "He has got to be the one to blame."

Des was unable to share Maurice's suspicions but nodded just the same to please his boss.

"You could be right there," he said, with little conviction in his voice.

"Of course I am," snapped Maurice. "He was always a hopeless salesman and this just proves it. Thank goodness we got rid of him when we did."

As coincidence would have it, at that very moment David was being toasted by his new colleagues at the Queen's Head for winning the Conningvale House order.

Chapter Twenty

The following day David took the bus to work. It was quite an adventure for a young man who had never used this form of transport in his life. The Chambers family, like most other Fellowship followers, travelled almost exclusively by car, which enabled them to steer clear of sinners who were unlikely to be saved by the Almighty.

Sitting on the top deck David enjoyed a panoramic view over parks and many other open spaces. For this first time passenger, it was a strange experience to be moving along the High Street and being able to look through upstairs windows or gaze down upon shoppers below. Then every hundred metres or so the bus would grind to a halt by the roadside and from his lofty height, he would watch as people of all ages climbed on and off. Finally the bell would ring out and the journey would continue again.

Fortunately David had allowed himself ample time. Although sitting on top of a red double-decker was quite entertaining it hardly moved at express speed. Not only were there all those numerous passenger stops but to add to the frustration, the bus seemed to go all around the houses instead of taking the most direct route.

To be truthful, David was relieved to see Robsons red bricked building come into view at long last. In what seemed to be an eternity on the bus, he had sat next to four different passengers and seen parts of Brockleby he had never known existed. The trouble was that for the latter part of the ride he had been breaking his neck to go for a pee.

Wesley Chapple was already at his desk when David walked into the office. However, he had yet to switch on his computer and was instead busy studying the sports pages of his newspaper. On his face there was a look of intense concentration.

"Good morning," called David, cheerfully.

For a few minutes there was no reaction. Then having finished his article at last, Wesley turned his head around and favoured his new colleague with a mischievous grin.

"How did you get on last night with Samantha?" he asked.

Unprepared for such a direct question David needed a few seconds to collect his thoughts. It was tempting to exaggerate and claim to have made a sexual conquest but a voice within his head was telling him to play the whole thing down. It was likely that any gossip would spread rapidly around the office.

"Both Samantha and I went home soon after you," answered David, casually.

"She didn't invite you back to her place then?" enquired Wesley, still hopeful that his colleague would have something juicy to report.

David, shook his head.

"No, we just went our separate ways."

David, however, was unable to kill off all speculation of a budding office romance. Therefore throughout the day and for the rest of the week he had to put up with plenty of banter in the Sales Department. Even Roger Green liked to contribute with the occasional jibe.

The good humoured teasing didn't trouble David too much. As the child of a family with rather quirky religious beliefs he had suffered far worse at school. His greatest concern was the possible embarrassment that certain comments might cause Samantha were she to become aware of them.

There was another reason that David would have preferred the banter to come to an end. The truth was that he already regretted his brief flirtation with the young secretary in the back of the taxi and was now keen to put the whole episode behind him. Although she was very beautiful there was no place for two women in his life. Things would just become too complicated.

Under the circumstances he decided to keep his distance from Samantha and allow the gossip to die down. He would act as though nothing had happened between them and treat her like any other colleague in the office. It occurred to him that if he were to show no further interest she was bound to get the message before too long.

Unfortunately things didn't turn out to be as simple as that. When David failed to ask her out as he had suggested in the taxi, Samantha made up her mind to take the initiative herself. It was only a matter of picking the right moment.

Finally the opportunity presented itself in the stationary room of all places. David had wandered in to find a box of staples when he suddenly turned around to find that he wasn't alone. Samantha had followed him in before silently shutting the door behind her.

"My flatmates and I are holding a party on Saturday night," she began with a beguiling smile. "If you are free would you like to come?"

Of course David knew he should be strong and refuse the invitation. However, at that precise moment he was simply mesmerised by the young secretary and his willpower deserted him. She was just too pretty to be resisted.

"What time does the party start?" he heard himself blurt out.

"People will be arriving any time after half eight," answered Samantha as she helped herself to a small notepad.

David looked thoughtful. As it happened Alison was visiting her aunt in the New Forest at the weekend which would rather leave him at a loose end. Of course he could spend Saturday evening with the other Labour activists but a party was certainly a more attractive option.

"I have shopping and various things to do in the day but I am free in the evening," he answered, finally.

"So will you come then?" asked Samantha, hopefully.

"Yes and thank you for inviting me," said David with a broad smile. "I will have to remember to bring a bottle of wine."

Samantha quickly scribbled something down on her new notepad.

"The address is number twenty-two, Station Road, but I've written it down just in case you happen to forget."

Very soon David began to feel glad he had accepted the invitation. Outside work most of his leisure time was now taken up with political campaigning and a party promised to offer a welcome change. He decided to stop feeling guilty about Alison and simply go and enjoy himself.

Up to this point everything had gone well for David since he had parted company with the Fellowship. He now enjoyed a good social life and was quickly widening his circle of friends. It was simply too perfect to last.

The bombshell struck just after midday on Saturday. David

was sat in the living room reading a newspaper when his two housemates returned home from their weekly surgery at the Village Hall. However, the expression on each man's face suggested that all was far from well.

"Have you spoken to a Mrs Dorothy Winter?" demanded George as soon as he came face to face with his newest lodger.

David was rather startled by the stern manner in which he was being addressed. It was difficult to gather his thoughts with both Kenny and George glaring accusingly at him. After a few minutes of searching his memory he finally had to admit defeat.

"The name does seem vaguely familiar but I just can't recall where I've heard it before," he answered a little uneasily.

"Perhaps you had a telephone conversation with this lady last Saturday about her broken window," suggested Kenny, with a hint of menace in his voice.

"I remember," replied David as it all came flooding back to him. "Mrs Winter told me she had been waiting nine days for someone to come and fix it."

"So you decided to be helpful and ring up a private company on her behalf," said George, bitterly.

David shrugged.

"I had to do something. She couldn't be left with a broken window for ever."

"But Mrs Winter was both a pensioner and a council tenant," fumed Kenny. "Therefore in this particular borough she was entitled to have somebody come down from the Town Hall and repair it free of charge. However, through your stupidity this poor lady was presented with a bill for over seventy-six pounds."

"I'm sorry I didn't realise," stammered David. "Look I'm happy to reimburse Mrs Winter out of my own pocket. If you have the address I will pop round to see her straight away and put matters right."

George who had stood holding a leaflet in his hand, suddenly slammed it down hard on the table in front of his new lodger.

"You're too late," he snapped. "Charles Dawkins has beaten you to it."

"But why?" asked David in surprise.

"To stick a knife in the Labour Party, with the ultimate intention of damaging the prospects of his main rival in the

General Election," explained George, angrily.

"You have probably helped him kill two birds with one stone," added Kenny, bitterly. "Your blunder won't just put an end to Jacqui Dunn's hopes of becoming an MP, it will probably destroy my reputation as a councillor at the same time."

"I don't understand," answered David, who was beginning to feel his stomach churning around.

"I think you had better read the latest literature that the Tories are putting out," replied George, pointing at the leaflet on the table.

David was left alone to digest Charles Dawkins' article. Suddenly hating the sight of their new housemate, George and Kenny had stormed off to the kitchen to make drinks. Speaking in loud voices, both were making it perfectly clear what they thought of dim-witted people who interfered in matters that didn't concern them.

As soon as David picked up the leaflet his blood began to boil. Under the heading 'Labour Councillor lands pensioner with huge repair bill' the Brockleby MP had gone straight for the jugular. Having assumed that Kenny was responsible for engaging the glazier, the article described the young man as heartless and uncaring. In contrast, Charles Hawkins had presented himself rather like a modern-day knight in shining armour riding up on his white horse to rescue an elderly lady in distress.

The two photographs particularly angered David. In the first the MP was standing alongside Mrs Winter with the sort of smarmy smile that would have embarrassed many self-respecting game show hosts. The look of gratitude on the pensioner's face on the other hand, resembled that of a person who had just been rescued in the nick of time from the jaws of a crocodile.

The second photograph was no less infuriating. A man in a white van was seen leaning out of the window and waving a cheque as though he was a jackpot lottery winner. Named as Andy Jackson, the glazier who had fixed the window, he was quoted as saying that 'Councillor Simpson needed a good kick up the arse'.

In despair, David decided to get as far away from the house as he could. Feeling totally confused he just wandered aimlessly along streets that he had recently delivered leaflets or even canvassed. His mind a blank, he had absolutely no idea where he was and in which direction he was heading.

Finally the fog began to clear. Dreading the thought of returning home to a hostile atmosphere he toyed with the idea of ringing the Brockleby Park Hotel. If there was a vacant room he could collect all his belongings and move in straight away. Of course it would only be a short-term measure until he was able to find something more permanent.

While pondering on this matter he became aware of a large figure coming towards him. As it got closer David recognised the features of a plump man with a shock of dark hair. It was Mr Chapman, his old History teacher.

"David Chambers!" he beamed, as he threw out a chubby hand.

"How are you?" smiled David, who was genuinely pleased to see a friendly face.

"I'm very well dear boy," replied Mr Chapman, as he firmly shook the hand of his former pupil. "I understand that you have taken up politics."

David nodded.

"How did you know?"

A sly grin spread across Mr Chapman's broad face.

"I happened to be driving by in my car last week and saw you and Alison Johnson delivering leaflets together."

"Yes I am now a fully paid up member of the Labour Party," admitted David, proudly.

"Just like Alison," said Mr Chapman, still grinning.

David realised what was being insinuated. However, although it was true that he had got involved in politics because of Alison he was too embarrassed to confess to the fact. Under the circumstances he decided to pretend that his motives were far more noble.

"Actually I joined the Labour Party because they want to keep Britain out of the Iraq War."

"Very good reason," smiled Mr Chapman, approvingly. "And are you enjoying your involvement in the General Election?"

"I was until an hour or so ago," replied David, sadly.

"Why, what happened?" enquired Mr Chapman, with raised eyebrows.

For a split second David hesitated. He was undecided as to whether to give in to a pressing need to unburden himself or just change the subject altogether. Finally he went for the first option and provided a full account of the broken window saga.

When David had finished, Mr Chapman smiled sympathetically.

"Look even the Prime Minister makes mistakes. If Labour lose this election the defeat is more likely to be blamed on the actions of Bruce Shaw rather than your tiny little blunder."

"That is probably true," replied David, gloomily. "However, the local activists may hold me responsible if Jacqui Dunn loses the Brockleby seat."

"Look, if your candidate doesn't win on Thursday it will be due to many reasons," laughed Mr Chapman, stepping aside on the pavement to allow a mother with a pram to pass. "Anyway if your so-called political friends continue to be nasty to you I suggest taking up another activity. Perhaps something that won't get you into trouble like fishing or singing in a choir."

"You can forget the second idea," grinned David. "I have got a dreadful voice."

Suddenly looking serious, Mr Chapman fixed his dark brown eyes firmly on his former pupil.

"Last time we met you were just about to part company with the Fellowship. I take it that now you are living with these two friends that the ties have finally been broken."

David nodded forlornly.

"The only Fellowship friends I have left are Simon and Rebecca Broadbent. Not even my parents want to know me anymore."

Mr Chapman placed his hand on David's shoulder.

"I just don't know how people can treat their own flesh and blood like that. Nevertheless, there is nobody now to stop you from following your dreams and training to become a school teacher."

"I remember we spoke about it at the reunion," replied David. "Unfortunately there has been so much going on in my life that I haven't had time to give it much thought."

"Well you have my number young man," smiled Mr Chapman, patting David on the upper arm. "If you need any advice don't hesitate to give me a ring."

Then with a cheery wave he continued on his way. Mr Chapman was one of those people who managed to radiate warmth to anybody he happened to come into contact with. As the large bulky figure disappeared into the distance David was already feeling that much more positive about life.

In this new frame of mind David decided not to book a hotel room for the moment. It seemed to make sense to leave it for one more day and see whether his two housemates mellowed towards him. With a bit of luck the whole thing might just blow over.

However, when David returned home later that afternoon George and Kenny continued to ignore him. Taking the hint he went up to his room and read for a while. Rather belatedly he began learning about the role of a local councillor from the small booklet with the red cover which Tony had given him. Soon he was regretting not having flicked through the pages before. It would certainly have stopped him putting his foot in it with the window saga.

One thing, however, was starting to become apparent to David. It would certainly be very difficult to do his present job, study with the Open University and perform the role of a local councillor all at the same time. Something he decided would have to be put on hold for the foreseeable future.

At six thirty the front door slammed shut. Gloomily David wandered over to the bedroom window and watched as his two housemates climbed into George's car. Generally at this time he would have been setting off with them to the club but tonight, quite obviously his company wasn't wanted.

Of course David did know where he would be welcome. After having a quick bite to eat in the kitchen he started preparing himself for Samantha's party. On no account did he intend to sit around the house moping all evening.

At a quarter to nine David arrived outside number twenty-two, Station Road holding a bottle of red wine. Having been raised in a Fellowship family, he had never been to an event where the idea is to dance to loud music while embracing members of the opposite sex and consuming large amounts of alcohol. Although it had to be said that his parents, like other followers, were not averse to getting drunk.

A torrent of sound greeted David as the front door swung open. For a brief moment a tall young woman with short frizzy hair stood and looked him up and down as though assessing his suitability for admittance. Finally with a casual wave of the hand she stepped to one side and allowed him in.

"I work with Samantha," said David in a voice just loud enough to be heard above the music.

"You must be her latest," replied the young woman, nonchalantly. "My name is Alex. I am one of Samantha's flatmates."

David called out his name to her as he was led down the hall and into a large kitchen.

"Help yourself to a drink while I go and tell Samantha that you are here," said Alex, just managing the faintest of smiles.

David put his wine bottle down beside a dozen or more others on the table in the centre of the room. There were a number of other people in the kitchen either helping themselves to drinks or just milling around. Without exception they appeared to be in their early to mid-twenties.

Due entirely to his total lack of experience as a party goer, David had come overdressed for the occasion. Quite clearly a suit looked out of place when all the other males he had seen so far were wearing jeans and casual open-neck shirts. It was yet another stark reminder of how much he still had to learn about the ways of the world. A further lesson was to follow shortly afterwards.

Samantha hurried into the kitchen with a wide smile. Dressed casually like everyone else with one notable exception of course, she immediately grabbed David by the hand and guided him towards the door.

"Come on," she called, excitedly. "Let's go and dance."

David followed his hostess into a semi-darkened living room. In the dim light he could make out a number of people facing each other in pairs. Each person was swinging their hips from side to side as though they were stuck to the floor and trying lazily to dislodge themselves.

Having never danced in his life David was feeling slightly apprehensive. Still holding his hand Samantha squeezed past several swaying couples before coming to a halt in a rather less crowded space in the corner. Then turning to her partner she

265

began performing similar body movements to those around her.

Feeling a little self-conscious David tried to imitate the other dancers. As a first attempt it wasn't a complete disaster, even if he resembled a boxer attempting to connect with a punch bag. However, his confidence soon began to evaporate when he noticed the amused expression on Samantha's face.

Instantly dismissing her partner as a dancing failure, Samantha decided to take the initiative. Moving one step forward and adeptly evading the flailing arms she clutched David around the waist before putting her lips close to his ear.

"Let's dance slowly together," she shouted above the music.

It was a suggestion that David was more than happy to go along with. This new dance hardly seemed to require any skill at all apart from embracing one's partner and gently swaying the body. In fact he quickly concluded that the only purpose of the exercise was to get intimate with a member of the opposite sex.

Gradually David was beginning to get aroused. He was allured by Samantha's sweet fragrance and her soft warm body nestling against his own. Under the dim light with their cheeks pressed lightly together he experienced a strong urge to make love.

People were still arriving at the party. It was a warm evening and as the room filled up with dancing couples so the temperature began to rise. Finally David, feeling hot and sweaty, decided that it was time to take a break.

First kissing Samantha on her pale silky neck he placed his mouth close to her ear.

"Let's go and get a drink," he suggested in a loud voice.

Samantha smiled agreeably as they withdrew their arms from each other. Then linking hands and, with David this time taking the lead, they began squeezing past a forest of moving bodies. However, with all the space in the flat taken up with people it took a while for them to negotiate their way back to the kitchen.

"Follow me," said Samantha when they had both got their drinks.

The couple yet again began weaving around bodies of all shapes and sizes. Cautiously carrying their glasses so as not to drench anybody who happened to get in the way, they slowly headed down the hall and into a large dining room, through a sliding patio door before eventually joining a scattering of people in the garden.

A gentle breeze did little to extinguish David's burning ardour. Once they had found a suitable place to settle he took Samantha forcibly in his arms and kissed her passionately on the lips. At that precise moment, driven by sexual desire, he was totally oblivious of a nearby couple who were casually watching on.

For a while they caressed while exploring each other's mouths with their tongues. Samantha seemed entirely responsive until David attempted to slip his hand beneath her T-shirt. Immediately she stopped the progress of his wandering limb by moving back a step.

"We need to be alone," she said, breathlessly.

David was brought to his senses with a jolt.

"Where do you suggest we go?" he asked, with his pulse racing fast.

Samantha shook her head sadly.

"There are too many people here tonight to get up to anything. We will just have to be patient for a little longer."

"When have you got in mind?" asked David, disappointedly.

There was a slight hesitation as Samantha gave the matter some thought. She knew that her flatmates were always prepared to make themselves scarce in a good cause. It was really just a case of making prior arrangements.

"Perhaps you could come around next week," she suggested, finally. "Which nights are you free?"

"Only Thursday is out," answered David, feeling frustrated that any sexual gratification would have to be put temporarily on hold. "I shall be tied up that night with the General Election."

Samantha raised her eyebrows in surprise.

"I didn't realise you were involved in politics."

David nodded.

"Yes and in fact I've been asked to put my name forward to be a local councillor," he replied, hoping to impress her.

Samantha shuddered.

"All that sort of thing is too heavy for me. I prefer to go out enjoying myself."

They continued to talk for a while until it grew too cold to stay outside. Then after returning their empty glasses to the kitchen they went back to the dance floor where space had become even in shorter supply than before. As a consequence couples had now abandoned all those expansive movements seen previously.

David and Samantha found themselves pinched up in a far corner of the room. Any conversation between them was now close to impossible as the music had climbed several decibels. In order to avoid jostling anyone around them, they were restricted to standing cheek to cheek and enjoying the sensation of having the other's body pressed up tightly against their own.

Just after midnight a trickle of people began to leave. Prompted by their actions, this quickly led to a mass exodus as the party began winding down. Soon clearing up operations were underway as black bags started appearing everywhere.

After a long embrace by the front door David reluctantly withdrew his arms from around Samantha's waist.

"I shall see you at work on Monday then," he smiled.

Samantha nodded.

"Hopefully by then I should have sorted out an evening for us to be alone."

As Samantha lived so close David had decided to travel on foot. It had the advantage of allowing him to drink as much as he liked and afterwards, enjoy a late night stroll before retiring to bed. Providing the weather remained dry, which it had, the idea seemed quite agreeable.

Walking along the quiet deserted streets in the dark prompted David to sing quietly to himself. His mood rapidly changed, however, as he approached the semi-detached house that had recently become his home. He was suddenly given a sharp reminder of a more painful side of his life.

The two councillor's cars were both parked in the drive. However, with the house in total darkness, David was relieved to know that he could probably creep up to his room without having to come into contact with the other housemates. He just felt the need to avoid yet another of those frosty silences.

For a while David lay awake taking stock of things. His thoughts now turned away from the isolation he was suffering in the house to the problem relating to affairs of the heart. Suddenly it was beginning to dawn on him that he was starting to play a dangerous game.

The plain fact was that he was cheating on Alison. Like it or not he was guilty of 'two timing' and unless Lady Luck was on his side he was likely to get caught before very long. Therefore he needed to make up his mind very quickly as to which of these two women was most important to him. Should he fail to make that choice, fate would doubtless do it for him.

Chapter Twenty-One

The following day was wet and blustery. David was woken by heavy rain lashing against the window while in the back garden a dustbin lid clattered about on the patio. Glancing at the clock by his bed he noted that it had just gone nine.

Voices from the kitchen indicated that George and Kenny had already surfaced. Pushing aside the duvet and placing his feet on the carpet David began wondering where he might be sleeping that night. He was determined to ring the Brockleby Park Hotel about a room straight away if his housemates continued to ignore him. It seemed better by far to live alone than remain in an unpleasant atmosphere.

Thankfully, unlike the weather conditions outside, the black clouds indoors had been swept away. No sooner had David reached the bottom of the stairs when he was greeted by the offer of a cup of tea. Having had time to cool down, the councillors no longer felt the desire to punish the new lodger for having made an innocent mistake.

"Last night we called in on Mrs Winter," George revealed, as the three housemates were about to settle down in the lounge with a pile of Sunday newspapers.

"Fortunately her daughter was there to give us the full story," chimed in Kenny. "She told us that originally her mother had tried to contact Charles Dawkins about her broken window. However, after leaving several messages with his secretary and hearing nothing back, she eventually decided to ring me."

"And that is when you happened to pick up the phone," said George, managing just the hint of a smile.

"But I shouldn't have interfered," answered David not wishing to avoid taking the blame for his blunder.

George shrugged.

"I suppose you only did what you thought was best. Mrs Winter had waited nine days for her window to be repaired and she was almost at the end of her tether. Therefore, feeling sympathy for this poor old lady and wanting to help, you promptly got in touch with a private company who were willing to fix it almost straight away."

Although not entirely at ease with himself, David was beginning to feel a little better. Undoubtedly he had made a silly error but at least it was appreciated that his intentions had been good. Ideas of returning to the hotel had now been dismissed.

"Of course I am still guilty of expecting Mrs Winter to fork out a lot of money, which she could ill afford," he admitted a little sheepishly.

At that point the two councillors exchanged smiles.

"I lied by telling Mrs Winter that one of us fully intended paying the bill ourselves," said Kenny a little guiltily. "However, I explained that once we heard Charles Dawkins had already stumped up there didn't seem to be much point."

David was still feeling distinctly uneasy.

"So Mrs Winter is now happy with us," he said, thoughtfully. "How about the rest of the council tenants that the Tories have targeted with this story. We still need to let them know that Labour acted in good faith over this matter."

Kenny nodded.

"Tony is already getting a leaflet printed today. It will accuse the Tories of using smear tactics and put Charles Dawkins in the dock for not dealing with the problem in the first place."

Happily back in the fold David was soon out canvassing. The rain had now stopped although it was difficult to walk at times due to the very high wind. Undeterred, however, he and several other hardy activists had teamed up to make 'follow up' calls. This meant making a second attempt to speak to residents who had been out when a party worker had previously knocked on the door.

Alison was amongst the notable absentees. She wasn't expected to return home from the New Forest until late that evening. There were, however, many new faces, as Labour supporters flocked in from surrounding areas to help fight this winnable seat.

Excitement was now at fever pitch. The General Election was only four days away and still every national opinion poll was predicting a close result. Locally, too, the outcome was far from certain, with Tony's canvass returns showing that Jacqui Dunn and Charles Dawkins were running neck and neck.

"It is vital that we get all our supporters out to vote on the day," said Tony for about the millionth time.

His remark was greeted with nods of agreement. It was now much later in the day and after Jacqui Dunn's most loyal devotees had been trudging the streets, they suddenly flaked out around the usual two tables placed together. There was a quiet satisfaction in the air from people who knew they had managed to push themselves to the very limit.

"Are you coming to the Count?" asked Jacqui, suddenly turning to David.

"Yes if I'm invited," answered the political rookie, who had only recently become familiar with the term.

"You are most welcome," smiled Jacqui, revealing a perfect set of white teeth. "I want everybody sitting here to be there on the night."

Forgetting his weary legs, Kenny suddenly stood up.

"I, the returning officer do declare that Jacqui Dunn has been duly elected to serve the constituency of Brockleby," he announced before raising his pint glass in the air.

Raucous cheers rang out around the bar. Having suffered many disappointments in the past though, few supporters were prepared to raise their expectations too high. Many were just hoping and praying that the voters of the town would elect their first ever Labour MP.

One member present though was an exception to the rule. Still angry that the Government were unwilling to support the Americans in Iraq, Sid Davidson wished nothing but ill on the Labour Party. However, since making himself a laughing stock in the presence of Bruce Shaw he had become rather subdued of late. Now he just sat scowling on his usual bar stool while making sure he didn't spill beer on himself.

At work the following morning Samantha had some disappointing news for David. Alex, her room-mate had developed a heavy cold and was unlikely to be venturing out of bed for a couple of days.

"At the moment it is impossible to plan anything for definite," explained Samantha in a low voice as she and David stood side by side at the photocopying machine. "I will probably have to leave it until the end of the week before inviting you around."

"What a shame it can't be sooner," answered David, in a voice more mournful than he had intended.

Having completed all her photocopying, Samantha stood to one side looking thoughtful.

"Is it possible that I could come over to your place?" she said in a low voice.

David immediately panicked. To do as she suggested would mean running the risk of smuggling her into the house while George and Kenny were out. As they were both loyal friends of Alison, his housemates would take a dim view of the situation were they to arrive home and find him alone with a strange woman.

A more experienced 'two timer' might have known what to do. For a rookie like David though, this was completely new territory and he needed a flash of inspiration from somewhere. His whole love life might depend on what he said next.

He needed to play for time. Seeing that Samantha had just turned her head towards the window, David discreetly gave an overfull rubbish bin a sharp back heel. Then still wrestling with his problem he slowly began gathering up the loose debris which was scattered on the floor. It was then that the answer came to him.

"I'd love to invite you around but unfortunately we are decorating at the moment," said David, forlornly. "The house is in total chaos and simply reeks of paint."

"Never mind," replied Samantha, cheerfully, as she collected up all her papers from the photocopier. "Perhaps I can take a look at your handiwork once it is finished."

"Yes of course," beamed David. "You are welcome anytime."

As he wandered back to his desk he felt an even more urgent need to come to a decision. Quite clearly, carrying on in relationships with two women was dragging him into a tangled web of deception in which he was certain to be caught out before too long. He needed to act quickly before things got out of control.

Workwise David continued to prosper. After clinching the Conningvale House order he had also made several other sales to clients of his previous company. In addition to that he had provided a hundred thousand pound quote for furniture to a women's refuge in the Midlands. Having had many dealings with the buyer in the past he had high hopes of seeing off the competition.

Office life at Robsons however was something he was still trying to come to terms with. Although the atmosphere was friendly, people were less respectful of each other than they had been at Fine Choice. This was certainly the case with the younger members of staff.

Wesley Chapple in particular, was forever playing pranks on his colleagues. Until he was tipped off by Roger Green, David had spent the best part of his second morning parading around the office with a 'For Sale' sticker attached to his back. On another occasion he had been sitting on the toilet when a wet towel had sailed over the top of the cubicle door and landed on his head. It was all good fun for everyone except the victim.

Away from work it was all politics. Like all the activists David was excited that election day had almost arrived, yet another part of him wished it was all over and done with. He was tired of spending all his spare time just tramping the streets.

Tuesday night Alison arrived at the club beaming brightly. Having enjoyed a weekend break in the New Forest it was the first time she had seen any of her comrades for a few days. David in particular felt a warm glow inside as they briefly kissed.

Now fully refreshed and raring to go she helped Tony to rally the troops. It was far from an easy task even with the finishing post in sight. The campaign had been long and now most activists were digging into their last reserves of energy.

"My legs are killing me," Carol explained, taking a pile of leaflets from Tony.

"It will all be worth it on Thursday night when Jacqui is elected," said Alison, cheerfully.

As the faithful were about to hobble out of the door, Tony had some parting words for everyone.

"Don't forget that we must try and squeeze the Lib Dem vote. Anyone wanting to keep Britain out of Iraq must vote for us."

"We may have a problem," said George. "Many see the Lib Dems as being rock solid against the war whereas our party appears to be divided."

"That's right," piped up Kenny. "There are too many bloody dissenters."

Tony was about to answer but Jacqui got in before him.

"Just say that as long as Bruce Shaw is Prime Minister this country will never enter into that futile conflict," she said with deep conviction ringing in her voice. "Also remind them that if they elect me as their MP there will be no fiercer critic in Parliament of American foreign policy."

Every activist present was fired up by the candidate's stirring words. Suddenly energy levels soared and aching legs ignored as they grabbed their leaflets and headed for the streets again. It was as though they had each been given a new lease of life.

David set off in a group of four. Eager as ever to get the job done, Tony seemed to be driving at almost breakneck speed. Anxious that they might be stopped by the local constabulary, Carol repeatedly cautioned him to slow down.

Tonight they were heading for the Gladstone Estate. Their mission was to deliver leaflets targeting council tenants in response to Tory allegations about the broken window saga. Despite constant reassurances from his fellow activists, it was still a subject which made David squirm with embarrassment.

The difficulty was that references to the incident were unavoidable. Worse still, Alison who had been away over the weekend, wanted a blow by blow account of what had transpired. Sitting quietly in the back David tried to put on a brave face as Tony updated her.

"Didn't you think to ask this old lady questions?" enquired Alison, turning to David with a look of amazement.

David shrugged.

"How was I to know that Mrs Winters was entitled to free repairs."

"I shouldn't worry about it," said Carol, deciding to come to David's rescue. "While the Tories are attacking us on one front they are keeping quiet on another."

At that moment the car screeched to a halt by the roadside. The fact that his three passengers had been jolted violently forward hardly seemed to bother Tony who quickly snatched the bundle of leaflets which had been resting on Carol's lap. They had arrived at their destination and the party organiser was anxious to get started. However, before starting the evening's work he briefly turned his head around to face Alison.

"This leaflet isn't just about a broken window," he said with a sly smile. "I have also written an article stating that if the Tories are allowed to drag us into the war, council rents will be going up fifty per cent to pay for it."

"That's rubbish," protested Alison.

"Of course," laughed Tony. "But you don't win elections by telling the truth."

Later that evening David drove Alison home as usual. Stopping off in their favourite spot they enjoyed another period of intimacy together, but always keeping an eye open for passers-by. In the darkness they kissed and tenderly fondled one another in blissful contentment.

"I'm sorry if I criticised you earlier," whispered Alison. "It was unkind of me."

"You were right," answered David. "I should have taken down a message from that old lady and passed it on to one of the councillors to deal with. To be perfectly honest I never imagined that there could be so much fuss over a stupid window."

"Everyone learns by their mistakes," said Alison, sympathetically. "Anyway I think it was kind of you to try to help somebody with a problem. That is what politics should be all about."

"I wish it were," replied David, bitterly. "Party politics to me seems all about people trying to outsmart each other."

Alison's body suddenly stiffened. From the little light that shone in the car, David could just make out a change in her expression. No longer smiling, she now seemed to look annoyed.

"Don't be cynical," she said, firmly. "Trust me there are many who are working hard in this election to try and make the world a better place to live in."

OK you win," replied David, who had no wish to start an argument.

"Anyway," said Alison, a little more cheerfully. "After the election I will have to invite you around for another meal."

"Sounds good to me," replied David as they continued to caress.

The following morning he received a similar invitation in the office. While waiting at the drinks machine watching steaming hot water gush into a white plastic cup, he suddenly felt the presence of somebody standing beside him. Turning his head sideways he found himself looking straight into Samantha's clear blue eyes.

"Alex has made a full recovery," she smiled. "I have managed to persuade both her and my other flatmate to make themselves scarce whenever you are free to come around."

Silently David withdrew his cup from the machine. After the previous evening he was tempted to drop a gentle hint that might be sufficient to bring the office romance to a close. The problem was though, that the further he drove down the road of deception the harder it became to do a reverse turn. In addition to that Samantha did have a rather tantalising smile.

"How about early next week?" he heard himself blurt out.

"Shall we say Monday evening about eight then?" suggested Samantha as she stepped up to the vending machine.

"Perfect!" replied David, thinking of all that wonderful spare time he would be able to enjoy once the General Election was over.

As he was about to walk away Samantha put a restraining hand on his arm. Instructed to stand facing the door he felt something being peeled off the back of his shirt. On turning around he saw the words 'HANDLE WITH CARE' printed boldly on a large white label.

"Bloody Wesley Chapple," he muttered, screwing up the label and flinging it in the direction of the paper bin.

**

Like Labour, the Tories were putting every last ounce of effort into the campaign. Although absolutely exhausted from the effects of knocking on countless doors with a clipboard and suffering a great deal of abuse in the process, Charles Dawkins was intent on speaking to as many voters as possible. On the last day before the country went to the polls, however, he decided to be kind to his weary legs and canvass by telephone instead.

Charles was not alone in this pursuit. A section of the bar had been converted into a miniature call centre with a telephone on six separate tables. The plan was that Tory activists could arrive throughout the day and take a turn in contacting households in respect of their voting intentions.

Both Charles and Adrian Thomas were on the early shift. It was monotonous work but somehow they managed to keep going for almost two hours without a break. Finally at twelve o'clock relief arrived as a second batch of Tory devotees prepared themselves for a similar period of pure drudgery.

Normally at midday the bar would have been fairly quiet. However, this was the eve of the most intriguing General Election for many years and it seemed that so many members just wanted to be involved in some way. Clearly there was a vibrancy about the place that had never existed before.

The two high-ranking Conservatives circulated amongst the troops for a while. Beaming broadly they lavished praise on anybody who appeared to be making some sort of contribution towards the campaign. A word of encouragement from the top brass could often do much to lift the flagging spirits of the average foot soldier.

Soon plates of sandwiches arrived from the kitchen. Made with loving care by several refined ladies they were small, triangular and crust free. Other refreshments quickly followed and almost immediately, all political activity ground to a halt as party workers queued up beside the buffet, laid out on four tables.

Having gathered up an assortment of food on tin trays, Charles and Adrian headed for two armchairs in a far corner. The monotony of telephone canvassing had dulled their brains and for a time they choose to sit and eat in silence. Eventually, however, a sudden thought prompted the Brockleby MP to rediscover the power of speech.

"I see that Labour have responded to my leaflet about the broken window," he said with a smile. "It amazes me that they managed to hit back so quickly."

"You obviously managed to hit a raw nerve," replied Adrian, a little distantly.

Having finished eating, Charles sat back in his armchair looking rather smug.

"I wonder what they think of our latest leaflet?" he said,

looking at his companion through half-closed eyes.

It was one of those questions that didn't really require an answer. Obviously a scathing personal attack on Jacqui Dunn was hardly likely to go down well with her party followers. Particularly as there would be no opportunity to reply before the General Election.

The leaflet contained a crude characterisation of the Labour Party candidate. Described as a 'loony leftie' she was portrayed as a champion of the shiftless. A woman who was hell bent on helping the work-shy to prosper at the expense of the industrious suburban middle classes.

In the article she was referred to as 'Red Jacqui'. A left wing extremist the writer claimed, who was forever in support of providing hand-outs to gay groups, unmarried mothers, the unemployed and just about anyone else who came along with a begging bowl. In short the woman was never happier than when she was dishing out other people's hard earned money.

"I can't imagine that Labour will be too happy with our comments," said Adrian as he was about to sink his spoon into a carton of yoghurt. "The atmosphere is likely to be pretty tense at the Count tomorrow."

"Particularly when our opponents realise that I have held on to my seat," answered Charles, looking even more smug than before. "In an affluent area like this many voters are likely to be frightened off by Miss Dunn's Socialist credentials."

Adrian gazed disconsolately at the MP.

"I wish we could have avoided making personal attacks. The Tories should win Brockleby without having to resort to those sort of tactics."

Charles was taken aback by his companion's negative response.

"Because of the boundary changes this constituency is not the Tory stronghold it was two years ago," he said with a warning look. "This leaflet is intended to put the final nail into Jacqui Dunn's coffin."

After his buffet lunch Charles began to feel sleepy. Then having strolled around in an attempt to rally the troops once more, he decided to slip home and spend an hour or two in bed in order to recharge his batteries. Later in the day he intended to be back for a marathon session on the telephones.

As Charles turned his key in the front door he was looking forward to a restful afternoon. No sooner had he crossed the threshold however, before it became apparent there would be little peace without a confrontation. Music which could hardly be described as easy listening blasted out above his head.

Grim faced with determination the MP stormed up the stairs. With every step the sound grew louder and more objectionable until he finally came to a halt outside a door at the end of the landing. Then deciding against rapping his knuckles against the wood he drew in a deep breath instead.

"Turn that bloody racket down," he demanded.

For a few seconds he stood boiling over with rage. Then angrier still when there was no instant reduction of the cacophonous din he barged straight into his son's room. With two strides he had reached the CD player and in a flash there was total silence.

"Oh Dad," protested Oliver as he lay stretched out on the bed.

"Why aren't you at school?" snapped Charles.

Oliver gave his father a look of long suffering.

"Because we always get two free periods on Wednesday afternoon."

"In which case you should be spending your time in the library revising instead of listening to that load of rubbish," shouted Charles, nodding towards the CD player.

Generally when the old man complained about his behaviour Oliver would just sulk and say nothing. This occasion was different though and as the teenager slowly got up from his bed there was a look of defiance on his face. For once it was him that was holding the trump card and he was just about to fling it on the table.

"You won't be putting up with me for much longer I suppose," he said, calmly. "After the election you will be going off to live with your girlfriend."

Charles was stunned. As far as he was aware, nobody in the family had an inkling about his affair with Madeleine. In fact he had done everything in his power to keep the matter a secret.

"What girlfriend?" he asked, attempting to conceal his alarm.

"The one that left a message on your mobile," smiled Oliver.

"It seems that this woman can't wait for you to divorce mum so that she can become the next Home Secretary's wife."

"How did you get hold of my phone?" asked Charles, realising the futility of denying the affair.

"I found it in the flower bed near the front door," replied Oliver, contemptuously. "It was the day after you damaged your car when you ran into that fox."

"Then why on earth didn't you hand it back to me?" asked Charles, angrily. "I have missed some very important calls."

Oliver shrugged.

"Mum put it away somewhere and told me not to say anything to you."

It took a few moments for this latest information to sink in. Charles was puzzled as to why Sally should choose to say nothing about his infidelity and just carry on as though nothing were happening. In their twenty-two years of marriage his wife had never shied away from confrontation before.

The situation made him feel uneasy as he slowly backed towards his son's bedroom door. Sally could be a wily old fox and he was concerned that she was hatching up some devious plan as an act of revenge. In his present weary state though, he was incapable of attempting to fathom out what might be up her sleeve.

"By the way," he said, gruffly. "I don't want to hear that so-called music blaring out again. Some of us lead hectic lives and need a little peace and quiet sometimes."

"OK Dad," replied Oliver with a little secret grin as his father slammed the door behind him. "Enjoy your rest."

Chapter Twenty-Two

The day of reckoning had finally arrived. The long bitter campaign was over and the nation now had to decide who would govern them for the next four or five years. The opinion pollsters were still reporting however, that many voters were still having difficulty in making up their minds.

The Government had two major factors in its favour. They were benefitting from the effects of a strong economy and the popularity of Bruce Shaw, the Prime Minister. On the negative side Labour were divided over the Iraq War and the electorate were alarmed by the arguments which were raging within the party. It was something that the opposition parties had managed to capitalise on.

The United States, too, seemed to be attempting to influence the result of the election. In retaliation for not supporting the so-called 'War on Terror' certain senators were calling on Americans to boycott goods from the UK. In fact on the other side of the Atlantic, Bruce Shaw was frequently accused of being a 'yellow bellied coward' and far worse. Unsurprisingly such jibes were eagerly seized upon in Britain by a hostile right wing press.

Grass roots activists of course could do little to control events at Westminster and beyond. Most just worked hard locally and hoped that those higher up in their party echelon didn't rock the boat. All too often a vote pledged to a canvasser one evening, can be lost by careless remarks made by those in Parliament the following day.

It was partly for this reason that David and his two housemates were gathered around the TV at five thirty in the morning. Sitting bleary-eyed and eating breakfast off plastic trays laid across their laps, they were anxious to watch the news. It was still possible even at this late stage that something could have happened overnight to determine the result of the General Election. After all, the polling stations had yet to open up.

Following the short musical introduction the news presenter

appeared on the screen grim faced. It was the expression that he generally reserved when announcing earthquakes, plane crashes and other similar disasters. On this occasion it was a suicide bomber who had blown himself up alongside many others, on a crowded street in the centre of Baghdad.

"The situation in Iraq seems to get worse all the time," said George when he felt that the following news stories were of no particular interest. "How much longer does this madness have to go on?"

Kenny nodded in sympathy.

"Hopefully this latest incident will help Labour's chances. Before they go off to vote today the British people will be reminded of the consequences of sending our troops off to fight alongside the Americans."

"I'm not certain," replied George, with a rueful smile. "I believe there are those who enjoy a good war providing they don't have to put their own lives on the line. Some people have a morbid fascination for hearing about the suffering of others."

"You are becoming very cynical these days," said Kenny between mouthfuls of cereal.

"Just call it experience," answered George, with a shrug of his shoulders.

For a while the housemates continued eating their breakfast in silence. However, the councillors quickly came to life at five to six when an attractive blonde appeared on the screen in front of a weather chart. Both George and Kenny had already been out in the garden to take a close look at the elements, but they were nevertheless keen for a more professional assessment.

Thankfully the forecast was very much to their liking. According to the expert who was waving her arms at the map of the UK, the rain would obligingly hold off until the weekend. There was even a slim possibility that certain parts of the country might even be treated to a glimpse of the sun on election day.

Kenny punched the air in delight.

"Brilliant!" he exclaimed.

"Were you planning a trip to the seaside?" asked David in amusement.

"We need a dry day for the election," explained Kenny. "Some of Labour's more apathetic supporters can't be bothered to turn out to vote in the rain."

"Many don't make the effort whatever the weather," added George, scornfully.

"But surely the Tories must have the same problem," said David, thoughtfully.

George scowled as he began collecting up the breakfast things.

"Those rich buggers from Upper Oakham would go out in a hurricane to vote," he said, acidly. "They know that a Tory Government can always be relied upon to look after their interests."

Kenny nodded.

"That is why it is important to get every single Labour supporter down to the polling station to vote, even if it means dragging them there by their hair."

George's lounge was soon crowded with people. It had been designated as one of the party's election rooms for the day. Amongst the battered cardboard boxes laden with council literature, would be a centre where operations would be co-ordinated.

Tony strutted around issuing instructions to anyone who caught his eye. However, most of those present were seasoned campaigners and took little more than a polite interest in what he had to say. Before long though, the election organiser managed to find a young man who provided him with a more attentive audience. Being a political rookie, David was keen to receive all the advice he could get in preparation for the ordeal ahead.

Once he got talking about his favourite subject Tony could go on forever. As it happened though, David was left without any of his questions being answered. It was really the fault of George who stepped in to remind the election organiser that he had an important job to be getting on with.

"Don't forget that the polling stations open at seven o'clock," said the senior councillor. "You need to make certain that there are tellers at each one otherwise we won't have a clue as to who has been out to vote."

Glancing down at his watch, Tony panicked. It was now twenty to seven and having little faith in the reliability of certain Labour activists he was keen to check that everyone was at their post. Therefore appreciating the need to race around Brockleby at breakneck speed he quickly headed for the front door.

No sooner had he left before Alison arrived. She and Carol were to sit in George's lounge and take telephone calls from people who needed a lift to the polling station. The message would then be relayed to people like David who had been given the role of taxi driver for the day.

"Did you get around to buying a mobile phone?" asked Alison, who had brought the subject up on several occasions.

David shook his head.

"Sorry but with work in the day and canvassing at night, I didn't get around to it."

"But what happens when people ring up for transport?" asked Alison with a look of frustration. "How am I supposed to get hold of you?"

David shrugged.

"I will just have to keep coming back here."

Immediately Alison took off her shoulder bag and began fumbling around inside. Then after a few minutes she produced a small grey metal object and held it out in David's direction.

"Here, use mine," she muttered.

David examined it a little cautiously. The truth was that he had never handled one before so it was yet another of life's great mysteries to him. According to Fellowship teachings the Devil is the lord of the air and because of that, followers are told to avoid using mobiles. Therefore the young man had been given a piece of equipment which he had no idea how to use.

Soon David was sent off to make his first pick up. On his chest he proudly displayed a large red rosette while the dreaded mobile phone nestled in his trouser pocket. Once the opportunity arose he was determined to discover how the damn thing worked.

His first client was a certain Mavis Small. An elderly lady with white wispy hair, she had the look of a person who was sleep walking with their eyes wide open. While hobbling along the garden path she suddenly grabbed hold of her young escort's arm as though fearful he might run away. However, nothing was said until they got into the car.

"Can we go to Sainsbury's first?" requested Mavis, cheerfully, even before David had a chance to switch on the engine. "I need to buy some meat for my dinner."

David was rather taken aback. Nobody had warned him to expect a request like this and he couldn't quite decide how to respond. Clearly as an ambassador for the party he needed to create a good image, but this was rather taking advantage of the situation.

"Very sorry but I'm in a bit of a rush," explained David politely. "After you there are lots of other people who require lifts."

"I fancy lamb today," mumbled the old lady, who seemed to be in a world of her own.

David could feel that he was being taken over by the better side of his nature. Therefore having decided that it would take less than ten minutes to pick up a joint of lamb, he turned the car around and headed for the High Street. He felt reasonably confident that Sainsbury's wouldn't be crowded at this time of the morning.

As he predicted trade was a little slack, at least until Mavis arrived. Instead of just stopping off at the meat counter, the old lady hobbled around the supermarket with her trolley gathering up, what seemed like a whole month's groceries. The situation got a whole lot worse when the prolific little shopper reached the check-out only to discover that she had forgotten her purse.

Once again David was in a quandary. Should he offer to lend Mavis the money or leave the shop assistant to put all the groceries back on the shelves. Finally he went for the first option but on the understanding that he was reimbursed later.

Unfortunately the nightmare was set to continue. Twenty minutes later David guided Mavis into a school hall, which was being used as a polling station for the day. Due entirely to his family's total rejection of the whole democratic process, he was under the impression that people could just turn up and vote where they liked. However a sign on the wall with road names underneath alerted him to the fact that things weren't quite as simple as that.

Suddenly a tall gentleman strolled up. He had been given the role of assisting confused and witless people to cast their vote. Needless to say that he was being kept fairly busy.

"Are you both OK?" he smiled.

"Which polling station do residents of Dorset Close have to go?" asked David. "This lady has forgotten to bring her card."

"I shall soon tell you," replied the official, turning his back and heading towards a nearby table.

Picking up a large blue soft covered book he began flicking through the pages. Then after casting his eyes down a long list of road names he finally came to the one in question.

"You need to go to Marlands Hall in Temple Street," he announced.

At that precise moment it occurred to David that he had no idea where to vote himself. Therefore deciding it was the ideal opportunity to find out he provided the helpful official with his parents' address. It seemed absurd to spend the day getting others to fulfil their duty in the ballot box if he wasn't going to do the same himself.

It was while David was driving Mavis to Temple Street that he detected strange musical sounds rising up from just below his waist. Stopping the car about twenty metres along the road he reached in his trouser pocket for Alison's mobile phone. However, after examining this strange gadget for a few seconds the ring tones suddenly ceased.

Of course David would have returned the call had he known how. Instead he drove on and tried to ignore the phone when it rang a second, third and yet a fourth time. Even Mavis came to life as a consequence of these frequent interruptions.

"Somebody is trying to get hold of you," she said, appearing to be under the impression that the driver had lost his sense of hearing.

"It's a friend trying to find out where the bloody hell I am," David snapped.

"I don't mind if you stop to answer your phone," said Mavis, cheerfully. "I'm in no particular hurry."

"Well I am," answered David, tersely.

Having cast her vote Mavis finally arrived home. Sitting on a stool in the kitchen she supervised David as he carried her groceries in from the car. Like some eastern potentate, she issued instructions such as "that needs to go in the fridge", "those should go on the top shelf" and so on. At times she was even quite sharp when items weren't put away exactly to her liking.

At last the job was done and David handed the old lady the bill.

"This is how much you owe me," he said, jabbing his finger at the total amount printed towards the end of the white till roll.

Having studied the figure for a while Mavis hobbled off to get her money. From the kitchen David could hear the sound of sliding drawers and shuffling papers. Eventually the old lady returned holding up a five pound note.

"This is all I have," she announced, without the slightest hint of an apology in her voice. "I shall have to owe you the rest."

"But your bill came to eight-six pounds and seventy-five pence," protested David, who was rather taken aback by the old lady's casual attitude.

"Come round next week," answered Mavis. "I may be better off then."

A younger person would have received some verbal abuse. However, having been brought up in a Christian family, David had always been taught to be respectful of the elderly. Therefore on this occasion he limited his anger to storming out of the house and slamming the door.

"Where have you been?" asked Alison when David finally arrived home. "I kept ringing the mobile but there was no reply."

"You won't believe it," began David, before relating the full story of his encounter with Mavis Small.

Carol who like Alison had been assigned to the election room for the day smiled sympathetically.

"I'll have a word with Tony and see that you get your money back through Labour Party funds."

"Thanks," answered David, who was already beginning to calm down now that he was back in the company of friends.

"But didn't you hear me ringing the mobile?" persisted Alison.

David suddenly looked sheepish.

"You had better teach me how it works. I've never used one before."

The two women looked at each other in amusement. Then still smiling, Carol retreated to the kitchen to make coffee for everyone leaving Alison to give David a crash course on the use of mobile phones. Gradually the political rookie was beginning to feel he could face the outside world again.

In a short while David had resumed his role as taxi driver for the day. Fortunately none of his passengers tried to take the same sort of liberties that Mavis Small had got away with. Most seemed very appreciative of the service they were getting.

At eleven o'clock he kept his appointment to pick up Mrs Cook and her friend Beryl. These two elderly ladies were not only about to provide Jacqui Dunn with two of the very few votes she was likely to receive in snooty Upper Oakham. They had even dared to display her name on posters in their upstairs and downstairs windows.

"Isn't this exciting," said Mrs Cook, as she scrambled into the front passenger seat. "I will be sitting on the edge of my settee until the early hours, waiting for the results as they come through on the TV."

"I wonder when we will know what has happened in Brockleby?" asked Beryl, as she tried to squeeze her great bulk into the back seat.

"Around about midnight unless there is a recount of course," replied David, repeating what he had been told by Tony.

"Oh I do hope that Jacqui Dunn wins," said Mrs Cook, turning her head towards the driver. "She looks so nice in her photographs."

David nodded as he switched on the engine.

"She's lovely," he said, proudly.

"Those Tories wrote some nasty things about her in their last leaflet," said Beryl after she had finally won the battle to fasten her seatbelt.

"Typical of that lot," said Mrs Cook, indignantly. "That smarmy smile will be wiped off Charles Dawkins' face tonight if he loses his seat."

The journey was a brief one. Beryl who had difficulty walking, gladly accepted the offer of David's arm and slowly the pair made their way into the polling station. As luck would have it, this happened to be the same place where the young man needed to cast his vote, too. Therefore strolling up to the desk he took his place behind the two elderly ladies he had just escorted.

Having issued Mrs Cook with a ballot paper the young lady behind the desk turned her attention to the next in line.

"Do you have your polling card?" she smiled.

"I'm afraid I don't," replied David somewhat sheepishly.

"What is your name and address?" she enquired, still smiling brightly.

"David Chambers of twenty-eight, Chestnut Avenue," came the reply.

For a few minutes the official ran her eye down a long list of names and addresses. Finally she looked up and shook her head.

"I'm afraid you don't appear on the electoral register," she said, apologetically. "The only names at the address you have given me are John and Hilary Chambers. There is nobody else mentioned."

"Does that mean I can't vote then?" asked David, anxiously.

The official nodded, sadly.

"I'm afraid so. You see a form is sent out to each household and it asks for all the names of persons resident at that address, who are eligible to vote at a certain date. Unfortunately it seems that you have not been put down," she explained.

"Is there anything I can do about it now?" asked David in desperation.

"Nothing at this late stage I'm sorry to say," replied the official, sympathetically.

David felt utterly disappointed as he moved away from the table. His anger immediately turned on his parents for depriving him of his democratic right, to take part in the most important ballot the country had faced in many years. Why he wondered had they failed to include his name on that form.

While waiting for the elderly ladies at the entrance he was suddenly struck by an unpleasant thought. Supposing that Jacqui Dunn failed to get elected by a single vote. Of course such a scenario was highly unlikely but anything was possible.

Although upset David tried hard not to dwell on his misfortune. He was determined to get himself on the electoral register at the earliest opportunity in preparation for the future. His aim now though was to assist other Labour supporters to cast their votes for the party.

Time passed quickly. Each time David happened to glance down at his watch another half-hour or forty minutes had slipped by. It was one of those days in his life when everything seemed unreal. By late afternoon he had driven so many people down to various polling stations that when thinking back later, many of the faces just merged into one.

David was of course receiving his instructions from Alison. Every so often there would be a call from her on the mobile providing him with the address of his next customer. As transport co-ordinator she would receive a request for a lift and then pass it on to one of several drivers.

When the phone rang at four thirty, David was surprised to hear another familiar voice speaking to him.

"Can you go down to Coronation Hall in Bow Street right away," requested Tony, anxiously. "Someone who promised to do some telling has let us down."

"How long for?" asked David, who rather welcomed a break from driving.

"Until Mrs Dickson comes along to replace you at six o'clock," replied Tony.

Coronation Hall was a small detached red bricked building. Local people often hired it for children's parties, meetings and twice a week harassed mothers could off-load their toddlers for a couple of hours at a playschool there. Today though, the premises was serving as a polling station.

When David arrived there were three tellers seated just inside the front door. All ladies and each with a different coloured rosette to denote their party loyalty, they were equipped with pen and clipboard. Their job was to approach people who had just voted and to record the registration number on their poll cards.

Despite differences in party allegiances the atmosphere between the threesome appeared cordial enough. There is a convention amongst tellers that anything is acceptable as a subject of discussion providing it is unrelated to the world of politics. Unsavoury incidents outside polling stations between rival loyalists would be of no electoral benefit to anybody.

The representative telling for Labour seemed pleased to see her replacement. Having been sat there in the same spot for well over two hours she was desperate to do something else with her day. Happily she handed over the clipboard and after a brief wave hastily disappeared through the swing door and into the outside world.

Left with two middle-aged ladies for company, David felt like an outsider. In their time together telling, the Tory and Liberal Democrat representatives had struck up a bit of a rapport. Apart from holding opposing political opinions they seemed to be in general agreement on just about everything else.

"I'm having steak and kidney pie this evening," announced the Tory.

"My favourite," revealed the Lib Dem, enthusiastically.

"Mine, too," smiled the Tory. "I like it with mash potatoes, peas and lots of thick gravy."

"Sounds heavenly," sighed the Lib Dem. "You are beginning to make me feel quite hungry."

"Did you happen to watch *Sporting Dancers* last night?" asked the Tory.

The Lib Dem nodded eagerly.

"I thought the footballer with the big ears was very light on his feet."

The Tory's face lit up.

"He did a marvellous Tango," she purred. "The only thing which put me off was the skimpy dress his partner was wearing."

"I'm afraid that rather spoilt it for me, too," agreed the Lib Dem.

Initially David listened with mild amusement. However, when it became apparent that this banal prattle was likely to continue for some time it began to get on his nerves. He made a mental note to bring earplugs the next time that Tony called on him to do some telling.

Finally his misery was brought to an end. An angel of mercy appeared in the form of a studious gentleman in his sixties who had arrived to take the place of the Lib Dem chatterbox. Once her newly discovered friend had departed the Tory became subdued. Possibly through some primeval instinct she may have had a gut feeling that neither David or the newcomer would appreciate a discussion on the glories of steak and kidney pie or skimpily dressed dancing partners.

At ten o'clock the polling stations promptly closed their doors. Soon the ballot boxes would be loaded on to lorries and quickly delivered to the Town Hall in preparation for the counting of votes. Meanwhile, the old building was already filling up with people who had some form of interest in what was about to happen.

As Brockleby was a key marginal seat it had attracted a great deal of national attention. All the major television organisations had sent camera crews along to interview anyone playing a prominent part in the election, as well as providing regular updates on how the count was progressing. A prime target for the media was Charles Dawkins of course, who had been widely tipped as the future Home Secretary.

Meanwhile, Jacqui Dunn and her supporters waited outside the Town Hall for a while. Before entering into the public spotlight the Labour candidate wanted to spend a few precious moments with the people who had worked so hard for her. She could hardly have asked for more from any of them. The greatest fear she had now was that their efforts could all have been in vain.

"I want to say just one thing to you all," she smiled. "If Labour don't win tonight in Brockleby, the fault will be mine not yours."

"Rubbish!" protested Tony. "We couldn't have wished for a better candidate. You have worked your guts out during this campaign."

Jacqui shook her head.

"The problem is that the Tories have branded me as a loony leftie and there may be some truth in that. You see I plead guilty to caring about the sick, the poor, the elderly, the disabled and all the other vulnerable groups in our society."

"In that case that makes me a loony leftie, too," said Alison, with obvious feeling in her voice.

"It probably sums up the lot of us," laughed George.

"Come on then you loonies," shouted Tony, taking the lead as usual. "Let's go inside now."

David was the last to start moving. He was feeling a strange mixture of excitement and dread as the little group made their way into the marble entrance of the Town Hall. It had been apparent from the very start that Dawkins and Dunn were the only two candidates with a realistic chance of winning the Brockleby seat. Now the moment of truth had almost arrived. Later that night one would pass out through those beautiful oak doors in triumph, while the other would emerge in tears.

Chapter Twenty-Three

Ryan Pritchard was Robsons' top salesman for September. To celebrate his success colleagues headed for the pub after work to enjoy free drinks at the company's expense. As it was election day though, there was one notable absentee. Less than half a mile away David Chambers was sat outside a polling station wearing a red rosette.

Not that the new salesman had been forgotten. In fact during the course of the evening his name would crop up quite frequently. Although not disliked, he came across to many of his workmates as a bit of an oddball. Someone they felt who had an unworldly innocence and didn't seem to belong in the twenty-first century.

"He was telling me that his parents never allowed him to watch TV," remarked Wesley Chapple, with a look of amusement.

"That bloke is really weird," chimed in Aaron Childs, a young sales assistant who had recently left school. "He knows nothing about football, music, computer games or just about anything else for that matter."

"It's hardly surprising," replied Roger Green, who knew more about David's background that anyone present. "His parents made him attend church once every day with the exception of Sunday when he was forced to go five times."

This revelation was greeted with gasps of surprise.

"Bloody Hell!" exclaimed Ryan. "That hardly sounds like a barrel of laughs."

Roger Green was the only one who could empathise with David. As a boy he had been dragged along to the morning service on the Sabbath day. He still had childhood memories of hard wooden pews, long monotonous sermons by a man in robes and elderly ladies in sombre hats.

Others gathered around the table were less inclined to be sympathetic. In David's absence they were eager to have a laugh at what they regarded as his peculiarities.

"The other day I told him that joke about the old girl who accidentally went into the men's toilet," said Wesley, with a broad grin. "I think he seemed to get quite upset with me."

Most of those listening, however, couldn't recall how the joke had finished. Therefore the sales assistant obligingly repeated it from the very beginning. This of course he did with great pleasure being the type of person who always enjoyed being the centre of attention.

In fact the joke was hardly hilarious. An elderly lady having gone into the wrong public conveniences had mistaken a urinal for a washbasin. Then having lined up beside a member of the opposite sex who was using it for its intended purpose, she had turned to him and asked to borrow the soap when he had finished with it. Now whether the poor old soul was myopic, confused or a bit of both wasn't made clear.

Much to Wesley's delight most of his audience laughed heartily at the joke.

"So what makes you think that David Chambers didn't appreciate the joke?" asked Ryan, with a look of surprise.

Wesley grinned.

"He told me I shouldn't make fun of old people."

Suddenly more laughter broke out from all those in listening distance. Ryan almost choked on his beer as colleagues sitting further away clamoured to find out what was causing all the amusement. Samantha who had been talking with the two older secretaries was as curious as anyone.

"I'll tell you another thing," chimed in Aaron Childs, keen to get in a few laughs of his own. "David Chambers doesn't even know who the England manager is. He actually asked me whether it was another name for the Prime Minister."

"You won't believe this," said Ryan Pritchard, with a sad shake of his head. "I told him the other day that my brother was a plonker. He only looked at me and asked whether that was another name for a plumber."

After more hearty laughter others waded in with more little anecdotes about their absent colleague. Had anyone around the table felt remotely sympathetic towards him, they made no attempt to come to his defence. It was rich entertainment and

Samantha in particular seemed to be enjoying herself.

Eventually the conversation switched to other matters, At his end of the long table, Roger Green was boasting about his sexual conquests he had made while on the road selling. It was his favourite subject when drinking and he could always be assured of an attentive audience. Not that anyone actually believed the stories but they were always fun to listen to all the same.

Suddenly Wesley dug Ryan in the ribs.

"Don't look now but you are being given the eye," he whispered.

"Who by?" muttered Ryan, while still keeping his gaze on Roger Green.

"Who do you think?" chuckled Wesley.

After a few minutes Ryan casually glanced around the table before his eyes settled on Samantha. Sure enough the young secretary was staring straight at him as she sipped wine from a long stemmed glass. As always she was attracted to the hero of the hour whoever that might be. Tonight it just happened to be Robsons top salesman for September.

Ryan headed straight for the loo. Then standing in front of the mirror he carefully checked his appearance while deciding on the best 'chat-up' line. Providing he played it right Samantha was his for the taking.

"Just act cool," he muttered to himself while adjusting his tie.

Before returning to the bar he needed to do one more thing. Reaching into his trouser pocket he produced a mobile phone and began calling up his home number. With luck he could be in for a long evening and that being the case, it was advisable to speak with his wife in advance. Nicola was generally happy enough if she thought he was out drinking with the boss.

Minutes later Ryan returned to his colleagues. Having spoken with his wife he had been given the green light to enjoy a few beers providing he returned home with a kebab. Under the circumstances it seemed a small price to pay for the sins he was hoping to commit.

***

Once the ballot boxes arrived at the Town Hall the count was soon underway. Five long lines of tables had been assembled where workers would spend a couple of hours or so wading through thousands of white voting forms. Without the use of technology to assist them it was a laborious task and accuracy was of the highest importance.

An assortment of people were milling around. As expected the media had turned up in force with large moveable cameras placed at strategic points. Then there were the candidates with their entourage of supporters huddled into groups.

In fact there were a number of names on the ballot forms. Brockleby being a marginal seat was therefore high profile and meant that entering the contest was an easy means for individuals and groups to draw attention to themselves. Most were representing serious causes but then there were the more frivolous ones such as 'Give Dogs The Vote Party'. The candidate being easily identified as a figure wandering about dressed as a giant Dalmatian.

The Conservative and Labour contingents kept their distance from each other. Accusations made by each side during the course of the campaign had created a great deal of acrimony between the two parties. In particular, scathing attacks made on both Charles Dawkins and Jacqui Dunn had been deeply resented in their respective camps.

Tony quickly got his troops mobilised. Activists might well have been working their socks off during the campaign but this wasn't the time to sit back. There was still one very big job left to be done.

"Keep an eye on the vote counters," he instructed. "Stand and look over their shoulders if you have to but make certain they know you are watching them."

"Quite right," agreed Jacqui. "There may be a rogue one amongst them who could be a Tory admirer. We need to make certain of fair play."

"If you see anything suspicious just let me know," said Tony. "I will go straight to the Returning Officer to report the matter."

Not surprisingly supporters from other parties were given similar instructions. Soon gangways between the long rows of tables were full of people closely monitoring operations. Those that looked the most anxious though were from the Labour and

Conservative camps.

As expected Charles Dawkins was much sought after by the media. Tall, well-groomed and dressed immaculately in a dark Savile Row suit, he was looking every bit a man destined for high office. If he was nervous it was well disguised behind his dazzling smile as he posed for photo shots.

Jacqui Dunn, too, was receiving a great deal of attention. As the only candidate who had a realistic chance of unseating the high-flying MP news reporters were only too well aware that she might be making the headlines in a few hours' time. Therefore a posse of media people clamoured around her to find out as much as they could about this attractive middle-aged lady councillor.

At twenty past eleven the count was still in full swing. However news was starting to filter through of results which had already been declared in other constituencies. The TV crews having received the details first were quick to share them.

"Labour have held on to Sunderland West and Hull East but have lost Basildon to the Tories," announced a cameraman with shoulder length hair and a red open-necked shirt.

"Has there been a big swing away from Labour?" asked Tony, anxiously.

"Less than two per cent," replied the cameraman. "There are early signs that we could end up with a hung parliament."

Tony wandered away to join his friends. Like everyone else he had given up on watching the votes being counted. Having been up since the crack of dawn he was mentally exhausted and quite content to put his trust in the people who were wading through those endless white forms.

"We've lost Basildon," he announced, gloomily.

"Let's hope Labour can take Brockleby then," replied George. "The Tories over there are beginning to look nervous."

"I'm pretty worried myself," admitted Jacqui, who looked perfectly composed on the outside. "Very soon I should know whether there are going to be monumental changes in my life or whether things will just go on as usual."

At twelve forty-five all the ballot papers had at last been counted. Putting a microphone to his mouth the Returning Officer called all of the candidates on to the platform. Those looking on watched in hushed silence as they assumed that the moment of truth was just about to arrive.

All eyes and the TV cameras were suddenly focused on three figures. Jacqui Dunn and Charles Dawkins standing side by side with the Returning Officer. The remaining candidates on the other hand looked perfectly relaxed as they laughed and joked amongst themselves. The 'Give Dogs The Vote' campaigner caused some hilarity by dancing around in his canine suit.

Soon the whole gathering on the stage disbursed. Grim faced, Jacqui Dunn returned to her supporters to update them on what was going on. However, before the parliamentary candidate could open her mouth the little Labour group were joined by a posse of media people desperate for information.

"The Tories got just thirty-two votes more than us so I've asked for a recount," announced Jacqui Dunn, managing a brave smile.

The news was greeted with groans of frustration. The activists on one hand were suddenly faced with the galling prospect of probably missing out on electoral success by a whisker. On the other hand the media crowd were upset that bedtime would now have to be a lot later than originally planned.

"We can still win," said Carol, cheerfully, as she sensed the feeling of despair amongst the other activists. "I'm sure some of the votes must have been miscounted."

"Quite right," said Tony, attempting to sound more optimistic than he felt. "Probably bigger majorities have been overturned in a recount."

Jacqui suddenly drifted off into her own private world. Appearing to stare straight through Tony she was already trying to come to terms with defeat. All the effort she had put into the campaign over the past few weeks would change nothing in her life. Worse still she would not be able to speak out in the House of Commons against the Iraq War or fight for any of the other issues that she felt so passionately about. Just a handful of votes looked set to bring her ambitions crashing to the ground.

"It's going to be a long night," she said, suddenly emerging from her trance-like state. "If anyone has had enough please don't feel obliged to stay."

Nobody moved. Most people in the group now longed for their bed but each and everyone of them was determined to stay to the bitter end. If Jacqui was to end up losing they wanted to be on hand to support her.

"Perhaps you should go for Amanda's sake," suggested Tony, turning to Alison.

Alison shook her head.

"She'll be fine with my mum."

"If we are going to stay on then let's make ourselves comfortable," suggested George, who was the oldest member of the group.

"That isn't a bad idea," answered Jacqui, who knew exactly what her fellow councillor had in mind.

Up to now they had all been standing. However, the large hall was mainly used for meetings and stacked up against the wall were plenty of wooden chairs. Following George's example the rest trundled over to collect one.

After a short break the ballot papers were being waded through for a second time. For both Conservative and Labour camps it mean more agony as they waited for the eventual result, whenever that might be announced. However, for the minor candidates and most of the media representation, a further count just meant another period of total boredom.

Results from the other constituencies continued to flood in. Kenny had brought a small radio in order to stay in touch with the situation, while the cameraman with the shoulder length hair also provided frequent updates. However there seemed to be very little good news for Labour supporters. The party was continuing to lose seats to the Tories and the situation was beginning to look grim.

David and Alison sat apart from the rest of the group. Both of them felt a need to talk about anything other than politics. In the case of one of them though, it also seemed the ideal opportunity to bring up a subject which would drastically affect their relationship.

"Do you miss your family much?" asked Alison. "You rarely ever talk about them these days."

David nodded sadly.

"It hits me most when I'm alone and have time to think. I miss that feeling of being part of a community. In the evening after church sitting down to eat with the family and any other

Fellowship friends who had just dropped in. At the weekends going to social events with people that I knew and then there were all the other little gatherings that happened all the time. It was a completely different lifestyle to what most of those in the outside world ever experience."

Alison looked thoughtful.

"You seem to be enjoying a good social life at the moment with your political friends and going to parties."

David gave her a surprised look.

"But I don't go to parties."

Alison smiled and playfully slapped his wrist.

"Apart from the one you went to on Saturday night in Station Road. You were seen there by a friend who had spotted us out canvassing together."

David was stunned.

"Look you were away last weekend and I had nothing else to do," he explained, anxiously.

"It doesn't matter," laughed Alison. "Anyway I heard you were getting on very well with one of the ladies who live in the flat. Is she nice?"

"I don't know," muttered David, rather stupidly.

"What's her name?" asked Alison, sweetly.

"Samantha," replied David, hardly able to believe he was having this conversation.

"And does she have any children?"

"No," answered David, suddenly realising what a hopeless 'two timer' he was turning out to be. Finally having been caught out he had simply no idea how to lie his way out of trouble.

"It sounds as though life would be a lot less complicated with her than it would be with me," laughed Alison.

A few moments of silence followed as David tried to collect his thoughts. Feeling absolutely exhausted after his long never ending day he was unable to decide where the discussion was leading to. What exactly was he supposed to say.

"But Samantha doesn't mean anything to me," he said, finally. "She is just a friend at work who was looking for a partner for the night."

For a moment Alison was close to tears but managed to remain composed. The time had come to drop a bombshell on the poor vulnerable creature who had recently entered her life. She had hoped his involvement with this woman might help soften the blow. However, she had now a gut feeling that it probably wouldn't.

"Look last night Mark and I had a long conversation," she began, hesitantly. "It seems that at last he wants to settle down and for us to get married. Mad as it sounds I am still in love with him, so during the last hour I have decided to accept."

David felt as though he had just been struck by lightning. The first thought that entered his head was that he was being punished by God for breaking away from the Fellowship. Then he wondered whether it was just a bad dream and the alarm clock would go off any minute.

"But I thought you said that Mark didn't want all the responsibilities that go with marriage," said David in bewilderment.

"He has decided to turn over a new leaf," replied Alison moving her legs slightly to allow a television crew member to pass. "Mark has managed to find a good job and wants to settle down with Amanda and me. He has promised to reform and put all those drinking sessions and parties behind him."

"I hope you will both be happy," said David attempting to sound magnanimous.

Suddenly Alison brightened up.

"Didn't you say that you were going down to Broadstairs at the weekend to visit Rebecca?"

David nodded without any great enthusiasm.

"I'm driving down with Simon."

"Now that Rebecca is a widow I think you should grab the opportunity to propose to her," said Alison, eagerly. "She would make a perfect wife for you."

Although deeply depressed David managed a faint smile.

"The Fellowship don't operate like that. For Rebecca to marry me she would require the approval of not only her parents but other leading figures in the church. That would hardly be likely with my current popularity ratings."

"Then ask her to break free of the Fellowship like you did," suggested Alison. "Tell her about your new life and what it is like to be free from religious dogma."

David didn't get an opportunity to reply. Throughout their conversation the pair had been sitting with their backs to the rest of the Labour group. Finally tired of being ignored, Carol breezed over and patted Alison on the shoulder.

"Look why don't you two be more sociable and come and join the rest of us," she said, with a trace of a smile. "I'm desperate for somebody stupid to talk to."

As soon as David seated himself next to Tony he was quickly updated on the latest election results. The Tories were continuing to pick up seats at Labour's expense but it was unclear whether they were on track to win an outright majority. There was still a great deal of water to pass under the bridge before the picture would become clear.

Not surprisingly the little group as a whole were downcast. The very best the party was likely to achieve now was to be part of a coalition Government. They needed Jacqui Dunn to lift their spirits by winning the Brockleby seat.

Finally the second count was completed. Having been called back on to the platform the candidates once more crowded around the Returning Officer. All those in the hall not involved watched on in hushed silence.

Suddenly Jacqui looked across at Tony and shook her head. Then with a look of resignation she joined the long line of parliamentary candidates that were stood facing the back of the hall and the TV cameras. The hearts of all her supporters in the Labour camp immediately sank.

In contrast, Charles Dawkins, had the contented look of a man who was on course to become the next Home Secretary. Anticipating victory, the smiling Tory supporters were preparing themselves for a noisy celebration once the result was officially declared. However, had the high flying MP been looking in the right direction he would have a seen a sly smile spread across his wife Sally's face. If her husband thought he could dump her just like that he would have to think again she mused.

The Returning Officer suddenly rapped his gavel on the table. Then after giving the all too familiar preamble he began naming the candidates and the votes they had obtained. As it happened the two with any realistic hope of winning just happened to follow one another alphabetically.

The first name to be read out was that of the 'Keep Brockleby Roads Safe' candidate. Two of the fifty-nine people who had voted for him clapped loudly from the back of the hall. Then there was a slight pause as the Returning Officer slowly put the microphone once more to his lips. It was suddenly so quiet it would have been possible to hear the proverbial pin drop.

"Charles Dawkins... 19,375 votes," came the announcement.

Predictably a loud cheer rang out from one section of the hall. However, the ecstatic Tories were quick to restrain themselves in order to find out how the other heavyweight in the contest had got on. The expressions on their faces suggested that they were feeling extremely confident.

"Jacqui Dunn... 19,344 votes," were words which received the biggest cheer heard in the hall for many a year. On one side the Tories were celebrating victory while on the other, Labour supporters were showing their admiration for a woman who had given everything to the campaign and had come close to winning. Patiently the Returning Officer waited for the noise to die down before reeling off the results of other candidates which were on the ballot papers.

Charles Dawkins' speech became an acrimonious affair. Raising his voice above the heckling he accused Labour of using smear tactics to discredit him. Then he launched into a bitter attack on Jacqui Dunn.

"As a councillor she has shown herself to be an enemy of hard-working families," he shouted, while looking in the direction of the television cameras. "Many of the half-baked schemes she has supported over the years would have forced up local taxes for many struggling Brockleby residents. Fortunately our Tory controlled council has sensibly rejected Miss Dunn's money wasting proposals.

"Therefore the people of this constituency have elected me because I happen to share the same values as they do. A belief in low taxation, free enterprise and justice for victims of crime. Like them I want to see a society in which the law works in favour of the innocent and not the criminal. It is therefore my intention to lead a crusade for the reintroduction of the Death Penalty. The vast majority of people in this country say they are in favour and I will help to deliver it to them."

Charles ended his speech in a crescendo of noise. Supporters of the re-elected MP were jubilant with what they had just heard, however, others were rather less impressed with the talented orator. Labour, Lib Dem, Green and various left wing groups joined forces to boo and hiss.

As runner-up in the poll, Jacqui Dunn was the next to take the microphone. Although looking calm and composed as ever, deep down she was fuming. Having lost the election she was determined to win the war of words.

"This has been a stunning result for Labour," cried Jacqui, triumphantly. "In the past this has always been a safe seat for the Tories but tonight, we just fell short of taking it from them. This is despite Charles Dawkins telling the voters that I was intent on turning Brockleby into a Marxist republic.

"What is most offensive is when he has the cheek to accuse me of being an enemy of hard-working families. During the campaign I met dozens of people who have written to our MP asking him to help them with their problems and never received a reply. They believe he is only interested in getting to the very top.

"Well I've got a message for Mr Dawkins. Unless he starts looking after his constituents he won't have a political future after the next General Election."

It was a powerful speech but unsurprisingly was greeted with a mixed reception. The other candidates were then invited to come forward to say a few words. In the case of the man dressed as a Dalmatian, he decided to express himself with a few loud barks instead.

Finally all the candidates left the stage. Charles Dawkins was instantly cornered by the media but the remainder joined up with their supporters unhindered. The TV companies and the press had little interest in the losers.

Jacqui tried hard to disguise her disappointment. Smiling cheerfully she threw her arms around each member of the little group and hugged them. Overwhelmed with emotion, nobody was able to find the appropriate words to express their feelings. Alison in particular, looked a picture of pure misery as she dabbed her eyes with a paper tissue.

It was now a quarter past three. David felt as though he had been awake for a week as he followed the dejected figures of

Jacqui Dunn and the others towards the exit. While behind him, the Tories were noisily celebrating their victory.

David quickened his step in order to catch up with Alison.

"Can I give you a lift?" he asked.

Alison turned and shook her head, sadly.

"Tony and Carol are dropping me off. Thanks all the same for the offer."

"It seems I'm the biggest loser of all tonight," David complained, miserably. "Suddenly it seems to have gone horribly wrong."

Alison squeezed his hand tightly. Her eyes were still red from the tears but she had managed to regain her composure.

"You're far too good for me," she smiled. "Rebecca would make a perfect wife for you. Trust me, I know I'm right."

David felt devastated as he climbed into his car. He had hoped for great things from Election Day but in the end it had all turned out disastrously. Finding out that Jacqui had been beaten by the Tories was bad enough but losing Alison was far worse.

At that moment though he felt too tired to think straight. It was just possible that after a few hours' sleep things wouldn't seem quite so bad. After all, work was still going well and of course there was always Samantha. He suddenly remembered that she had invited him round for a meal the following week. Perhaps everything would turn out well in the end he told himself.

Chapter Twenty-Four

The following morning the weather changed for the worse. Under dark skies heavy rain fell steadily while great gusts of wind tore leaves from their branches and hurled them away at high speeds. It was a stark reminder that summer had slipped by for yet another year.

David arrived at the office wondering how he would survive the day. Having managed to squeeze in little more than three hours sleep he felt that all the life blood had been drained out of him. In a desperate attempt to revive himself he collected a black coffee from the drinks machine.

"See Labour lost last night," commented Wesley Chapple, looking up from his newspaper with a big grin.

"Looks like it, although there are still a few more results to come in," replied David, preparing himself for a few taunts.

However, he was to be spared for the present. Wesley's attention was distracted when he spotted Ryan Pritchard walking in his direction. Immediately his grin grew even wider.

"Did you score last night?"

"I lost count in the end," answered Ryan, with a lecherous smile.

"Lucky bugger," said Wesley.

"Could be your turn next time," said Ryan as he passed by on his way to the photocopier.

David took a sip of coffee. He had no idea what his colleagues were talking about but, the word 'score', suggested that there might be a sporting connection. With this in mind he made the error of taking a friendly interest.

"Was Ryan playing football last night then?"

"I hardly think so," answered Wesley, folding up the newspaper and putting it away in his desk drawer. "He was drinking down the pub with the rest of the sales office as it happens."

"So where did the scoring come in?" asked David, a little

bemused.

A broad grin spread across Wesley's face. His weird colleague had come up with a classic this time and he couldn't wait to spread it around the office. On second thoughts though, he wondered whether to save it up until Robsons next booze up.

"Last night Ryan took Samantha home from the pub and gave her a good..." Wesley began, before deciding to change his intended phraseology for the benefit of the simpleton he was talking to. "...had sex with her."

David couldn't believe his ears. If Ryan wasn't exaggerating then, it seemed that everyone was given a turn with Samantha as though she were a ride at the fairground. In his mind's eye he saw a long line of his male colleagues queuing up for tickets.

"Let's hope you get a go before long then," said David, managing to keep the bitterness out of his voice.

Wesley stared suspiciously at him through half-closed eyes.

"Not jealous are you?" he asked. "I seem to remember that you took Samantha home last week."

"Of course not," David replied, indignantly. "Women like that don't interest me."

Wesley was about to speak when his phone rang. While his attention was diverted, David took the opportunity to glance around at the secretarial department. He wanted to take another look at the nymphomaniac who benevolently divided her time between the young men of the office, and possibly some of the older ones, too.

Samantha was sitting demurely at her desk. From a distance the young secretary could have passed for a woman of great virtue as she gazed serenely at her computer screen. Perhaps even a nun who had just fitted herself up with a chastity belt in order to stay pure.

Sickened by the sight of her, David began to work. He had no wish to become one of Samantha's playthings and take turns with Ryan Wesley and the rest of them. Those left in the competition were welcome to her as far as he was concerned.

**

The hostile weather conditions continued into the following

308

day. Shoppers in Broadstairs battled to keep their balance as howling winds blew in from the sea. Any attempt at holding up an umbrella was doomed to failure.

The seaside town had looked so different on David's last visit. At the end of August, throngs of scantily clad holidaymakers had strolled leisurely along the streets and promenade in sun hats, while holding erect large dollops of ice cream at the end of cornet wafers. Now the pleasure seekers had finally returned home, it was probably just the locals who could be seen scurrying around in rainwear.

It was slightly after midday when Rebecca opened the door to her two guests. Smiling cheerfully she looked radiant even without the aid of make-up, which Fellowship women were forbidden to wear. Dressed in something other than plain uninteresting attire she would have been quite stunning.

The hostess led her visitors into the lounge and offered them an aperitif. As a delicious aroma wafted in from the kitchen the little gathering relaxed with their drinks while exchanging the latest news. Much had happened in the past few weeks.

"David was telling me that he was made to work hard during the election campaign," said Simon, turning to his sister.

"Yes I'd heard you had joined the Labour Party," said Rebecca, taking a sip of sherry. "I often feel like getting involved in politics myself. There is so much injustice in the world."

"There is no point in thinking about it," grinned Simon. "The Fellowship won't even allow you to vote."

Rebecca scowled. She was continuing to borrow books from the library, which were filling her head with new and exciting ideas. Reading about various forms of Government had convinced her that democracy was far and away superior to anything else yet devised. Ironically though, the Fellowship rejected the electoral process even though it was the one system which allowed them the freedom to worship as they pleased.

"Anyway, what happened finally?" she asked, determined not to dwell on the bigotry of the Fellowship. "I know the results were still being announced as late as yesterday afternoon."

"The Tories managed to get an overall majority of five," answered David, sadly.

"Close," smiled Simon, downing the last drop of whisky in

his glass. "They hardly got a resounding endorsement from the country."

Sick of politics, David was keen to change the subject. Other than football his housemates talked of nothing else and he had looked forward to his day with the twins for a welcome respite. Then he suddenly remembered Rebecca's recent bereavement.

"Have the police managed to trace the motorist who killed Malcolm yet?"

Rebecca shook her head.

"They probably never will. Had there been any witnesses willing to give evidence, they would have come forward by this time."

"I wish I could get my hands on that cowardly bastard," said Simon, angrily. "He should have had the guts to report the accident."

"It hardly matters now," replied Rebecca, heading towards the kitchen to check on how the meal was progressing. "Nothing can bring Malcolm back."

Soon the three of them sat down to eat. As they tucked into some very fine home cooking, Rebecca updated David on the changes that were taking place in her life. Most it seemed were for the better.

She had now got a job. Although married Fellowship women are forbidden to work, the rule doesn't apply to widows. Therefore after Malcolm's tragic death a member of the local church offered Rebecca employment in his company. Doing menial office tasks hardly taxed the brain but, even so, it was far more stimulating than sitting at home all day.

In fact her life in general had become a whole lot more interesting. Living alone meant that there was no longer any need to hide library books behind the wardrobe and she now read without fear of being caught in the act. Then one Saturday afternoon in an act of sheer bravado, she jeopardised her eternal soul by taking a trip to the theatre to watch a production of *Hamlet*.

Simon's news was rather more negative. Without looking too perturbed he announced that there would be no arranged marriage involving himself and a certain young lady from Devon. Apparently the other party had decided to wait for a more suitable gentleman to come along.

"I can't understand why all these women reject you," said Rebecca with a puzzled expression. "I would have thought you were a very eligible bachelor."

Simon grinned.

"I tell them that I wet the bed. That always seems to put them off."

"But why?" asked Rebecca in bewilderment. "Don't you want to get married?"

"Not to the sort of women our parents introduce me to," laughed Simon, almost choking on his lunch.

David couldn't be sure whether his friend was joking or not. Claiming to be a bed wetter was hardly likely to do wonders for a person's image. On the other hand it was preferable to have a tarnished reputation than to spend a lifetime with some old bag from the West Country.

Finally the Broadbent twins looked expectantly at David. Both were curious to know what had been happening in his life over the past few weeks. After all they had never known anyone who had broken away from the Fellowship.

David provided his friends with a brief summary. However, not wanting to admit to being a two timer, he deliberately made no mention of Samantha. He felt certain that Rebecca would disapprove of such behaviour.

"Things seemed to have gone wrong in the last thirty-six hours," said Simon.

"You must have had a nasty shock to learn that Alison was getting married," said Rebecca, gazing sadly at her guest. "Are you in love with her?"

For a while David didn't reply. Deep in thought he and Alison were gently embracing in the front seat of his car. He could feel the warmth of her body and the soft hair on his cheeks as they kissed. Outside in the black of night the only sound was that of rustling leaves as a gentle breeze brushed through the trees.

It was only a fortnight ago. After a drink at the Labour Party Social Club they were driving home and had stopped off at their favourite spot. Looking back it was a magical time when everything seemed unreal. Sadly now though, the dream was over and all that remained were the memories.

"Yes I suppose I am in love with her," replied David, finally. "But we had a relationship that was probably never going to last. I think that Alison was just waiting for Mark to commit himself to marriage and that would be the end for me."

"Apart from that though, are you still enjoying your new life?" asked Simon, having just swallowed the last mouthful of his main course.

"Yes I think so," answered David, thoughtfully. "Although it is very difficult to adjust to the ways of the big wide world."

"Would you ever consider returning to the Fellowship?" asked Rebecca, gathering up the empty plates now that everyone had finished eating.

"Possibly," answered David, closely studying his fingernails. "You know there are times when I feel like an outsider. I just don't fit in anywhere."

"Perhaps you need a period of reflection in which to find yourself," suggested Rebecca, as she set off for the kitchen with the dirty crockery.

"You are speaking to someone who spends his whole life in contemplation and never arrives at a conclusion," replied David, ruefully. "I just get carried along by events."

"You made the decision to leave the Fellowship," smiled Simon.

David conceded the point. However, deep down he understood what had really prompted him to turn his life upside down. Firstly the need to avoid an unwanted marriage and secondly to pursue the love of his schooldays.

The afternoon passed by blissfully enough. Sat comfortably in the lounge David was updated on what had been going on in Fellowship circles since his departure. Although nothing had radically changed there was no shortage of gossip.

The most serious news concerned a good friend of David's mother. Apparently Mrs Jenkins had slipped over in the rain and bruised her arm. In fact the injury was so painful that the poor old soul hadn't been seen in church for a week.

Things weren't going so well either for the Evans family. Robin had been caught speeding on the same day that Enid had lost her purse in the High Street. Somebody suggested that the Lord must be testing their faith.

"By the way," said Simon, suddenly. "I was shown a postcard the other day that Scott and Helen had sent to your parents. It seems that they are enjoying their travels around the country."

David smiled as he remembered his Australian friends.

"I enjoyed their company so much when they were staying with us. They were great fun," he said, fondly.

"Being Fellowship isn't all doom and gloom," replied Simon, sipping his tea. "Had you still been one of us we three could have paid them a visit next year."

All day David had been waiting anxiously to speak with Rebecca alone. Just after tea he finally had the opportunity when Simon strolled out to his car to fetch something. Knowing that his friend was unlikely to be gone for long he decided to be brief and to the point.

"Alison thinks you would make a perfect wife for me," he blurted out.

Rebecca was mildly amused.

"I wonder why she should say that?"

David could feel his cheeks burning.

"She didn't say but I tend to agree with her."

Rebecca was lost for words. For a few moments she sat staring at the wall on the opposite side of the room while David waited for her response. He was praying that she would speak before Simon returned.

"I've only just buried my husband," she said at last. "It is impossible for me to even consider marriage to anyone right now."

"But what about in the future?" asked David.

"You are forgetting one thing," said Rebecca, with a wry smile. "I'm Fellowship and you are not. We can't possibly marry under that arrangement."

David glanced quickly out of the window. Much to his relief he discovered that the conversation would be allowed to continue for a little longer before being interrupted. A low brick wall surrounded Rebecca's front garden and over the top, he could see Simon still rummaging around in the boot of his car.

"Would you ever consider deserting the Fellowship like I did?" he asked, hopefully.

Rebecca shook her head firmly.

"I've got too much to lose. My family, job and even this bungalow. You see Malcolm was given an interest free loan from the Fellowship when we bought it, and I am far from paying them back what is owed."

"So are you happy to go on deceiving everyone then?" asked David, accusingly.

"Why do you say that?" replied Rebecca, in surprise.

"Because you are a sceptic," answered David. "Deep down you question the Fellowship's narrow-minded beliefs as much as I do."

"Of course I do," replied Rebecca, scornfully. "On the other hand I am perfectly content with things as they are. I have my family, friends, a good social life and there is always someone to help me when things go wrong. In comparison the outside world seems a cold and selfish place where people just live for themselves."

Suddenly there was the sound of heavy footsteps outside. Having found what he wanted, Simon would be ringing the doorbell at any moment. David reckoned on having just enough time to squeeze in one final question.

"Would you marry me if I returned to the Fellowship?" he blurted out.

Rebecca's mouth fell open in surprise.

"You know the Fellowship don't operate like that. Other people have a large say in who you can and can't marry."

"But what if nobody objected?" David persisted.

Rebecca stood up as the doorbell rang for a second time.

"I would need to think long and hard about it," she answered.

Simon returned carrying a leather photograph album. Having finally tracked it down in a plastic carrier bag he was ready to show his sister and friend pictures of a recent Fellowship fund raising event in Brockleby. With the wave of his arm he motioned them to sit either side of him.

As Simon turned the pages, David recognised many familiar faces. There smiling up at him were family members and friends he had known all his life. Suddenly he felt a tinge of sadness at seeing all those good gentle people again. For the first time the rebel who had broken away from this tightly knit community realised how much he missed them all.

The following day David started to catch up on the national news. In the aftermath of the General Election the country had acquired a new Government with the right honourable Jonathan Canning at the helm. Furthermore, the previous Prime Minister, Bruce Shaw had announced that he would be standing down as leader of the Labour Party once a successor had been chosen.

After breakfast, David casually wandered into the lounge. Much to his amusement, George and Kenny were surrounded by Sunday newspapers that they were attempting to scan while watching the news on TV. In addition to that the two councillors were even managing to conduct a conversation at the same time.

"A crowd of us are out delivering leaflets this afternoon," announced George, as soon as he set eyes on his newest lodger. "I trust that you are free to lend a hand?"

David looked aghast.

"You can't be serious. Everyone has worked their guts out during the past few weeks. Don't' we all deserve a break now that the campaign is over?" he protested.

"Labour can't afford to relax," answered Kenny, briefly glancing up from the *Sunday Telegraph*. "There could be a General Election at any time. The Tories won't be able to govern for long with only a five seat majority."

"And the next time we will be in a strong position to win Brockleby," beamed George.

David took a look out of the window. He had no intention of joining a bunch of fanatics to tramp the streets in torrential rain and gale force winds. Thankfully though the inhospitable weather conditions of the past two days had given way to sunshine and blue skies.

"Very well," he said, wearily. "What time are we going?"

***

The Prime Minister finally decided on who would be serving in his new cabinet. The names were released to the media just as many people were about to tuck into their Sunday lunch. Among those appointed to high office was Charles Dawkins who as widely predicted, had been given the job of Home Secretary.

Madeleine who was working in the kitchen when she heard

the announcement punched the air in delight. Dressed in a plastic apron she was preparing an evening meal for two in celebration of Charles's election victory. It was also her intention to use the occasion to bring up the subject of their future marriage.

That afternoon the glamorous model devoted her time to domestic chores. As she polished and dusted every piece of furniture in sight for the benefit of a very distinguished guest, her mind was far away. With Charles at her side she was stood on the White House lawn with the American President and his wife. Close by cameras were flashing as the world's media watched on.

Madeleine's daydream was brought to an abrupt end by the doorbell chimes. Thinking that Charles had arrived earlier than planned she discarded her duster and hurried eagerly along the hall. She couldn't wait to set eyes on one of the country's most powerful men.

Throwing open the door Madeleine's face immediately dropped. It wasn't Charles's tall imposing figure which stood before her, but a slim middle-aged woman in a dark coat. From her appearance she could have been mistaken for a Jehovah Witness who was out spreading the word of the Lord.

"My name is Sally Dawkins," she said, without the trace of a smile. "I wonder if I might have a word with you?"

Madeleine's pulse began to race. Sooner or later she had expected an angry confrontation with Charles's other half and now it appeared that the moment was just about to arrive. Fortunately though, her rival seemed far less formidable than she had feared

"You had better come in," replied Madeleine, pulling back the door for her visitor to enter.

Soon the two women sat facing each other in the lounge. Sally was older by some ten years but the wrinkles had yet to encroach on her soft pale skin. Although not unattractive it was highly improbable that she would ever have been considered for a career in modelling like Madeleine. There was something about her high forehead and sharp intelligent eyes that would have looked out of place on the catwalk or the fashion pages.

"Thank you," said Sally, as she accepted a cream biscuit that was offered to her on a plate. "I'm glad I've finally met up with you."

316

"How did you know where I lived?" asked Madeleine.

Sally smiled.

"Having suspected that Charles was having an affair I hired a private detective to follow him."

"So have you come here to ask for him back?" asked Madeleine, with a wry smile.

Sally shook her head firmly.

"No far from it. I was just interested to find out what sort of person you were and also to offer my sympathy."

Madeleine was taken aback.

"Why should I need sympathy?"

Sally was deep in thought as she nibbled on her biscuit. Feeling vindictive towards the other woman she was savouring the opportunity to deliver some shattering news. It was just a matter of saying it in a manner that would have maximum impact.

"You know my private detective, a chap called Doug by the way, actually joined the Brockleby Conservatives in order to keep a watchful eye on Charles," she smiled. "In fact he was becoming quite a keen activist."

"That was nice for him," remarked Madeleine, acidly.

"Anyway one Friday evening Charles was sat talking in the bar with Adrian Thomas," continued Sally, with the smile now gone from her face. "They were both drinking quite heavily and when it was time for Charles to leave he seemed quite unsteady on his feet. What he didn't realise, however, was that Doug, who had been sitting on another table, was about to follow him home."

Madeleine's heart rate began to soar as she guessed what was coming.

"Go on," she said, anxiously.

"In short, there was a fatal accident," explained Sally. "Doug saw Charles run down a young man and then just drive away."

Madeleine saw the room spin around before her eyes.

"So does Doug intend to go to the police?" she asked, nervously.

Sally shook her head.

"That would be in nobody's interests," she laughed. "Anyway after Doug witnessed the accident he parked outside our house just waiting for daylight. Then slipping into the drive he started taking photographs of the damage done to Charles's car. For the purposes of DNA testing he also scraped a patch of congealed blood off the tyres and placed it in a plastic bag."

"Are we talking blackmail here?" asked Madeleine, suspiciously.

"I suppose you could say that," replied Sally, thoughtfully. "Anyway it wasn't until yesterday that Charles was told there had been a witness to the accident. It didn't seem fair that he should have that on his mind while fighting the election. So last night I invited Doug around in order that the three of us could have a nice little chat."

"Must have been fun," said Madeleine, disdainfully.

"To cut a long story short," continued Sally, ignoring the interruption, "Doug and I agreed to keep quiet about the accident on two conditions. Firstly that Doug was given a lucrative position at the Home Office and secondly that my husband agreed to stay married to me. You see, everyone is a winner except you of course."

Madeleine was silent for a few moments as she tried to find flaws in this arrangement. She could see how everyone would benefit from keeping their side of the bargain but there was something they had definitely overlooked. Suddenly a triumphant smile appeared on her face.

"Aren't you forgetting me?" she said. "I know about the accident."

Sally stood up in preparation for leaving. It had always been her intention to make this a brief meeting and now there wasn't very much left to say.

"If you so much as breathe a word your modelling career is finished," warned Sally. "Charles in his position has a great deal of influence and he will make sure that you never get another contract. Anyway even if you do speak out you don't have a shred of evidence to support your claims. People will just conclude that you are publicity seeking."

Long after the visitor had departed Madeleine sat staring into space. At first she felt deflated at having lost the man who would have brought her fame and fortune. Gone were the dreams of socialising with Her Majesty and all those visits to the White House. There would be no banquets with world leaders, television interviews or travelling around the world in luxury. She would remain just a second-rate model as Sally Dawkins had so aptly put it.

Then Madeleine had an idea. Wandering off into the hall she picked up the *Yellow Pages* directory from under the telephone table and began searching for the category headed 'Detective Agencies'. It was time she decided to have a little meeting with Doug.

Chapter Twenty-Five

Monday morning David had his regular one-to-one tête-à-tête with Roger Green. So far these meetings had been going well but on this occasion the atmosphere was less cordial. The sales manager was clearly frustrated with his new member of staff.

"You have dozens of contacts from your previous firm. Why aren't you managing to extract more orders from them?" he demanded.

"I'm trying my hardest," protested David. "It's just that nobody is looking to buy furniture right now."

Roger flung his pen down on the desk in frustration.

"Look you are on an excellent salary and the company expects results. Therefore I suggest you get on the phone and start bringing in more business."

David felt disgruntled as he left the boss's office. In all his five years at Fine Choice he had never been spoken to so harshly. For all his many failings, Maurice Hopkins, his old sales manager, always treated those beneath him with the greatest respect.

Throughout the morning David remained in a bad mood. Apart from the acrimonious meeting which continued to weigh on his mind he was growing increasingly irritated by some of his colleagues. For no apparent reason Wesley Chapple had started to call him 'Bonzo' and the name had caught on around the office.

About eleven o'clock David sauntered over to the drinks machine. While waiting for his cup to fill up with hot water he heard footsteps approaching from behind. Turning around he came face to face with Samantha.

"Look I need to speak with you about tonight," she said, hesitantly.

Anticipating what was coming, David decided it was time to make a small dent in her over-inflated ego.

"What is happening tonight?" he asked, with a look of surprise.

Samantha seemed taken aback.

"I invited you around for a meal. Don't you remember?"

Pretending to be searching through his memory bank David stood looking thoughtfully into space. Then as he snapped his fingers a broad smile appeared on his face suggesting that it was all coming back to him.

"You know I'd completely forgotten. There are so many things going on in my life at present that it's hard to keep track of them all."

"Therefore you won't be too disappointed to learn that I will have to cancel the invitation," said Samantha, haughtily. "Something important has come up."

David shrugged.

"Never mind," he said, casually, removing his cup from the coffee machine. "As it happens, there is a programme that I want to watch on TV this evening."

"Enjoy yourself then Bonzo," replied Samantha, frostily.

David made no reply as he strolled away. The thought did cross his mind to turn around and call her a tart but he decided against it. He was concerned that all her male admirers in the office might suddenly turn on him.

That evening David arrived home to find that Tony's car was parked outside the house. On opening the front door he heard voices coming from the lounge and was just about to join the gathering before being stopped in his tracks. Suddenly he realised that they were talking about him.

"I believe that David may have cost us the election," Kenny was saying. "Expecting that poor old pensioner to pay for her broken window couldn't have gone down well on the council estates."

"When you think that we lost by a mere thirty-one votes that could well be right," replied Tony.

David didn't want to hear any more. Feeling totally mortified he turned around and hurried upstairs to his bedroom. Suddenly it felt as though the whole world was turning against him.

For a while he lay on his bed staring up at the ceiling. Normally after work he would sit down to eat with his housemates but this evening there was something more important on his mind. Was it time he wondered to repent and return to the Fellowship.

David felt he needed to talk his problems through with

someone before arriving at a decision. However, he realised that it was important to find the right person who would listen sympathetically and provide him with some considered advice. So after some thought he decided to turn to his oldest and most trusted friend. He would therefore ring Simon at work the following day and try to arrange a meeting.

It wasn't long before David heard footsteps on the landing. Recognising George's little cough he needed no script to guess what was about to happen next.

"You had better get ready," called the landlord. "We are all meeting up in half an hour to deliver leaflets."

Suddenly David had a sense of déjà vu. Several weeks earlier his father would have been warning him not to be late for the evening's Fellowship meeting. It was as though nothing had really changed at all.

"Sorry but I'm not coming," David called out. "I've had a rather tiring day."

Immediately the bedroom door swung open and George's head appeared.

"Look everyone is feeling tired but this is no time to slacken off. The next election could be only a few months away and we need to be fighting that campaign now."

David could feel the anger boiling up inside.

"Perhaps you would be better off without me," he said, bitterly. "It seems that it was all my fault that Labour didn't win in Brockleby last week."

George looked sheepish.

"You must have been listening to our conversation downstairs."

"Yes and I'm furious to hear your comments after all the work I put in for the party during the last campaign," replied David, bitterly. "In fact I'm sick to death of delivering leaflets and discussing politics every minute of the day."

George shrugged.

"For people like Kenny and myself that just happens to be the way we are. Politics has got into our blood and we'd be lost without it."

David who was now sitting on the edge of the bed began to calm down.

"I have decided to move back to the hotel," he announced after a few minutes. "Thanks for providing me with a home here but now I feel the need to be by myself for a while."

"Very well if that's the way you want it," answered George, with a sad smile. "So when do you want to move out?"

"Tomorrow evening if that is all right with you," replied David. "Just let me know how much rent I owe."

"We'll sort it out when I get home," said George, before his head disappeared behind the door.

By eight o'clock the following evening David was comfortably installed back at the Brockleby Park Hotel. Having just eaten a three course meal in the restaurant he returned to his old room to watch some television. Laying back on his bed he felt a wonderful sense of freedom. For the moment there was nobody around to bully him into going to Bible Study meetings or to deliver a bundle of leaflets.

David also enjoyed having a television all to himself. Being the sole user of the remote control allowed him to watch any programme he liked without provoking an argument. Just as importantly he was now at liberty to switch the set off whenever it became an unwanted distraction.

Just after nine there was a tap on the door. Immediately David leapt up and began straightening the duvet that he had been sprawled out on. He wanted his room to create a favourable impression.

Simon was punctual as always. Earlier in the day David had rung his friend up from work and asked him to come to the hotel urgently. In their brief conversation he had made it clear that he was desperate for some guidance without going into precise details.

"I am thinking of returning to the Fellowship," David began when they were seated in the two matching armchairs at either side of the window.

Simon didn't show any visible signs of surprise at this sudden news. Instead he sat back in his chair and surveyed his host through half-closed eyelids like a psychiatrist about to analyse a patient.

"But I thought you wanted to be free to think and do as you pleased," he said with a faint smile. "Why are you giving up on your new life so soon?"

David gazed gloomily into space.

"It's not working out," he replied, with a shake of the head. "Outside Fellowship circles I'm like a fish out of water. Worldly people just don't know what to make of me and I don't really understand them either."

"But you must have known from the start that going out into the big wide world was never going to be easy," answered Simon, as he took a sip of tea that his host had made for him.

"You never know what things are like until you try them," replied David. "Anyway at the time I was desperate to free myself of Ruth and leaving the Fellowship seemed the only escape route."

"And of course there was Alison Johnson, the girl of your schoolboy dreams," laughed Simon. "Suddenly she seemed to be within your reach and you were prepared to sacrifice everything to grab her."

David took a sip of tea. He knew only too well that what his friend had just said was perfectly true. However, Alison's memory had become very painful and he was keen to change the subject.

"I need to leave the past behind and look to the future," explained David. "That is why I would appreciate your advice. Tell me what would you do in my position?"

Simon didn't reply immediately. Instead, wishing to take in his new surroundings, he allowed his eyes to wander around the room. It was the first time in his life that he had ventured inside a hotel.

"You seem to have all you want here," commented Simon at last. "En suite bathroom, tea making facilities, comfortable furniture and even your own television up on the wall. It must be costing you a fortune to stay here."

David shrugged.

"It's only a temporary measure."

"And then what?" asked Simon. "Sharing accommodation with people who don't understand you or living alone like a hermit?"

David stared blankly at his friend.

"I'm trying to decide which is the least of the two evils."

Simon quickly glanced at his watch. At nine forty-five he was expected home to join his parents in a Bible reading session. He decided that he would stay another few minutes but no more.

"Many people are praying that you will return to the Lord," he said, gently, laying down his cup and saucer on the coffee table beside him. "Shall I speak with Ian Porter and see if I can arrange an informal meeting between the two of you?"

David gazed thoughtfully at his fingernails for a few seconds.

"Go ahead then," he answered. "I suppose there is no harm in listening to what he has to say."

"I'll ring you at work when I have spoken to Ian," said Simon, suddenly standing up in preparation for leaving. "Sorry to dash off so soon but mum and dad think that I have just popped out for some petrol."

David continued watching television once Simon had gone. Having become an obsessive viewer he regarded the TV as the only real plus in his new life. Everything else had promised so much but had now turned sour on him.

At ten o'clock he switched over to the news. Not surprisingly the new Prime Minister had made the headlines by announcing that British troops were to be sent to Iraq. Facing the cameras at a press conference he attempted to justify his decision.

"We must stand by our American allies in the War on Terror," he announced, rather dramatically. "Freedom is precious and it would be foolish of us to ever take it for granted. Therefore I believe that Britain must be prepared to stand up and protect the way of life that we all enjoy."

It was only a brief statement. Once he had finished, Jonathan Canning strongly argued his case when he was cross examined by journalists. Then the TV cameras switched from the Prime Minister and focused on a political expert from the BBC to provide an analysis of the situation.

David was not persuaded by Jonathan Canning's argument for entering the conflict. The new Prime Minister seemed convinced that Saddam Hussein had possessed a huge stockpile of lethal weapons that could fall into the wrong hands if they were not discovered. This belief he claimed was based on reliable information that had come from sources who had once been very close to the former dictator.

"Failure to act," he had warned one reporter. "Could put our whole national security in jeopardy."

Then the second news story happened to be strongly related to the first. A suicide bomber had created carnage in the centre of Baghdad by blowing himself up alongside many innocent victims. There were scenes of great distress as grieving relatives were trying to come to terms with what had happened to their loved ones.

Ever since the General Election Labour had seemed to be changing their position on the Iraq invasion. After Bruce Shaw had announced that he intended to stand down as leader of the party once a successor had been chosen, many contenders for the coveted position began to speak out in favour of supporting the Americans and their allies by sending out the troops.

David's thoughts quickly turned away from politics. There were just too many things going on in his own life to concern himself over events which were outside his control. He had problems that just went around and around in his head and simply refused to go away.

Simon managed to arrange for David to meet Ian Porter on Thursday evening. Pulling up in his car outside the priest's house just after nine o'clock, the young breakaway was feeling apprehensive. In fact part of him wanted to turn around and drive straight back to the hotel. However, quickly putting all such thoughts behind him, he strode boldly up the garden path.

"How nice to see you again," smiled Ian, warmly, before guiding his guest into the lounge.

"Good to see you, too," replied David, as he entered the room, which immediately brought back memories of his last visit that had ended in such acrimony.

Soon the two men were sat facing each other and exchanging pleasantries. Yet again the guest would be denied refreshments because of the priest's refusal to eat with the ungodly. Therefore Mrs Porter senior had been given strict instructions not to appear with tea and biscuits.

"So Simon tells me that you may be ready to repent," said Ian, suddenly looking serious.

"I'm considering it," answered David, hesitantly. "I've become disillusioned with the world and what it has to offer."

"And what about the young lady that you were seen with?" Ian enquired. "Are you prepared to give her up?"

"I'm afraid that our relationship has ended," replied David, attempting to disguise his sadness. "She is now engaged to marry somebody else."

Ian nodded thoughtfully.

"You have had a lucky escape in that case. The Devil is always trying to lure us off The Path Of Righteousness. Knowing our weaknesses he puts temptation in our way and hopes that we will succumb."

"So is it likely that the Fellowship will take me back?" asked David.

"The Lord is always prepared to show mercy to those who seek forgiveness," replied Ian, with a serene smile. "However, whether you will be permitted to return to the Fellowship in the near future is not my decision alone. First I will have to consult with other people on the matter."

David had a fair idea who Ian would be speaking to. Without doubt he wouldn't be inviting the opinions of women or males below a certain age, but rather senior men of the faith who were generally regarded as being in possession of sound moral judgement. Good solid types like his father for instance, who had never been known to question anything the Fellowship had ever preached to him.

"So how long do you think it will be before I get an answer?" asked David.

"I hope to have some news for you within a week," answered Ian. "By the way, where can I get in touch with you?"

David had to think quickly. Other than the twins he didn't want anyone else within the Fellowship to know that he was employed by Robsons. Samuel Boswell would be most upset to learn that one of his former salesmen had gone to work for a rival company.

"Actually I can't be contacted in the day so perhaps you could ring me at my hotel after six in the evening," said David, as he quickly scribbled the number down on a scrap of paper.

The two men talked for a while. As they hadn't seen each other for a few weeks, Ian was keen to find out how his guest had been coping in the big wide world. David on the other hand was very selective in the information he gave away.

That night David went to bed feeling easier in his mind. Feeling pretty confident that the Fellowship would soon accept him back in the fold he looked forward to being reunited with his family and friends again. Then for the first time in a while he said his prayers before finally falling asleep.

***

It had taken a number of phone calls before Madeleine managed to track down her man. She had rung a dozen or more detective agencies which were advertised in the *Yellow Pages* before meeting with success. Finally a rather bubbly receptionist advised her that the company she worked for did in fact employ an investigator by the name of Doug.

Several hours later Madeleine was sat alone in a waiting room alongside a pile of glossy magazines. Normally she would have been perfectly content to wade through the gossip columns and discover what the celebrities were getting up to. Today though she had more important things on her mind.

Madeleine was feeling impatient. For the third time in less than ten minutes she stood up and checked her appearance in an oval mirror hanging up on the wall. She had been told that Doug Quentin was currently with a client but was expected to be free very shortly. However, this information which had been given to her over half an hour ago was clearly inaccurate.

To make matters worse the waiting room was hot and stuffy. Madeleine tried to prise open each of the two windows but neither would budge. For a split second she considered breaking the glass with the heel of her shoe but then thought better of it.

If Hedges and Associates were making plenty of money out of their clients there was no outward sign of it. The company operated from a rather shabby three bedroom semi-detached house, which had been home to various families over the years. The waiting room having previously served as a lounge.

Eventually the bubbly receptionist arrived with a beaming smile and some welcome news.

"Mr Quentin will see you now," she announced.

Madeleine was led up a flight of narrow stairs, which were

covered in a green threadbare carpet. Stood on the landing waiting for her was a short man in his late fifties wearing a red cardigan and grey baggy flannels. His scruffy appearance blended in well with the surroundings.

Doug Quentin shook hands with his visitor before ushering her into a large office, which had once served as a bedroom. Then after uttering a few words of thanks to the receptionist he shut the door and took a seat behind a desk covered in papers and files.

"So what can I do for you Miss Kingsley?" asked the private detective.

"I've come to talk about Charles Dawkins," replied Madeleine. "A gentleman I believe you know well."

Doug nodded.

"Probably not as intimately as you do though," he smiled. "I discovered from my investigations that he paid you frequent visits."

"Look I'll come straight to the point," said Madeleine choosing to ignore the jibe. "We both know that Charles killed an innocent young man and I believe he should be made to pay for it."

Deep in thought Doug tapped the tips of his fingers gently on the desk.

"Are you proposing to go to the police?" he asked.

"Actually I was thinking more in terms of the press," replied Madeleine, with a smile. "One of the tabloids would pay a fortune for a story like that. Can you imagine headlines like Home Secretary is guilty of manslaughter."

Doug sat back in his chair and looked slightly puzzled.

"I assume you are capable of producing evidence Miss Kingsley. The press aren't interested in allegations which can't be substantiated."

Madeleine favoured the private detective with her most seductive smile. She was disappointed that the little man who could hold the key to her future happened to be so repulsive. Nevertheless she was not prepared to allow such minor details to get in the way of her ambitions.

"I don't have any proof of what happened on the night of the accident but you do," replied Madeleine, enthusiastically. "Therefore my idea is that we work as a partnership."

Doug looked mildly amused as he sat with hands behind his head.

"And what would you be contributing to this partnership?"

"That depends entirely on you," replied Madeleine, switching on her seductive smile again.

Doug's expression suddenly became serious as he straightened up in his chair.

"Sorry Miss Kingsley but you are wasting your time. I sold all my evidence yesterday to Sally Dawkins for a sizeable fee."

Madeleine looked visibly shocked.

"I'm sure any newspaper would have paid far more than you got," she gasped. "Not only that but you have probably allowed Charles Dawkins to escape a prison sentence."

Doug stood up and strolled over to the window. He was one of those fidgety people who could never be still for more than a minute. It was as though he was totally incapable of relaxing.

"I have no wish to see Mr Dawkins become incarcerated," said the private detective, lifting back the net curtain and peering down on the street. "It is good to have a friend in high places."

"Particularly when they can find you a highly paid position in the Home Office," said Madeleine, disdainfully.

"I start at the beginning of next month," answered Doug as he strolled back to his desk. "It will be wonderful to get away from this dive."

"Lucky you," said Madeleine bitterly. "Having looked forward to becoming the Home Secretary's wife I will end up being dumped without even an apology."

"I'm afraid you may have been deluding yourself Miss Kingsley," said Doug, shifting around restlessly in his chair. "Charles told me that he was growing tired of you with your shallow conversation and stupid painted face."

"You are lying to me," replied Madeleine, indignantly.

"I'm telling you the truth," said Doug as he tapped his foot on the floor.

"The bastard," retorted Madeleine, angrily, as she stood up and headed for the door. "I will make him regret saying things like that about me."

***

It was just after midnight when Charles Dawkins arrived home. Having spent the best part of Friday evening in the bar with many of the Tory faithful, the high flying minister had managed to introduce a fair quantity of alcohol into his bloodstream. However, for once he had no worries about being stopped by the police as Brian was driving.

One of the perks of his new position was to be given a chauffeur who doubled up as a bodyguard. His privileged position in Government also entitled him to a ministerial home in Downing Street, which he'd decided to reside in during the week. Then when parliamentary proceedings had been concluded on Friday he would depart for Brockleby to spend the weekend with his family.

It had been a punishing day for Charles. Suddenly being promoted to head of a major Government department was even more demanding that he had envisaged. There were constant meetings, piles of documents to be read and at the same time overseeing the drafting of a bill to reintroduce the Death Penalty.

"What time should I pick you up tomorrow sir?" asked Brian as he pulled up outside the minister's front gate.

"Make it about one o'clock," replied Charles. "I have to hand out prizes at a church fete in the afternoon."

Brian looked slightly surprised as he turned around to look at his passenger sitting on the back seat.

"Aren't you doing your usual Saturday morning surgery sir?"

Charles shook his head.

"I need to spend a little time with the family so I've asked Adrian Thomas to cover for me. Anyway, being the Council Leader he is far better on local issues than I am."

"Sleep well sir," said Brian, as his passenger scrambled out of the car.

"Good night," answered Charles.

Brian decided to wait for a few minutes before driving off. Aware of how much Charles had been drinking he wanted to make sure that the great man found his way indoors. As one of several bodyguards to the minister he didn't want to see the poor chap having any nasty accidents on his watch.

As Charles strolled down the garden path he reflected on his achievements. Already tipped as the next Prime Minister he could see his name written in the annuls of history alongside that of Disraeli, Churchill and all the other great Tory leaders. However, instinct told him he could be even better than any of them.

Suddenly Charles stopped. With his head in a drunken stupor he began fumbling around in his pockets for the front door key. Then having finally located it, the tiny metal object slipped from his fingers and dropped to the ground.

From the glow of the street lighting, Brian watched on with a look of amusement. He was just about to climb out of his car to offer assistance when a woman passed by on the pavement. Tall and blonde she was in her thirties and wore a dark fur coat.

Brian was taken by surprise when the woman pushed open the gate that Charles had just gone through. Not totally familiar with all of the Home Secretary's female relatives he wasn't entirely sure how to react. However, something inside was prompting him to lay his hand on his gun.

"Excuse me madam but do you live here?" he called out.

The woman appeared not to have heard. Instead she quickened her pace towards the bent figure of Charles who was still searching for his key on the garden path. Then without stopping she placed her hand inside her coat and produced a knife with a long gleaming blade.

Brian fired his gun but he was too late to save the Government Minister. With his neck drenched in blood, Charles was the first to hit the ground while a split second later the assassin collapsed on top of him. It was rather like one of those gory scenes from a Shakespearean tragedy.

Although stunned, Brian had the presence of mind to instantly produce his mobile phone to call an ambulance. He had no sooner begun to speak, however, before Sally Dawkins, dressed in her night clothes, had thrown open the front door and stormed over to where the two bodies were lying in a heap. Then a look of horror appeared in her eyes when suddenly the assassin's head gradually turned around to face her.

"Why?" shrieked Sally.

"Justice," croaked Madeleine, before her eyes shut for the very last time.

Chapter Twenty-Six

Jonathan Canning was woken up at one o'clock in the morning by the sound of his bedside telephone. For the next few minutes he listened in disbelief as a junior Home Officer minister explained how Charles Dawkins had been murdered in his front garden. For the first time in his long political career the newly elected Prime Minister was almost lost for words.

"Do you know who this woman was?" asked Jonathan, raising himself up in bed.

Alan Cavendish who was a rising star on the Tory benches smiled to himself.

"She was Charles Dawkins' mistress until he suddenly gave her the elbow."

"It gets worse," groaned Jonathan. "The last thing I need is for the tabloids to uncover a sex scandal involving one of my senior ministers. I'm only grateful that they won't be calling on me to sack him."

"Bit late for that," agreed Alan.

Mrs Canning who lay alongside her husband was listening with some interest. Normally when Jonathan received a call in the middle of the night it concerned some boring matter and she would pull the bed clothes over her head. A love triangle which ended in murder, however, was something she could get her teeth into.

"It's a pity the bodyguard didn't react sooner," said Jonathan, bitterly.

"Apparently he had been drinking with Charles and that must have slowed his thought processes down," answered Alan.

"I could strangle that stupid bastard," snapped Jonathan. "Not only has the Government lost a Home Secretary but it also means that the Tories now have to fight a very difficult by-election. The party will have to defend a seat with a wafer thin majority."

"Won't be easy Prime Minister," said Alan.

Jonathan cursed as he switched off the bedside lamp. Like

himself, Charles was a right winger and would have been a staunch ally in all those cabinet meetings ahead. Finding a suitable replacement to fill one of the top positions in Government wouldn't be easy.

The Prime Minister shut his eyes and settled down beneath the covers. He needed to get some sleep for the following day promised to be even more hectic than usual. Apart from all his other duties he would now need to spend part of his time speaking to the media about the assassination.

"I feel sorry for Sally Dawkins," piped up Mrs Canning. "Shouldn't you call her right away to offer your condolences?"

"I shall do it tomorrow," answered Jonathan, irritably.

***

Unlike the Prime Minister, David had to wait until the morning to find out about the murder. Switching on the television he was a little surprised to see the face of his MP staring at him from across the room. The picture disappeared and was replaced by a young man standing outside the gate of a large detached house.

"Just after midnight Charles Dawkins, the Home Secretary was stabbed to death here in his own front garden," announced the reporter. "His killer is understood to be a Miss Madeleine Kingsley who was herself then shot dead by Mr Dawkins' bodyguard. At present it is unclear what the motives were for this fatal attack, but it is rumoured that the pair may have been former lovers."

David couldn't believe what he was hearing. He and others had flogged themselves to death in an attempt to destroy the political career of Charles Dawkins during the election campaign. Now suddenly, possibly a jilted mistress had done the job with just the thrust of a knife.

Turning off the television David went down to the restaurant for breakfast. It was Saturday morning and as he sat down to eat it suddenly occurred to him that he had nothing planned for the weekend. It was pleasing to think that for once there was nobody around to organise his life for him. He was free to do exactly as he pleased if only for two days.

After leaving the hotel David headed straight for the High Street. The weather was getting colder and he decided it was time to look around for a winter coat. For a while he wandered in and out of clothes shops but there was nothing that really took his fancy. Finally tired of being pestered by over-zealous sales assistants he made up his mind to call off the search until another day.

David now turned his attention to buying a paper. Fascinated by the dramatic events which had occurred during the night he was keen for as much information as possible. It was while he was on the lookout for a newsagent that he happened to pass the Odeon, Brockleby's only cinema. Stopping for a few moments he began studying a poster stuck to the glass doors.

Printed in bold capitals was the word 'Braveheart'. It was a film that Wesley Chapple had seen during the week and had spent a great deal of working time discussing it with his colleagues. So having been given a favourable review, David was eager to acquire a ticket.

The young man had never been to the cinema before. Watching films in such places was yet another of those worldly pleasures that the Fellowship condemned. They believed that this decadent form of entertainment was successfully employed by the Devil to tempt the Godly from the paths of righteousness.

Not surprisingly David was curious to find out what Satan had to offer. Then after briefly studying a poster listing the performance times he wandered away to continue his search for a newspaper. However, he planned to be back at the Odeon by the time the doors opened at one o'clock.

The High Street had now become crowded. Suddenly amongst the sea of faces David spotted an attractive one that he recognised. Samantha was less than twenty metres away and heading in his direction. She was not alone, however, but was strolling along hand in hand with a tall fair haired young man.

David immediately became intrigued. He wondered whether the stranger was a regular boyfriend or merely somebody who was being given a turn. Just as interestingly, did the poor devil appreciate the fierce competition that he faced from practically the entire male workforce of Robsons.

David chose to acknowledge his colleague with just a half

smile before passing by. Then after having purchased a copy of the *Guardian* he decided to wander down to the park to read about the murder. He also felt the need to escape from the hustle and bustle of Saturday morning shopping.

Before long he was sitting on a bench overlooking the lake with its small woody island in the middle. The ducks were gliding gracefully over the surface of the water as ever but, today, there were no parents with small children to throw scraps of bread at them. In fact because of the chillier weather there were few people around at all.

It had been several weeks since he had ventured down to the park. On that occasion he had just fallen out with the Fellowship and was planning a new independent life for himself. Then having come face to face with his sister-in-law Kate and little niece Gemma, the pair had fled from him as though he were a carrier of the Bubonic Plague.

David settled down to read the murder report. However, he had barely got past the first two paragraphs before he heard somebody calling out his name. On looking up he saw a plump man with a shock of dark hair heading towards him.

"David Chambers, good to see you dear boy," boomed out Mr Chapman as he flung out a large chubby hand.

Standing up respectfully David greeted his old History teacher with a warm smile.

"It's good to see you again," he replied.

"Are you all ready for the by-election then?" asked Mr Chapman, jovially, as the two men lowered themselves on to the park bench at the same time.

"Certainly not," answered David with a shudder. "I'm sick of politics right now."

Mr Chapman nodded sympathetically.

"I remember when we last spoke you didn't seem too happy with some of your fellow party workers. They seemed to be upset with you about a broken window."

"They actually put the blame on me because Labour didn't win Brockleby in the General Election," replied David, indignantly. "After I'd worked my guts out for them as well."

"So have you given up politics for good then?" asked the History teacher.

David nodded.

"There seems little point in me continuing if I am seen as a liability."

For a moment Mr Chapman's attention became distracted. A black Labrador had just bounded up with the sole purpose of sniffing his overcoat. Then having satisfied itself the animal hurried away to have a paddle in the lake.

"And what about Alison?" enquired the older man, suddenly remembering he was in the middle of a conversation. "Is she upset that you won't be going out canvassing with her anymore?"

David shrugged.

"I doubt whether she cares. Alison is getting married next year to the man she used to go out with."

Mr Chapman looked thoughtfully at his former pupil.

"It sounds as though you are having a pretty rough time of it at the moment."

David nodded, gloomily.

"The problem is that I don't understand the way worldly people think and behave. Away from the Fellowship I'm like a fish out of water."

Mr Chapman began searching around in his overcoat pocket. Then after a few moments he produced a pipe with a curvy stem, a tin of tobacco and a silver lighter. A nifty bit of finger work followed before the History teacher's head partially disappeared behind a great billow of smoke.

"So are you considering returning to your former life?" he enquired, after finally withdrawing the smouldering pipe from his lips.

"Yes," answered David, wearily nodding his head. "I've already spoken to somebody about going back and the matter is now under consideration. Apparently certain senior Fellowship members will need to give their approval."

A look of disappointment spread across Mr Chapman's kindly face.

"Surely you aren't giving up on your new life so soon. I was hoping you were going to fulfil your ambitions and become a teacher."

"What is the point if I am just going to be miserable," replied David. "I miss my friends, family and also being part of a close

337

network of people who are always there to support each other."

There was a slight pause in the conversation as Mr Chapman attempted to light up his pipe once more.

"I can appreciate your plight," he said, reflectively. "However please give it some more thought. Remember you are making a vital decision that will affect the rest of your life."

"I appreciate that," smiled David. "If I return to the Fellowship they will expect me to marry and have children. Then there really will be no turning back."

Mr Chapman stood up and flung out his chubby hand once more.

"I must be going and leave you to read your paper," he smiled, affably. "Remember to give me a ring if you need any advice."

"Certainly," replied David. "I still have your number."

The young man felt a tinge of sadness as he watched the great bulky figure stroll away. The thought suddenly occurred to him that perhaps his old school master was able to emphasize with his problem much better than most. As a homosexual, he too would have known what it felt like to be an outsider.

When the Odeon opened at one o'clock David was the first in the queue. Followed by a stream of eighty or so people he strolled over to the cashier who was seated inside a small glass enclosure and bought his ticket. Then after leaving the foyer he passed through two sets of swing doors before eventually finding himself in the auditorium. For the first time cinema-goer it was all very new and exciting.

"Sit anywhere you like," smiled the middle-aged usherette in a blue uniform.

David was spoilt for choice. There were rows and rows of red upholstered seats, which matched in colour, both the carpet and also the giant curtains that were draped in front of the screen. The high walls and ceilings in contrast were light pink.

After a little indecision David went and sat near the front. Soon a scattering of people began occupying neighbouring seats and on several occasions, he had to stand up to allow others to pass in order to take their places further along his row. Then a young woman in a white coat slowly paraded down the centre aisle carrying a tray of ice creams, stopping every so often to sell her wares. In a while soothing music began wafting out from somewhere in the auditorium.

Finally the lights dimmed. Then as the music stopped playing there was a hush in the audience as the two giant curtains suddenly started to roll apart. In the semi-darkness all eyes were focused on the big screen that was now revealed.

The performance started off with commercials. A number of local businesses used the cinema as a means of promoting themselves with some rather bland advertisements. Then it was on to the trailers of films soon to be shown at the Odeon. Each one of these forthcoming attractions strangely enough were described to the audience as being 'unmissable'.

At last to everyone's relief the word 'Braveheart' appeared on the screen. Having been advertised as an heroic drama, it was based on the life of William Wallace, the Scottish nationalist leader of the late thirteen century. It was a sympathetic portrayal of a man who, against the odds, had taken on the might of Edward the First and his English army with some considerable success.

David was fascinated by the film. Having read about the battles of Stirling Bridge and Falkirk he was now able to watch these gory events being re-enacted before his eyes. Also being so close to the big screen made him feel as though he was actually there.

David was disappointed when the film finally came to an end. While following the crowd out of the cinema, mentally he was fighting out there on the battlefields against his treacherous enemies. He was for the present a valiant Scot attempting to defend the independence of his country.

It was late afternoon when David returned to the hotel. However, on arriving at the reception desk to collect his room key the freedom fighter was quickly reminded of the real world. The proprietor presented him with a scrap of paper with a message scrawled on it, 'please ring Ian Porter', followed by a telephone number.

As soon as David entered his room he switched the kettle on. Then while waiting for the water to boil he attempted to get into the right frame of mind for making the call. Finally armed with a cup of tea he felt ready to do the deed.

"Hello, Ian Porter," said the familiar voice.

A little apprehensively David announced himself.

"Look I've now had a chance to speak with some of the Fellowship," began Ian, cheerfully. "Naturally everyone would like to see you return to the Lord. However, firstly we want to give you a little trial period."

"That sounds good to me," answered David, as he sipped his tea.

"Well it's just that we need to be certain that you really are repentant," explained Ian. "Anyway as you are aware Jeremy Wright has agreed to buy your house but he isn't ready to move in just yet. In any case until the contract is actually signed the property is legally owned by Ruth and yourself. So the idea is that you go and live there for a week."

"How am I to be tested then?" asked David, rather taken aback.

There was a pause as Ian tried to carefully choose his words.

"Various Fellowship friends will be calling on you throughout your week's trial. Then finally we will all gather together to decide whether you really have managed to triumph over the Devil."

"But I can't live in that house at the moment," David protested. "There isn't any furniture, gas or electricity."

"All those things will be in place by the time your probation period begins," said Ian, reassuringly.

David looked down doubtful at his teacup.

"And when will that be?"

"Very soon," answered Ian. "Don't worry. I will keep you informed."

The remainder of David's weekend was rather uneventful. Apart from a walk in the park, he spent most of Sunday either watching TV or reading one of the many books that guests of the hotel could borrow. Free of having a minder around to tell him what to do he was able to enjoy a thoroughly lazy day.

Problems were about to beset him on Monday, however. David's one to one meeting with Roger Green was even more acrimonious than it had been the previous week. This time the gloves really were off.

"What is happening?" snapped the sales manager. "Over the last fortnight you haven't managed to introduce any business at all into this company."

David shrugged.

"The customers are just not ready to buy at present."

"Bring your leads in here," ordered Roger, with a look of exasperation.

The thought crossed David's mind to resign on the spot. Instead though he stood up and trudged disconsolately back to his desk and grabbed a little red box. Inside, stacked in an upright position were piles of cards with the contact details of his former clients from Fine Choice Furniture.

Soon Roger was busy sifting through the contents of the box. On the back of each card were notes that David had made each time he had rung the client. Comments written down were useful details that might possibly help to secure future sales.

"What is happening with this lead?" asked Roger, with an accusing glare. "There is a note on this card stating that the home is looking to buy furniture at the beginning of October. We are now approaching the middle of the month and nothing has been written down here to suggest you have made a follow-up call to the customer."

"I must have overlooked that one," answered David who was determined not to appear intimidated.

Roger scowled at his newest member of staff.

"This has gone too far. I pay you a lot of money for just keeping an eye on a box of cards and trying to spot a selling opportunity when it arises. What could be simpler than that?"

David chose to remain silent. In fact he was angry with himself for not having removed the card the previous week. Now he was feeling rather stupid.

When Robsons had offered him a job it had been a godsend. However, circumstances had changed and suddenly his continuing employment in the company was starting to create a major headache for him. Stealing customers from Fine Choice Furniture could rebound on him in the future were he to be given his old job back.

"I'm going to give you one last chance," continued Roger, sternly. "I want you to go through this box and…"

David wasn't prepared to sit back and be lectured to anymore. He was heartily sick of the company and most of the people who worked in it. The time had come he decided to put an end to his misery. Suddenly he stood up and glared angrily at the sales manager.

"You can stuff you bloody job," he shouted. "I resign."

Suddenly the main office fell into silence. Although Roger's door was closed, David's raised voice could be heard by the entire staff sitting outside. Then red faced with anger the culprit appeared and headed straight for his desk.

"Everything all right Bonzo?" enquired Wesley Chapple who for once was minus his big wide grin.

"No!" snapped David, as he gathered up a few personal belongings from his drawers.

"What is the problem?" asked Wesley, with a look of surprise.

David couldn't be bothered to reply. Instead watched by many curious eyes he started to make his final departure from Robsons. Then without glancing back he hurried out of the building and into his car.

David felt a sense of relief as he drove back to the hotel. Although now jobless it was nice to think that he would never have to work with Roger Green and his sales staff again. No longer would he be addressed as 'Bonzo' or be laughed at because he didn't know the name of the England football manager.

There was another thing that he had to gloat about. In his briefcase was a rather weighty printout that could prove very useful were Samuel Boswell to re-employ him at Fine Choice Furniture. It was a copy of the database containing every customer that Robsons had ever dealt with. More importantly there were even printed notes against certain names and addresses stating when they were intending to purchase furniture again.

***

Like many people Doug Quentin had been shocked by the news of the Home Secretary's murder. For the private detective however, the death of his distinguished friend was certainly going to have unfortunate personal consequences. It threatened to derail the gravy train that had been heading full steam in his direction. As the contract had still to be drawn up, the lucrative position at the Home Office that he had been promised now looked in jeopardy.

Senior civil servants had been far from happy with Doug's proposed appointment. They saw turmoil looming as it meant promoting a newcomer over the heads of worthy people who had worked in the department for many years. However, there was nothing anybody could do if the Home Secretary insisted on getting his own way.

In addition to the new day job Doug was also to be provided with an interesting sideline. Concerned that he might lose his seat at the next General election, Charles Dawkins intended to pay the experienced sleuth out of parliamentary expenses, to investigate the activities of Jacqui Dunn. He was to try and uncover anything that might discredit the Labour councillor.

Suddenly Doug was back to square one. The success and riches that he had been counting on had all gone up in a puff of smoke. The Home Secretary was dead and would never repay the favours that he owed.

He now bitterly regretted having done a deal with Sally Dawkins. The evidence that he had collected, proving that Charles was guilty of manslaughter could have made him an extremely wealthy man. Any newspaper, tabloid or otherwise would have paid a fortune for such a sensational story.

However, Doug's luck was to change. On Sunday evening he happened to call in on the Conservative club for a quiet drink. Not surprisingly, as it was less than forty-eight hours since the murder of the Brockleby MP, there was only one topic of conversation being discussed amongst the members.

Immediately he showed his face though, Doug was cornered by Howard Phipps. A notorious bore, he was one of those people who talked endlessly in a flat monotonous voice, which invariably sent the poor listener into a trance-like state. Understandably most club members did their best to stay clear of him.

Amazingly, however, the insufferable old gas bag happened to say something which made Doug's ears prick up.

"What was that?" he asked.

"I was just saying that Sally Dawkins wants to sell Charles's Mercedes," replied Howard.

Doug sipped his beer thoughtfully.

"What is the asking price?" he enquired after a few minutes.

"Fifteen grand," answered Howard. "Expensive. Mind you it's a lovely car."

Doug endured another five minutes of mindless prattle then left. He could think of better ways of spending his time than listening to a tedious halfwit suffering from verbal diarrhoea. One was imagining spending all that lovely money when it eventually came his way.

Doug knew he had to act quickly. After leaving the club he set off for Musselworth to call on his sister. She seemed the obvious choice to help him achieve his ambitions.

At present Jean was living alone in a council flat. Although a happily married woman she hadn't seen a great deal of her husband lately. It was just those precious hours every week when the inmates at Wormwood Scrubs were permitted visitors.

"I need you to buy me a Mercedes," began Doug when they were both seated with cups of tea.

Jean gaped at her brother in astonishment.

"I'm in arrears with my rent. How the bloody hell do you expect me to pay for an expensive car?"

"Tomorrow morning I will arrange for a fifteen thousand pound transfer to be paid into your bank account," explained Doug. "You then need to ring a woman by the name of Sally Dawkins and arrange with her a time when you can view the car."

"Look I'm not your bloody servant," protested Jean. "Why don't you do it yourself?"

Sitting back Doug clasped his hands behind his back.

"Because I don't believe Mrs Dawkins would sell the car to me. She would probably question my motives for wanting to buy it."

"Look I am totally confused by all of this," answered Jean. "So if you want my help I suggest that you tell me what this is all about."

After taking a deep breath Doug got to his feet. Then as he began providing Jean with the full story he started to pace up and down the room like a caged lion. His heavy footsteps putting a great deal of strain on an already threadbare carpet.

"And that's about it," said Doug, finally, as he lowered himself into his chair once more.

Jean stared at her brother in disbelief.

"It's an incredible story. First you witness Charles Dawkins commit manslaughter, then you conduct an interview with his killer the day before he is stabbed to death. The newspapers would love it."

"And I propose to provide all the facts to the highest bidder," laughed Doug as he rubbed his hands together.

Suddenly Jean decided to add a note of caution.

"It's a while since Charles Dawkins ran that young man down. Are you sure that the evidence will still be there on the car?"

Doug nodded confidently.

"The victim's DNA will be written all over the underside of the chassis. I just need to get hold of that vehicle."

"So really there is no time to lose," said Jean, excitedly. "You need to buy it before someone else does."

Doug gave his sister an imploring look.

"Would you ring Mrs Dawkins now and make an appointment to see the Mercedes in the morning?"

"I'm supposed to be at work tomorrow," protested Jean. "Can't you find someone else to do it?"

Doug fidgeted anxiously in his chair.

"I don't trust anyone else. It has to be you."

Folding her arms Jean glared at her brother through half-closed eyes.

"What is in it for me then?"

Doug lifted up his cup and took a sip of tea.

"How about this?" he replied, gazing fondly at his sister. "Two hundred quid up front. Ten percent of any fee I receive for my story. Finally, as you were planning to visit your friend in Eastbourne next week, I will take you down there in the Merc."

Jean clapped her hands in delight.

"Give me that telephone number," she cried, excitedly.

Chapter Twenty-Seven

David had never been unemployed before. Although it wasn't an unpleasant experience he discovered that his present state of idleness did create certain feelings of guilt. It wasn't just that he no longer had a job to keep him active during the day. As a hotel guest he no longer even had to concern himself with mundane domestic chores such as catering or cleaning his room.

However, having nothing to do had compensations. David enjoyed the freedom of getting up when he pleased and then taking a leisurely stroll down to the restaurant for breakfast. The rest of the day could then be spent reading, watching television and going for a walk whenever it suited him.

One evening he went to the cinema again. The Odeon was showing one of those attractions which the trailers had described as 'unmissable'. It happened to be a low budget science fiction film with second rate actors which the connoisseur would have avoided at all costs. However, David who possessed less sophisticated tastes, was enthralled throughout the whole performance.

Time slipped by steadily. Thursday morning, three days after his departure from Robsons, David had still not heard from Ian Porter. Suddenly he was beginning to grow anxious. What if the Fellowship were feeling vindictive and had decided not to welcome him back into the fold, he wondered.

At eleven o'clock he finally got the long awaited call. Driven out by the cleaner who needed to straighten up his room, David was about to take himself off for a walk. However, while passing the reception desk he was stopped in his tracks by the proprietor.

"Could you ring Ian Porter," he smiled. "Your friend rang about thirty seconds ago."

David shortened his intended walk and returned to the hotel in less than twenty minutes. With his room now looking immaculate once more he sunk down on the bed and lifted up the telephone. Feeling a little apprehensive he slowly dialled the number that he had learnt off by heart.

"Thanks for ringing back," said Ian, cheerfully. "Look the good news is that your probation period begins whenever you are ready. You will be pleased to know that your house is now equipped with some essential furniture, gas, electricity and hot running water."

David had to stop and think for a moment. He had paid in advance for two more nights at the hotel and it seemed a shame to lose all his money. On the other hand he was keen to return to his old life as quickly as possible. Finally he decided to come to a compromise.

"Sounds good," answered David, enthusiastically. "Could I move in tomorrow?"

"Of course," said Ian. "Do you need any assistance with transporting all your belongings?"

"Thanks for the offer but I can manage," replied David.

There was a slight pause at the other end of the line.

"When I left a message with your hotel reception desk I didn't expect you to get back to me so soon," said Ian. "Did they contact you at work?"

David hesitated for a moment. In his last meeting with Ian Porter he recalled telling the priest to ring after six as he couldn't be contracted during the day. Therefore it seemed an ideal opportunity to put the records straight.

"I'm out of work," answered David. "It was difficult working for a worldly employer so I resigned from my job on Monday."

"I can appreciate your problem," said Ian, without sounding surprised. "Let me speak with Samuel Boswell. I'm sure if you return to the Fellowship he'd be more than happy to employ you again with Fine Choice Furniture."

David felt a sense of relief as he put down the phone. The isolation that had engulfed him in this strange new life might soon be over. Before long he could be back in the bosom of a community of people who understood him. All he needed to do was to convince everybody that he was worthy of being welcomed back.

That afternoon David lay on his bed and watched television. Above all else this funny little box which provided a continuous source of entertainment, was the one thing he would really miss in the future. There seemed little likelihood that the Fellowship top dogs would ever permit their followers to bring such an evil influence into their homes.

Soon David became engrossed in one of those black and white films. He must have been one of those rare people of his age or above who had never heard of *High Noon* let alone seen the great classic western. Therefore like millions before him he was moved by the gripping story of a lawman who had bravely chosen to take on four killers in a gunfight rather than run away.

Once the film had ended David decided to switch channels to avoid the adverts. However, before he reached over for the remote control the familiar face of the former Brockleby MP suddenly appeared on the screen. Then after a few seconds the cameras turned on a serious looking presenter.

"Police are investigating a claim made in a national newspaper that the recently murdered Home Secretary Charles Dawkins, may have been guilty of manslaughter several weeks before his death," he began rather dramatically.

Like other viewers who had not read the story, David was taken by surprise. However, he was totally unprepared for the startling revelation which was to follow. It seemed unbelievable.

"DNA found on the undercarriage of the former Home Secretary's car is now being examined," the presenter continued, "and may be that of Mr Malcolm Baverstock who is understood to have been from Broadstairs in Kent."

Now sat upright on the bed David was glued to the screen. Viewers were told that a local detective had witnessed the fatal accident and had now come forward. Downing Street however, were unwilling to comment on the matter until the police had completed their investigations.

When the news bulletin ended David's thoughts immediately returned to Rebecca. What would her reaction be if she was suddenly put under the public spotlight he wondered. It seemed inevitable that she would receive some media attention if only from the local press.

David resisted the temptation to ring Rebecca straight away. For one thing he wanted to choose his words carefully before making the call. Then it occurred to him that she would probably still be at work in any case.

The following morning after breakfast, David started to pack up his possessions. Looking around his room for the very last time he suddenly began to have misgivings about whether he was doing the right thing. The freedom that he had enjoyed since moving into the hotel would be gone forever. Soon the Fellowship would completely take control of his whole life once more.

David quickly dismissed all such negative thoughts. Having made up his mind he decided that there was no turning back. Deep down he felt that the privilege of being able to please himself was greatly outweighed by the benefits of returning to his former life.

Stepping into the hall David shut the door behind him. Then staggering slightly from the weight of two suitcases he slowly made his way down the stairs before checking out at the reception desk. It was with a fond smile and a little sadness that he handed over his key to the proprietor's wife.

Within twenty minutes David was back in the property that he still owned jointly with Ruth. As he went on a tour of the house he could see that someone had been busy getting things ready for his short stay. There were curtains up at every window, rugs on all floors and one bedroom intended for him was well furnished. Most of the other rooms were almost bare apart from a few essentials, like a three piece suite in the lounge and a freezer in the kitchen, which was well stocked up with food.

Something else that the Fellowship had provided was a microwave. It was while using this appliance to heat a ready prepared meal for lunch that David received his first visitors. Maurice Hopkins and Des, his former colleagues from Fine Choice Furniture had dropped in to deliver a dining room table.

As ever, neither Maurice or Des were in a rush to get back to work. After eating, David spent the best part of the afternoon talking and drinking tea with his old workmates. It was early on in the conversation, however, that the subject of a job vacancy was raised.

"Sam Boswell has decided to promote Des to Assistant Sales manager," said Maurice, smiling proudly at a man who had recently risen up in the world.

David tried hard to keep a straight face. He had lost track of the positions that Des had held in the company before being moved on. Quite obviously the powers that be were forever looking to find a role for their most inept employee, in which he could do the least harm.

"Anyway," continued Maurice, "that means we are looking to fill your old position. Therefore I wonder whether you would be interested in joining us again?"

"Is Sam Boswell agreeable?" asked David, warily.

"Yes," beamed Maurice, enthusiastically. "Providing that the Fellowship are ready to take you back of course."

At this point Des produced a tube of mints. After taking two himself he returned the remainder to his trouser pocket without offering them around. Clearly sharing with others wasn't one of those Christian principles that he adhered to.

It was four o'clock when David's guests climbed reluctantly to their feet. Maurice decided that it was time for him and his newly appointed assistant to put in an appearance at work. More importantly he needed to rescue his briefcase before the building was locked up for the weekend.

"By the way I have a message for you from Ian Porter," said Maurice, as he slipped on his jacket. "He wondered whether you are free to help out tomorrow. As you may remember, the Fellowship are in the process of building a church in the Canterbury area."

"Very well," answered David, successfully managing to conceal a sudden feeling of gloom. "What time do I need to be there by?"

For a moment Maurice fumbled around in his inside jacket pocket. Finally he produced a crumpled up sheet of paper and handed it to David.

"The time and the address are all written down here for you," said Maurice. "Will you require a lift?"

David shook his head.

"I'll find my own way there thanks."

"Very well," answered Maurice, as he prepared to leave. "Anyway it was good to meet up with you again."

"Will I be seeing you both tomorrow?" asked David.

Des as ever winced at the very idea of manual work.

"Not with my back," he replied, with a shudder. "It's been playing me up recently. I couldn't possibly lift anything heavy."

Maurice looked sympathetically at his new assistant.

"I'm afraid I won't be there either," he said, sadly. "My foot is painful whenever I try and stand on it for too long."

David smiled as soon as his visitors had gone. He had never known either of them offer their services in assisting with any of the Fellowship's building projects. They always managed to conjure up some physical complaint which excluded them from helping out.

The following morning was bitterly cold. The very thought of working out in the open air had little appeal for David as he forced himself out of his warm bed. However, he appreciated that it wasn't in his long-term interests to let the Fellowship down. To be accepted back into the fold he needed to create a good impression.

With a map of Kent as a guide, David found the site without too much difficulty. Volunteers had been requested to arrive about eight o'clock and although he was on time, many had already started work. A group were in the process of erecting scaffolding, others were busy gathering up bricks while a rather large man in a woolly hat operated a cement mixer.

David recognised many familiar faces. A few lived in the Brockleby area but most were from further away. It was likely that all those present were Fellowship, however, sometimes specialists from outside the faith were drafted in to assist.

Suddenly David heard his name being called. Turning around he saw Ian Porter heading swiftly in his direction with a clipboard.

"I've put your name down for scaffolding," he boomed out.

"Fine," replied David, attempting to sound far more enthusiastic than he was actually feeling.

Ian smiled as he marked a tick on his sheet.

"By the way. Breakfast is being served in that portable cabin over there," he said, pointing his finger. "It's never advisable to do manual work on an empty stomach."

David didn't need to be told twice. Immediately he headed off towards a steel structure with a flat roof at the far end of the site. Painted in blue it had a door in the middle and was probably about thirty foot in length. It served not only as a kitchen but was also used as an office where all the paperwork was done.

Strolling up to the cabin, David opened the door. In spite of wearing some heavy clothing he was still feeling frozen. It therefore came as a welcome relief to be instantly transported into a warm atmosphere. The source of the heat was a large electric fire in the corner of the room.

"Fancy seeing you," exclaimed a young woman standing by a large tea urn.

David was taken aback. Much to his surprise Rebecca was in charge of handing out breakfast to the workers. Other than his old school friend though there was nobody else around.

"How are you keeping?" he asked.

Rebecca smiled.

"Can't complain. How about yourself?"

"I'm fine," replied David.

"I was surprised to find out that you wanted to return to the Fellowship," said Rebecca. "I thought that we had lost you forever."

David shook his head as he helped himself to a bacon roll.

"Nothing has been decided yet," he replied. "Next week I should find out whether the Fellowship are ready to take me back."

"And is that what you really want?" asked Rebecca.

"I think so," answered David, as he peeled open his roll and shook a bottle of tomato sauce over the bacon. "I don't seem to fit in with the outside world so there doesn't seem to be any alternative."

"Just as long as you don't have any regrets later on in life," said Rebecca, as she stooped down to gather up crumbs off the floor with a dustpan and brush.

David sat down on one of the several armless dining chairs in the room. The prospect of starting work was distinctly unattractive so he was determined to stay put for as long as possible. In addition to that there were a few things he wanted to discuss with his old school friend.

"Of course I have regrets," he said, bitterly. "I am sorry that I was born into a family that has prevented me from feeling at home in the big wide world. One that expects me to choose between them and being free to think for myself."

"So are you absolutely certain that you are making the right choice?" asked Rebecca, with a look of concern. "If the

Fellowship take you back you can hardly break free again. Otherwise you will end up going around and around in circles."

"I've made up my mind now and I'm sticking to it," said David, resolutely.

"Well that's a relief," smiled Rebecca. "By the way, would you like a waffle before starting work?"

"Sounds good," replied David, with a broad grin.

Rebecca strolled over to a large freezer and took out a red cardboard box.

"I'll put it under the grill for you."

"You'd make a good wife," said David, with a look of admiration. "What a pity that your parents would be unlikely to ever accept me as a future son-in-law."

Rebecca stopped what she was doing and turned around.

"I think they are probably right. It would be a mistake for us to marry."

David was slightly taken aback.

"I should have thought we were ideally suited."

"Of course we are but that is the problem," replied Rebecca, taking a seat opposite David. "Both of us think too much and that isn't helpful if you happen to be Fellowship. Do you understand?"

David nodded.

"What you mean is that as a married couple we could have a negative effect on each other. I would put doubts into your head and you would do the same to me."

"Precisely," answered Rebecca. "And before very long we would feel alienated from our family, friends and the only life we were comfortable in."

"So are you happy to marry a man without a mind of his own?" asked David.

Rebecca shrugged.

"I did it before," she sighed.

For a moment they sat in silence. Both were reflecting on Malcolm's tragic death and the recent sensational revelations following on from it. Finally Rebecca stood up and wandered across to the cooker to turn the waffle over under the grill.

"I can't believe that your husband was killed by the Home Secretary of all people," said David, as he finished off his bacon roll. "I understand the police have now confirmed it."

353

Rebecca turned around with tears in her eyes.

"It's bad enough losing Malcolm," she sobbed. "Now I'm being pestered by people who believe that they have a perfect right to pry into my life."

"Like who?" asked David in surprise.

"I am getting called from TV companies, radio stations, the press, women's magazines and just ordinary members of the public," replied Rebecca, angrily as she sat down again. "Perfect strangers just knock on my door and ask questions."

"Why don't you move in with your parents for a while?" suggested David.

Rebecca shook her head.

"They live too far away from my job," she replied, after blowing her nose. "The only solution is to stay with nearby friends for a while."

David reached out and touched her hand.

"If only I could look after you," he murmured.

Rebecca stiffened and pulled her hand away.

"We are friends and that is all there is to it," she said, firmly. "It is futile to imagine what could be."

David had no opportunity to respond. Heavy footsteps could be heard outside and suddenly the door flew open. There standing on the threshold was the sturdy figure of Ian Porter.

"So are you ready now to give us a hand?" he smiled. cheerfully.

Immediately David climbed to his feet. As he was on probation with the Fellowship it hardly seemed wise to upset anyone at that particular moment. He just regretted having to leave his waffle for someone else to enjoy.

After the warmth of the cabin it now seemed colder than ever in the open air. Wearing a forced smile David reluctantly followed Ian up to meet with the scaffolding team. However, the foreman greeted his newest hand with a look of suspicion.

"Done this sort of work before?" he asked.

"No," replied David, firmly, hopeful that he might be given less arduous work.

"You had better work under Joseph then," replied the foreman thoughtfully. "I'm sure he could use a little extra help."

Sure enough Joseph was grateful for a healthy young labourer to do plenty of lifting and carrying. Enviously, David watched as Ian Porter hurried away with his clipboard in order to get somebody else organised. As the co-ordinator he seemed to have been given the best job on site.

Joseph was short and wide. A man with a cheerful disposition he went about his work singing hymns for much of the time. Not over keen on excessively exerting himself though, he was a master on the art of delegation as David was soon to find out to his cost.

However, within a short space of time, David was beginning to enjoy himself. The physical activity warmed him up and he liked the friendly camaraderie between the workforce. In fact he had a sense of belonging in the present company.

That evening David's body ached. Unaccustomed to manual labour he had put a great deal of strain on muscles that were generally inactive. However, he was consoled with the knowledge that the discomfort was only temporary.

As he sat drinking tea his thoughts turned to Rebecca. In their brief conversation she had made it perfectly clear that she would never consider marrying him. In a strange way he felt disappointed but hardly overcome with grief. Deep down there was only one woman that he yearned for and he had lost her to another man.

***

At three o'clock Mark finally left the pub. It had been an intensive drinking session with some of his acquaintances who regularly frequented the Queen's Head. After downing each round of drinks somebody in the group would be immediately picked upon to go up to the bar to order another.

Following their engagement it had been decided that Mark should move into Alison's maisonette. With the aim of saving money for their future it made perfect sense to pay rent on just one residence rather than two. Unfortunately though, any economies made by this shrewd move were being frittered away on alcohol.

In fact things generally were not going well between the engaged couple. Although he claimed to have changed his ways,

Mark appeared to be as irresponsible as ever. Having walked out of a job the previous week he seemed to be making no obvious attempt to look for further employment.

As soon as Mark arrived home he flaked out on the settee. He was expecting to spend a peaceful afternoon asleep but, unfortunately in his drunken, state he had forgotten what day of the week it was. Alison didn't work at the library on a Saturday and usually took Amanda out in the buggy if the weather was fine.

Mark quickly dozed off and didn't hear the front door as it creaked open. However, moments later he was woken up by loud shrieks followed by a sharp pain in the middle of his chest. Lost in a drunken fog he was unable to comprehend what was happening. All that he was aware of was a weight of some description perched on top of him.

As the pressure was sufficient to restrict his breathing he began to panic. Instinctively he raised an arm and managed to push the offending object off his body. Immediately there was a loud thud followed by a shrill scream.

"What the hell are you doing?" shouted Alison, as she scampered across the floor to pick up her daughter. "Amanda only wanted to play with you."

Mark looked dazed as he attempted to collect his thoughts.

"Why didn't you stop her from jumping on me?" he protested.

"Don't blame her," snapped Alison, indignantly. "If you hadn't been down the pub drinking yourself stupid, none of this would have happened."

Mark sat up and held his head in his hands.

"Stop going on," he groaned.

"Don't worry, you won't be listening to me for much longer," Alison muttered to herself.

Mark gazed silently into space. Had his head have been clearer he would have noticed that Amanda's screaming had now given way to a whimper. However, at that precise moment all he could think about was going back to sleep.

"I'm tired," he moaned, with his eyelids now closed.

Alison decided it was time to act decisively. Taking Amanda by the hand she headed straight for the bedroom and began packing Mark's clothes. There was a grim determination about her as she went about the task.

In a while Mark was woken up again. Aware that someone was talking in a loud voice, he looked up to see that Alison was standing over him with hands on hips and a fixed expression on her face. At her feet was a large suitcase, which he vaguely recognised as being his own.

"I've just phoned your mum and explained that you are now homeless," began Alison, firmly. "Thankfully she has agreed to put you up for a few nights."

Mark was clearly shaken.

"But I want to stay here with you," he answered in surprise.

"Sorry but I am evicting you," Alison replied, coldly. "Amanda and I would be far better off living on our own."

"But we are getting married next year," replied Mark in astonishment.

Alison slipped off her ring and handed it to him.

"I'm afraid you are mistaken. It's all over between us now."

Mark pocketed the ring and unsteadily got to his feet. Having checked his watch he decided that he might as well go sooner rather than later. After all, the boys were expecting him down at the Queen's Head later that evening.

Chapter Twenty-Eight

David woke up feeling stiff. While hobbling downstairs in some considerable discomfort he decided to employ his father's favourite remedy for such a complaint. After breakfast he would lay soaking in a hot bath to ease away his aches and pains.

In fact David was expecting a leisurely day. There was no need to venture out in the cold as visitors would be calling on him at various times. The plan was that he and certain Fellowship members would sit and read texts from the Bible together. It was part of the test to discover whether the lost sheep was ready to be re-admitted to the fold.

Each session was likely to be short and sweet. As it was Sunday the Fellowship would be expected to attend church on five separate occasions. Therefore being busy on a worshipping spree left precious little time for anything else.

David received his first caller at about eleven o'clock. A gentleman in his eighties, Mr Clough was always in a permanent state of confusion. Amongst his many mental failings was an inability to remember names.

"It's good to see you again, Derek," he said, sitting himself down in an armchair.

"The feeling is mutual," replied David, who decided to settle for his new name rather than go to the bother of correcting his guest.

"I see you've cleared away most of the furniture in here," said Mr Clough, casting his eyes around the room. "Are you about to do some painting?"

"No," replied David. "The place is pretty bare because I am living here on a temporary basis. I shall move once you and other Fellowship members have judged whether I am ready to join you again."

Mr Clough blinked hard.

"I thought you couldn't get to church today because of your arthritis."

"Whatever made you think that?" asked David, trying hard to keep a straight face.

"That is what I was told," said Mr Clough. "And you do seem to be having some difficulty in walking."

"That is because I am stiff from working on a building site yesterday," explained David, with a broad grin.

Reaching into his inside jacket pocket Mr Clough produced a crumpled scrap of paper. There then followed a long drawn out silence as the elderly gentleman attempted to read his own writing. Finally a smile appeared on his face.

"I'm getting you mixed up with Mrs Crump who is on my list to see this afternoon. You are the one who needs rescuing from Satan I see."

"That's me," said David, managing to contain a snigger.

"Well let's get going," said Mr Clough, as he took a long hard look at his watch. "I'm in a bit of a rush."

"Fine by me," replied David, amiably.

Mr Clough opened his Bible and began slowly turning the pages.

"I am going to read a passage from Luke," he announced.

David sat upright and waited to be entertained. However, after some considerable delay it became apparent that Mr Clough was unable to find what he was looking for. In fact he appeared to be getting quite agitated.

"Now where is my marker?" he muttered to himself. "I know it is here somewhere."

"Perhaps you could read something else," suggested David, helpfully.

"Good idea Donald... er... Dennis I mean," said the senior Fellowship Follower, clearly grateful for the advice. "I have a passage in mind that either comes from Amos or Jeremiah."

Soon he was furiously page turning again. After a while though it became obvious that the latest search was unlikely to be any more successful than the previous one. Finally with a deep sigh he took another long look at his watch before closing his Bible.

"I'm afraid we will have to do this another time," he said, apologetically. "Mrs Clough will be expecting me home for lunch soon."

David tried to look suitably disappointed. It was far from shattering news but he was eager to make a good impression. He didn't want the Fellowship to think that he was indifferent to hearing the word of the Lord.

"Please don't keep your wife waiting on my account," smiled David, politely. "You go home and I will sit here and read the Bible alone."

"Very kind of you Donald," replied Mr Clough, as he stood up to leave.

Once his visitor had gone David picked up the Bible he had been given as a child. Bound in black leather it was a gift that he had been told to treat with the utmost respect. According to his father it was the most important book ever written.

David soon lost interest. Trying to interpret texts that were often incomprehensible hardly compared with the delights of watching TV. Needless to say of course that the Fellowship had failed to provide him with a set in his temporary home.

That afternoon he had two more visitors. When he opened the door on this occasion he was confronted by both his father and Ian Porter. It was with a feeling of apprehension that he showed the pair of them into the lounge. The last time the threesome had sat down together the atmosphere had been decidedly hostile.

However, David needn't have worried. There was genuine warmth in John Chambers' eyes as he greeted his son with a firm handshake. Ian, too, seemed to be in one of his more jovial moods.

"I've just been telling your dad how hard you worked yesterday," smiled the priest, amiably. "That is once I had managed to drag you away from the refreshments."

"Takes after me," laughed John, heartily. "I can never get myself going without a good breakfast inside me."

Ian nodded.

"The Lord doesn't expect us to build his houses on empty stomachs."

Suddenly John's expression changed. He had allowed himself to become a little too flippant, but now it was time to get down to business. What he had to say after all was very important.

"I am so glad that you are attempting to pull free from the clutches of Satan," he said, smiling proudly at his son. "However

I fear that your soul is still in great danger from the forces of evil."

Ian nodded gravely.

"Once Satan senses weakness he will always be trying to tempt you away from the paths of righteousness."

David tried to hide his amusement. Once they got into their stride his two visitors became a very effective double act. Given the right script he felt, they could have made a good career for themselves on the stage.

"I shall definitely be on my guard this time," promised David, solemnly.

"I am impressed by your determination," replied John glancing quickly across at Ian as though checking that he was still there. "Unfortunately some of us find it difficult to fight the Devil by ourselves."

"You see Satan is aware of our vulnerabilities," explained Ian. "Last time he managed to snare you with an ungodly woman, so your dad and I want to protect you in the future."

"Thank you," replied David, totally unaware of what was in store for him.

The two older men turned to each other and smiled.

"I think it is time you told your son the good news," grinned Ian.

"Very well," answered John, before noisily clearing his throat. "Last night I had a long telephone conversation with Ruth's father. Anyway to cut a long story short, I wondered whether he was still willing to allow his daughter to get back together with you again."

David was alarmed at the very suggestion of such an idea.

"Ruth is far too good for me," he blurted out.

"Nonsense," chimed in Ian. "There is nothing wrong with you that a strong god fearing wife couldn't put right."

"But I'm sure Ruth wouldn't contemplate marrying me after the terrible way that I've treated her," replied David, voicing his hopes rather than any sound reasoning.

A twinkle appeared in John's eyes.

"Now that is where you are wrong," he chuckled. "Ruth is ready to forgive you. She believes that Satan was to blame for putting sinful thoughts into your head."

"A fine Christian lady," said Ian, gently smoothing down the hair at the back of his head.

David was feeling distinctly uneasy. He had a strong suspicion that the Fellowship were about to insist that he married Ruth as a pre-condition of being received back into the fold. Were that to be the case he would be forced to reconsider his future.

"I'd certainly like to think about it before committing myself," he said, trying to play for time.

John gave his son a warning stare.

"He who hesitates has lost. In your place I would ring Ruth up straight away before she discovers somebody else."

"But I need to be sure I am doing the right thing," protested David.

The two visitors exchanged furtive glances. They were like two of the conspirators who were waiting for the right moment to draw their knives and assassinate Julius Caesar in the Senate.

"I am concerned that you may find marriage partners hard to find," warned Ian, fidgeting nervously in his armchair. "Because you deserted the Fellowship to go out into the world many parents may wonder whether you would make an ideal husband for their daughter."

David shrugged.

"I could always remain a bachelor."

"Not advisable if you wish to be saved," replied John without hesitation. "On your own I don't believe you are capable of resisting Satan and his temptations. That is precisely why you need the support of a strong Christian wife."

"That's nonsense," objected David.

"Then why were you seen queuing up outside the cinema only a few days ago?" demanded Ian, accusingly. "What are we to make of someone who says that he is ready to repent yet continues to enjoy worldly pleasures."

David was taken aback. It had never occurred to him that prying eyes might be watching as he stood waiting to go into the Odeon. His only thoughts centred around the film he was about to see.

"Look I just went out of curiosity," he mumbled, having quickly decided that it was futile to deny his little misdemeanour.

"The truth is that you succumbed to temptation," said John,

sternly. "And I fear you always will without the support of somebody stronger."

David decided it was time to ask the all-important question. Clearly he would find out at some stage so it might as well be sooner rather than later.

"If I don't marry Ruth will I be received back into the Fellowship?" he asked, hesitantly.

"Were it my decision alone the answer would be no," said John emphatically. "However, there are others who must also have their say."

"I'm in agreement with your dad," added Ian. "But believe me, we both have your well-being at heart. Neither of us would wish you to miss out on the glories of salvation."

David felt deflated. He had come to a fork in the path of life and both of the roads ahead were almost certainly going to lead to grief and misery. It was either a case of being trapped in an unhappy marriage or living as an outsider in a cold mysterious world.

"You must give me a chance to consider the matter," he pleaded with more than a hint of desperation in his voice.

The two older men glanced across at each other and nodded.

"You must make up your mind by Wednesday at about four o'clock," warned Ian. "That is the time I shall be ringing you. The meeting to discuss your request to rejoin the Fellowship is to take place later that evening."

"I'll let you know by then," promised David, just relieved that he had been spared from having to make an immediate decision.

"Anyway I thought we might read from the scriptures now," said Ian, quickly glancing at his watch. "I promised to call in on Mrs Crabtree in about half an hour. The poor lady is suffering badly with her lumbago recently you know."

Soon the threesome sat with Bibles on their knees. Ian was reading aloud a passage from the Book of Revelations, while the two Chambers followed the words on the page as they were spoken. However, part of David's mind was already wrestling with the vital decision he would shortly have to make.

Ian loved the dramatic finale to the New Testament. Revelations reminded him that in the last days the Devil and his followers would get their comeuppance, while God's devotees would be rewarded with a bucket full of bliss for the whole of eternity. It was also reassuring to reflect on the fact that rejecting all that worldly pleasure would pay dividends in the end.

Clearly chapter nine had been carefully selected. Ian was intent on frightening his wayward young listener with the horrors which awaited those who hadn't repented of their sinful ways. However, at that precise moment David was more concerned with problems in his present life rather than the threat of hell and fire in the next one.

During the following two days David received more Fellowship callers. Each one was a senior member of the church and people that he had known all his life. As with Ian Porter and his father they would sit down for a short chat and then read the Bible with him.

By Wednesday morning David had sunk into a deep depression. There were now only a few precious hours before the Fellowship meeting which would determine his future, yet he still couldn't decide what to do. Was he going to agree to marry Ruth or not.

David put on his coat and set off for a brisk walk. He hoped that the exercise coupled with the fresh Autumn air might help him to think more clearly. Perhaps he could find that flash of inspiration, which would solve all his troubles.

It was a fine day although a powerful wind blew in sharp short bursts. Without any conscious planning David headed directly for the park with the scenic lake. From a child its stillness and tranquillity had always attracted him like a magnet.

Passing through the wrought iron gates he was vaguely aware that the landscape had changed colour. No longer predominantly in shades of green, it was speckled with brown, russet and golden leaves both on the trees, and scattered over the ground. There was however, little sign of life but for the ducks and an elderly gentleman walking a dog.

David's spirits were temporarily lifted by his new surroundings. However, although this improved state of mind had the effect of assisting the thought processes, he was still unable to decide which path to follow in his life. Under normal circumstances he would have sought advice from Simon. On this occasion though, his closest friend was currently enjoying a holiday in Seattle and wasn't due back from America for another week.

Finally his thoughts turned to more mundane matters. Having strolled around the lake at least three times David suddenly remembered that he needed some razor blades. Almost reluctantly he set off for the High Street leaving the park with its rich array of colours behind.

Soon he was mingling with the morning shoppers. David was just about to go into Boots to buy his blades when he felt somebody touch him on the shoulder. On turning around he came face to face with a tall bearded gentleman.

"Tony," he cried in surprise. "Good to see you again."

"Everyone down at the club has been wondering what has happened to you," answered Tony, with a broad grin. "We were beginning to think you had gone off to join the Tories."

"No likelihood of that," laughed David.

Suddenly Tony's expression became serious.

"Actually the date of the Brockleby by-election has just been announced," he said, stroking the tip of his beard. "It has been set for the last Thursday in November. So if you happen to have any spare time we'd appreciate some help."

David looked dubious.

"You'd be far better off without me," he smiled, sadly. "Labour lost some precious votes at the General Election because of my stupidity. It never occurred to me that a poor old pensioner might be exempt from paying for her broken window."

The conversation briefly came to a halt. The two men quickly moved aside as they realised that the entrance to Boots was hardly an ideal place to stand. Particularly when a steady stream of shoppers were attempting to get in and out of the store.

"You weren't to blame for our defeat," answered Tony, when a more suitable position had been found to continue the discussion.

"That's not what I overheard you and Kenny say just after the Election," said David, accusingly. "You were both in agreement that it was my fault that Jacqui Dunn didn't win."

Tony laughed.

"Everyone took their share of criticism for the result not going in our favour. In fact as campaign manager, I took more of the flak than anybody."

"That's not fair," protested David. "You worked your guts out for the party."

Tony shrugged.

"That's all water under the bridge. I now have a golden opportunity to put matters right by seeing that Jacqui wins this time. Will you help me?"

David shook his head.

"The problem is that I have a lot going on in my life at present. I have some major decisions to make and politics is the last thing on my mind."

"After the group have been out canvassing one evening, you could always join us at the club for a drink," suggested Tony, as he sidestepped a young mother with a pram.

"I'll see," replied David, wary of committing himself to an actual date. "Anyway, how is everyone from the old crowd?"

Tony had to stop and think. The interest he showed in his friends from the Labour Party rarely extended beyond how they performed as political activists. Their personal lives were of little concern to him. Then he just happened to remember something that his wife Carol had mentioned the previous evening.

"Alison's engagement is off," he said, finally. "Apparently she and Mark had a big argument at the weekend."

David was shocked. It had never really occurred to him that Alison would be anything other than a married woman in a few months' time.

"Do you think they might get back together again?" asked David trying his level best to appear nonchalant.

Tony shook his head firmly.

"Not from what Carol was telling me. For some reason Alison hates Mark's guts and doesn't even want him to see Amanda anymore. Therefore I think we can safely assume that it is all over between them."

"Sorry to hear that," said David, who was far from being honest.

"Anyway must be off," said Tony, quickly glancing at his watch. "Hope to see you up at the club one evening."

Having bought his razor blades David wandered up and down the High Street several times. He was overcome by a powerful urge to drop in at the library and invite Alison out to lunch. However, the more cautious side of his nature, which he eventually heeded, warned him against acting on impulse.

Back at his temporary makeshift home, David spent the best part of the afternoon reading. Having purchased a copy of the *Guardian* from WH Smith's he was keen to catch up on the news. No longer with access to a television set he felt strangely cut off from the big wide world.

The headlines concerned British troops that were about to be deployed in Iraq. During the following week several battalions were to be sent to Basra, which was south of the country, as peace keepers. However, Jonathan Canning, the new Prime Minister, was attempting to reassure the British public that the region was much less dangerous than Baghdad where the Americans were based.

There was also another story on the front page concerning the war. It related to the former Iraqi President and his alleged weapons of mass destruction. Trying to allay fears that Saddam Hussein had vanished for good and that his lethal arsenal had never existed, a White House spokesman had promised that both would be uncovered by Christmas.

Newspapers were yet another worldly pleasure that the Fellowship rejected. Therefore having read his copy of the *Guardian* from cover to cover, David put it straight into the boot of his car. It was the one place he felt confident would not be detected by prying eyes.

Something that David had been provided with was a telephone. Surprisingly the Fellowship didn't regard this invention as a tool of the Devil to corrupt the soul. Instead they considered it to be an essential means by which the faithful could communicate with each other to do the Lord's work.

At four o'clock David received a call. He was rather taken by surprise, for although the telephone had been installed two days earlier, this was the first time it had actually rung.

"It's Ian Porter," said the all too familiar voice. "How are you?"

"I'm fine thanks," replied David, who was in fact feeling a little apprehensive.

"So what have you decided to do about Ruth?" asked Ian.

"Will you agree to marry her?"

David hesitated for a split second as he braced himself to give a reply that was unlikely to be well received.

"Sorry but the answer is no," he replied, firmly. "There is no point in marrying somebody that I don't love."

There was a brief silence on the other end of the line. Clearly it wasn't the response that the priest had expected.

"But you must have been attracted to Ruth once," he said, finally. "Not so long ago you were engaged to her."

David decided it was time to make a confession.

"That was all due to a crazy misunderstanding," he explained. "The day my parents took me up to Birmingham I had too much to drink. Anyway I became lost in a drunken stupor and didn't listen to what dad was saying to me. Then the next thing I know is that I'm engaged to be married."

Ian was shocked at this sudden revelation.

"But why didn't you say something once you had sobered up?"

"Because everyone became so excited I hadn't the heart to disappoint them," said David. "Then I found myself caught up in a whirlwind. People were furiously making arrangements and before I knew it I was being dragged around looking at houses. I just had no idea what to do."

"Perhaps you were being guided along by God and didn't realise it," suggested Ian. "He knew that marrying Ruth would be the best thing for you."

"In that case he was wrong," said David, acidly.

"You are the one who is mistaken," said Ian, sternly. "Anyway, very shortly I shall be off to the meeting which will decide your future. Somebody will call in this evening and give you the verdict. It won't be me, however, as I have to meet some friends from Gatwick Airport later on."

As soon as Ian had rung off David wandered into the kitchen and switched on the kettle. Making cups of tea was a task he did frequently since moving into his new surroundings. Somehow it just helped to relieve the monotony.

David desperately needed some intellectual stimulus. In the absence of television the only alternative was to study his black leather bound Bible. However, after a few minutes of consideration he chose to leave the good book where it was and go for a bath instead.

At nine o'clock Sam Boswell arrived. He had been the one nominated by the Fellowship committee to call on David and report back on what had been decided. As he entered the lounge though, it was obvious from the grim expression on his face that the news wasn't good.

"The Fellowship believe that you are not ready to return to the Lord just yet," began Sam, solemnly. "We feel that you are not truly repentant and that Satan is still controlling your life. Also that redemption for you at present will only be possible with the help of a wife with strong Christian convictions."

"I see," answered David, appreciating that there was little point in arguing.

"Anyway it isn't all bad news," said Sam, quickly brightening up. "Jeremy Wright doesn't get married until January and he is happy for you to stay here even after the contracts are signed. However, in return he would like help with decorating this place."

David nodded his agreement. Knowing Jeremy very well he rather suspected that there would be strings attached to his generous offer.

"In that case I need to sit down with him to find out what he wants me to do," he said, thoughtfully.

"I will get him to ring you to discuss it," replied Sam with a smile. "By the way, I understand that you are out of work at the moment."

"That's right," replied David, gloomily.

"Perhaps we could help each other out in that case," said Sam, eagerly leaning forward in his armchair. "Since you left Fine Choice sales have dropped off a bit. Now I know it isn't the fault of Maurice Hopkins because he is working tirelessly to bring in more orders. However, something is going wrong."

With difficulty David managed to restrain himself from smiling. There seemed no limit to the faith that Sam Boswell had in his ineffectual son-in-law. Like the peace of God referred to by St Paul, it passed all understanding.

"What exactly do you want me to do?" asked David.

"I would like you to be a telemarketer," answered Sam. "You are to ring potential customers with a view to bringing in some business for the company."

David's face broke into a broad smile. The offer of a job at that precise moment was the answer to a prayer. Particularly as he had a secret weapon in the boot of his car, which was certain to bring him great success. It was the massive printout he had taken with him from Robsons listing out all the names and addresses of their clients.

"Very well," agreed David. "When do you want me to start?"

"Tomorrow at nine if at all possible," replied Sam, beaming broadly. "We can discuss the salary and terms and conditions of your employment in the morning."

As the two men stood up to shake hands, Sam suddenly took on the expression of a person who had just remembered something.

"By the way," he began, earnestly. "Like last week, the Fellowship are looking for volunteers to help build their church near Canterbury. Would you be available to lend a hand on Saturday?"

David wanted to curse out loud. However, having just been offered a much needed job at Fine Choice Furniture he felt rather obliged to offer his assistance. He just hoped that the weather would be a lot milder this time.

"I'll be there," he replied, somehow managing a half smile.

Chapter Twenty-Nine

David felt more than a smidgen of disappointment when he was introduced to his new office. Located towards the rear of the warehouse, the room was little more than a windowless box containing a table with a telephone perched on top, an armless unpadded chair and a small bookcase crammed with yellow telephone directories. While outside the sliding wooden door stood rows of pine wardrobes which were waiting to be sold.

Cut off from his former colleagues the job looked to be a lonely one. However, he would soon make new friends with some of the manual workers who were employed to shift furniture around as and when required. Other than first thing in the morning, when they were busy loading up the vehicles in preparation for despatch to customers, these good hearted men were always ready to stop and chat.

Complete with telephone and weighty printout purloined from Robsons, David quickly got into his stride. As a very experienced cold caller he knew the value of drafting out a script for himself before ringing around. It was always advantageous to prepare a sales spiel before actually speaking with potential clients.

The first day went particularly well. Not surprisingly there were many who were unhappy with the products which they had purchased from Robsons in the past and were willing to consider switching suppliers. Therefore these people would be sent a Fine Choice Furniture brochure and then earmarked for a follow-up telephone call in a week or so. Of course although the early signs were encouraging, only time would tell whether many orders would be placed as a result of David's efforts.

At ten to five Maurice Hopkins called in on the latest addition to his sales team. Now working in separate buildings they had seen very little of each other throughout the day. Meeting up had also become more difficult as David, now non-Fellowship, was barred from using the staff canteen whenever God's chosen ones were eating in it.

"What exactly is that great stack of paper you have there?" asked the sales manager, who was unfamiliar with computer terminology.

"On the pages of this printout is a very large database which should be very valuable for this company," explained David, patiently.

Maurice looked puzzled as he craned his upper body over David's shoulder. In fact the company's former rep had been asked to get in touch with his old clients rather than explore new territory. Des had actually been sent over earlier in the day with all the names and addresses. What he had brought were the very index cards that had once been given to Roger Green for photocopying.

"Where did you get all this information from?" gasped Maurice, as he studied the sheet at the top of the mountainous printout.

"It really doesn't matter," replied David, dismissively.

Maurice, however, wouldn't be fobbed off so easily. In front of his eyes were comments such as 'clients wish to refurbish their entire premises in the next two months'. Phrases always likely to arouse excitement in furniture salesmen.

"This must belong to one of our competitors," said Maurice, suspiciously.

"Robsons as it happens," answered David, as he casually opened up his briefcase and wedged the printout inside. "Although they don't own it anymore."

"How on earth did you happen to acquire it?" asked Maurice in astonishment. "I don't want to see Fine Choice taken to court for stealing other people's property."

David put a consoling hand on his senior colleague's arm.

"You have nothing to worry about. The printout was taken from Robsons by a disgruntled employee when he left their premises for the very last time."

Maurice was shocked by what he was hearing. He would have sat down had it been possible but the office was too small for a second chair. Therefore he chose instead to lean up against the wooden door.

"If that great heap of paper has been stolen we have a duty to return it to the rightful owners," said Maurice, indignantly.

David shook his head firmly.

"We can't do that. I have been writing notes on it all day while phoning Robsons clients. The wisest thing is just to allow sleeping dogs to lie."

"But what you have in your briefcase is vital information," Maurice protested. "Robsons sales staff will be looking high and low for it."

"That is where you are wrong," answered David with a broad grin. "The employee who took the printout had been told to shred it the day before he left. You see it was out of date and the computer had already produced a current one."

Maurice checked his watch. It was almost five o'clock and as always he was eager to go home. Not only that but having to stand up for even the shortest time had a tendency to wear him out.

"Look I'll leave the matter to you and your conscience," he muttered while sliding back the wooden door. "See you in the morning."

Like his boss David had no intention of working overtime. During the day he had decided to spend the evening campaigning for the Labour Party. The thought of delivering leaflets wasn't exactly appealing but he was willing to put up with a little hardship. He was keen to meet up with his old political friends again. Particularly the Greek goddess with the flaxen hair.

Less than two hours later David pulled up outside the Brockleby Labour Party headquarters. The last time he had set eyes on the large detached Victorian house was the day of the General Election. On that occasion there were rather more cars on the forecourt than there were at present.

As he entered the front door David felt a little nervous. Quickly glancing around he recognised only two familiar faces amongst the dozen or so people who had arrived before him. At the far end of the room Tony and Jacqui Dunn appeared to be engaged in an earnest discussion.

David wandered over to the counter for a drink. While waiting for service he happened to look up at the photograph of Bruce Shaw hung on the wall. It suddenly dawned on him that the former Prime Minister's smiling face would soon be replaced by that of another Labour leader's, once the party had taken part in a ballot.

Having bought a pint of bitter, David went over to study the noticeboard. It was while his attention was focused on the latest fund raising events, such as the Halloween dinner and dance, that he received a hearty slap on the back. Upon turning around he came face to face with George.

"Good to see you again," grinned the councillor. "Have you come to give us a hand tonight?"

David gave his old landlord a smile.

"I want to help Jacqui Dunn win this time."

Immediately the expression on George's face changed. The eyes had turned cold as he directed his stare towards the window.

"This is going to be the most important by-election for many years. If the Tories lose this seat they will see their overall majority in the House of Commons sink to three. In that situation Jonathan Canning will have major difficulties in trying to run his Government."

David looked thoughtful.

"You'll have to forgive me but I have been out of touch recently. I can see from all the posters in the bar that Jacqui will be our candidate again, but who have the Tories selected to fight the seat for them this time?"

"Adrian Thomas," replied George. "He is the leader of the council and a very popular man locally."

"As a fellow councillor then I suppose you have come to know him very well," said David.

George nodded.

"He is from the more caring wing of the party. Adrian is not the type to think that the poor should be left starving in the gutter."

The conversation came to an abrupt halt. Out of the corner of his eye David saw two figures approaching him with some purpose. Turning his head sideways he recognised the two smiling faces of Tony and Jacqui Dunn.

"How are you?" beamed the Brockleby Labour candidate.

"I'm fine thanks," answered David, as he received a kiss on the cheek.

"Our young friend wants to lend a hand this evening," smiled George.

"The more help we get the better," said Tony, grimly. "We

374

aren't getting much support from the top. Other than Bruce Shaw, most prominent Labour MPs seem unwilling to campaign for us. Fearing that a new leader will back the Americans in Iraq, they are keen to distance themselves from an anti-war candidate."

David was taken aback.

"But I should have thought they would have been desperate to beat the Tories."

"Unfortunately there are too many politicians who are happy to put their career prospects over their principles," replied Jacqui, sadly.

David struggled to find words to express his outrage. By the time he had thought of something appropriate, Jacqui's attention had been diverted elsewhere. She was suddenly waving enthusiastically at a large woman in a red coat who had just arrived.

"Kenny won't be out helping tonight," said George, turning to Tony. "The Housing Committee are holding a meeting."

"Carol and Alison will be missing, too," replied Tony. "They've gone shopping but will be joining us up here later for a drink."

Despite the three notable absentees the bar was now quite full. However, most of those present had not come in just to buy drinks but were preparing to go out on the streets supporting the party they loved. A lot were grassroots activists from other constituencies, who unlike most of their party leaders, were not put off by the anti-war candidate.

Something prompted Tony to check his watch. Deciding it was time for action he quickly headed to a table by the window, which was piled high with leaflets. He couldn't afford to allow the troops to stand idly by when there was work to be done.

Soon David found himself walking the streets with three strangers. As the only local person in the group he had been given the task of acting as a guide to the others. During the evening he discovered that his fellow deliverers had travelled down from North London on the train. They were three male university students who proved to be entertaining companions as they tackled their work together.

The last leaflet was delivered as a nearby church clock struck nine. Then after dropping his new-found friends off at the station,

David drove back to headquarters. Having walked continuously for very close to two hours he was desperate to sit down with a pint of best bitter.

Many of the other delivery teams had finished early. Upon entering the bar through the swing door, David was completely taken by surprise to see so many people. All the tables were occupied and those forced to stand were packed solidly together.

Having negotiated his way past a forest of bodies, David finally managed to join the drinks queue. While waiting to be served he gazed around in the hope of seeing his friends. However, with the crowds blocking much of his view it was never going to be easy. Then suddenly he felt a tap on the shoulder.

"Here is fifteen quid," said George in a voice just loud enough to be heard above the general hubbub in the bar. "Get three bitters, two white wines, a coke and whatever it is you want yourself."

"Where are you sitting?" asked David.

George pointed to a table about thirty feet away. Seated on the near side were Tony, Carol and Jacqui while facing them it was just possible to make out Kenny's boyish profile, now back from his meeting. Next to the young councillor David could see a bright red jumper but, at present, the wearer was hidden from view.

His heart began to beat rapidly. All of a sudden he felt impatient with anyone who stood ahead of him in the queue. He was now desperate to discover the identity of that obscured person.

Tonight his prayers were answered. Alison looked up just as David joined his friends carrying the long awaited drinks on a black plastic tray. As their eyes made contact there was a warmth in her smile. She looked stunning with her shoulder length hair laying gently over the rolled up collar of her red jumper.

"Alison was saying that you know Rebecca Baverstock," remarked George, as he stood up to assist in the distribution of drinks.

"That's right," replied David, as he sat down on the chair at the end of the table, which had been reserved for him.

"Do you happen to know whether anyone connected to the Tory Party offered this lady compensation after her husband was killed?" asked Tony.

David looked blank.

"Not that I am aware of."

"It's just that we are looking for issues to campaign on and this could be a good one," explained Jacqui. "Particularly as Charles Dawkins happened to run Mr Baverstock down in this constituency."

"Do you know how we can get hold of Rebecca?" asked Alison.

David stopped to consider the matter. At the weekend Rebecca had complained of being pestered by people from the media over Malcolm's fatal accident. Under the circumstances he wanted to avoid making the situation worse by helping to create yet more publicity for her. On the other hand he wondered how she might feel about receiving a large donation from the Conservative Party.

"Let me speak to her," said David at last. "As it happens I should be seeing her next Saturday."

The rest of the group offered their appreciation and the conversation moved on to other things. Of course nobody had any inclination to discuss subjects unrelated to the forthcoming by-election. For David it was just like old times.

Given the chance the group would have gone on talking all night. However, for Alison that wasn't an option, as she was expected home at a reasonable hour to relieve her mother of baby-sitting duties. Therefore shortly after ten thirty she stood up to put on her coat, which had been draped over the back of her chair.

"Can I give you a lift?" enquired David, before anyone else had an opportunity to volunteer their services.

Alison smiled.

"Thank you. It will give me an opportunity to catch up on all your news."

After going around the table and kissing her friends goodbye, Alison followed David to the door. Leaving the bar was much easier than it had been to get in now that many of the activists from outside Brockleby had left. Those that remained were mostly regulars.

"And what about you and Rebecca?" asked Alison, as soon as the car set off.

"How do you mean?" asked David.

"Are you two intending to get married?" enquired Alison, with a hint of mischief in her voice.

"No we're not," answered David, rather taken aback by the directness of the question. "What makes you think that we might be?"

"Don't you remember our last conversation?" asked Alison. "I suggested that Rebecca would make a perfect wife for you."

David nodded.

"I haven't forgotten."

"So why haven't you asked her then?" enquired Alison, taking a sideways glance towards the driver.

David hesitated for a few moments. The question was straight forward enough but he couldn't decide how to respond. It was so easy to say the wrong thing, particularly after having recently consumed a pint and a half of best bitter.

"I did ask her to marry me but she refused," he said at last. "Knowing that her parents and the rest of the Fellowship would disapprove she wasn't even prepared to consider the matter. You see they all believe that my faith is weak and I might easily lead Rebecca into wicked ways."

"Why doesn't Rebecca just tell them all to mind their own business?" said Alison, angrily. "What right do they have to interfere?"

"None whatsoever," answered David. "However, if she decides to marry against their wishes, her family and the rest of the Fellowship are likely to cut her off as they did with me."

"I feel so sorry for you both," sighed Alison.

At that moment they passed the spot where the two of them had enjoyed intimate pleasures together on a number of occasions. David longed to stop again but he was concerned that Alison might not be receptive to the idea. Therefore he just kept on driving.

A heavy storm had been widely predicted for that evening. As if to prove the weather forecasters had got it right heavy drops of rain suddenly began splattering against the windscreen. Across the road a young man taking the dog for a late night walk quickly darted beneath the nearest tree.

"I'm not disappointed that Rebecca turned me down," said

378

David, as the rain got heavier and was now hammering down on the roof of the car. "We are good friends but our feelings don't go any deeper than that. Anyway I happen to be in love with somebody else."

"Not that woman who was seen with you at the party is it?" Alison giggled.

"No," answered David, indignantly. "Samantha isn't interested in a permanent relationship. She just wants to flirt with any man who takes her fancy at the time and then move on to somebody else."

"So have you found a new girlfriend then?" asked Alison, excitedly.

David slowed the car down as he approached a main road. They were now less than half a mile from Alison's home but he wanted to prolong the journey for as long as possible. Every moment he spent with her was precious.

"It is somebody that I have known for a very long time," said David, feeling the emotion building up inside. "The truth is that I've never really wanted anyone else."

Alison gazed thoughtfully ahead. The windscreen wipers were steadily swinging from side to side, instantly clearing the torrent of rain that was lashing down against the glass. However, at that precise moment she was hardly aware of the inclement weather conditions.

"Where did you meet her?" she asked, softly.

Suddenly David's throat felt dry. Fearing that his voice would sound gruff he swallowed hard.

"We were in the same class at school," he replied, longing to stop and take her in his arms but not daring to. "I used to think about her all the time. She was my very own Aphrodite."

Alison needed no further clues. David had once revealed he had often thought of her as the Greek goddess of love. She remembered that he had said it before they had enjoyed intercourse together for the very first time.

"It could never work between us," she replied, gently. "I tried to tell you before that we live in two different worlds."

"But I hate my world," protested David, bitterly. "I want to be in yours. My dream has always been to qualify as a teacher, get married and have a large family. We would live in a nice house, have plenty of money and our children could have anything they want. Is that so very much to ask?"

Suddenly Alison brushed a tear away from the corner of her eye.

"I've just broken off my engagement to Mark," she said between sobs. "I'm just not ready to start a relationship with anyone right now. Let's just be friends and leave it like that for the time being."

The journey ended in silence. The rain had eased off but both of them were too locked up in their own private thoughts to notice. After all in the grand scheme of things, a passing storm pales into insignificance against the emotional turmoil that these two people were suffering just then.

"Sorry if I made you cry," said David, finally resuming the conversation. "The last thing I wanted was to upset you."

"I know," replied Alison, dabbing her eyes with a handkerchief. "It's just that I am feeling rather depressed at the moment."

"I understand but please answer one question," said David, gently. "Is it possible that you could ever love me?"

Alison leaned over in her seat and kissed him lightly on the cheek.

"I'm sorry but I'm too confused to be able to think about such things," she answered, while at the same time opening the car door.

David had mixed feelings about the situation as he drove away. On the one hand he felt frustrated at being denied clear answers to his questions, however, on the other, he was pleased at not being rejected out of hand. As things stood he decided to be patient and just hope for the best.

Saturday morning meant an early start. David had little appetite for returning to the building site and toiling away as a manual labourer. Having just recovered from the aches and pains he had suffered the previous week, he had no desire to inflict yet more agony on himself. The only consolation he could think of was that at least the weather had warmed up over the past few days.

Before starting work he headed straight for the portable cabin. Apart from being tempted by visions of bacon sandwiches and waffles dripping in fat he was keen to have another word with Rebecca. He wanted to ask the one question or possibly two that Tony had wanted answered. Whether the Tories had compensated her for Malcolm's death and if not, was she willing to allow Labour to make an election issue out of it.

However, as soon as he pushed open the door his heart sank. It wasn't the beautiful Rebecca who stood behind the counter serving out breakfast but a much older woman with long silver hair. Rather dejectedly he helped himself to a plate, before joining a line of three men eagerly waiting a share of the fried sustenance that was on offer.

"No Rebecca today then?" he asked, when finally arriving at the front of the queue.

The woman casually shook her head.

"I'm afraid not. When I left home she was just about to tackle a big pile of washing."

"Has Rebecca moved in with you then?" asked David in surprise.

"Just for a while," replied the woman. "She is staying with me while all this interest in her is going on."

"I can't understand why she is getting so much attention," answered David.

"These people are always pestering her," complained the woman, angrily. "Of course Rebecca refuses to open the door anymore but it is still threatening when there are strangers keeping a watch on your home."

Suddenly heavy footsteps could be heard outside the cabin. In a few seconds the door was flung open and in stepped a ruddy faced man in white overalls. While helping himself to a plate he made a cheery remark to a little group who were stood eating in a corner.

Not wanting to keep others waiting, David quickly made his food selection. Having handed over his plate, he watched as the silver haired caterer removed two succulent slices of bacon from under the grill and laid them inside a roll. To this was then added a lightly browned sausage and a potato waffle.

"Look I'm a friend of Rebecca," said David, eyeing his breakfast with some relish. "How can I get in touch with her?"

The woman looked thoughtful. Then having considered the

matter, she scribbled something down on a scrap of paper and handed it to David.

"I'm her Aunt Rose," she said. "This is my telephone number which you can speak to my niece on but don't give it out to anybody else. I don't want the press sniffing around my home as well."

"Thank you very much," answered David with a smile. "However, I do have one final question for you. Has Rebecca ever been offered compensation for the death of her husband?"

Aunt Rose shook her head firmly.

"Not a penny and the sad thing is that she needs the money. Some people have advised her to take legal action but she just ignores them. Actually I don't think she wants all the hassle of going to court."

After he had eaten, David was set to work as a bricklayer's labourer. As somebody unused to carrying a weighty hod about he soon discovered that his arms and back were beginning to ache. In fact by the time he arrived home his whole upper body was in agony.

Suffering as he was, however, David still decided to spend the evening delivering leaflets. Much of the time it was a tortuous process just to lift his arm up to the letterboxes but, stoically he continued to the bitter end. Finally having gone back to the club for a drink he gently lowered himself in a seat opposite Tony and took a large gulp of best bitter.

"Have you managed to speak with the lady who lost her husband yet?" asked Jacqui Dunn who was sitting next to him.

"No but I did have a brief conversation with her aunt," replied David, feeling a dull ache in the arm as he lifted his beer mug to take another gulp of bitter. "I have found out that the Tories haven't paid Rebecca any compensation, however, there is no way we should be making an election issue out of it."

"But why ever not?" asked Tony in surprise. "Your friend could end up with a lot of money."

"Because I am concerned that Rebecca might have a mental breakdown," explained David. "You see she has already left home in order to avoid being hounded by the media. Therefore it hardly seems right to push her still further into the public spotlight."

Several people around the table nodded with a resigned look

on their faces.

"It seems a shame if poor Rebecca has to miss out on what she is entitled to," said Alison, sadly.

"I may be able to help," said Jacqui, thoughtfully. "There won't be any votes in it but that doesn't matter. Politics isn't all about getting yourself elected."

David was interested in finding out more. Unfortunately as often happens in social gatherings, somebody happened to change the subject and he wasn't able to question the local councillor. Therefore it would be several days before all would be revealed to him.

Chapter Thirty

When David woke up the following morning he could scarcely move. For a while, stretched out in bed, he tried to assess which parts of his body had been partially incapacitated by paralysis. His early findings, however, suggested that most of his muscles ached unmercifully.

While struggling to climb into his clothes David began to curse. This was the second successive Sunday in which he had felt like a man who had fallen off the top of a high-rise block of flats. Every inch of him seemed to be screaming out that he was not suited for strenuous activities on a building site. It was time he decided to sit up and take notice.

After breakfast David took a hot bath in an attempt to alleviate the stiffness. While lying contentedly in the warm soapy water the young man calculated that in the past two months, he had moved home on no less than four occasions yet still had no permanent place to live. He was beginning to feel like he had the roots of a nomadic tribesman. Some stability he decided was urgently required.

Later on David ventured down to the park again. It was a bright but chilly morning and intermittent gusts of wind blew the autumn leaves in all directions. Undeterred by the inclement weather conditions, however, two small children stood by the side of the lake feeding the ducks. Further away in the distance several older boys, with coats for goalposts were playing football.

As David sat down on a bench his thoughts turned to Alison. Once more he attempted to relive those precious moments in the hotel when they had made love for the first time. It was a wonderful experience that would always remain in his memory and deep down he knew that he had found the one person in the world who could make him truly happy. Without her his life was empty and meaningless.

That afternoon he had two visitors call on him. With no television and having just finished the *Observer,* which he had earlier bought from a nearby newsagent, David was grateful for some company. Even if it did come in the shape of his father and Ian Porter.

"We were just wondering whether you have changed your mind about Ruth," began Ian, when they had all settled down in the lounge. "Are you sure that you don't want to marry her?"

"Quite certain," replied David.

John Chambers smiled sadly at his son.

"Your mother misses you. Why don't you marry Ruth if only for her sake?"

"Because I have no desire to spend the rest of my life with somebody I don't love," answered David, firmly. "As for mum, she can come and visit me anytime she wants. I'm not stopping her."

"She is keeping away because her son has turned against the Lord," explained Ian.

"It's because the young man that she raised has succumbed to the temptations of the world," added John.

It was the old music hall double act again. Were they a singing duet, Ian and John would have doubtless sung in perfect harmony. They were like two heads sharing one brain.

Ian gave John a quick glance before addressing the younger Chambers.

"How do you feel about Geraldine Stone?" he enquired.

David shrugged.

"No strong feelings one way or the other."

"As you have obviously lost interest in Ruth, how would you feel about marrying Geraldine then?" enquired John, apparently deciding it was his turn to ask a question. "It's just that we both believe that she is another strong Christian woman who would make an ideal wife for you."

"The pair of you are wasting your time," said David, wearily. "The truth is that I'm in love with somebody else and she isn't Fellowship."

The double act exchanged glances that expressed their disappointment.

"Who?" they asked in unison.

"If you must know, it's the lady with the blonde hair," replied David.

Ian looked amazed.

"But I thought you said she had got engaged to somebody else."

"Well things have changed," snapped David.

For once the two great minds did not think alike. John who had heard just about enough from his wayward son stood up to leave, while Ian on the other hand sat perfectly still. The priest it appeared was not prepared to abandon the lost sheep just yet.

"I'm afraid that Satan is using this young woman to guide you away from the paths of righteousness," he said in the gloomiest voice he could manage.

"Are you suggesting that Alison is in league with the Devil?" asked David, who felt he might be about to explode at any minute.

"We have no means of knowing," replied John, who had suddenly resumed his seat again. "She has certainly become a very bad influence on you."

"I fail to see why," answered David, indignantly.

"Because she is leading you astray and might cost you a place in Heaven," explained Ian, sadly shaking his head.

"She is destroying your faith in the Lord," added the other half of the double act.

Throughout his life David had allowed himself to be lectured and spoken down to by these two sanctimonious individuals. However, on this occasion something suddenly snapped inside and finally he decided to fight back. It was time to defend not just himself but also the woman he loved.

"Why do Fellowship followers always feel morally superior to everybody else?" he began, bitterly. "The set of rules which govern your lives are merely based on a narrow interpretation of a two thousand year old book."

The two guests looked aghast.

"I can't believe that you are starting to question the word of the Lord," said Ian when he had finally managed to recover from shock. "I will pray that this woman disappears from your life before too long."

"Alison is a sweet and gentle person," answered David, feeling a sudden warmth for his Aphrodite. "It is true of course that she doesn't give up much of her time to worrying about Salvation. She is far more concerned with all the people who are suffering right now on this Earth."

John immediately turned to his Bible that he had been holding in his hand. Well-worn through continual use, the black covered book was a constant travelling companion whenever he went anywhere. Quickly thumbing through the flimsy pages the senior Chambers finally found the passage he was hunting for.

"Corinthians two, chapter six, verse fourteen," he announced after clearing his throat. "Be ye not unequally yoked together with unbelievers, for what fellowship hath righteousness with unrighteousness and what communion hath light with darkness."

"I'd rather a woman who wanted to save the world than one who was only interested in saving her soul," replied David, turning up his nose.

Ian finally gave up on the lost soul who was obviously beyond redemption. Seeing that John was up on his feet again in preparation for leaving the priest decided he would follow his friend's example on this occasion.

"We will pray for you," he muttered while buttoning up his coat.

David shrugged.

"Please yourself."

"By the way, I almost forgot," said Ian, just as he was about to turn around and follow John through the lounge door. "Jeremy Wright would like to call in this evening and discuss the decoration of this house with you. Are you likely to be in?"

Alarm bells immediately started going off in David's head. It had completely slipped his mind that he had agreed to paint and wallpaper some of the rooms before Jeremy moved in. Of course were that promise to be kept, he would be left with very little spare time to campaign for the Labour Party and more importantly, stay in touch with Alison.

"Could he come around tomorrow evening instead?" he pleaded, while instantly considering the idea of finding a new home over the next twenty-four hours. "I have to go out shortly and won't be back until quite late."

"Very well," answered Ian. "I will ask Jeremy to ring you at work tomorrow and arrange a convenient time for him to call round."

That evening the Labour activists were sent out canvassing.

Afterwards as they sat drinking back at the club David managed to briefly steer George's thoughts away from the subject of politics. Feeling slightly embarrassed he approached the all-important question.

"Have you found a lodger for my old room yet?"

George shook his head.

"It's been vacant ever since you moved out a couple of weeks ago. As you know I only rent it out to friends who are desperate for somewhere to live."

"In that case you are looking at a person who fits that description," replied David, who could feel his cheeks burning.

"When would you be looking to move in again?" asked George, who didn't appear unduly surprised at what he had just heard.

"Early tomorrow evening if that is possible," answered David without hesitation. "It really is a bit of an emergency."

George turned to Kenny who was sitting alongside him.

"As a fellow lodger, have you any objection to David moving in with us again?"

Kenny grinned.

"Just as long as he doesn't try to interfere with my council business, I don't mind one little bit."

David smiled.

"I promise to concentrate on my own problems from now on."

The arrangement was informally ratified as three beer mugs touched one another in mid-air. Then unsurprisingly everybody returned to the subject of the Brockleby by-election and matters relating to it. The fact was that nobody was prepared to give much thought to anything else as the big day got ever nearer.

The following morning Des wandered into David's tiny office. As always the newly appointed Assistant Sales Manager looked like a man with all the time in the world to kill. It therefore came as a disappointment to him to discover that there was no spare chair to sit down on.

"Are you having much success with the cold calling?" he enquired, while unpeeling the navy blue wrapper from one end of a chocolate bar.

"Yes I am getting quite a favourable response," replied David with a smile.

Having taken a sizeable bite from one of a number of his mid-morning snacks Des looked thoughtful for a few moments.

"After you left Fine Choice Furniture I was asked to ring some of your clients," he said, finally.

"I imagine somebody would be given that unenviable task," laughed David.

"Oh everything is always dumped on me," answered Des, resentfully. "Anyway what puzzled me was the number of these clients who had been told that you had gone to work for Robsons."

David gave his colleague a surprised look.

"Now where on earth would they have got a crazy idea like that from?"

Like Maurice had done the previous week, Des leaned back against the wooden sliding door to rest his weary body. Having taken an instant dislike to this poky little office with its lack of creature comforts for the social caller, he decided to make his visit brief.

"Some were saying that you had told them," he answered, hesitantly.

"Perish the thought," said David, dismissively. "Could you imagine me working for a second rate company like Robsons?"

"I suppose not," replied Des, as the last piece of chocolate disappeared into his mouth. "Out of interest though, where were you working over the past few weeks?"

Before David could answer the telephone rang. As he reached over to lift up the receiver, Des slid back the wooden door and wandered off in search of another colleague to waste some time with. One he hoped who could offer him a comfortable chair to sit down on.

David immediately recognised the voice of Jeremy Wright on the other end of the line. After taking a deep breath he prepared himself to deliver some rather disappointing news to his caller.

"Would it be all right if I called round about half eight tonight?" asked Jeremy.

"Please do but I suggest that you bring your key," answered David, smiling to himself. "By the time you arrive I will have moved to another address."

There was a brief silence on the other end of the line as this information sunk in.

"But I thought that you had agreed to help me paint and decorate my new house," answered Jeremy at last.

"I can give you a hand but it won't be until the first week in December," said David, who was starting to enjoy himself. "You see until then I shall be out night after night canvassing for the Labour Party."

"Don't bother," answered Jeremy, sounding rather disgruntled. "No doubt I can get other people to lend me a hand."

David shrugged his shoulders as he put down the phone. He had absolutely no intention of feeling guilty at letting anyone down. Having spent two back breaking Saturdays on a building site, he now felt under no obligation to anyone within the Fellowship for providing him with free food and a few creature comforts in recent days.

That evening he had to excuse himself from canvassing duties. Not only was there a little matter of transferring his belongings into new lodgings but he also needed to drive down to the supermarket to stock up on food. Finally at ten to nine, having scoffed down a ready prepared meal in front of the television, he set off for the club to join his political friends.

Once again the bar was packed when David wandered in. Surrounded by a sea of strangers he slowly negotiated his way towards the drinks counter to buy a pint of bitter. As he was about to tag on to the end of a queue, Jacqui Dunn suddenly blocked his way.

"I've got some good news," she said, excitedly. "This afternoon I managed to have a word with Adrian Thomas who, as you know, is the Tory candidate in this by-election. Anyway I enquired whether his party intended to compensate your friend Rebecca for the death of her husband, seeing that he was killed by one of their most senior MPs."

"What did he say?" asked David with wide eyes.

"Apparently under pressure from one of the tabloids, the Tories have tried to give Rebecca a cheque for fifty thousand pounds," Jacqui beamed. "Probably they were concerned with what could turn into an election issue. The problem has been though, that nobody in the party has been able to speak to your friend for more than five seconds."

"I don't understand," answered David, with a puzzled expression.

"It's as though she doesn't want to come into contact with anyone," explained Jacqui. "A number of people have tried ringing her but she just hangs up the moment they speak. Then when local activists have called around, Rebecca never answers the door even though it is obvious she is in the house."

David couldn't help smiling as everything suddenly started to fall into place.

"You see, since it was reported that Rebecca's husband was killed by the Home Secretary certain reporters from the media were keen for her to do an interview," he began, after collecting his thoughts. "However, although they were turned down, one or two of these people persisted until Rebecca just refused to speak with strangers either at the door or on the phone. Finally, tired of being harassed she moved out of her home and is now staying with an aunt for the time being."

"How awful," exclaimed Jacqui. "And after having just lost her husband, too."

David nodded.

"Let's hope this large sum of money can go some way towards easing her misery."

"Why don't you ring her straight away?" suggested Jacqui, enthusiastically. "My office is free if you want to use it."

David immediately took up the offer even though it meant having to wait for his first pint of bitter of the evening. Soon he was following the Labour councillor out of the crowded bar, up a flight of stairs and through a partly opened door at the end of the landing. Once inside he was surrounded by notices and posters on the walls, while roughly a third of the floor space was taken up by a pine desk and beside the window stood a grey metal filing cabinet.

"This is the telephone number of Charles Dawkins' wife," said Jacqui, placing a slip of paper on the desk. "Sally is keen to meet up with Rebecca and present her with the money."

David sat down behind the desk once Jacqui had left the room. Then having taken a few minutes to decide what he was about to say he finally lifted up the telephone. Naturally Rebecca was delighted as soon as the good news was relayed to her.

"Apart from receiving a much needed cheque I might also be able to go back home," she said, happily.

"Worth giving it a try," replied David. "Hopefully most of the people making a nuisance of themselves before were Tories trying to give you money."

They continued to talk for a while. However, when David described the most recent changes he had made in his life Rebecca began to show some concern. It had been little more than a week when they had last met in the portable cabin, and then he had spoken of his desire to rejoin the Fellowship. Now it seemed he wanted to be part of the big wide world again.

"It's as though you are on a merry-go-round," said Rebecca, sadly. "You don't seem to know what you want. I just wish you would settle down for a while."

"The merry-go-round is about to grind to a halt," answered David, firmly. "From now on I am going to follow my dreams. I shall make a start once this by-election is over by finding out from Mr Chapman how to set about becoming a teacher."

"When we last spoke you told me that you were desperate to return to the Fellowship," said Rebecca. "Not only were people in the big wide world making you feel like an outsider, but also because you were missing your friends and family. What has changed in such a short space of time?"

David sat gazing at a large photograph in a gold frame hanging up on the wall ahead of him. The two people that smiled down on him were Jacqui Dunn alongside Bruce Shaw before being deposed as Prime Minister by the electorate. Together they made a very attractive couple.

"Because the Fellowship attached a precondition to my being accepted back into the fold," explained David, as he studied his fingernails closely. "It was that I should marry a strong willed woman capable of keeping me out of the clutches of Satan."

"And of course you weren't prepared to be tied down to some overbearing battle-axe for the rest of your life I suppose," chuckled Rebecca.

The conversation continued on for a time. When it finally came to an end David hurried downstairs to join his friends in the bar. As ever, there was one he was eager to see in particular.

***

The following Saturday morning Rebecca drove up to Brockleby. She was eager to see Simon who had just arrived back in England after having returned from his holiday in Seattle. However, there was another reason for her wanting to make the journey up from the Kent coast. Once she had spent most of the day with her family she intended to leave their house about ten to three and then call on an even larger property only a few roads away.

Rebecca drew in a deep breath as she rang the doorbell. There had been something rather intimidating about the woman she had spoken to over the phone. Sally Dawkins had one of those haughty voices so characteristic amongst the upper middle classes. She had sounded like the type of person who was used to being obeyed by those of an inferior station in life.

Moments later the door slowly opened and the two women came face to face. In a flash Rebecca's apprehension deserted her because of the warm welcoming smile she was greeted with. In the flesh Sally Dawkins was far less formidable than her brusque telephone manner had seemed to suggest.

"Of course you are one of the Fellowship," commented Sally, as she watched Rebecca remove her black headscarf in the hall.

Rebecca smiled.

"Fellowship women wear it whenever they are out," she explained.

"Yes I've heard that somewhere before," said Sally. "Actually I'm Church of England myself. Every Sunday I always go along to the evening service."

Soon the two women were getting along well. Once again as she did when entertaining David, Rebecca ignored the rule that Fellowship should not sit down to eat with non-believers. Having read in chapter nine of St Matthew, verse ten that Jesus had partaken food with sinners and publicans, she felt such a course of action was fully justified. It meant also that she could avoid offending her hostess while at the same time, enjoy a slice of mouth-watering fruitcake.

After a while Sally's expression changed. Having been

393

talkative and bubbly up until that point, she obviously decided it was time to be serious. Her eyes that had sparkled suddenly became sad as she gazed thoughtfully into space.

"I have an apology to make to you," she said in a quiet voice. "I knew all along that Charles had accidentally killed your husband but it was never really my intention to report it to the police. All I ever thought about was protecting Charles's career and how this terrible occurrence could be used to save our marriage."

Rebecca looked blank.

"How could Malcolm's death have saved your marriage?"

"Because Charles was having an affair and knowing what I did about the accident gave me great power over him," explained Sally, with a sad smile. "It was made absolutely clear to him that unless he finished with this woman the whole world would get to know what he had done. Were I to do that of course, he would have likely ended up doing a long stretch in prison with his career in tatters."

"And wasn't it his mistress who stabbed Charles in your front garden?" asked Rebecca, who had found herself taking a morbid interest in the murder at the time.

"It was Madeleine all right," replied Sally, without a trace of malice in her voice. "My husband had promised to marry her you see and she must have been looking forward to being the Home Secretary's wife in place of me. Of course once Charles had been forced to call the whole thing off, she took her revenge in the most savage way possible."

"She must have been out of her mind," said Rebecca, with a shudder.

Sally didn't answer. Once again she was reliving those horrifying moments in the front garden when two blood soaked bodies had laid at her feet. Those memories were just as vivid in her mind now as they had been on that dreadful night a few weeks earlier.

"Madeleine may have been mad but she still triumphed over me in the end," said Sally, with a faint smile. "That woman was determined to snatch Charles away from me so she decided to take him to the grave with her."

"Anyway I forgive you for not going to the police," said

Rebecca. "Even had you done so it wouldn't have brought Malcolm back to life."

Sally attempted to brighten up.

"Thank you for being so understanding," she smiled, while holding her guest a slip of paper. "Anyway I didn't invite you here to talk about myself. Here is the cheque that I promised you."

Rebecca blushed as she reached out her hand to accept the gift. She had never felt entirely comfortable in taking presents from strangers. Particularly when they were from non-Fellowship people.

"Thank you," she said in an almost guilty voice. "You are most generous."

"It isn't my money," answered Sally, with a laugh. "You are being paid out of Conservative Party Funds. Central Office weren't too happy in coughing up but I left them with very little choice."

"I don't understand," said Rebecca.

"Let me put it this way," began Sally as she sat back in her armchair. "As the wife of a cabinet minister you can find out some very interesting information about why the Government acts in the way it does. For example I have printed evidence stating that the Prime Minister's decision to invade Iraq had little to do with weapons of mass destruction. It was all about protecting British economic interests by going along with the American President."

"That's dreadful," said Rebecca, indignantly.

"I mustn't divulge more," said Sally, with a shake of her head. "But believe me, one of these days the truth is going to come out."

Rebecca drove home and put the car away. Now living back in the bungalow, she was relieved that all those unwanted strangers were no longer knocking on her door or making unwelcome phone calls. Everything appeared to be back to normal.

The problem she faced now was how to spend her windfall. Rebecca was determined to keep most for herself but she was also considering giving money to a good cause. Deep down she knew that Malcolm would have wanted her to make a donation towards the building of the Fellowship school in the Broadstairs area.

However, a nagging voice inside was saying something different. Finally the rebel in her triumphed.

"I am going to give four thousand pounds to Oxfam," she said out loud to herself. "Why should that money be used for a bunch of privileged kids when it could help feed many starving people in the world."

Chapter Thirty-One

It was now less than a week before polling day. The canvass returns for both Labour and Conservative parties were indicating that it was likely to be yet another close result. Desperate for victory, activists on both sides of the political divide were now pushing themselves to the absolute limit.

The only two candidates with a realistic chance of winning the Brockleby seat each had their problems. In their election leaflets the Tories were gloating over the fact that few senior figures in the Labour Party had been in the constituency to lend their weight to the campaign. The conclusion they were drawing was that the shadow cabinet as a whole, regarded Jacqui Dunn as being too left wing for their tastes.

Adrian Thomas on the other hand had no reason to feel complacent. He had always been known as an enthusiastic European and for that reason the UK Independence Party was mounting a strong challenge for the seat. Of course, the only likely effect that the candidate William Court would have on the by-election was to split the Conservative vote.

David was throwing his heart and soul into the campaign. However, as the big day grew nearer he was beginning to feel increasingly frustrated with his parents for not including his name on the electoral register. Night after night he was trying to persuade others to vote for Jacqui Dunn, while knowing all the time that he probably wouldn't be able to do so himself.

So far he had kept his problem to himself. However, the thought nagged away in his head that even at this late stage it might not be too late to put matters right. Finally he decided to seek the advice of his two housemates.

"There isn't enough time left for you to become registered," said Kenny, who was dividing his time between listening to David and watching the news on TV.

George on the other hand sat thoughtfully with his head bowed.

"All may not be lost," he said after a few minutes. "Tell me, is anyone at your home address registered to vote?"

"Mum and Dad are," answered David. "I found that out on the day of the General Election in the polling station. You see I wanted to cast my vote but was told that only the names of my parents were listed."

As George digested this information a sly smile spread across his face.

"Weren't you telling me that the Fellowship don't vote?"

David nodded.

"They think that the laws passed through Parliament rarely take the teachings of the Bible into account. Therefore they prefer to have nothing to do with the ballot box."

"Excellent!" exclaimed George. "If your father is on the electoral register then it is possible that you could use his vote."

Kenny gave his fellow councillor a warning look.

"If David should get caught he will get into serious trouble. Surely you can't be suggesting that he should risk being prosecuted?"

"I am prepared to chance it for the party," said David, boldly. "But don't I need a polling card in order to vote?"

His two housemates didn't reply immediately. For a while they were transfixed by a news item that was being announced on TV. A car bomb had exploded in the centre of Baghdad killing over thirty people and injuring many more. Images of the carnage then appeared on the screen before focusing on grief stricken relatives and stretchers carrying away the dead and injured.

After cursing the present Prime Minister, George turned to face David.

"It is better if you have one," he replied. "There is less chance of an official asking for some form of identification."

Later that evening David pondered on the problem. Having been effectively barred from his parent's home it would be impossible to acquire either John Chambers' polling card or some proof of his identity. In order to be successful he would need to break into the house when it was unoccupied and rummage through the drawers.

Then David had a flash of inspiration. Surely he reasoned, if none of the Fellowship wanted to involve themselves in the democratic process then any one of the followers could provide him with a polling card. That being the case there was one person who just might be persuaded to oblige he told himself.

The following morning David sat back at his desk trying to decide how he should phrase his strange request. It was hardly common practice to ring up a friend and ask to use his polling card in order to go off and vote. For one thing such an arrangement was strictly against the law. Finally he picked up the phone and got through to Simon's office.

"You must be out of your mind," gasped Simon. "We could end up spending time together in a prison cell."

"Look there is absolutely no chance of us getting caught," replied David, reassuringly. "If I walk into the polling station with your card nobody is going to take the time to check my identity. It just won't happen."

There was a slight pause on the other end of the line as Simon carefully considered the situation.

"Actually I threw my card away with the rubbish yesterday," said Simon, finally. "However, it should be possible to retrieve it. As far as I recall the bins don't get emptied until next Thursday."

"So can I have it then?" asked David, eagerly.

Simon sighed.

"I suppose so but let's get one thing straight. What you are proposing to do is fraudulent so don't implicate me if you get caught."

"I promise," answered David, gratefully.

"OK so if this card can be found amongst all the dirt and grime by what means do I get it to you."

"Post it to me," answered David, before giving out his home address.

"Very well," said Simon, with a chuckle. "But I must warn you it could be smeared in tomato sauce or perhaps something far worse. Hope they will appreciate that down at your polling station."

David had considered asking Simon to deliver it to the house. However, with the demands of canvassing being imposed on him night after night he decided to leave the invitation until after the by-election. Socialising he decided, would have to be put on hold for a while.

Politics though was not the only thing currently on his mind. Alison was becoming distant and seemed to be treating him like any other Labour activist. Either by accident or design on her part, at no time did he get an opportunity to be alone with the woman of his dreams. After drinking in the club of an evening she always chose to be taken home by Carol and Tony rather than him.

On the positive side Alison didn't appear to have anybody else. It was for that reason that David continued to tell himself that he needed to bide his time and just play the situation by ear. Nevertheless he still longed to kiss and hold her tight.

As the big day got ever nearer, bodies began to get weary. Finally on the eve of the election David and his fellow activists, having just bought drinks at the bar, collapsed into those wooden chairs having done their very last stint of canvassing in the campaign. Everyone was now well aware that it was up to the voters to decide which of the candidates would represent them in Parliament.

Each of them in the group, however, knew that their work was far from finished. If they were to help get Jacqui Dunn elected there was still more to be done. It was something that Tony, looking even more harassed than usual, was at pains to point out.

"It is imperative that we get all our supporters out tomorrow," he said, while squeezing the tip of his beard. "Don't forget Kenny that it is your responsibility to ensure that there are tellers at every polling station throughout the entire day."

Kenny nodded wearily but remained silent. Like everyone else around the table he had just heard Tony repeat himself for about the millionth time. If he wasn't familiar with his election day duties now he was never likely to be.

Tonight Jacqui seemed particularly subdued. Although looking perfectly composed she must have been wondering what the next twenty-four hours or so was going to bring. Was she finally about to achieve her lifetime ambition and become an MP or would it all end in disappointment yet again.

The little group all drifted away a little earlier than usual. They each knew the importance of getting a good night's sleep in preparation for what was to come. The following day would be long and hard, particularly if a recount was going to take them into the early hours of Friday morning.

It was five thirty when David opened his eyes. Having experienced an Election Day only weeks before as a party worker he had a better idea of what was expected of him on this occasion. It meant driving numerous strangers to and from polling stations for hours on end. This time though he was determined not to get deceived into taking crazy old ladies down to the supermarket to do their weekly shopping.

Today though there would be one important difference. Now being in possession of Simon's polling card David would be able to cast his vote for the very first time. The fact that he wasn't doing it under his own name seemed neither here nor there.

The clear skies suggested that it might remain dry throughout the day. However, those that were hoping for a Labour win weren't entirely happy with the weather. A bitterly cold November wind they feared, might discourage half-hearted supporters from turning out to vote.

Time slipped by very quickly for David. However, until the polls closed at ten o'clock that evening little that he did would be memorable in the years ahead. As an unpaid taxi driver it was just a case of being aware that countless strangers were climbing in and out of his car.

There was one memory though that would always stand out in his mind. Lining up behind a queue of people, waiting to be issued with a sheet of paper just to mark a cross on, was indeed a nerve wracking experience. He had an irrational feeling that everyone in the polling station suspected him of being a voting cheat.

Finally it was David's turn to present himself before the middle-aged woman sitting stern faced behind a long wooden table. Taking the polling card that was being held out to her, the council official began slowly turning the pages of a soft covered book containing long lists of name and addresses. Then at long last she looked up.

"Simon Broadbent of number fifty-four Westwood Avenue?" she enquired, without the trace of a smile.

David's throat felt parched and dry as he prepared himself to reply. Struck with panic for a split second the idea flashed briefly into his head to turn and run. However, he somehow managed to put all such misgivings behind him.

"Yes," he heard himself answer in a hoarse whisper.

Gratefully David took the slip of paper he was given and made his way towards one of the six cubicles. Once inside he studied the list of candidates and was a little shocked to see how many people were actually standing. Without bothering to count he guessed that there were at least about twenty.

Jacqui Dunn's name happened to be third from the top. However, wary of putting his cross in the wrong box it took David an age before he was certain enough to apply pencil to paper. Then having finally done the deed he felt a great sense of relief.

The little group of Labour activists arrived at the Town Hall after ten thirty. All eyes were on the left wing candidate and her supporters who made a late entrance. Tonight Jacqui Dunn, dressed in a red trouser suit looked even more stunning than usual.

The count was already well under way. As at the General Election there were five long lines of tables at which workers were sifting through piles of voting forms. It was only early stages in the operation and the result was unlikely to be known for at least two hours. For supporters of the two main parties it would be a long anxious wait.

Yet again the media were there in force. Camera crews from all the television news channels were lined up against the back of the hall, while a posse of reporters tried to interview everyone of any notoriety at all. The star attractions of course being Jacqui Dunn and Adrian Thomas, the only candidates with any realistic hope of being elected.

Time passed slowly in that tense atmosphere. David and others stood behind the chairs of those employed to count those endless sheets of paper to ensure that they did their job properly. Both Conservative and Labour supporters were aware that every vote could well be crucial.

Finally just after twelve forty-five the Returning Officer put the microphone to his lips.

"Would all candidates please come up on the stage," he announced.

Almost immediately about twenty or so people from all parts of the vast hall began heading in the same direction. Those that stood out most were the frivolous ones such as the 'Give Dogs A Vote' candidate dressed in his now familiar Dalmatian suit. Having stood for the Brockleby seat at the General Election he might possibly have been hoping to improve on the twenty-two votes received on that occasion.

David's heart was in his mouth as he watched Jacqui Dunn and the other candidates gather around the Returning Officer. He was well aware that the votes had now been counted and all those standing in the election would be given the final result of the ballot to see if any of them demanded a recount. Everyone else in the hall, however, would have to wait just a little longer to be informed.

Suddenly all eyes were either on Jacqui Dunn or Adrian Thomas. Those watching on were looking for facial expressions or any sign at all which might give a clue as to which way the contest had gone. For all those closely involved the tension was unbearable.

"Bloody Hell I think we have won," whispered Tony, excitedly. "Adrian Thomas has just shook his head at the Tory agent."

"And Jacqui Dunn has suddenly started grinning like a Cheshire cat," added Kenny.

"Let's wait for the result before we start jumping to conclusions," warned George, who was determined not to get carried away until the exact position had been confirmed.

Finally all the candidates were organised into a long line on the stage. Once in place the jolly faced man standing for the Raving Loony Party took off his brightly coloured hat and waved it at spectators. Not to be outdone for frivolous behaviour the large Dalmatian dropped down on all fours and gave a little yelp. Seemingly unimpressed with such nonsense the Returning Officer placed the microphone to his lips once more.

The official began by making a little speech. After that it was on to his main duty of the evening, which was to name the candidates in alphabetical order along with the votes cast for them. With over twenty individuals on the ballot paper it was likely to take a little while.

The first two people listed must have just entered the contest for the fun of it. After their names had been announced along with the meagre number of votes they had each received, there followed a few half-hearted cheers and some polite applause. Then the hall fell into total silence.

"Jacqui Dunn... 23,426 votes," called out the Returning Officer.

The glamorous Labour candidate waved at her excited party workers. Clearly many people who had not supported her at the General Election had turned out to do so on this occasion. At that very moment she was wearing the contented smile of someone who had just achieved their lifetime ambition.

The tension was now unbearable. Everyone was desperate to find out who the people of Brockleby had chosen to send to Westminster as their representative. However, before they were able to discover how the other heavyweight in the contest had fared, the names of thirteen other candidates needed to be read out.

Finally the moment of truth arrived. It would have been possible to have heard a pin drop before the Returning Officer blew loudly into the microphone.

"Adrian Thomas... 21,954 votes," he called out.

Immediately there was ecstatic shouts and screams from one section of the hall. Filmed by television crews, pictures of celebrating Labour Party workers were immediately transmitted around the globe. People from thousands of miles away would have witnessed hugging and kissing on a grand scale.

"You see all that hard work paid off in the end," smiled Carol, happily as she brushed a tear from the corner of her eye.

"Bloody right it did," replied Kenny, raising his clenched fist into the air. "We've given the Tories a thrashing."

David couldn't trust himself to speak. Overcome with emotion he just contented himself by throwing his arms around anyone who looked willing to share an embrace. One of those people just happened to be Alison.

"Will you take me home tonight?" she whispered into his ear.

David was rather taken aback. In the past week or so she had gently refused all his offers of a lift. Instead she had always chosen to travel with Tony and Carol.

"Of course," he replied, eagerly.

Suddenly the Returning Officer called for order. Jacqui Dunn had almost certainly topped the ballot but the proceedings were not yet over. The names of the remaining candidates still had to be read out and then there were also speeches to come.

Further raucous Labour cheers followed when Jacqui Dunn was declared the newly elected MP for Brockleby. Then after an appreciative wave to her adoring supporters she stepped forward and took the microphone. Once again the hall fell into total silence.

"This is a victory for Socialism," she began, proudly. "By electing me the people of this wonderful town have sent a clear message to the Government. They want their taxes to be spent on hospitals, schools and elderly care rather than killing innocent Iraqi citizens in an illegal war. During this campaign Tories and even people within the party that I have spent my life working for, have accused me of being a left wing extremist. If that means being on the side of the poor, the sick and the vulnerable then I plead guilty."

David could feel the hairs standing up on the back of his head. The speech was being delivered with great passion and like many others that were listening he felt certain that Jacqui was destined for great things. Could she even be Labour's first woman Prime Minister he wondered.

When proceedings on the stage had finally ended Jacqui came over to join her supporters. Then throwing her arms around each one in turn she thanked them all personally for their help. While the men fought hard to hold back tears the women didn't even try.

David was the last one to receive a warm embrace. Then standing back one pace Jacqui took the recent Labour Party recruit by the hand.

"As you know I shall be giving up my council seat now," she smiled, warmly. "Are you interested in standing for it?"

David shook his head sadly.

"This evening you have achieved your lifetime ambition and I must start aiming for mine. Now the election is over I am going to train to be a teacher so that will take up much of my time. Perhaps one day though I might become a councillor."

"I wish you luck in pursuing your dreams but please don't give up politics. You know there are so many causes worth fighting for," smiled Jacqui, before she was called away to do her first television interview.

It was now ten to two in the morning. As the newly elected MP faced the cameras her little band of loyal supporters decided to set off home. There would be plenty of opportunities to celebrate in the near future but right now everyone was eager for a few hours' sleep.

David had been looking forward to having Alison in the car with him. It was a while since they had been alone together and tonight his passenger seemed less distant with him than she had been in recent weeks. The two young political activists were talking excitedly about the evenings events when they came to a part of the journey that had become so familiar with them both. It was the place beneath the trees where they had shared many intimate moments.

"Can we stop here for five minutes," requested Alison. "I need to ask you a question."

David was taken by surprise but readily agreed. Something was telling him that what he was about to hear would be of great importance. As it turned out his instinct was absolutely correct.

For a few moments Alison sat staring straight ahead. It was a frosty November evening and although the heater warmed up the interior of the car she sat huddled up in her thick outdoor coat. Not a soul was about and the world around them was in total silence. Everything was still and there wasn't even a slightest rustle of leaves from the overhanging branches.

"Do you still love me?" asked Alison, finally.

"I will always love you," answered David, feeling a sudden surge of warmth inside as he spoke.

"I love you too," whispered, Alison.

David couldn't believe what he had just heard. Simultaneously they released themselves from their seatbelts and fell into each other's arms. For a while they kissed tenderly and were given a glimpse of what it would be like to be in Paradise.

"I can't understand why you love me," said David with tears of joy in his eyes. "In the real world I'm a social disaster."

Alison giggled.

"I'll sort you out," she promised. "Before very long you will be as crazy as everybody else."

All that happened seven years ago and now in 2010 things have naturally moved on. Soon after coming to power in 2003 the new Tory Government lost its overall majority and were replaced by Labour two years later after another General Election. Roy Donaldson who had succeeded Bruce Shaw as leader of the Labour Party, now became Prime Minister and immediately pledged that British troops would continue to support America in the Iraq War.

Roy Donaldson was never a popular figure either with his party or the country as a whole. However, it still came as a shock to the nation in 2007 when he announced his resignation on the grounds of ill health. Many political experts assumed that with a General Election some three years away at the most, he had decided to step aside and allow someone else to establish themselves before the country was asked to go out and vote again.

By now support for the Iraq War was falling both in Britain and the USA. Many saw no end to a conflict that was proving to be costly, both in terms of money and lives. So it was hardly surprising when Labour selected Bruce Shaw to once again lead not just the party but also the country. Once in charge the first decision that the new man took was to bring the troops back home.

Jacqui Dunn's political career suddenly received a massive boost. She had been re-elected in the 2005 General Election with an increased majority and soon she had a very powerful friend at Number 10 Downing Street. Somebody who, like herself, had always opposed the War.

Bruce Shaw didn't disappoint. Wanting to fill as many Government posts as possible with his allies, Jacqui was appointed as a junior minister at the Foreign Office. At the Labour Party headquarters in Brockleby the news was greeted with great excitement.

Nobody was happier after learning of Jacqui's success than David. After several years of hard work he is now a qualified teacher and practices his new profession in a local secondary school. Although the job is challenging he finds it rewarding and has no desire to do anything else.

His personal life, too, couldn't be better. Having married Alison not long after the by-election he now has three wonderful children. There is Amanda, the step-daughter that he dotes on and a boy and girl of his own. While still living in Brockleby the family moved to a three-bedroom house with a big garden which is ideal to play in.

Sadly neither Alison or the children have ever met David's parents. Hilary and John Chambers have been sent a number of family photographs and to be fair, have often responded by putting gifts of money in the post. However a number of invitations made to them to come and visit have all been ignored.

In contrast David sees his mother-in-law practically every day. Alison's mum is always on hand to babysit or to help out in any way she can. The children all adore her and could be forgiven for believing that she is the only grandparent that they have.

David and Alison are still keen Labour Party activists. After an evening out canvassing they like nothing more than to sit and talk politics in the club with all their old friends. Then when driving home later they have been known to stop in their favourite spot and enjoy some intimate pleasures together.

Ever since his marriage David has become a different person. Now a keen Crystal Palace fan, he spends many a Saturday afternoon down at Selhurst Park and loves talking football with anyone who has an interest in the game. Most evenings he enjoys watching TV and occasionally accompanies Alison to the cinema if there is anything worth seeing. In fact these days he is a very well-adjusted member of a crazy world and makes friends very easily.

David is still very friendly with the Broadbent twins. When he married Alison, Rebecca was actually there in the church watching the wedding service with tears rolling down her cheeks. Part of her was regretting that things had to be the way they were. How she longed to be the bride, standing up there at the altar with the one man she had ever truly loved.

However, thankfully she has now found happiness in her life. Three years ago she married a Fellowship gentleman called Graham and much to her great joy became pregnant soon after. All along she had blamed herself for being infertile. Suddenly it became evident that it was Malcolm, her first husband who had been the cause of the problem.

Recently Simon also got married. Having been introduced to a young lady from Yorkshire he finally discovered somebody who took his fancy. So on this occasion he left out the lie about being a serial bed-wetter. Even better news is that he has now become a father-to-be.

The last footnote belongs to the Fellowship. After years of preaching that computers are sinful they have finally begun to use them in their businesses. Once the church hierarchy gave the green light Fine Choice Furniture were in fact one of the first companies to show an interest in acquiring them.

Samuel Boswell, the company's senior partner decided to appoint an IT manager. Now having built up a reputation as a technical wizard, because of his ability to fix the drinks machine whenever it broke down, Des seemed the ideal candidate. The fact that he was a feckless, work-shy good-for-nothing had miraculously escaped the management's notice for many years.

Anyway Des has had many discussions but to date, there has been very little advancement towards introducing computers into the company. It can only be hoped that progress is made in that direction before this type of technology becomes obsolete in the future.